ALMODIS

ALMODIS

The Peaceweaver

Tracey Warr

First Published 2011
by Impress Books Ltd

Innovation Centre, Rennes Drive, University of Exeter Campus,
Exeter EX4 4RN

© Tracey Warr 2011

Typeset in Garamond by Swales & Willis Ltd, Exeter, Devon

Printed and bound in England by imprintdigital.net

British Library Cataloguing in Publication Data
A catalogue record for this book is available from the British Library

ISBN 13: 978–1–907–60505–5 (paperback)
ISBN 13: 978–1–907–60509–3 (ebook)

CONTENTS

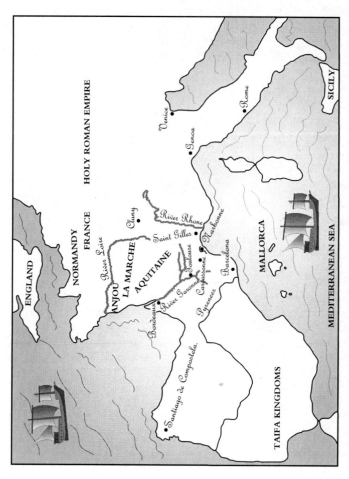

Medieval Europe at the time of Almodis

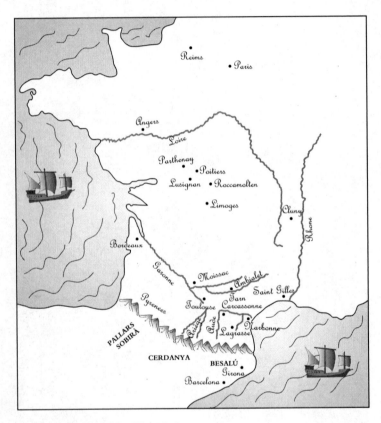

Occitania south of the River Loire

Prologue

I stand on the precipice wrapped in bulky grey and silver furs. My eyes are trained, like a hawk at hunt, on the steep road snaking up the mountain towards me. I feel the bitter cold of the granite ledge through the thin leather of my shoes, and I slide my feet forward inch by inch towards the edge, to get a better view. I turn my head to the faint sound of men's voices wafting up through the clear air and the sudden shift in my balance makes my foot begin to slip on ice. Fumbling desperately for a hold on the rock, I wrench my wrist as I pull myself back from the drop. I take two fast breaths and unclench my teeth. Fear and adrenaline taste of metal in my mouth. My hot breath billows in a white cloud around my frozen cheeks and nose. Perhaps I imagined the voices. I can still see nothing on the road. I am waiting for the arrival of the man who will be my husband. I am looking out for the arrival of my independence.

Winter has come so fast this year. Only a few weeks ago I was swimming in the river with my sister and a lukewarm autumn sun touched our goosebumps. The sunlight danced between the surface of the water and the trees' fabulous display of orange, red, brown, green, gold. The harvest doesn't seem long ago, when the peasants gave me the honour of being the maiden who would cut the last stand of corn. Now, over to my left, I see sunlight sparkling on vast sheets of ice where the water trickles down the mountainside for most of the year. In places it is frozen in enormous stalactite shafts, poised over the sheer drop like giant glass lances waiting to fall on the heads of any travellers risking the road. I shiver and wrap my furs around myself more tightly. Holding my hands inside my cloak, I touch my bruised wrist and grazed fingertips, run my index finger up and down between the knuckles of my left hand, feeling the slight bumps of three old star-shaped scars. I trace the gold and garnets of the betrothal ring on my little finger and twist the ring around and around.

The female troubadour's song that I heard in Toulouse last Easter runs through my head:

> Now we are come to the cold time
> when the ice and the snow and the mud
> and the birds' beaks are mute
> (for not one inclines to sing);
> and the hedge-branches are dry –
> no leaf nor bud sprouts up,
> nor cries the nightingale
> whose song awakens me in May.
>
> My heart is so disordered
> That I'm rude to everyone . . .

'Almodis! Come away from that edge! Why did you come out without me?' My twin sister's voice is close behind me.

I step back from the precipice and turn to take Raingarde's hands affectionately in my own. I look into my sister's face, the same face that I see myself in the smooth surface of the summer river. The same long tumble of dark gold hair. The same dark green eyes.

* * *

The aged female troubadour, Dia, breaks off her story momentarily, sets her harp down across her knees, and takes a sip of wine. She looks to her patron, Lady Melisende, who is the chatelaine of this Castle of Parthenay. It is the last night of the old century,

31st December 1099, and Dia has finally agreed to tell the whole story.

'I can see your mother, Almodis, and your father, Hugh, in your face,' Dia says. 'This part of the story that I have just told you . . .'

Melisende nods.

'. . . when your father came to claim his bride. That took place in the blood month of November, and in the year 1037, after the Great Famine, at the Castle of Roccamolten, in the county of La Marche in northern Occitania, not so far from here. The troubadours, or *trobairitz*, as we female storytellers are rightly called, we are both historians and poets. We find *and* make our songs and stories.'

Melisende nods again.

Dia picks up her harp and positions her fingers on the strings. 'But where to begin,' she says, 'since we are always in the middle apart from when we are at the beginning and the end and even then we may be in the middle?'

Part One

AQUITAINE

1026–1040

1

Easter 1026

If I try to cast my mind back to my earliest memories I am always caught screaming silently at the burning when I was six years old. There must be other memories before that, memories of my family in Bellacum and Roccamolten, memories of my sister, before I became a child hostage at my grandfather's court in Aquitaine. But every time I try to remember I am always thrust there – to the execution ground of Lady Elisabeth and I cannot think back beyond that one raw memory. Before the burning there is only blankness. So I don't like to remember at all but I must begin and that day at the Easter Assembly, at the Castle of Montreuil-Bonnin, is the beginning for me.

My eyes are screwed tightly shut and my small hand is being crushed in Geoffrey's grip, but I can still see, seared onto my eyeballs, his mother's terrified and agonised face as the flames leap around her and the charring tatters of her wedding dress. The awful inhuman screeching has stopped now and my heart is starting to slow down but I think I will hear the echo of her screams resonating in my ears forever. How can birds still sing now? Hot tears squeeze out and filter through my eyelashes, running coldly down my cheeks. I open one eye slightly, enough so that I know how far to turn my head in order to avoid a peripheral view of Elisabeth's charred remains hanging off the stake. I look instead up at Geoffrey. His eyes are wide open, staring at his mother's grisly corpse. His jaw muscles clenching and unclenching are the only mobile feature in his whole face and body. That, and the hand that seems to be systematically crunching the bones of my hand. His nostrils are flared and I realise that the air smells and tastes like burnt pig. Geoffrey looks down at me with dark blank eyes and I glance in supplication at his fist. He lets go of my hand abruptly, as if it were burning him. A black plume of smoke dirties the pale blue of the spring sky. How can the blossom trees still wave pink in the breeze?

I want to turn my back on the execution site and fall to the ground weeping. I want to drag Geoffrey away and comfort him as he comforts me when I skin my knee or graze the palms of my hands falling in the courtyard. Instead we stand rooted here, he staring ahead unflinching, and I staring at the view of the ground and my feet swimming in tears, my nose running.

'Come with me now, Geoffrey, Almodis.' My grandfather's voice is gentle and low and I feel a wave of merciful relief as he turns Geoffrey around by the shoulders and I happily turn with him. Geoffrey staggers a little as if unable to bend his knees. I put my uncrushed hand into Grandfather's and we walk away, passing Geoffrey's father, Fulk the Black, Count of Anjou, who still stands, consuming the sight of his adulterous wife's charred body.

We reach the door to Geoffrey's chamber and Grandfather tells him that he can have time off from his studies today. Geoffrey nods mutely and closes the chamber door quietly behind him. What tempests might occur behind that door? If I were Geoffrey, would I be most furious with my mother, for her adultery, if it is true. Or would I be most furious with my father, and his pretty mistress, Hildegarde, who might now become the new countess?

Grandfather and I stand on the threshold of his Great Library. This collection of books and manuscripts is one of the splendours of all Europe. Even the monks in Cluny are sitting envious, dreaming of our books here, my grandfather says. Not long after I had arrived in Montreuil-Bonnin, he had shown me to the library. 'Might I live here, Grandfather?' I asked him earnestly, in love with the promise of the books and hopeful that I might escape his wife Agnes' unkind surveillance. 'I could place my bed under this desk here.' Grandfather roared with laughter at me, but he pointed out the books that were my own, that Grandmother Adalmode had left to me in her testament. Today as I step into the room with its high ceiling and see the shelves of parchments and scrolls rising up around me and the glint of sunlight on the polished wood of the reading table and on the golden and jewelled covers of the books, I do not feel my usual excitement as if I have stepped into a magical world. I just feel sick and sad and angry.

'I don't think I can do any reading today, Grandfather,' I whisper.

'Then I will read to you and heal your heart, darling,' he says, tipping my chin up towards his face. I focus my eyes on the soft white curls of his beard. I don't want to look into his eyes. After all he, the Duke of Aquitaine, could have stopped it if he wanted to.

'This is a very hard thing that you have seen today Almodis. Men go into battle, but this can be a dangerous world for princesses too.'

I already know that. Duke Guillaume isn't after all my real grandfather. He is my step-grandfather, since he married my grandmother by force after killing her first husband, Count Audebert of La Marche, who *was* my real grandfather. But I love the duke nevertheless. And I know it is a dangerous world for women. Haven't I just seen the Duke's third wife, Agnes, screaming in labour as she gave birth to their new daughter as I ran in and out of the room with clean water and cloths? My stomach lurches at the idea that I might myself one day face what Elisabeth of Vendôme has just suffered. My mind races for defences. Elisabeth left herself open to the charge of adultery even if it were not true. She was openly fond of a man who has also died a grisly death. She was not adequately protected by her kin against Fulk. I would ask my father or my brother for help if I were ever threatened so, and they would rescue me. Perhaps. I think again of Geoffrey's feelings now about his mother and his father, but it is hard for me to imagine that. I can barely remember the faces of my own parents, or of my two brothers, Audebert and Eudes. Only my twin sister Raingarde's face can remain clear in my head, far away, but growing day by day the same as my own. I look up at my grandfather to show him what I think about his story of battles and princesses.

'Do not accuse me so with those big green eyes, Almodis. I know you are thinking I should have prevented this. Could have. But Fulk must do what he will with his own wife. I am his over-lord, yes. He gives me fealty and must do my bidding but some-times a lord has to judge what he must not ask for, else his closest ally may become his bitterest enemy.'

It is a pretty speech and, of course, Fulk would be an enemy to fear but I am not distracted from my accusation. Alas, for the first time I see something I do not like in my beloved grandfather. For the first time I see that I am ranged on another side, separate from him, on the side of women.

'Come and look at this, sweetheart.' Duke Guillaume is sit-ting at the reading table with Bede's history of St Cuthbert open before him. He beckons me and I climb up onto his knees but I cannot look with my usual delight at the tumble of blue and yel-low flowers and the green tendrils travelling down the margins of the page. I wind a tendril of my tumbling gold hair around and around my finger, let it spring out of its tight knot, and then begin the twirling again. Grandfather turns the pages slowly and I give a little of my attention to him and the book, but everything is changed. Our shared delight in the stories and word-hoard of the library, our game that they wait patiently ranged on the shelves for us to choose them today and voice them together, seems crumbled to dust. I can still taste ash and smoke in my mouth and smell it in my hair. I look quickly and fearfully at grandfa-ther's precious parchments in case they should crumble or burn because I am imagining that in my anger.

My grandfather loves me undoubtedly. I lean back against the warmth of his chest and roll my head back and forth against the soft blue velvet of his tunic, as my pony snuggles against me when I have an apple for him. I imagine the Duke's smile at my gesture. He would never burn me at a stake, no matter what I did. His wife, Agnes, however, my foster-mother, yes she would like to throw me on the kitchen fire anytime. She hates me because I am the granddaughter of Duke Guillaume's first wife, Adalmode. Adalmode's son, my uncle, is the heir to Aquitaine standing in the way of Agnes' own children. The Duke makes no secret that Adalmode was his great love and that he sees his two subsequent wives as mere heir breeders. He says so often, in front of Agnes, keeping her in her place. A man can't have enough sons he always says. Agnes passes her fury onto me, treating me as if I am a servant girl rather than the daughter of a count and an honoured hostage at the court, the granddaughter of the Duke's only love, the niece of the heir.

Next time my betrothed husband, Hugh of Lusignan, comes to court I will take a good look at him and see if he is the kind of man, like Fulk, who might take a mistress and burn his wife. I shudder and Guillaume pats my hand, turning the pages on Bede's words. I stare at the dust suspended in a shaft of sunlight, unable, today, to give my attention to the worlds conjured by the books.

2

Easter 1032

This morning I caught sight of myself in the large mirror in Agnes' room and thought at first it was Raingarde standing in the doorway and I gestured to her with joy to come into my embrace. Agnes laughed long and loud at me when I confessed my mistake. There Raingarde was (in fact me), standing in a blue gown with a gold tasselled belt at her waist, a gold border at the hem and gold lining showing on voluminous turned back sleeves. A short, red silk cloak around her shoulders was held in place with the saucer brooches that father gave me when I left home. (That is when I realised it was my image instead.) My loose hair fell to my waist in thick gold kinks. The outline of my knee was visible in the sculpted folds and creases of my skirts and my breasts were just beginning to fill out my bodice and give me a shapely defined waist and hip. I held a thick book in my hand.

'Did my husband give you permission to run around with that in your grubby paw?' Agnes asked.

'It's mine,' I said. 'My grandmother left it to me.'

'Everything here belongs to my lord and to me.'

I walked out quickly before she could snatch it from me and went to find Bernadette, my new maid, to dress my hair. I found her screeching in the solar at the sight of a perfectly harmless garden spider that had spun its web in our window.

'Seeing a spider in the morning brings bad luck, Lady,' she says.

'How can you say that, Bernadette? Look at how beautiful is the dew on its perfectly round web.'

I write letters regularly to Raingarde and never send them. After all she cannot read and if they fell into the wrong hands or she had to ask a dishonest cleric to read them for her, then my inner thoughts might be exposed. They pile up inside my locked chest as the years of our separation pass, but I think that sometimes she must know a little of what I write to her.

Today I wrote:

> *My new maid, Bernadette, has arrived from Paris and unfortunately she is a Northern dolt. She is about ten, has wiry black hair and is short and podgy. Agnes of course chose her, unkindly, for me. She speaks no Langue d'Oc and knows nothing of southern ways. She knows her job well enough with my clothes, my jewellery, my person, and she loves to run errands to the kitchen. I am tired to death of hearing how her mamma in Paris sets about marinating a leg of lamb and how she is such a good brewster . . .*

As she brushes my hair, Bernadette asks me about my betrothed husband and I explain to her that my real grandfather, Audebert, ruled both the counties of La Marche and Périgord, having inherited the one from his father and the other from his mother, and then he gained a stake too in the rich city of Limoges through his wife, Adalmode. I picture the jigsaw of fought-over territory in my mind's eye, trying to explain it all to Bernadette. 'As Adhémar of Chabannes tells in his book,' I say, 'Audebert, in league with Fulk of Anjou, successfully invaded Poitiers and this castle belonging to my step-grandfather, the Duke of Aquitaine. But Audebert's successes were halted by an assassin's arrow in the forest and then step-grandfather worked hard to break up what Audebert had put together. First he married my grandmother, taking her Limoges wealth for himself and gaining guardianship of my father who was a small child. When my father came of age my step-grandfather allowed him only La Marche and not his full rights to Périgord and half of Limoges. My step-grandfather was a hopeless soldier by all accounts but he lacks nothing in strategy. And his final masterstroke was me.'

'How so, Lady?' asks Bernadette, yawning.

I am getting quite tired myself having to speak in Langue d'Oil to her all the time. I frown at her open maw and she shuts it up. 'My grandmother had thought to circumvent some of her second husband's destruction of the La Marche fortunes by confirming me as her heir, to her Limoges wealth at least.'

Bernadette perks up at that. 'So you're rich?' she says, brush in hand, her eyes wide.

'In theory,' I say, 'but my step-grandfather took me as a hostage here when I was five, as guarantee of my father's good behaviour.'

'And Piers, too,' she interrupts.

'And Piers too,' I say, cross that she is already flirting with my other servant. 'When I was five Duke Guillaume betrothed me to Hugh of Lusignan, who owns good lands but is a minor lord. It's a way of controlling the La Marches you see?'

She shrugs her ungainly shoulders and says, 'Women don't rule on their own or own property where I come from. We leave that to men. Much safer that way.'

I roll my eyes to the ceiling in despair.

When she leaves me, I continue my unsent letter to Raingarde: *So you see what a hopeless confidante this Bernadette will make.*

She was more interested in hearing about Piers than me, her mistress. 'He came with you as a hostage too when he was a little-un did he?'

'Yes.'

'And he's your father's son?'

I was about to shout at her angrily at that but what is the point in denying it. 'All noble houses are swarming with bastards,' I said instead which silenced her. I suppose that Piers has told her that my father is his father, wanting to impress the foolish chit.

Now we are all waiting outside the entrance to the Great Hall for the party of riders sighted from the tower. The Aquitaine family is ranged across the top of the steps, preparing to formally greet the visitors, but it is taking a long time for them to reach us and I am getting bored. I try out the skipping steps of the dance that the *jongleur* performed in the hall last night.

Agnes buffets my head, knocking the careful concoction of my plaits. 'Stand still! Do you want your mother-in-law to think you are a capering idiot?'

I stand still and try to push my wound plaits back into place under my head veil but they won't be perfect now. This is the first time that I have worn a woman's head veil – a *couvrechef* – and I am mortified that Agnes has ruined its appearance. I plunge my hand into the deep pocket of my gown where two of my ivory alphabet tiles click softly against each other. I feel their letters: A for Almodis (and unfortunately, Agnes), H for Hugh. Across the courtyard there is still no sign of the riders at the castle gate. Grandfather gave me the tiles. They were his when he was a child. He told me that I am quicker at my letters than everyone, quicker than his eldest son, Guill (my uncle), who is a tall, fat man, standing next to grandfather; quicker than Eudes, who is seventeen and the son of grandfather's second wife, Sancha. We all learnt to read and write together at the cathedral school, with Geoffrey too, using a psalter and a book of grammar called *The Back Sparer*, but I had no need of back sparing. I loved my lessons and learnt fast. It was the best part of my day.

Eudes stands on the other side of Agnes, trying to keep her seven-year-old twins, Pierre and Guy, from falling down the steps. A maid stands behind Agnes holding her baby daughter. I glance up at the dark, red coils of Agnes' hair under her fine head-veil edged with gold stitching. She made me brush her hair last night, and that is a servant's job. The thick, dark red mane crackled and sparked under the hard strokes of the brush like a wild animal, like a fox. It is the only thing about Agnes that I like.

Agnes looks down, turning her reddish brown eyes on me. 'Well, here comes your lordling.'

I grit my teeth against her insult. Grandfather likes to tell me that I, the daughter of a count, am to marry a mere lord, because I am 'The Peacemaker', settling years of bitter disputes between the three families of Aquitaine, La Marche and Lusignan. I try to find excuses for Agnes' meanness. It must be hard for her, a young girl, married to an old man, more than thirty years older and anyone can see that the duke loves me a great deal more than Agnes who just serves him in bed. She is unkind, jealous, gleeful in her power. I have to stop my thoughts in their tracks. It is not christian or dignified of me to think like that about my foster-mother.

'Hugh owns the largest castle in Aquitaine,' I say sullenly, 'and rich lands.'

Agnes opens her mouth to respond with another mocking comment.

'Silence, ladies,' the duke commands, as the horses enter the bailey and clatter rapidly to the bottom of the steps.

I watch Hugh dismount, help his mother, Lady Audearde, from her horse and then kneel to my grandfather. This muscular, black-haired man bears no resemblance to my vague memories of a lanky boy holding my hand in the betrothal ceremony seven years ago. Whilst my grandfather and Agnes welcome the guests, and Lusignan and his mother make the customary responses, I study him and feel glad at what I see. He is tall, six feet perhaps, which is good because I am already tall. I wrote in a letter last night to Raingarde, how foolish we would look if our husbands are shorter than we are. Hugh's hair is truly black, not just dark brown, but a thick, shiny black with a tufted texture. I imagine how pleasant it might feel to run my fingers over his head. His beard is the same black and cut short to his face. I am glad to find that my betrothed husband is strong and handsome. I am startled from my reverie as his eyes alight suddenly on me: gentle black eyes. He soon turns back to my grandfather and I become conscious that my mouth is open and I have been holding my breath as he looked at me. What does he think of me?

His mother, Lady Audearde, is very thin and her hair is dark grey under her veil. After the recent death of his father, Hugh is now the fifth Lord of Lusignan. He is here to give his fealty to the duke and to pay his respects to me, his bride-to-be. He is of age now, twenty, but at twelve, I am still too young to marry. Perhaps it would be good to escape soon from Agnes' household and command my own.

Hugh turns smiling towards me and I smile shyly back and then look up at my grandfather who is also pleased and squeezes my hand. Suddenly I feel a terrible pain slash at the side of my leg. I scream and fall clutching my leg, wailing. Anxious faces crowd above me blotting out the sun.

'What is it darling! What's the matter?' grandfather cries.

I feel nothing but the pain. Raingarde. When I am conscious

again to what is happening around me I find that Hugh is lifting me from the ground and carrying me into the Great Hall. He perches me on my grandfather's throne and calls for a doctor to examine me. Everyone is offering suggestions. Has she been stung by a hornet? Is it the onset of a sickness? Now that the pain and my gasping have subsided, I can look at them all again. Hugh's mother Audearde, is standing back from the anxious crowd of people with a look of great disapproval on her face.

'Nothing wrong there,' the doctor finally announces.

'Nothing?' echoes the duke looking with puzzlement at me.

'She is seeking attention as usual,' Agnes pronounces and I watch with dismay as Audearde nods her head, her lips grimly set in a line.

'I feel fine now,' I say. 'It must have been Raingarde. Something bad has happened to her leg. May I send a messenger to ask if she is alright Grandfather?'

'What is the child babbling about?' Audearde asks. 'Does she have a fever?'

The doctor shakes his head.

'Raingarde is her twin,' Duke Guillaume offers the explanation in the direction of Hugh. 'It is said that twins do feel each other's pain at a distance.'

Hugh's black eyebrows arch.

'What blasphemous nonsense!' Audearde exclaims. Agnes smiles smugly and pointedly at me. 'Some say that twins are the seed of two men – of adultery,' Audearde continues, 'and others that they are the offspring of the Devil.'

I look with dismay at the frown forming on Hugh's face. Is he frowning at his mother's words or at me?

'It is those sayings, Lady Audearde, that are nonsense!' my grandfather says swiftly. 'Do I not have twin sons myself?' he asks and the smirk on Agnes' face disappears as she is anxious not to be implicated in my contagion. 'Almodis is a good girl, the apple of my eye,' Grandfather tells Hugh.

I want to explain how I can sometimes feel Raingarde though I have not seen her for seven years. 'It . . .' but the Duke has clamped a big hand over my mouth and is staring into my eyes meaningfully. When he removes his hand I stay silent.

What do they know? They know nothing. I hope ardently that Raingarde's leg was something simple – like a bee-sting – nothing serious. Hugh smiles at me again, but now his smile is lopsided, uncertain. I leap to my feet to show that I am fully recovered and curtsey to him. 'I am recovered my Lord. I thank you for your care of me.' They laugh at my womanly gestures as I intend.

That night I lie in my curtained feather bed thinking of my husband-to-be. He has given me an exquisite white-enamelled swan on a golden chain. He seems kind and he is beautiful. During the feast Agnes whispered mockery in my ear at every opportunity, pointing out how Hugh still demurs to his mother's lead 'as if she were still regent of his *large* castle' and how 'the old harridan' would rule both Hugh and his little wife. No, I thought, she certainly won't. Probably she will be dead by the time I marry and go to Lusignan, and if not, well I will better that old lady. I mean to be an excellent wife. I am learning the duties of a chatelaine avidly and I carry my girdle with its jangling keys with pride, even though they are only the keys to my own casket at present. I will attach the swan there to sway against my hip.

3

November 1036

Dramatic changes in the weather began three years ago with torrential rain, and the ground has been waterlogged all this time, impossible to plough or sow. A terrible famine began and the people were compelled to eat grass and acorns. Weeds covered the fields at harvest time. Men, women and children died in thousands. Many dead lay out in the open because no one in the villages had the strength left to bury them, and the corpses were eaten by wolves. Survivors left their homes and migrated west in search of food. We heard that Odilo, the Abbot of Cluny, had buried ten poor children dead of cold and hunger in his own cloak. Mass pilgrimages set off to the Holy Land from Limoges and many other cities, desperately seeking God's mercy in these dark days. My grandfather became a little crazed with the bad news we heard day after day. He came back from a visit to his coastal holdings saying that he had seen the sea and the rain turn to blood. Agnes looked on his increasing age and feebleness with a smug smile that she directed at Geoffrey too often for my liking. We all began to think about the succession, when my grandfather might no longer be able to rule his Duchy.

Not long after Hugh and his mother visited us, my grandfather went away to the monastery at Maillezais, and my uncle Guill became the new duke. I sobbed loudly when grandfather prepared to leave.

'I am tired and old, little one,' he remonstrated as I clung passionately to him. 'My son needs to take control of Aquitaine and grow into his command. It is time. He is a full-grown man and I am a sick old man.'

In the long winter nights, I had stroked his hair when he fell asleep by lamplight amongst the books, his white head resting on the gold letters of a manuscript that was a gift from Cnut, the Norse King of England.

'But you're not sick or old Grandpapa,' I wailed, 'you're just middle-aged. And you'll look really silly with a bald patch shaved on your head.'

He laughed at my carefully thought-out objections, with tears in his eyes, and then left me with Agnes. I knew that I would never see him again.

I like my uncle Guill, now Duke of Aquitaine, and his wife, Eustachie, is young and has been kind to me, but now I watch as Eustachie wrings her hands in despair at the scroll that I have just read to her.

'Three million kroners!' exclaims Eustachie again, looking in bewilderment to me. Even the rich lands of Aquitaine cannot muster such a high ransom for my uncle who has been captured and imprisoned by my childhood friend, Geoffrey of Anjou. The Geoffrey I had known disappeared after his mother's burning and never came back. He seemed deadened and stiff all the time. He turned his attention to developing new fighting games that he called 'tournaments' and, worst of all, he began to flirt with hor-rible Agnes, a widow after my grandfather died in the monastery, and hungry for a new young husband.

There was something between them even before Grandfather died. I caught Agnes one morning kissing Geoffrey in the stone passageway. I looked away quickly, but I had seen that his hand was up her skirts and hers was in his clothing. She called me to her room later, but before she could speak I said, 'You don't need to worry. I would never betray Geoffrey and I would never betray a woman,' (even you, I thought) 'to the anger of a man.' She considered me gravely, wondering if she should threaten or cajole me; but eventually she nodded, decided to hold her tongue, and dismissed me. She treated me more kindly, of course, after that.

When Agnes married Geoffrey last year my first reaction was a desperate jealousy that she should have my friend, but then my jealousy turned to anxiety when I thought of Agnes' ruthless ambition combined with Geoffrey's famed prowess on the battlefield. Agnes never made a secret of the fact that she wanted her own son to rule Aquitaine even though my grandfather had left two other heirs, Guill and Eudes. Now Geoffrey and Agnes had captured my uncle Guill and set a ransom so high that it was impossible to meet. Duchess Eustachie handed out justice at the Assemblies with assurance in the first months of her husband's absence and her Regency, but if Agnes and Geoffrey took this opportunity to invade, I doubted that Eustachie would prove much of an adversary for them.

'Should I send to my father and brother for support?' I ask.

'What! Do you think Geoffrey and Agnes will bring an army here?' Eustachie looks terribly alarmed.

'It's possible,' I say slowly, not wanting to send her into more panic. We are surrounded on all sides by Anjou allies. If Geoffrey rose against Eustachie and tried to take the throne of Aquitaine for Agnes' young son, we are not in a good situation. 'I should write and inform my father how things stand and ask for his advice. We should ensure that the outlying garrisons all have full musters and that we have spies out to tell us if Geoffrey is preparing an army.'

'Yes, yes, will you give those orders?' she says. 'Where would I be without your good sense?'

I nod and go to seek out the steward.

But Geoffrey and Agnes did not come that summer. Geoffrey had other military business in the North where he was intent on extending his power towards Saintonge. My uncle Guillaume mouldered somewhere in a black dungeon behind the towering Roman walls of Angers, that was if they hadn't already murdered him. I thought of him often and sadly. He would not manage captivity well and I doubted that he was being kept in good conditions. Whilst Geoffrey has been brought up by Fulk in the harsh Roman way – seriousness, modesty, plainness – Guillaume was a man who had luxuriated in rich food and beautiful things. In truth, I was not certain which way the wind would blow with my father and brother. The La Marches had been allies with the Anjou family, successfully waging war against the Aquitaines, until my step-grandfather had murdered my real grandfather. It was possible that my father would side with Anjou, but on the other hand he would not be happy to see Aquitaine in the hands of Agnes and Geoffrey, who had such strong inclinations and connections with the northern Capetian king.

For three summers Eustachie ruled in her husband's stead, no news came of Uncle Guillaume, and I grew taller and taller and thought of Raingarde doing the same. The time of famine has passed and the harvests these last few years have been especially celebrated when the people remember their deliverance from that earlier devastation. Last year Geoffrey's father, Fulk, went on pilgrimage to the Holy Land, perhaps, I thought, seeking forgiveness for what he had done to poor Elisabeth, and, I added tartly in my head, I hope he doesn't get it. Fulk had left Anjou in his son's command, giving us all the more reason for disquiet at what Agnes might push Geoffrey to do about Aquitaine; but again, Geoffrey's military exploits were focussed in the North, towards Normandy and not towards us in the South. Perhaps he refuses to comply with his horrid wife's wishes, but I knew that this was just a delay, that sooner or later, Geoffrey and Agnes would come for Aquitaine.

A messenger is hurrying into the hall, running down the aisle towards us, scattering the *jongleurs* unceremoniously to either side. Eustachie holds up her hand for a halt in the music. Clearly the messenger brings important news and I recognise him as one of the spies that Roland, our steward, had sent to keep watch on Geoffrey. The messenger kneels and Eustachie waves him, Roland and me, back into the curtained chamber to hear the news in private. I can already see from the messenger's face that this is good rather than bad news.

'Is my husband released?' Eustachie asks.

'No Lady, but Count Fulk has returned from pilgrimage and was mightily displeased with his son's rule,' the messenger says, his gasping breaths evidence of his hurry to get here. Eustachie nods and the messenger continues.

'He required Lord Geoffrey to relinquish rule back to him, and Geoffrey refused and revolted against his father.'

We all gasp at that. Geoffrey's nickname is 'The Hammer' because he is undefeated on the battlefield, but his father is also an unrelenting warrior, basing his tactics on the Romans, brandishing Flavius Vegetius Renatus' manual of war, *De Re Militari*. To rise against his father was a rash move on Geoffrey's part and I frown, longing to ask if he is dead. I don't want him to be dead, even though he is our enemy now.

'Count Fulk has prevailed and defeated his son,' the messenger announces and we see, from the glee on the messenger's face, that there is more news to come. 'Count Fulk subjected his son to the Roman ritual of trampling the defeated!'

'What is that?' Eustachie turns to me. 'Is he dead? Will my husband be freed?'

I know the ritual. I read the Roman books of war with my grandfather but before I can reply the messenger continues cheerfully with his eyewitness account.

'The Count's son had to carry his own saddle on his back for several miles, and then he had to kneel at his father's feet and the Count placed his foot on his son's back and declared, "You are finally conquered"'.

Eustachie puts her hand to her mouth. 'Oh humiliating!'

My first thought is for the humiliation of Agnes. How she would bridle and ache at that: her husband in the dust in defeat; but then I think of Geoffrey, first compelled to watch his father burn his mother, and now this. How would such things twist and turn a good man into a bad one?

The messenger allowed Eustachie some moments of exclamation and then tells her the bad news. 'The ransom for your husband still stands the same my Lady. Fulk is in agreement on that with his son at least. And Lady, I urge you to release him soon. I could not get to see him but there are rumours that he is very sick. I believe there is truth to the rumours.'

Eustachie hangs her head in distress and I put my arms around her shoulders. 'We nearly have the ransom now, Aunt, and we will treat with Count Fulk for Uncle Guillaume's release and he will be more just with our negotiations than Geoffrey and Agnes have been.' I try to sound as confident as my words, but in truth, we are a vulnerable woman and a girl. Fulk could easily take Aquitaine for his son and his wife now if he chooses.

4

Easter 1037

I rein my horse at the top of the rise to wait for my companions and to look down on the walled city of Toulouse in the valley below. I bounce impatiently in my saddle, feeling that I am on the brink of life as well as on the brink of the steep incline. It is a beautiful crystal-clear morning with tiny wisps of cloud high up in an azure sky. I look back at the rest of the party. We have been riding for many days to arrive in time for the Easter Assembly and most of the group look bedraggled and exhausted. My Aunt Eustachie was forced to hand over the massive ransom to get her husband back. He more than earns his nickname: Guillaume 'The Fat'. His fine clothes strain over his stomach and thighs. Four years in a dungeon has ruined his health and now he lacks the arrogant confidence that a Duke of Aquitaine needs.

I regard my uncle with candour. Guillaume, the sixth Duke of Aquitaine and third Count of Poitou, looks like an overstuffed cushion. He is at home on a sumptuous bed, and not on his muscled and massive horse. His black hair stands up on top of his head in lush waves and one curl hangs down his forehead. His mouth and eyes look tiny in their bed of lavish flesh and hanging chins. Eustachie, riding next to him, is as thin as he is fat. Her eyes and mouth are edged with a network of deep lines. Since Guillaume had been kept so long in captivity by Agnes and Geoffrey there has been no chance for Eustachie to conceive, and now perhaps with Guillaume ill and prematurely old, she never will. Guillaume's half-brother, Eudes, is the heir to Aquitaine and likely to remain so.

My gaze sweeps over the group of servants and focuses on my own two, Bernadette and Piers, riding side by side. Five years Bernadette has been with me and she is still having difficulty adjusting to our different southern ways. As usual, she is looking cross and complaining about something. Piers has a semblance of attentiveness fixed on his face as he leans towards her. Now that I am nearly of age perhaps I must get a new, more contented, maid. Bernadette is good at her work but I cannot abide her whining. Piers, my horse marshal and falconer, looks handsome with his brown hair and beard glinting in the early morning sunshine. He smiles, meeting my glance, sharing my pleasure in the ride.

I turn to look down again on the walled city with its red-tiled roofs and smoke rising from countless chimneys. Most of the city is on the near side of the great blue bend of the Garonne river. I can see the white and yellow sails of boats and tiny figures moving across the city's two bridges. To my left, the dark pink walls of the castle of Toulouse, the Chateau Narbonnais, rise up near one of the city gates, towering above the other buildings. Close to another of the city gates, I can see the oval of the old Roman amphitheatre with its tiered seating. I am so excited to be here, close to this city that was the hub of the Roman and Visigoth Empires in the South. Somewhere down there is my family: my father, my brother and oh, my sister. I have not seen them for twelve long years.

I inhale the cold morning air. It smells of spring and wood smoke. I kick my horse and steer him with my knees toward the steep incline. We pick up speed and are soon travelling at breakneck pace down the hill. I hear startled shouts behind me and laugh aloud, relishing the rush of the cool breeze against my face.

As I wait again for the group to catch up with me at the St Étienne Gate, I watch the traffic of peasants, entering the city with their *tallage*, their tax payments in grain, chickens, cakes of beeswax, pigs. They file past the guards and occasionally make way for loud groups of noble visitors on horseback.

My aunt and uncle finally arrive and I listen with a fiction of a demure, penitent face as Eustachie admonishes me for the reckless ride down the hill. I fall into line behind them as they prepare to enter the city with dignity. My uncle will be the most important visitor to the assembly. A servant straightens my uncle's fur-lined red cloak around him on the horse. He pulls a coronet studded with green jewels out of a leather bag and passes it up to the duke who nests it precariously in the bouncing crest of his hair. Guillaume carefully nods his head in command and we all move forward towards the gate.

Once inside the city we pass the church of St Étienne and then ride straight down towards the river. Ahead, I can see boatmen unloading onto the crowded pier. Brightly painted pink, green and yellow houses line the opposite side of the river, with their lower levels in the water so that boats can pull directly into their basements. The upper storeys of the houses hang over, and are reflected in, the water's surface. We turn left and follow the river towards the Narbonnais Gate. As we reach the huge sculpted gateway another group of nobles are approaching and at first attempt to force precedence. I exchange a horrified glance with Aunt Eustachie as I recognise Agnes of Mâcon and Geoffrey of Anjou. At the last moment, when I thought my uncle would have to exert his right to enter first, Geoffrey reins his horse and puts a holding hand out to Agnes. He bows sardonically to Guillaume as he passes and then I feel his eyes on me.

'Good morning, my beautiful Lady Almodis of La Marche. A glorious morning.' Geoffrey's voice is loaded with self-satisfied sarcasm.

I merely nod my head without looking at him as I pass. I am not *your* beautiful lady, I think furiously. Geoffrey is quickly forgotten however as I emerge into the cobbled courtyard of the bailey and my excitement rises at the thought of being reunited with my family. Inside there is a scene of vast confusion as peasants queue with animals, and visitors are directed to their quarters.

A servant tells my uncle: 'I have lodging in the east wing for you and your household, my Lord. I understand that I am to take Lady Almodis to the Count of La Marche's lodgings?'

'Yes,' Guillaume answers, dismounting stiffly, puffing and groaning. The folds of his face are now an unhealthy and livid red, with streaks of white at the sides of his nose. The fashion for short tunics and hose gartered below the knee so as to show off a finely shaped leg, does not, I observe, suit my uncle much.

Piers murmurs to me that he will take care of my horses and falcon. He disappears into the melée of people, moving in the direction of the stables with the reins of the horses in one hand and my treasured peregrine falcon balanced on his other gloved fist. I turn to Guillaume and Eustachie, trying to control the emotion tightening my throat. My eyes are welling with tears as I embrace them. Since I was five my grandfather, and then they, have been as parents to me. I cannot remember what my own mother and father look like.

'There, child. Wipe your face,' Eustachie tells me. 'Don't spoil those fine eyes. Your father will be looking on you soon enough. Go settle into your lodging with Bernadette, and we will speak with you later in the company of your father.'

I follow a servant into the hall, along narrow passageways and up winding stone staircases. This castle is like a maze. I cannot find my way back. I can only go forwards now.

I stand with Bernadette in the doorway to a small dormitory room on the upper floor. There is no one there, but clothes and travelling chests are dispersed around the room. Three curtained beds are crowded close together and there are straw pallets on the floor for the servants. I step into the room looking for signs of my sister.

An ivory tric-trac set, on top of a large chest of dark embossed wood, looks likely to belong to my father or brother. On the far side of the room, on the bed closest to the wall, I see a small gold casket. This must be Raingarde's. I move over to it and run my fingertips across the gorgeous blue enamelled carvings. It is similar to my own casket, both of them made in the famous workshops of Limoges. The images on my sister's casket tell the story of our great-aunt Emma who was kidnapped by Viking raiders but returned safely after three years when a ransom was paid. I smile at the carving on the lid showing Emma stepping from the Viking long boat to her husband, waiting on the shore. Two servants arrive in the doorway with my travelling chest and I direct them to place it next to my sister's. Seeing the two similar caskets side by side fills me with inarticulate emotion.

Sunlight stripes into the empty room through the *meurtrières*, the narrow slits high up in the wall. Although they are not present, I can almost see the ghosts of my family, recently in this room, laying out the possessions they have brought with them from the eagles-nest castle of Roccamolten. I imagine them debating over who will take which bed. The one my sister has chosen, which I will share, is close to a window slit giving a narrow view of the green countryside beyond. I am tempted to open Raingarde's casket and look for clues about the twelve lost years of our lives apart.

I sink suddenly onto the bed in despair. I don't know these people: my father, Bernard, Count of La Marche; my brother Audebert, who is twenty now; my twin, Raingarde. What will they think of me? Will they be disappointed? Under my fingers I feel the thick brown fur of the bedcover. I know these furs come from Roccamolten. It is one of the few things I can remember: snuggling up with Raingarde on a freezing night, giggling as our frigid toes touch together and our warm breath caresses each other's cold cheeks. My mother, Amelie, has not come to this assembly and is at home in La Marche. I strain with my eyes closed trying to remember her. The vague, pale face with yellow hair that swims into my mind is probably an image from a painting or a tapestry and not my mother's face at all.

'Why these tears, my Lady,' asks Bernadette, 'on this happy day when you will greet your father again after such a while?' She dabs at my face delicately with a handkerchief.

I open my eyes and smile feebly at her. I take the handkerchief and blow my nose loudly. 'Yes, you're right.' I spring up from the bed and wipe the last of my tears away. 'I'll go and see if I can find them while you unpack.'

At the doorway I hesitate. I have no idea of the layout of this castle, so different from the Aquitaine stronghold of Montreuil-Bonnin. I follow my instinct left, come to a narrow passageway cut into the cold, pale stone and slide into its slender darkness. It takes me to an open balcony where I can look down on the

25

continuing confusion in the courtyard. I see with satisfaction that Geoffrey and Agnes are still waiting for the servants to show them to their accommodation. Geoffrey's angry impatience is being transferred into the nervous and dangerous prancing of his warhorse in the crowded space.

Safe in my unseen eyrie, I observe Geoffrey. The last time I saw him he was a young man. Now he is in his early thirties and powerfully built. His straight black hair is combed back from his pale face and cut short at the neck, soldier-fashion. His eyes are deeply set and an intense golden brown. They seem to bore into everything he looks at. His nose is large and curved. I have heard that he keeps three concubines besides Agnes. She must hate that. He is close friends with the northern French King, Henri. 'Anjou,' uncle Guillaume declares, 'is a treacherous man in every respect, inflicting assaults and intolerable pressures on his neighbours.' His clothes are plain black and brown but made from fine cloth. His only ornament is a great saucer brooch of Viking design, holding his cloak at one shoulder. The tense and ready way that he carries himself speaks more of his blood line than any fine clothes might.

Agnes, however, has tricked herself out like a queen. A coronet glints beneath her head-veil. Jewels hang from her ears. Her fur-lined cloak is held in place at the shoulders with two huge black brooches in the shape of eagles and a thick gold chain hangs between them. Agnes is a decade older than Geoffrey, but she is still a fine-looking woman with her dark red hair, yet her face looks well lived in. The worry over his philandering and her own ambition, perhaps.

Donkeys laden with goods are being led across the cobbles of the courtyard or are stubbornly leaning backwards, holding their place, as their owners pull and pull on the reins. Soldiers in livery with large horses clatter towards the stables. Maids run frantically from kitchen to hall with loaves of bread and flagons of wine. This is an important assembly with much business to be conducted. Apart from the usual paying of taxes and legal rulings, the new Count of Toulouse will be crowned; since I am seventeen and nearly of age, I will be formally handed back to my father; and my sister will be betrothed to Pierre, heir to Carcassonne.

The noble families from all across Occitania and Catalonia are gathering to witness these events.

I turn from the scene in the bailey and continue out of the sunshine and into the chill gloom of the narrow stone corridor, impatient now to find my family. I take a staircase that leads down into darkness. The steps wind round and round, worn unevenly in the centre by the passage of many feet. With one hand I hold up the hem of my dress and my other hand follows the cool contour of the spiralling wall. Then, with dismay, I see the top of a woman's head below me. One of us must go all the way back up or down as there is no room to pass. The lady below is looking down at her feet and has not heard my steps. As we come face to face, hand to hand, bathed in bright light from an arrow slit, she exclaims 'Oh!' at the unanticipated encounter, and, after a moment of staring into my face, 'Oh!' again. I am looking into the loved and longed for face of my sister.

'Raingarde!'

She moves up another step, as close as possible in the narrow and precarious stairwell and we hug each other tightly for a long time, as if we will never let go.

'Almodis! I can hardly believe it's really you, and not the phantom that I've hugged every night these many years!'

Then we are silent and regard each other without blinking, holding hands, until I pivot suddenly and begin to go back up the stairs, pulling Raingarde behind me.

'Slow down!' she shouts. 'I can't keep up.'

'Yes you can,' I call back and our laughter and running steps ricochet off the walls in the cramped space.

We are quickly back on the open balcony, pause briefly to look at the bustle below, then speed along the passage to our bedchamber where we can talk together for hours.

'My Lady,' Bernadette begins, as we burst into the room, and then she stops with her mouth open. I am delighted to see the look of amazement on her face as she takes in the two ladies standing laughing before her, *both* apparently her Lady Almodis.

The following morning Raingarde and I are walking through the Toulouse market. I smell warm bread and apples, spices and perfumes.

'Bernadette!' I call behind me. 'Keep up!' The investiture begins in minutes and father will be furious if we straggle in late.

I am holding hands with Raingarde. People stop and stare at us as we pass and some cross themselves. We still look exactly the same and I see them having to force themselves to look away from our twoness. We are wearing new green gowns, gifts from our father for this reunion. We are in heaven to be together again after so long and haven't stopped talking since we found each other yesterday, even whispering behind the bed curtains last night until Father shouted at us to be silent for pity's sake. We talked about all the things that happened to me at the Aquitaine Court and about Raingarde's betrothal. Raingarde told me what has been going on in La Marche all the time that I have been away. 'Father continues to hold the Occitan frontier against the greedy northern French,' she said. Or, 'Do you remember that old brown cow with the white star on its forehead that kicked Audebert when he tried to milk her? She died last winter.'

The stalls we pass are crowded into the rectangle of the marketplace. They have colourful awnings – red, green, blue, white – protecting the stallholders' stock from the spring sun. I poke herbs and spices laid out on one stall, seeing the promise of a gold sauce in the saffron, pink in the garlic, and luminous red in the dyer's bugloss. I breathe in my favourite scents of cinnamon and vanilla. Another stall has fine woollen cloth, silks, embroidered bands and thin leather shoes dyed bright green and blue. And another has silver and gold bangles glinting temptingly in the sunlight. I stop at a display of long ropes of *saucisson* dusted with white flour, salamis cut in half and tied at one end with string. The *patissier* has a fine array of bread and gorgeous smelling pies. One is in the shape of a rabbit and another has a picture of a castle moulded onto it. I am starving but we don't have time to pause and have to hurry on.

Arriving at the imposing barbican of the Chateau Narbonnais, I say to Raingarde, 'Look at the size of this entrance.' I swing her hand backwards and forwards, staring up at the huge decorated arch and the jagged teeth of the portcullis suspended above our heads.

'Well I would,' Raingarde laughs good-naturedly, 'if you'd left us any time to do so, but now we have to hurry past and get to the Great Hall.'

It is my fault that we are late. I was too long exercising my horse and bird this morning and Bernadette was grumbling and moaning about how impossible it was to get me presentable in time and get the twigs and tangles out of my hair.

I push open the heavy door and find my place at father's side ignoring the reproachful stares from the roomful of strangers as our entry disturbs the solemn ceremony. The bishop is young and nervous and his arms are shaking with the weight of the crown raised over the head of the kneeling count. The frown on my father's face soon disappears at the sight of me, his newly reacquired daughter.

'By the power vested in me,' the bishop says, 'I confirm you, Pons, as Count of Toulouse.' The hovering crown comes down on the grey head. The new Count of Toulouse rises in his heavy robes and turns to face us. He is not a pretty man. He has an enormous, hooked nose and his mouth is all hanging wet red flesh. My own face is scrunching up at the thought of that mouth slobbering near my neck. I feel sorry for the young woman standing there next to him.

'Poor little Majora,' I whisper to Raingarde, 'she was only eight when she married him.'

I look sadly at the small woman holding the hand of that awful man with a mouth like a whiskery old horse and teeth to match. She looks miserable. The door creaks behind me and I am surprised to see that someone else is even later than we were. It is a formidable looking old woman with a face all angles and sharp edges and a tall boy with bright blond hair and a splendid blue tunic, as blue as his eyes.

'Now *he'll* make someone a good husband soon don't you think?' I whisper again but Raingarde frowns at me to be silent. He *is* a beautiful, confident-looking boy.

I see my father nod formally at the pointy old lady. She must be someone very important then for the Count of La Marche to give her a courtesy.

'Who are they, father?'

He tells me, close to my ear, 'Ramon Berenger, Count of

Barcelona, and his grandmother, Ermessende of Carcassonne, who stands regent for the boy.'

There is a free hour before the coronation feast and my father sits in the bedchamber holding my hand, gazing into my face. My brother, Audebert, and Raingarde are sitting nearby and the servants have been dismissed from the room.

'I know the contours of your face, of course, darling. I've been looking at them every day despite your long absence,' my father says and we all smile at this. 'And yet you are a stranger to me my dear daughter. I haven't watched you grow from grubby imp to beautiful woman, as I did with your sister. I know nothing of what your life has been, the deepest desires and griefs of your heart, the business of your days.'

I look back into my father's face. Many strong men might flinch at such a view but I gaze at him with fearless love. He has spent his life on horseback, defending the rights of our family, taking and losing territory, hacking at men and being hacked at. His short hair is iron grey. He has lost one eye and the socket is a red hollow of fearsome scarring. A scar slashes down his face from left eyebrow to right cheek. There is an ugly knob of mangled flesh where his right ear should be. To look at his face is to hear the ring of swords, the screams of horses and men. The bland, good looks of Audebert are an indication of what my father once looked like, before such havoc was wrought on his features.

I know what the purport of my father's words are. He means that I should give him and Audebert a thorough debriefing on everything I know about the Aquitaine family that might be of use to them. I have waited for this day, storing up my observations and information, impatient to contribute to the La Marche family strategy, to show that I am mindful of the needs of my kin. At the Aquitaine Court I was treated by my grandfather as a little pet, and by Agnes as an annoying nuisance. I was at the court for so long that everyone forgot that I was a cuckoo in the nest, a La Marche spy. Or perhaps it was because I was a young girl that they paid me no attention. The Aquitaine family conducted their business in my full view and now I will tell my family all about them. Focussing on the undertow of my father's words, I decide to dive in and give my full report. It is true that father and Aude-bert do not know me and I want them to see who I am.

'My uncle Guillaume has returned from his long and cruel captivity in ill health,' I say. 'He and Aunt Eustachie have been kind to me, but I fear that the duchy is likely to pass to Sancha's son, Eudes, before too long.'

'Guillaume may yet recover his health and his wife may yet conceive an heir,' says my father with a slight question in his tone.

I make no response but I see that he has read in my face that these possibilities are no possibilities. As if I had spoken, he nods and taps the back of my hand.

'And was Lady Agnes so kind to you?' asks Audebert.

'No,' I reply shortly. 'She never showed me kindness or care, though father gave me into her care, but her husband, old Guillaume the Great, was always kind to me. I studied at the new cathedral school with Bishop Fulbert, along with the Aquitaine children.'

'Well you know more than me then,' laughs Audebert. 'Will you take your learning into a nunnery sister?' he says provocatively.

'No, I won't,' I snap, turning fiercely to him, but then tempering my words as I feel a gentle pressure from my father's hand. 'I will use my learning to good account in furthering the fortunes of my kin and my husband.'

My father smiles and nods at this. 'Very well child. And Eudes? What sort of man is he?'

I try not to let a proud smile bloom on my face, as I realise that my father values my opinion, even if my brother sees only opportunity for jokes. 'Eudes is a good man,' I say with decision. 'He is intelligent and brave. He will be well-inclined to us I believe.'

'Well-inclined to you perhaps sister?' asks Audebert, laughing again.

Father and I form an alliance in ignoring this remark.

'Well-inclined is one thing,' says Bernard, 'but he will not be kin to us as Guillaume is.' Guillaume is father's half-brother, sharing as they do the same mother, Adalmode of Limoges.

'No,' I agree and pause, wondering if I dare venture the real thing that I want to tell my father. 'Agnes and Geoffrey will not be well-inclined to us, or to anyone else.' I swallow at my temerity and the stillness that descends on my father in response to my words. 'They will open the door for the northerners to overrun the South if they have the chance.'

'How is this, little sister?' asks Audebert slowly. 'The Duke of Aquitaine is Guillaume VI, our kin, and you already have him and his half-brother, Eudes, dead and buried, Agnes installed and King Henri Capet with his feet under our table?' Yet I hear a new note of respect replace the previous mockery of Audebert's tone.

'I learnt a great deal at the Aquitaine Court,' I say. 'I read the books in the Duke's famous library. I listened to all around me and I learnt to play chess . . . very well.'

Father smiles broadly at this and says, 'You are looking for the moves of the red queen, eh?' he says, meaning Agnes.

'Eudes would do well to get himself a wife and an heir fast and cut Agnes' spawn out of the succession,' Audebert says, arching his eyebrow and nodding his head in my direction.

I shake my head in irritation with my brother. 'I am already betrothed, and in any case, I am related to Eudes. The church would never sanction such a marriage.'

'You are only related by marriage, not by blood,' Audebert says stubbornly.

'Even if Eudes did marry right away,' I say, 'a child heir would be no deterrent to the vaulting ambition of Agnes and the Hammer.'

'No,' Audebert responds, 'but a strong Regent would be. She's wasted on Lusignan, father!' I am flattered that he thinks I would be a strong regent but his strategy is not sound.

'I gave my oath to Lusignan,' father says and it is clear that there is an end to any other possibility. My father stands up, pulling me to my feet with him. 'Very good. We will speak more of this. Now we will eat, drink and rejoice that we are reunited.' He takes Raingarde's hand and moves to the door with us, his identical daughters. Audebert steps out to intercept me and kisses my cheek. 'You have done well sister. Please excuse my jesting.'

5

The Mews

I slip out of bed without waking Raingarde or Bernadette and slide my feet into thin leather shoes, pulling a fur wrap around my nightshift. I rake my fingers through my hair and step out into the chill dawn air. The courtyard that had been so frantic yesterday is now deserted and silent. An old black cat sits by the well eyeing me. I take a tin cup from its hook and dip it into the well bucket. The cold water revives me and I am hungry but first I need to check on my falcon. I walk towards the arch in the far corner of the bailey and find my way to the falconry mews, adjacent to the stables. Passing the stables I hear the horses chomping softly on hay, shifting their positions.

I duck inside the dark mews and exchange a morning greeting with Piers who is already here about his work, cleaning harnesses and leather straps. He and I have an easy relationship now. He does his work very well and I try to forget our fight in the stables in Aquitaine when we were newly arrived as child-hostages. I was dressed up in all my best clothes and jewellery and playing queen. It was a game I played at home with Raingarde. He came in and sniggered at me. 'You won't ever be a queen,' he said. 'All you'll be doing is laying on your back with your legs open being fucked and having babies.' That was when I punched him and his nose bled, and I got the scars on my knuckles and a thrashing from Agnes.

I pick out my peregrine falcon in the dark rows of birds on perches and begin talking gently to her and feeding her a few titbits of quail that Piers has prepared for me. The dim light of the mews dims further as someone else enters behind me. The new occupant murmurs a greeting: 'My Lady.' I hear the Catalan lilt in his accent. Like me he is attending to his falcon, ensuring that she feels secure with her owner's voice in this strange mews. I sneak a glance at the newcomer as he talks to his own bird, a magnificent gyrfalcon. He is the tall blond boy who entered the investiture behind us yesterday with his grandmother: Ramon, Count of Barcelona.

He turns suddenly to me, deliberately catching me in the act of studying him and we both laugh. He makes me an elaborate bow and I can see that he is also in his nightshift beneath a very resplendent blue cloak with a border of elaborate silk embroidery. Even in the gloom of the mews I can see the blue of his eyes. I am suddenly conscious that my hair is hanging loose and uncovered down my back and that my own white undergown is visible below my fur cloak. But what does it matter. He is only a boy after all.

'May I take the liberty, my Lady, of introducing myself and asking your name? I am Ramon, Count of Barcelona.'

'I am pleased to meet you. I am Almodis of La Marche.'

'Ah! Were you not recently at the Court of Aquitaine?'

He is very well-informed for a boy! 'Yes I was there for the last twelve years and am only just returned to my father.'

'My felicitations on your reunion with your family, and with your honoured father, Count Bernard. At the Court of Aquitaine you must have known the two dukes, the old Guillaume V, The Great, and now his son, Guillaume VI?'

'Yes, the old duke was my guardian all through my childhood. I was privileged to have access to his Great Library and share his passion for music and poetry.'

Ramon shows no surprise at my implication that I can read. 'Ah! Won't you tell me something of that library?' he asks, inviting me to sit on a bench behind us.

I picture the shelves of the duke's library in my mind. I count off the books I can remember on my fingers. 'He had many bibles. And Augustine's *City of God*, Orosius' *History of the Ancient World* and Eusebius' *Church History.*'

'And did you read all these heavy tomes, Lady?'

'Yes,' I say. I am about to carry on with my catalogue of the library but realise that I have heard a tone of humour in Ramon's question. I look up quickly at his smiling face. 'Are you laughing at me?' I say abruptly.

'Indeed no.' His expression sobers. 'I am simply delighted to find someone who shares my passion for books. Parchment and gold are so costly. Even more so than months and months of a scribe's time!'

I nod and carry on with my list, although wary now that he is perhaps laughing at me after all, despite his assurances. 'He also had Saint Gregory of Tours' *History of the Franks*. Oh yes, and Apicius' treatise on cookery. He paid 200 sheep, and an enormous pile of rye, wheat and millet for that one.'

'We have a few books in Barcelona,' Ramon says, 'but I would like many more. And to build a library would be a fine thing.'

'I have a few books of my own,' I say, 'and I intend to collect more and be a patroness to writers and book-makers.'

Ramon arches his eyebrows at that. He has a mobile, expressive face. 'Excellent,' he says.

'My grandmother, Adalmode of Limoges, left some books to me and my father has just given me Adhémar of Chabannes' *Chronique*. I could show it to you if you like.'

'I would like that very much. I can bring you a literary surprise in return that I think will please you.'

'What is it?'

'Ah,' said Ramon, 'but then it won't be a surprise will it?' He rises to his feet, bowing. 'I must go now, Lady Almodis, or my grandmother will think I have been kidnapped by Moors!'

We laugh again and he takes his leave. I remain seated on the bench for a moment. I know that his grandmother, Ermessende, is famed for her military and political stratagems and no doubt she has schooled Ramon well. My empty stomach rumbles and I move to leave, passing Piers who is still standing in the semi-darkness polishing leather.

Back in the chamber, Bernadette fusses, scolding me for being absent so long and now being late to get dressed again, until I snap at her. 'Mind your tongue, girl. I'll do as I please and you will like it or you can find employment elsewhere.'

I am sitting alone in the chamber in the afternoon as my sister, father and brother have gone to meet Pierre and his mother to seal the details of Raingarde's betrothal. I sigh heavily at the thought that I will only be reunited with my sister for a few brief months before we each marry and are separated again. There will be a great distance between us once more.

'Sighing my Lady?' Ramon asks quietly. He has come in so silently that I am startled. Bernadette, is standing next to him with her mouth open. He has pre-empted her attempt to announce him properly. Ramon is, of course, considerably more formally dressed than when I encountered him in the mews in the morning. He is wearing a short brown tunic and a jewelled sword under his blue cloak. Now that I am meeting him in daylight, I see that his blond hair is bright and short and his eyelashes and brows are brown. A pink blush is visible under the tanned skin of his cheeks, almost as if they have been delicately brushed with paint. His nose and mouth are shapely. A slim black-haired woman with olive skin, wearing a yellow tunic, stands behind him holding a musical instrument. I force a smile onto my face as Ramon bends to kiss my hand.

'I am thinking how I must soon be parted from my sister.' I gesture to two stools for Ramon and the woman to take. 'She is to be wed to Pierre of Carcassonne and I to Hugh of Lusignan in a few short months when we are both of age. So our reunion is very short but sweet.' The woman has taken out a wax tablet and stylus and is writing something down.

Ramon notices my glance and introduces his companion and her activity. 'This is Mistress Dia,' he tells me. 'She is my surprise for you. She is a troubadour and one of great skill.'

Dia laughs at his words without looking up from her scribbling. I like the sound of her laugh. She sounds as if she acknowledges her own worth and is appreciative, but not obsequious, about Count Ramon's assessment of her. A female troubadour!

'And no doubt,' continues Ramon, 'she is scribbling about you already. The dolour of two beautiful twin sisters sadly parted is excellent fodder for poetry.'

'Forgive me, my Lady,' Dia says, putting aside her tablet and stylus and standing to give me a formal curtsey. 'I am remiss. I am honoured to meet you. Count Ramon has told me about your great learning and love of poetry.'

I blush at that. 'Great learning seems some flattery, Count,' I say to Ramon, 'but yes, love of books and poetry I will admit to. So I am pleased to meet you, Dia. You are the first female troubadour I have met!'

'We female troubadours are called *trobairitz*, my Lady. I am from Andalucia where there are many *trobairitz* and troubadours.'

'Will you let us hear some of your work?'

Dia places the harp on her lap. It is a golden boat-shaped instrument with a long handle bending back towards the body of the harp like a crook. She begins her *razo*, her introductory summary of the songs she will sing. 'Troubadour means finder and inventor,' she says in a melodious voice, strumming the harp. 'How much I have found and how much I have invented I must leave you to decide.'

> It greatly pleases me
> When people say that it's unseemly
> For a lady to approach a man she likes
> And hold him deep in conversation
> And whoever says that isn't very bright . . .'

I raise my eyebrows.

'She's warming up,' Ramon says.

Dia clears her throat and sings a beautiful lay about my Aunt Emma kidnapped by Vikings, and than another about my grandmother Adalmode.

'Are all your songs of women?' I ask her.

'Many are,' says Dia. 'I have songs about Brunhilde; Hildegarde, wife of Charlemagne; and the Empress Judith.'

I am delighted with Dia's songs and with Dia herself. Ramon looks pleased with the encounter. 'Fetch my book, Bernadette,' I order. Bernadette opens a chest and draws out the heavy book wrapped in sacking. She carries it over to a small table underneath the light from a window slit and unwraps it. We step up to the table to look at the Adhémar de Chabannes book together. The thick wooden boards of its cover are decorated with silver plate and encrusted with coloured jewels. I turn the pages slowly and carefully.

After a while Dia exchanges a glance with Ramon and asks, 'May I sing you one more story of a great lady?'

'Yes please do.'

We resume our seats and Dia sings about Ramon's grand-mother, Ermessende of Carcassonne. She is acknowledged by all men of Catalonia and Occitania as a strong and just ruler, laying the foundations for the might of Barcelona today.

'I have a *rotulus*, a scroll of my poems I would like to present to you as a gift if it pleases you, Lady Almodis,' says Dia.

I say that I will be more than pleased to receive such a gift.

'Perhaps your maid could accompany me to my chamber and bring it back to you as I must take my leave now? The Count of Toulouse has asked me to sing at the feast today.'

'Yes, go with Mistress Dia, Bernadette. I am grateful for your gift and for your songs.'

Bernadette rises to follow Dia out of the room, but hesitates on the threshold when she sees that Ramon has not risen from his seat. She looks questioningly at me.

'Don't dither Bernadette!' I say firmly. 'You will lose Mistress Dia and then lose your way in the maze of passageways.'

Now Raingarde's maid, Carlotta, is sitting in the corner of our chamber with a worried face, twisting her hands around and around in her apron, as I have just announced to my sister that I have a tremendous secret to tell her. Carlotta is just a simple country girl. Bernadette on the other hand is perched on the bed with us, hanging on our every word. Bernadette had left me alone with Count Ramon for half an hour or so whilst she went to fetch the scroll of poems from Dia.

'You should have asked father or Audebert to be here, Almo-dis,' Raingarde is telling me. 'You shouldn't receive strangers alone like that.'

I carry on with my story. 'He is that tall, young, blond-haired boy. You know, the one we saw at the investiture with Ermes-sende of Carcassonne. He is really rather charming for a boy.'

'Well, what did he want?'

'We talked about the Aquitaine Court and about Geoffrey of Anjou and Agnes. He asked me what I think about Toulouse, and he told me about Barcelona and about how his grandmother had been regent for his father and now, for him. He said that he would need an effective woman like her as his countess soon. Those were his words! An effective woman!'

'But isn't it strange to be asking a girl such things?' Raingarde asks.

'Of course not. I had plenty to say on those subjects. But mostly I think he came to gawk at me. I have made a conquest of a toddler!'

I laugh at my own joke but Raingarde looks at me with consternation and asks, 'Does he know you are betrothed to Hugh?'

'Yes, he seemed to know all about that and he is betrothed as well – to Blanca of Castile he says – but she really *is* a toddler.'

'Almodis, be careful! He may be only a boy but he is the Count of Barcelona all the same. You should not have seen him on your own. Promise me. At least I must be there another time.' Raingarde sighs loudly at me.

'And did you notice that ugly old Count of Toulouse staring at us in the investiture?' I ask her.

'Everybody stares at us Almodis,' Raingarde replies.

'Yes but he looked like he should like to lick our faces like two candied apples.'

'Oh fie Almodis! You slander the poor man,' Raingarde tells me.

I am laughing and shaking my head in disagreement, but then I become thoughtful and say, 'You know, Raingarde, I do believe that the Count of Barcelona is intending to propose marriage to me.'

There is a long pause whilst they all take in this flabbergasting piece of information. Raingarde looks at Bernadette. Bernadette looks at Carlotta who looks at her apron. They all look back at me.

'But Almodis you must tell father and Audebert now. It's important.'

'No, Raingarde.' I am imperious suddenly. 'And you will promise me not to speak of it to anyone. And you, Bernadette.' (I do

39

not bother to include Carlotta who can hardly string two words together anyway.) 'I do not wish to embarrass Ramon. He is sweet and rash and he means nothing by it. He is just a child.'

'I can't see how your extra four years puts you in a position to patronise the Count of Barcelona so,' says Raingarde. 'He may be only thirteen now but he is going to be a very rich young man in a few years time. What answer would you give him if he does propose? You must tell father at once! He must deal with it.'

'No need,' I say. 'I will thank him very graciously of course for the great honour he does me but assure him I cannot receive his proposals as I am solemnly contracted to Hugh, Lord of Lusignan, and will be married next month. I know that in betrothing me to Hugh, who is noble but yet not on a level with our own family, Aquitaine are seeking to control us, to keep La Marche from growing too proud and powerful. I know that. Look at you. You are marrying a count but I am merely marrying the Sire of Lugisnan and I am the heiress to Limoges, to our grandmother's rights and fortune! I know that an alliance with Barcelona could be a great opportunity for me and for La Marche.' I pause thoughtfully again and they all wait in suspense on my decision. 'Yet I could never break my solemn vow to Lusignan. Ermessende holds the reins of Barcelona and Ramon will have a battle on his hands, like his father before him, to wrest that control from her. He may not succeed. I will have to tell him that I regard my oath of betrothal to Hugh of Lusignan as seriously as would any man swearing homage to his lord. That will convince him to desist,' I finish with satisfaction.

'But Almodis, father may wish to consider this proposal don't you think? Barcelona is a great deal more powerful and rich than Lusignan and . . .'

'I had no idea you were so mercenary, Raingarde,' I interrupt. 'We won't speak of this anymore. Father would never countenance me breaking my troth and his oath. Next month I will be of age. I need a man, not a boy, for husband,' I say, remembering the muscles of Hugh's arms when he picked me up in Montreuil-Bonnin, his beautiful black hair and eyes, the red fullness of his mouth. To underline my statement, I sweep out of the room, feeling queenly, with my skirts swirling after me, wondering whether

Raingarde will tell our father or whether she will keep faith with me, her twin.

The next day I feel foolish when we hear that Ramon and his grandmother left Toulouse at daybreak. No proposal came and I am a little disappointed to find myself wrong in my expectations, even though I had resolved to say no.

6

November 1037

He has arrived, my husband-to-be, Hugh, travelling up the steep, icy road to Roccamolten, but Raingarde would not let me stay outside to see him come.

'It's freezing out here. You will see him soon enough.'

'He's really beautiful, Raingarde,' I tell her enthusiastically. 'Imagine when someone you love holds you; it must be like riding fast in a cold wind: you feel you *are*.'

Now he walks up the aisle in the Great Hall towards us, the La Marches, sitting on the platform, and I am pleased again at his powerful build and his well-shaped face. My father invites him to take a seat and a servant places a bowl for him to wash his hands, and puts wine and bread on the table. My view of the Lord of Lusignan is partially blocked by my brother, mother and father seated between us.

'My son, Audebert, will accompany Almodis to Limoges for the marriage,' father is telling Hugh. 'I must accompany her sister, Raingarde, to Carcassonne. It is all change now, in our family and I am sore at heart to lose my daughters.' Mother pats Father's hand.

'It will be my part to take good care of your daughter now, sire.' The interesting sound of Hugh's voice distracts me from my sadness at parting again from my family. I lean forward to catch another glimpse of him and he is looking back at me, with a cup half-way to his mouth. He smiles at me, but then he frowns as his eyes stray past me to Raingarde. 'I understand that she can read and write?' Hugh says to my father.

And what can you do, my lord, scuff a cross with your foot in the dirt? I am cross that he speaks of me as if I am not sitting there, an intelligent being, not an inanimate piece of furniture.

'Yes she reads and writes Latin, Langue d'Oc and Langue d'Oïl,' father responds proudly. Leaning slightly forward, I watch Hugh frown again at that information. I study his anxious features. He has two nicknames: Hugh the Fair and Hugh the Pious.

'What say you, Count,' he asks, 'of these claims that twins are the seed of two men, of adultery, or that they are the offspring of the Devil'.

I feel my mother shift on the bench, and I squeeze my sister's hand under the trestle, struggling to stay silent with my eyes downcast as I know my mother would wish.

'Don't be foolish, man,' father responds. 'Do they look like the seed of two men to you?' He pauses and glances at us for dramatic effect. 'What you are looking at *here*,' his arm sweeps across in front of me and Raingarde, 'are two fine *heir* breeding girls.'

I drop my head to conceal my amusement and hear a faint snicker escape from my sister. Beneath the trestle our joined hands clench and jiggle up and down on our knees, like laughter. My thigh is pressed tightly up against Raingarde's. I have to work hard to compress the glee on my lips into a demure shape before raising my head to see how Lusignan is taking my father's crude description of us. I wish then that I hadn't looked up because the sight of his face, dark pink with embarrassment, threatens my barely controlled humour. He wants me. The recognition is sudden and pleasing. I feel the heat of my own face. But my father is going about this discussion in all the wrong way. I will have to help. 'My Lord Hugh.'

My father, brother and Lusignan all turn towards me in surprise and Raingarde clutches my hand in warning. The 'heirbreeder' will speak.

'I have debated this question of the godliness or no of twins myself with our chaplain,' I say, fast and certain, before anyone can find the wit to stop me. My mother has placed a hand against her mouth as if to say 'Be silent!' I can feel Raingarde willing me to shut up, but Hugh is looking at me with interest.

'Indeed? And what does your chaplain say of it?'

'He has told me of twins in the bible who were blessed and of twins who have held holy office or been of noble birth and repute,' I say, making it all up on the spot, my eyes wide with innocent earnestness. It is what he wants to hear, what he wants to see.

'Indeed,' Hugh says again.

I let go of Raingarde's hand which has been tightly clutched inside my own, and shift my position so that our knees are no longer touching.

'We have a shrine to Our Lady in the walled garden that I would show you.' I point towards the door and allow a smile to bloom slowly on my mouth. 'We could speak there of Father Jerome's advice regarding twins.'

Hugh lurches abruptly to his feet, his eyes on my mouth. 'Yes, let us speak of this further, my Lady.'

I exchange the slightest glance of understanding with my father who is looking surprised but impressed with my initiative. I rise serenely, nearly matching my suitor in height. I place my white hand, with its long shapely fingers and its near-invisible knuckle scars, on the blue linen of his sleeve and steer him towards the garden.

7

Bernadette: A Parisienne in Roccamolten

I'm so relieved to be staring at the curling parchment that my Lady Almodis is pinning down on cook's floury table and reading out to me and Raingarde and all the assembled kitchen servants.

'In the year 1037 Anno Domini, Hugh V of Lusignan, contracts to marry Almodis of La Marche, daughter of Bernard I of La Marche and Amelie of Montignac. For that I, Hugh, respecting the authority of the Scriptures, guided by the counsel and exhortation of my friends and aided by heavenly piety, defer to the general custom concerning marital association,' she pauses to gulp in a breath and we are all laughing excitedly, and then she rushes on, 'out of love, and according to ancient usage, I give you, my gentle and most gracious sponsa,' she breathes again, and points a finger at herself nodding theatrically to us, 'by the authority of this sponsalicium, by way of dowry the *third* of my estates.' She draws that out emphatically, beams at us and then finishes in a great rush, 'This is given with the agreement of my mother and brothers and given to you for your lifetime. After death these properties shall come back to the children who shall be born of us!'

I push cook's hip out of the way so's I can get a better look at Lord Hugh's signature on the bottom of the document and Count Bernard's, along with their coats of arms. The Lusignan badge is boring: just a shield shape with silver and blue stripes, but the House of La Marche has a regal-looking badge with three lions prancing along a red stripe with a blue background and golden fleur de lys.

The relief is obvious on Raingarde's face, after the worry Almodis put us through at the Toulouse Easter Assembly over that Count of Barcelona. Well she is rich indeed now. A third of all of Lusignan, an eighth of Limoges inherited from her grandmother, and the gift of estates from her father too for her marriage. And it can't be all bad for me, either, with such a wealthy mistress!

When I first arrived in La Marche, I couldn't get over having to look at those two faces, Almodis and Raingarde, exactly the same and never knowing which was which. Now I'm used to it. More than that, now I can tell them apart by a difference in the aura that comes into the room with each of them. She, Almodis, my mistress, is all confidence. Swagger even. More like a lord than a lady. Raingarde, her sister, she's much more timid and demure, like a lady should be. Piers says that Raingarde was sequestered properly with her mother and the women since she was twelve like a girl should be, but nobody at the Court of Aquitaine put a halter on Almodis when she was that age. She grew up with the freedoms and education of a young prince, Piers says, and it shows. When I first got here, I used to have to wait for one of them to do or say something before I could tell which was which. Sooner or later, she will say or do something that Raingarde just never would say or do. But now I can tell it from the different things they do to the air around them. I'm usually right.

Amelie, their mother, comes into the kitchen announced by the chinking of the keys and needles on the short chains of her chatelaine belt. She is followed by the nursemaid with my Lady's two little sisters in hand, Lucia who is three and Agnes who is two. 'There you both are! What are you doing with that marriage contract rolling around in grease and gravy Almodis? Roll it up at once and make sure you put it back in your father's chest where it belongs. Now I need you all to help me with the preparations for tonight's wedding feast. Bernadette, go and lay fresh rushes in the hall and clean covers on the trestles, and then come back here and I will show you which of the glass beakers to lay out on the high table.'

I gulp at that and look up at those beakers ranged on a high shelf. I'm not relishing the idea of being responsible for carrying those fragile beauties. There's a bright blue glass drinking horn there in the middle of the shelf and on either side of it are pale green claw beakers. I've got a vision running through my head of them smashed in smithereens at my feet.

'Come on, then, Bernadette! There's lots to do,' Almodis tells me. She picks up the rolled marriage contract and tugs me out of the kitchen with her, like I'm her pony.

I told him I'd meet him at the old ruin but now that I am here and he hasn't arrived I wish I hadn't come. The evening is drawing in. The cold is penetrating my thin cloak. It is the twilight hour – *entre chien et loup* – between dog and wolf. The black rooks are circling in the pale sky. From this side of the hill I have a clear view across to the castle perched on the mountain top like an eagle's nest and the village clustered around it. The lower part of the village is shrouded in the rising evening mist. The buildings with their red roofs circle haphazardly around Roccamolten. In the far distance I can see more black mountains set against the darkening sky. How many mountains between me and Paris, my old home? I am just about making up my mind to leave when he arrives.

'Bernadette,' he calls to me softly picking his way carefully around the fallen stones in the long grass. 'But you are freezing, darling,' he says taking off his cloak and wrapping it around me. His mouth is on mine before I've had time to say a word. I open my mouth to his tongue. I am no longer cold in his arms. 'I have a present for you,' Piers says, his hand stroking my face and hair. From inside his tunic, he produces a tin bracelet with a decoration of blue glass and slips it onto my wrist. I turn my arm around and around, pretending to admire it, but I am disappointed. Only tin. It will tarnish and leave green marks on my white skin. I will never wear it after today.

'It's so strange here,' I say to Piers as he traces the contours of my face and neck with his finger. 'I can't understand what anyone is saying. I don't understand the speech of Raingarde, Audebert and Count Bernard.'

Piers' finger has strayed down to trace the outline of my breast

47

through the thick layers of my clothes and now it reaches my nipple. I slap away his hand. 'Are you listening or just groping?'

'Oh definitely listening, sweet Bernadette. Are we so different from you northerners then?'

'As different as ducks from chickens!'

His smiling lips are wide and wet against the silky brown of his beard and I long to kiss them; but my mother gave me a very long lecture on men before I left home. Looking into Piers' face I know that I am looking at the trap she described. 'They love you. They leave you with child. You lose your place. You and the child starve to death,' she'd told me over and over again, until it was like a nursery rhyme in my head. Piers has a long, large face framed by floppy brown hair. His eyebrows are thick and black above pale blue eyes. The blue is relegated to the edges now as his pupils are huge with desire for me.

Piers is the only real friend I have here. He and Almodis are the only people who can speak my northern French – Langue d'Oil – as well as their native Langue d'Oc. The Aquitaine Court was bilingual, facing in both directions, north and south. But here in the La Marche household, everyone speaks only Langue d'Oc, the language of the South. Piers told me that Occitan requires the mouth to be in a different shape to northern speech. I spent days listening to and imitating the sounds of the other servants shouting and singing: 'burb b burb b burb b,' I sang to myself with my mouth in what I imagined to be an Occitan shape as I wandered around the castle, doing my work. I will have to master it eventually but for now every conversation in this alien tongue feels like a catechism to me and I am tired out trying to understand it. These conversations with Piers in my own language are my only chance to relax.

'You will grow to love the South,' he says. 'The mountains are beautiful. As beautiful as you. And you will get used to the Occitan eventually, the accent *chantant*.'

I screw up my nose. Who cares about beautiful mountains? They are cold and rainy. There are no markets and few people to talk with. The conversation of rural folk is hardly to my liking after what I was used to in my mother's tavern in Paris. I couldn't care less about pigs and weather and crops.

Piers' rude finger wobbles my protruding bottom lip. 'You are pouting, Bernadette brown eyes,' he teases me.

'Well what is so exciting about some cold mountain?'

'Roccamolten Castle is not on just some cold mountain!' he laughs. 'La Marche is the frontier country. The count holds the frontier of Occitania against you northern French as his father and grandfather did before him. We are a proud race of warriors.'

He kisses me again and starts to undo the clasp of one of my shoulder-brooches that fasten my gown.

'You rush me, Piers,' I say, pushing away his hands.

'*You* rush me, Bernadette,' he says laughing. 'So let's find somewhere warmer and talk.' He pulls me into a part of the ruin that is more intact, where there is some protection from the cold wind, but the ground we sit on is cold and hard even with his cloak spread beneath us.

'How goes it with your mistress?' he asks, continuing his work on my brooch. One side of my gown falls down and I am embarrassed to see my breast emerge with its red nipple erect in the cold air. His hand closes over my breast and warms me. I know I should stop this now. I try vainly to recall my mother's advice but the feelings coursing through my body as his mouth covers my nipple are overwhelming. With an effort I push him away and hold my gown up against me.

'Piers stop that. My mistress talks to me harshly and expects me to turn her out like a queen when she behaves like a stable boy,' I say, hoping to distract him with what I know is his favourite conversation.

'Aye, she ignores and is rude to me too, little Bernadette.'

'And most ladies don't go gallivanting in their best gowns in the mud at all hours. I'm sure Raingarde doesn't,' I say.

'Aye, they two are different alright. Like as can be to look at, except for Almodis' scars, but different as can be in temper.'

'What scars?' I ask. I've bathed my Lady often enough in her padded tub and I've seen no scars on that perfect body. Piers reddens and I wonder if he has been peeking somewhere he shouldn't.

'On her left hand,' he says. 'Three small scars between her knuckles.'

I've never noticed them myself and wonder why he has.

'All that time she spent as a hostage at the Aquitaine Court has gone right to her head and she thinks she is the very Queen of the Franks, the very Queen of Charlemagne himself. I never saw such self-assurance in a young woman in my life,' I say to him, but as I say it, I realise that I'm starting to feel just a bit impressed with her. The count has still made no move to acknowledge Piers as his bastard and he projects his bitterness at this onto my mistress. 'She is more like a man than a woman with all her reading, hunting, talking politics and striding around in boots with her brothers.'

'Aye,' says Piers, his hand now roaming on my knee and pushing up my skirts. 'She is that. Mannish.'

The sensation of his hand on the soft inside of my bare thigh, above my hose, is glorious. I try to squeeze my legs together and squash his hand away but that only seems to increase the pleasure for both of us. Instead of removing his hand I am wriggling against it and feeling hot waves of desire. I pull myself away from his hand, sitting up against a sharp rock behind us. I should leave now.

'She will have to mend her ways when she is a wife,' I say, a little breathlessly. 'She will have to be obedient and submissive, then.'

'Yes, but I doubt that Hugh is the man to tame Almodis and put her right,' says Piers, his mouth on my neck and ear and his hand undoing my other shoulder brooch. My gown slides down exposing both my breasts to the cold night air.

'You think him weak?' I gasp in a last vain attempt to distract him and stem the desire coursing through me, but he does not answer and I can say no more as he pulls me down on the ground, pulls up my skirts and mounts me and I am moaning now in pleasure.

It is full dark when I walk home. He has waited behind for a while so that we should not be seen returning together. I feel the dampness and soreness from him between my legs. I worry that I might be with child, but then Piers will marry me and I will have myself a fine husband with noble blood. I look doubtfully at the cheap tin bangle on my arm. I take it off and put it in my pocket.

8

Hugh the Fair

For our feast before I leave home for my marriage, I am seated next to Hugh and sharing his trencher. He helps me politely to food. My father and then my brother are seated to Hugh's right. My other brother is away from home, training at the Court of Périgord. My mother is sitting on my other side. Raingarde has been veiled and banished to the children's table lower down the hall, out of sight. The servants have cleared away the first courses of the meal and now they are parading in with the roasted hare and lamb.

'Well, here you are my child, the Peaceweaver,' says father, looking with satisfaction at the bowls of pink and black sauce in front of him. 'As you know, Lord Hugh, there have been many years of fighting between our three families: Aquitaine, La Marche and Lusignan. First one of us encroached on another's territory or took another's castle or killed a kinsman and then there were the needful revenges. Those arguments went on for two generations, back and forth, but now this joining of you and my daughter will put an end to it.'

I have grown familiar with my father's gesture of leaning back to savour his wine, and his stories of old times. It is expected at a wedding feast, to tell something of the stories of our kin.

'Your ancestors, Lord Hugh, and mine, were bodyguards to King Charlemagne himself,' father says, 'and we hold our lands proudly, independently. Since Charlemagne, there has been no central power and each man has put his trust in his own sword.'

My father is tempering his language for Hugh's sake. Usually he is forcefully abusive about his neighbours but now he is choosing his words carefully in order not to re-open old wounds and revive old arguments. Eye for eye, kin for kin vendettas have been the way for decades between our three families. Peace was ever precarious.

'My father invaded Aquitaine, intending to dispossess Duke Guillaume V of Aquitaine, old Guillaume the Great, but my father took an arrow after the battle of Gencais and died of his wound at Charroux. The troops captured his brother, Gausbert, and cruelly blinded him for good measure. My mother, Adalmode, held out against the duke for weeks right here in the castle of Roccamolten but when he finally took the fortress she was forced to marry him and abandon me here under the guardianship of my uncle Boson. I was a mere babe at the time.'

I smile at that. It is hard to imagine my burly, battle-scarred father as a baby. He wipes his greasy fingers on the tablecloth and continues his story. 'My mother willed her inheritance of Limoges to my first-born daughter, Almodis here, in order to protect Limoges and La Marche from the ambitions of the Aquitaine family. And then on your side, sire, your family were great castle builders.' Father pauses politely to let Hugh take up the story.

'Yes, my great-grandfather, Hugh II, built the castle of Lusignan which is the largest in all Aquitaine, Lady,' Hugh says addressing me. I nod encouragingly but he says no more.

'According to some doctors,' Audebert interrupts, yelling a little too loudly down the table and holding up his brimming beaker, 'wine will give you good blood, good colour, strengthen your bodily virtues and make you happy, good-natured and well-spoken.' He raises his cup to Hugh who nods politely but makes no rejoinder to Audebert's humour. Hugh is drinking slowly, taking small mouthfuls and, unlike Father and Audebert, he is mixing water with his wine. It is a very good wine from Burgundy so it can't be the taste that is causing him to be so moderate. Perhaps he is being careful in potentially antagonistic company.

'Your father, Hugh the Brown, now he fought hard for his rights against both Aquitaine and myself.' Father pauses again to see if Hugh wants to give his own account of his notoriously bellicose and land-hungry father but he still says nothing so father goes on. 'He fought for many years with me and had many arguments and resentments with Aquitaine and others too.'

'Yes,' says Hugh, 'but these arguments seem most complex and difficult to unravel, with Fulk Nerra, Count of Anjou, the Vicomtes of Limoges and Geoffrey of Thouars also involved.'

'Oh they were complex alright,' yells father, laughing down the table in the direction of Audebert. I shift in my seat, hoping that father will not get carried away with his stories of old battles and say something to offend Hugh.

'Your father claimed the lands of Thouars as his but Guillaume of Aquitaine, that wily old bastard, he thwarted your father at every turn,' father says.

'So I understand,' says Hugh. 'My father used to tell me how the Duke of Aquitaine said to him, "If all the world were mine I would not give you what I could lift with my finger"'.

'Your father threw Thouars' men from the keep in one of the battles,' father says, 'and so Geoffrey of Thouars burned your father's fortress at Mouzeil, captured his horsemen and cut off their hands.'

A pained expression creases Hugh's forehead, but he still seems uninterested in giving his own version of his father's exploits.

'Then your father was trying to lay claim to Vivonne and to Civray, which were mine, of course,' father continues. 'Guillaume forced your father against his will to give me allegiance. The duke said to your father, "You are so dependent on me that if I told you to make a peasant your lord, you ought to have done it". That's when Duke Guillaume required four hostages of me as surety for my good behaviour. So I sent my little Almodis here and three others. He demanded her specifically of course because of her inheritance. Your father was incensed when I regained Civray and he demanded my hostages from Guillaume in recompense. Thankfully the old duke did not hand her over.' He caresses my hand.

'So how did the betrothal come about?' asks Audebert politely. We all know the answer, but this telling of the story at the wedding feast is also expected.

'Guillaume insisted on a truce between us at the court assembly at Blaye. I got word of this truce rather late,' father says, somewhat fudging the facts. 'I was besieging your mother, I'm afraid Hugh, in your family's fortress at Confolens, so Guillaume insisted then that my daughter Almodis, should be betrothed to you, to make the peace. I was obliged to leave Almodis continuing as a hostage at the Aquitaine Court after the betrothal, as a surety that I would hold to my promises.'

'Peace is what we should all wish for,' says Hugh, finally speaking out. 'I have subscribed my name to *Le Trêve de Dieu* – the Truce of God. There has been too much fighting and bloodshed.'

'Aye, aye,' says my father, sitting there with his face a patchwork of livid battle scars. He and Audebert exchange glances.

'What is the Truce of God?' I ask.

'It is the initiative of Bishop Clermont Etienne and Bishop Bégon. It imposes constraints on the private wars between lords, on those *bellatores* whose way of life is war,' Hugh tells me. 'The Pope has blessed the truce against these bad customs.'

I regard my husband-to-be. He looks like a warrior and yet he is none. He looks like a strong man and yet he talks like a monk. Peace is good but not if there is reason against it. I would not sign such a pact. There are those who would sign it in hypocrisy, and take advantage of the false security it promised to others.

'It's true enough that we have seen plenty of battle with foreign raiders, without continually stoking the battle between ourselves as well,' says Audebert and Hugh nods his head in agreement.

In the decades before my birth France and Occitania suffered continual and brutal invasions from Muslims in the South, from Hungarian Magyars in the East, and from Viking attacks on settlements on the coasts and up rivers. Intensive castle building and fortification of towns and villages has been the result.

'The country bristles with walls and palisades that are the visible symbol of our great anguish,' I say.

'Yes,' says father. 'The times of order and security that we knew under the Romans and then under Charlemagne are long gone.'

'But they will come again with the Truce of God,' says Hugh.

'Amen to that,' says my mother.

Father, Audebert and I hold our tongues and avoid looking at each other. The La Marche family has not succeeded for so long in holding the embattled frontier by succumbing to such feeble wishful thinking. I take a spoonful of quivering custard tart. 'The dariole is very good,' I tell Hugh.

'What of the Capetians, Lusignan?' Father asks.

'They seem to have no ambitions to the South and confine themselves to the northern country.'

Henri, the Capetian king rules France, north of the Loire. In the South, in Occitania and Catalonia, we have no king. Instead we have the independent dukes and counts: Gascogne, Provence, Auvergne, Aquitaine, La Marche, Toulouse, Barcelona and Carcassonne amongst them.

'My father met Hugh Capet and his son, Robert,' father announces and Hugh turns to him with interest.

'They expected him to bow down to them: Audebert, Count of La Marche!' Father guffaws. 'They were mightily surprised when he just said to them, "And who made you kings?"' Father, Audebert and I laugh heartily at our ancestor's famous quip. 'Who made you kings?' Father repeats, louder.

Hugh is not laughing. 'But might not a unification of north and south under the Capetian king bring us peace,' he says, 'and put an end to this constant rivalry between the southern lords?'

Father stops laughing.

'Unification!' splutters Audebert, too infuriated to be polite. 'Don't be stupid, man. The North is another country with its own tongue and culture. There is no possibility of unification. That would only be the death and the end of us: the South, Langue d'Oc, Occitania! When the Moors captured Barcelona, Hugh Capet showed his colours and refused to give the city any assistance. The counts of Barcelona and Auvergne have refused to acknowledge the authority of the Capetians and rightly so.'

Hugh is silent again, and mother skilfully turns the talk towards less controversial topics. The rest of the feast passes in friendly but dull talk of the foundation of new abbeys and monasteries in the region. Hugh is more animated on this topic. What need of a peaceweaver if my husband is already such a man of peace?

9.

May 1038

I am stepping into the Abbey of Saint Martial in Limoges and a sudden silence descends on the crowd of large men clad in dark leather that I see ahead of me, looking incongruous against the loops of fragile May flowers adorning the church. My usual confidence deserts me. I feel tiny in this soaring stone vault. I imagine that I am sitting on one of the huge beams far overhead looking down on my miniscule, distant self, weighed down in this heavy wedding dress, stared at by strangers.

If I had to speak right now nothing would emerge from my mouth. I try to swallow down the gag that seems to be filling my throat. Goosebumps rise on my arms and legs as I contemplate the necessity of walking alone up this long aisle to be wed. I scan the faces of these men looking for the one I know: my brother, Audebert.

'Ah, and here is the bride,' my brother's voice identifies his position.

I swallow down the fear in my throat and look in his direction. Eudes, the new Duke of Aquitaine, stands next to Audebert smiling at me. Both my father and my uncle Guillaume died a few months ago so that everything familiar is now strange. I feel angry with myself for this sudden and ridiculous timidity. Why should I, Almodis of La Marche, feel timid and small. What can I be afraid of? When I spoke of my coming marriage at home, when my father was still alive, it seemed like a good game and I was in control of it but now it is a concrete reality. I must have this man,

Hugh, in my bed, in my body. I will have to render my marriage debt to him and I will have to give birth to his children. I know that in time I will make a fine new game of all this too but for now I am miserable at the loss of my mountain home and, above all, the loss of my sister, like a limb hacked off, a raw absence at my side.

Audebert and Eudes, these young untried men are the rulers now. I know that my marriage will make important bonds in this new regime between La Marche, Aquitaine and Lusignan. I know that by marrying this man, Hugh, I will seem to please them all but I will please myself. I will make my family safe in La Marche. How far away home is. How strange and cold is this vast church. I see boys swinging censors on long chains. I hear the burr of a bird's wings high up in the roof.

I find a way to force myself forward. I focus on Eudes, holding his gaze, lift my stiff skirts with one hand and walk straight ahead to stand in front of him, not thinking about or looking at the others. I know that if I glance to either side or do anything other than fixate on the duke I will turn and bolt back out of the door behind me, that I will run to the stables, leap onto my horse and ride out of this place at a gallop. I am wondering if I can do it. Could I? I watch my feet in their white slippers stepping on the jewels of red- and blue-coloured light that play on the floor as the sun filters through the stained glass windows. I am arrived already in front of Eudes. I feel a smile curving my lips that only seconds before had trembled as I crossed the threshold. 'My Lord Eudes,' I say, standing before him, lowering my eyes demurely.

'Ah, lovely cousin, Almodis,' he takes my hand and strokes it as if he might be my new husband instead. Then I feel him place my hand into another hand, a large, cold hand and the panic begins to rise again. I am suddenly conscious that I have not looked at Lusignan at all yet.

I look up at Eudes, then at Audebert, who is smiling encouragement to me. Our two tow heads stand out in a sea of dark brown hair and beards. I try to keep the panic out of my eyes. I am glad of the thick white veil covering my face and hair. I find myself rolling my lips inwards on themselves and stop and pout them out again. I swivel my neck to look straight at him. I am not afraid. I am not. Hugh is looking directly at me through my veil. I register the startling solid black of his eyes. I look at my hand in his. I am pleased to find there is no trembling in my loyal hand. I cannot say the same for my knees but nobody can see them.

I will not be afraid of him, not I, but I do wish that my sister were here. My brother has judged that Raingarde must stay at home with my mother who is unwell. Raingarde will be travelling soon to her own marriage, affording Audebert another opportunity to strengthen his alliances as the new Count of La Marche. My mother told Audebert that he must avoid reminding Hugh of his superstitions about two girls who look the same, who do everything together – except this. Raingarde! I say in my mind, and fear that I might have said it aloud.

The bishop blesses us and begins the words of the marriage ceremony. I can't focus on the words that the bishop and then the man holding my hand are starting to say because I am still trying to decide whether or not to flee. Would I trip in this enormous gold and white dress with its stiff layers of dense embroidery? Could I extract my hand quickly enough to take them by surprise? Will they catch me before I reach the door, or before the stable, before I am struggling to rise into the saddle? Would it be best to shrug off the dress at the door and make my escape in my linen? Images of escape and possible captures flash in my mind and I see nothing with my eyes. The sound of the bishop speaking my name recalls me to the scene in front of me.

'Almodis of La Marche, do you consent to marry Hugh, Lord of Lusignan?'

A silence descends on the abbey. I smell damp. I hear a chink of metal on metal as someone shifts their position. I notice that the speaking has stopped and that the duke and Lusignan are looking at me expectantly. My brother's boot nudges the tip of my slipper quite hard.

'Oh, I do,' I say. Why did I say that! Tears of frustration and confusion spill off the edge of one of my eyelids and trickle down my cheek. Just a few. They reach the bottom of my chin and hang there, getting unpleasantly cold. I feel a strong need to sniff but I know that my brother would be mortified if I did such a thing in the middle of my wedding in front of all these nobles and rivals. The bishop is sprinkling Hugh and myself with holy water.

The question of my bolting is still hovering in my head, like a loose thread, a name I can't quite remember that is on the tip of my tongue and then, so quickly, the ceremony is over and Hugh lifts up my veil. His big hand holds my wet chin and tilts my face up towards him and he kisses me. He moves his mouth and face away from mine and I find myself smiling at him. His mouth is soft and red in his dark beard. I lift my eyebrows and open my mouth a little in surprise to find myself married.

10

Morgengebe

The door to the bedchamber stands open, as it must, so that the wedding party might, at least symbolically, appear to be witnesses to the consummation. The ruckus of drunken guests, with my brother and Duke Eudes among them, has withdrawn back to the Hall of Lusignan Castle and the bedchamber is suddenly silent and still. The room is brightly lit with many tall candles. The bishop made the sign of the cross on our foreheads and over the bed. I am naked on the bed and I shiver. Hugh has also been stripped by the carousing guests and sits on the other side of the bed. The expanse between us seems substantial. I feel a damp patch of holy water under my thigh. I swallow and turn to look at my husband. I am conscious of my thick, golden hair loosed down my back and soft on my shoulders. Hugh is not looking at me but instead has his eyes fixed down on the bedcover. I *am* proud of my embroidery but aren't I a better feast for his eyes? It took me two years to sew that quilt. My sister would have sewn such an item in a solid three months of patience and skill. She has taken four such bedcovers with her to Carcassonne and many other items of her beautiful needlework, but I picked this bedcover up and put it down repeatedly in irritation over the last two years. My needlework is fine enough but it bores me after a while and I rarely finish anything. My mother and sister had to help me with the final stages of this cover.

Since Hugh isn't looking at me I can allow my eyes to stray over him. His skin is a smooth olive brown sliding over the prominent muscles of his arms and thighs. In the centre of his chest there is a disk of curling black hair. His body is cupped to itself protectively. Should I touch him? I have no fear of coupling. I have watched horses and dogs mating. I inadvertently came across Piers once tupping a maid against a wall while we were still in Poitiers. I stayed and spied on them, curious, intrigued at the expression on the maid's face and the sounds she made and the rhythmic thrusting of Piers' buttocks. I want to bear strong sons, to be an excellent wife and chatelaine. I want to help the fortunes of my husband's family rise.

Hugh clears his throat. 'You do me great honour, Lady. You are indeed beautiful.'

I am a little irritated at this formula, especially since he hasn't looked at me yet. I have begun to realise that my husband, habitually, says little. Communication with him is not easy. If he were not so beautiful it would be possible to sometimes feel that he is barely present.

'Would you have me lie down, my Lord?' I ask tentatively. His mouth twitches and he clears his throat again. My confidence is beginning to desert me. I do not understand the tension I feel in the air. I cannot read it.

'The priests say that new married couples should abjure carnal relations for the first three days,' he says looking up at me briefly and then back down at the bedcover.

I am momentarily dumb-founded. If I do not produce the evidence in the morning that he has taken my virginity, what will my brother say, Duke Eudes, my mother-in-law Audearde? They will all blame me. 'And yet, my Lord,' I say gently, 'is it not our duty to get an heir for Lusignan?'

He nods but his whole body speaks of dejection not desire. I feel desperate with disappointment and fear of being shamed, but I cannot give up.

'Shall I blow out the candles and put the curtains warm about us?'

He nods again and I rise swaying carefully to display my naked body as well I might. Approaching the last candle I see that his eyes are raised at last, but not to me. Instead he looks to the large crucifix on the wall.

61

Dawn begins to seep into the bedchamber as I lie listening to the cockerel crowing and the soft breathing of the man beside me. I sit up and begin to pull on my shift, cloak and slippers. Hugh stirs behind me. I speak with my back to him. 'I believe it would be best if our guests understand that the consummation has taken place and that the morning gift can be given. Do you agree?'

'Yes, but . . .'

'I will take care of it.' I stand abruptly and move to the door without looking at him. Walking down the dim passage beyond the chamber my misery and resolve mingle. In the privacy of the passage I allow emotion to melt the forced serenity of my face. As I emerge into the early sunshine in the bailey I see Bernadette at the well, and the emotion is instantly erased again and I assume a smile of greeting. Could I trust Bernadette with the task? No. I can trust no-one. I wave away her enquiry and move towards the falconry mews. Let Piers not be there yet, I pray. Let his head be as sore as a bear's arse from last night's 'celebrations'. My prayer is answered and only the unblinking golden eyes of ten falcons turn to my entry. I make straight for the feeding tray where Piers has laid out freshly dead mice, rats and small birds. What would bleed enough? What would Piers not miss? I pick one of the larger rats up by its tail and quickly fold it into the cloth I have carried from the bedchamber. I push the other rats a little to conceal the gap and turn back, hearing my peregrine cry hungry behind me.

Later in the great hall I smile and smile as Audebert and Eudes clap Hugh on the back. The muscles of my face ache. 'May we remove this now my Lord,' I ask gesturing to the bloodied sheet that Piers and Bernadette have been holding up for all to see, and remembering Hugh's look of horror as I slit open the belly of the rat above the sheet in the bedchamber.

'It'll be twins, I wager,' Eudes tells Hugh. 'And what will you give your Lady in return for her virginity?'

Hugh gestures to a servant who comes forward and sets a small box in front of me, and the bedsheet is at last rolled up and stowed away. I open the box and exclaim with delight as I pull out an intricate green and blue jewel on a very fine gold chain. It is a tiny mermaid. I lift out and read a parchment from the box and find that Hugh has given me the deeds to the castle vineyard as my *morgengebe*, my morning gift. I thank him for his gifts.

'And maybe another little gift already, eh, Hugh?' laughs Audebert.

My mind is racing. What will I do if I cannot mate with my husband and prove my fertility. I will be put away in a nunnery as a sterile wife. I clench my fists and bite my lip at the unfairness of it. I do not want to be a nun! A marriage could be dissolved if impotency were proved but that would be humiliating for both of us. There must be another way. I could find another man to get me with child. I could ask Piers. I close my eyes briefly, appalled with myself. I must entice my husband, that is all. Once the guests have gone we can take time to get to know each other. I will have to guard against the jealous prying of my mother-in-law who has a fierce *contempus mundi*, a contempt of the world that I cannot share with her. I wonder how Raingarde has fared on her wedding night and pray that she is happy.

My brother has left to return to Roccamolten and Duke Eudes hurried back to Poitiers alarmed by news that Agnes and Geoffrey are mustering an army in the north. With the guests gone and less need for a sustained charade of married bliss I feel more at ease. I still have to keep a serene face to Hugh's mother, Audearde, and his two brothers, Rorgon, who is a priest, and the youngest brother, Renaud. I like Renaud. He is open and lively and near my own age. We ride and take our hawks out together most days. I feel Audearde and Rorgon watching me, looking for errors, for chinks in my armour. She is of the opinion, which she likes to tell us all often, that the world is not our real home, that living is a fraction of existence, a blink of an eye, whilst death is eternal, life merely interrupts the continuity of death. Audearde was regent for Hugh for five years after her husband's death and has never really let go of the reins. Hugh, my gentle Hugh, demurs to her opinions. Audearde is walking bitter envy of my possession of her son.

'Every utterance, Daughter,' she says to me, 'is an indictment of humanity.'

'No, Mother,' I counter, 'every utterance is a statement of presence in this beautiful, God-given, world.'

A week after my marriage, I am sitting breaking my fast on the raised platform in the hall. Audearde sits next to me and we watch Hugh and Renaud leave. They are going hunting together this morning. Audearde and I rise from the table and step towards the edge of the dais. I wait until she has stepped down from the platform, whilst I remain on it. 'The castle keys, Mother . . .' I begin.

Audearde turns to me with a kindly smile on her wrinkled face. 'You have a great deal on your mind at the moment, Daughter, getting used to a new place and your new position as wife to my son. I will take care of the household for now as usual whilst you make yourself at ease here.' She starts briskly down the hall, the chatelaine keys clinking at her hip.

'Thank you madame.' My voice rings down the hall arresting Audearde's progress and forcing her to turn back to face me. 'You are very kind. Nevertheless I will take the castle keys and my responsibilities now.' I inject the steel of command into my voice and hold out my hand. I have spent my childhood around the Aquitaine family who carry themselves as royalty and I have watched how my father commands his men. Audearde opens her mouth to protest, 'My dear . . .'

I interrupt her immediately bringing a new note of imperious irritation into my words, 'I will take them, *now*, Mother.' I say the last word as if it were a threatening insult. I have already resolved that if she gives me trouble I will find a way to give her her heart's desire: a cell in a nunnery. Audearde cannot turn to Hugh for support since I have deliberately waited for him to leave the hall. My mother-in-law walks slowly back towards me, her face betraying her failing attempts to find a convincing reason for refusal. She arrives in front of me with anger plain in her frown and the purse of her mouth. She unclips the heavy bunch of keys from her girdle and slaps them into my palm. I nod graciously in thanks as if she has volunteered them cheerfully. She turns abruptly and walks back down the hall, her girdle looking empty now with just her needles and threads suspended from it. Whilst her back is turned, I allow my mouth to curve up in a brief smile for my own benefit. I know that I will have to engage in such skirmishes with my mother-in-law over the coming weeks and I know that I will always win them.

64

It began as soon as I arrived, when I was carefully unpacking my books in my chamber with Bernadette. I was thinking that now I am a wife with my own lands and wealth I can buy more books. Audearde came into the chamber behind us.

'Books, Daughter,' she said, as if she was looking at a pile of steaming horse dung. 'You will have no need of them as wife of my son. I will arrange for someone from the priory to come and collect these. A monastery is a castle built against Satan.'

I curbed my anger and made my face bland before turning to her. 'No you will not,' I said simply. 'Orders regarding my possessions, whatever they are – my books, my servants, my lands, my tithes, will be made by me, Mother, and not by you or anybody else.'

'Your husband will give orders regarding all this,' Audearde told me smugly.

'No,' I said, 'he will not. Or you, and he, will find that I will be returning to Roccamolten and my wealth and possessions with me. My brother and the Duke of Aquitaine will hardly be pleased should I find the necessity for that.' I lifted one eyebrow and stared my mother-in-law down.

She stepped back to the doorway as if I had slapped her, and then left. I learnt early that bullies often respond best to being bullied. They live in the security that no one will dare treat them as they treat others, so that if you do surprise them with just that, they turn instantly into cowards. Over the next few days I had shown Audearde the bare minimum of respect and the flash of my temper at the slightest contradiction. The tactics seem to be working. On the occasion of my books, I had to resist the urge to celebrate my win with Bernadette who was grinning gleefully at me. That would not have been dignified. I returned to my unpacking and gradually quelled the shaking of my hands.

Now I look down at my new trophy, the bunch of keys and the chatelaine seal of the Lady of Lusignan. On one side the seal depicts the castle. On its other side there is a curious design of a sinuous serpent's head with a woman's face, rearing up out of the castle moat. Time to show the household how I mean to run things, to make some changes and establish my control!

I call Bernadette to come with me and then I go directly to the kitchen to examine the supplies and give orders to the servants, following the advice my mother gave me at home in Roccamolten. The kitchen is hot and full of people who turn surprised eyes upon me. I tour around with Bernadette, finding out who does what here. High piles of wood have been neatly stacked against the wall by the *souffleur* whose job it is to mind the fire. Servants are struggling in from the well with pails and pails of water. I speak kindly with everyone and see that they are amazed. After the great black shroud of Audearde weighing them down, I am like the early summer sun streaming through the window.

The stock of eggs, flour and cheeses are near depleted and need increasing. I give orders for rose water, borage, sugar, almonds, chestnuts and coriander. The kitchen staff look perplexed at some of my orders. They have never heard of a few of the items I require them to cook with, but Bernadette assures me that she will 'sort this out'.

'I know all about cooking, Lady, from my mother's tavern in Paris.'

'Yes, excellent dear,' I say. I don't want her to start that story again which I have heard a thousand times.

I ask the cooks to lay out the spices that we might see what else we need: pepper, ginger, cassia buds, grains of paradise, cubeb, cumin, nutmeg, mace and cloves.

'It's important,' I tell them (echoing my mother again), 'to cook for the eyes as much as for the palate.' Then I tell them what I want for the menu today, to please my husband, to show him what an excellent wife he has.

'The first course will consist of the Grenache wine from Banyuls and green apples to open the stomach. The second course will be pumpkin soup, sautéed mushrooms with spices and chicken with lemon. The third course will be spit-roasted hare with black pepper sauce and parsley-studded lamb with pink garlic sauce. The fourth course – the *entremets* – will be Italian Blancmange from Foreign Parts, cheese fritters and Torta Bolognese. For *desserte* we will have whole pear pie and dariole.'

'What is dariole?' asks Mabila, one of the cooks.

'It's a custard tart. Watch how Bernadette makes it and then you will know to instruct your assistants.' Both Mabila and Bernadette are pleased at the importance I give them.

'And what is Italian Blancmange from Foreign Parts?' Mabila asks, her front teeth visible in bewilderment on her bottom lip. Everybody laughs at the funny name.

'It's delicious,' I tell her. 'We'll make it from shredded chicken, rice and goat's milk, topped with sugar and pork fat.'

'You can tell when it's cooked right because it quivers like a junket,' Bernadette says and wobbles comically to underline her point.

We all laugh at her and I continue with my menu. 'For the *issue de table* we will have Hypocras and marzipan tart and then, Maurice,' I tell the Seneschal, who looks up, keenly, 'lay out some cardamon and anise seeds for the *boute-hors* to close the stomach and cleanse the breath.'

'Yes, Lady,' Maurice says, pleased with his task and that I have already learnt his name. Armed with their instructions, the servants scatter each to their jobs and each with their young helpers. The *potier* and his assistant are fussing with the pots and wooden spoons. Cauldrons, crocks, frying basins and spits are readied. Terrines are set out so that later they can be placed to cook in the embers. The sauce cook is laying out the *étamines*, the bags that he strains the sauces through, and for making almond milk. The *broyeur* is mashing and bruising parsley with her mortar and pestle. The *hateur* is skinning hares and preparing to roast them on the spit and her assistant begins to pluck and bone a chicken that will be set to soak in hot water. Delicious smells and colours are already beginning to assemble in the busy kitchen as Maurice grinds the spices: cinnamon, ginger and galangal.

'Bernadette,' I say, 'go and change the rushes in the Great Hall. Take some basil.' I load each herb into her basket as I speak. 'Balm, costmary, cowslip, sweet fennel, hyssop, lavender, pennyroyal and tansy. See if you can improve on the old beer, grease, bones, spit and cat shit that I can smell and see poking through at the moment. And when you are done with that ask some of the men to help you lay out the tables and then you can lay the cloths on them.'

'Yes my Lady.'

'There's more when you've finished that, Bernadette,' I say, 'if you can remember it all.'

Audearde has kept a austere household. She did not allow *jongleurs* and musicians. I am determined to rectify this by sending out an invitation to performers. Audearde believes that we are close to the end of time. Over dinner she talks of the apocalypse brought on by everybody's wickedness. 'The human race,' she says, quoting the Cluniac monk, Ralph Glaber, 'is like a dog that returns to its own vomit.' She says there are signs of The End all around us in plagues, eclipses, earthquakes and battles. I am disgusted with her ideas and the sway they hold over my poor husband. I believe in the future and in living life. You don't wait for destiny to happen to you, you make it and you have to create your own life. I mean to do that for myself and for my Lord. I believe that our lives are narratives we spin ourselves, and then they collide with accidents and the narratives of others and we navigate those collisions. I mean to be a new broom in this cold castle. But then there is Hugh. How am I to manage his apparent repugnance for me? I have no armoury or strategies for this. And how to manage the bitterness of my own disappointment?

Returning to the hall from the kitchen, I notice the arched opening to the stairway that goes up to the battlements and feel an irresistible urge to run up there. The staircase winds round and round, making me giddy as I emerge abruptly into dazzlingly sunshine. I run to the outer wall and lean on it, regaining my balance, looking at the distant countryside, breathing the air through my mouth in great fresh gulps. I feel as if I have been suffocating the last few weeks. Lusignan Castle is huge, light and airy. I have three generous adjoining chambers to myself as well as the bedroom that in theory I share with Hugh although he has not come there since our wedding night two weeks ago. It is not the castle that is stifling me or my daily routines of instructing servants, giving alms, receiving guests. It is the watchful eyes of Audearde and Rorgon. I suspect that some of the servants report my every move to them. I instructed Bernadette to check all the walls and floors and ceilings of my chambers for squints and eyeholes and we have plugged up any suspicious gaps and whorls in the wood. The pressure of maintaining the charade of my marriage distresses me. What should I do? Should I ride out, leave, go home to my brother? But I would have to prove that the failure of the marriage is Hugh's fault if I do that and I would become a repudiated wife, a woman with no power at all.

I pace around the battlements, looking out over the territory that I now rule with my husband. The Lusignan lands extend for fifteen miles in every direction. The castle stands on the western bank of the River Vonne. It is a brilliantly clear day and to the north I see the road to Poitiers disappearing into dense forest. If I travelled along that road for ten miles I would reach the formidable castle of Montreuil-Bonnin, my childhood home, where Eudes now rules as Count of Poitou and Duke of Aquitaine. To the north-west are the mountains of La Gâtine and nestling at their far edge I can just make out the town and abbey of St-Maixent. Looking south, there are fertile fields and meadows. Beyond them, where I cannot see, is La Marche, and far further to the south I imagine Raingarde standing on the battlements of Carcassonne, looking north to me. Raingarde will be feeling my grief. She will know. Keep sending me your news, Raingarde, I think, that I might imagine another life. When I fought with Piers many years ago and hurt my knuckles so badly punching him, Raingarde told me she felt a sharp pain in her own hand. When Raingarde's leg was scalded by hot water, far away in Aquitaine I had screamed and mystified the doctor with a pain that had no obvious cause. I long to see her, to sit on a shared bed and talk over the problems of my marriage. I gaze back to the fields that lay close to the castle. They are well ordered and I can see the peasants working there with a plough and oxen. What would it be like if I were just a peasant girl, married to a man who loves me? Perhaps not getting the things you want doesn't matter in itself since you are irrevocably changed by the wanting of them. Self-pity serves no useful function. I will ride out, hunt, fly my falcon, visit the hamlets, distribute largesse. I will get out onto my estate and find some relief in performing my duties as chatelaine. Now that Raingarde has her own clerk to read her letters, I will write and tell her something of my unhappiness and solicit news of how she fares.

11

Bernadette: Lusignan

What a godforsaken place we are come to, me and my Lady. The days grow at the pace of a flea. Piers hasn't spoken a word to me since we left Roccamolten, well since that night in the ruins in fact. Not on the journey here, not in Limoges during the wedding when I was wearing my best dress and had white flowers twisted in my black hair, and not here in this vast castle. I have no one to talk to now. I half-expected this from him but that doesn't make it any easier on my heart. Once I got the message in Limoges that he wasn't interested anymore I've put a brave face on it. I won't let him see how much he's hurt me.

Most of the servants here speak Langue d'Oc and treat me coldly as a newcomer. Anyway they are beneath my attention. I am the maid of the chatelaine now and far more important than they. Lord Hugh is fine-looking but a cold fish. He hasn't spoken a single word to me and speaks few to my Lady either. 'Perhaps he's slow to speech and slow to anger,' I tell her, trying to cheer her up. Lord Hugh's clothes are black and drab, hardly different from his priest brother's. He is praying and whispering with his mother and that brother all the time. It's a castle full of whispering corners, most of it against my poor Lady I'd wager. What has she done except be beautiful as a May day and run this household with an assurance that I have to admire and so should they?

But today she got herself a new ally and she seems well pleased with that. At midday a woman arrived on horseback with an escort. I recognised that Spanish poet woman, Dia, that we met in Toulouse. Almodis was delighted to see her and Hugh made her welcome. After Dia had taken some refreshment in the hall with them she gave us all quite a surprise and I thought that old harridan, Audearde, would die of a fit on the spot which would have been very nice for us all I'm sure.

'You are very welcome, Dia. Is your Lord well?' asked Almodis.

'He is my Lady, yes. Count Ramon sends you both felicitations on your marriage and he sends me to you with a wedding gift.'

'He is very kind,' said Hugh.

Dia then passed to Almodis a box and the box itself was a thing of great beauty made from finely carved bone. I craned my neck over my Lady's shoulder to see what was inside. There were two lovely palm beakers: pink with golden lines dribbled onto them. They were, as my Lady exclaimed: 'Exquisite!' and Hugh smiled his agreement. Nestling between them was a small scroll of parchment: a wedding poem by Dia perhaps? Almodis unfurled and scanned it quickly. A massive smile spread on her face at once, all the way up to her eyes and she beamed it at Dia. I hadn't seen her smile like that since she found Lady Raingarde in Toulouse.

'I will read what it says, Hugh,' she told him. He had to smile back at her. She was like a young girl in her happiness, with all the heavy weight of her responsibilities lifted off her suddenly. 'Count Ramon writes: Greetings Lord Hugh of Lusignan and Lady Almodis of La Marche. I hope that this small marriage gift will give you pleasure. The beakers are the finest Catalan glass. Lady Almodis, I venture to make you one more gift for yourself. My messenger is my gift to you. I loan her to you for as long as it should suit you both. I know that you will have much joy of her and I meanwhile, will pace my silent hall in Barcelona having to compose my own poor poetry till you should deign to give her back to me.'

Almodis and Dia both laughed at that and Hugh smiled politely. I was grinning too and immediately turned my eyes on Audearde and Rorgon who, sure enough, were looking far from pleased at being under the same roof with an Andalucian poetess! I would have kissed Ramon's mouth myself if he'd been there just for the gift of the expressions on their faces!

'Count Ramon belies himself,' said Dia in her matter-of-fact way. 'His poetry is quite good.'

'You must take food and rest Dia, after your long journey from Barcelona,' said Almodis. 'Bernadette, show Mistress Dia to my rooms and find her a place to sleep and stow her belongings. Would you be kind enough to play for us at dinner tomorrow that my Lord might hear what a good gift I have in you?'

'I would be delighted, my Lord, my Lady,' Dia said, curtseying low. What a welcome sight she was in our frosty grey hall with her gorgeous, yellow silk dress contrasting with the darkness of her skin and hair. Round the hem of her dress ran an embroidered border of orange phoenixes and she was like an exotic bird herself. I held my breath for a beat wondering if Audearde would start up some objection. But Almodis had been quite clear and firm in her acceptance of the 'gift' and so the old battle-axe was forced to hold her bitter tongue and I felt triumphant myself as I conducted Dia upstairs.

The next day an hour before we were due to dine in the hall, we were seated in my Lady's chambers and Dia had been telling Almodis about Barcelona and Count Ramon. 'Ermessende and Ramon have finished building a new cathedral in Vic. The county of Barcelona is prosperous and its craftsmen are highly skilled. Ramon chaffs at the iron control that his grandmother keeps over his domain though,' Dia told us. 'She was the same with his father too. What rightly should have passed directly to Ramon's father, instead his grandfather left in his will to Ermessende, and even when Ramon's father came of age, she did not relinquish control to him. He was merely her puppet, doing her bidding. She never allowed him to rule fully. Ramon fears that she intends to try the same with him.'

'I think she might find more difficulty with the grandson than with the son perhaps?' said Almodis.

'Yes, I think you are right Lady Almodis,' said Dia. 'Even though he is young, it is already clear that Ramon will be a very great ruler, but his first fight will be with his grandmother. I would like to warm up my voice and instrument before I perform before your Lord at dinner. May I sing a song for you and Bernadette?'

'Of course,' said Almodis, and I nodded enthusiastically although nobody needed my permission in truth.

Dia sang:

> Of things I'd rather keep in silence I must sing,
> So bitter do I feel toward him
> whom I love more than anything.
> With him my mercy and fine manners are in vain,
> my beauty, virtue and intelligence.
> For I've been tricked and cheated
> as if I were completely loathsome.
>
> My worth and noble birth should have some weight,
> my beauty and especially my noble thoughts;
> so I send you, there on your estate,
> this song as messenger and delegate.
> I want to know, my handsome noble friend,
> why I deserve so savage and so cruel a fate.
> I can't tell whether it's pride or malice you intend.

Dia paused. 'The song does not please you Lady Almodis?'

I looked at Almodis and saw that there was indeed a look of unhappiness on her face. 'No, no,' she said, blushing. 'It isn't the song. It is excellent, but it's too sad for my mood today. Will you play us something different?'

Dia nodded her head calmly, although I was quite put out not to know the rest of what the lady had to say to her neglectful lover. It put me in mind of Piers and me, and I thought if Dia had continued the bad lover might have got his come-uppance: died or got a pox that wilted his manhood or developed an unsightly tumour on his nose.

Dia next began to sing us a story about Melusine who was half-human and half-fay. Almodis and I smiled at each other, settling down to listen with fascination to this story. Melusine, Dia told us, strumming her instrument all the while, was the eldest daughter of the fairy, Pressine, and King Elinas of Albany. Melusine imprisoned her father on a mountain and was cursed by her mother to become a serpent from the navel down every Saturday. Almodis and I gasped.

'Unless,' sang Dia smiling at our reactions, 'she could find a husband who promised to never see her on those days. Raymond, Count of Lusignan,' Dia nodded significantly to Almodis when she sang that part, 'was hunting in the forest and he heard a maiden singing beautifully and found her sitting at a fountain. He fell in love with Melusine and she agreed to marry him on condition that he did not see her on Saturdays. She bore Raymond many children but they all had some defect. Her husband violated his oath one Saturday and she turned into a winged serpent fifteen feet long. She mounted the window-sill and flew out, leaving the print of her foot in the stone. She flew around the castle three times, uttering a piercing cry every time she passed the window of the room where she had been betrayed. She returned daily to visit her children and supervise their nurses. Since Raymond had broken his promise, Melusine was cursed now to stay in her serpent shape and she had to appear before the castle that bore her name for three days every time its lord changed or a man died who was descended from her line.'

We clapped enthusiastically at the end of this song.

'Did you make this story up for Lusignan?' asked Almodis looking a little perplexed as well she might. It was a strange and disquieting tale.

'No Lady. It is a song well known amongst the troubadours and it is no story but truth,' said Dia.

We both looked at her in astonishment.

'Truth?' echoed Almodis in disbelief. I pulled a face to show that I agreed with her.

'Yes. I'm sure if you ask your Lord and his family they will know of it and perhaps they saw or heard Melusine when Hugh's father died. Her footprint will be somewhere on a window-sill in this castle,' she said, moving over to Almodis' window to examine the smooth stone there.

'You are joking with us, Dia,' Almodis said with certainty after another pause.

'No Lady. I assure you that Melusine is no joke. You will hear her yourself when you give your Lord an heir.'

'If that ever happens,' said Almodis, her face immediately falling.

I exchanged a glance with Dia. I had noticed my Lady's depression on this topic before now.

'But Lady Almodis, you have barely been married three months,' Dia told her. 'There is plenty of time yet before you need worry.'

'Yes,' said Almodis but her eyes glistened with tears. I will speak with Dia later, I thought, about my concerns for my Lady. It would be wrong for me to speak to her myself on this subject but perhaps Dia can. She is no servant and she is a woman who has seen the world. I know herbs that can help my Lady conceive. I will tell Dia. She doesn't talk much outside of her songs, but she listens eloquently, my Lady says. Dia has songs for every occasion: *alba* for the dawn, sewing songs, *planhs* or laments, debates, May songs, *balada* for dancing, battle stories and, of course, love songs, especially *winileodas* – the unhappy love songs.

I was working in the hall a few days later on my sewing when I heard a great racket of horses and shouts out in the bailey. Visitors! And many of them by the sounds of it. I stowed my needle, picked up my skirts and ran to the door that I might take the news quickly to my Lady. There was a great melée of horses and people and two carts. I saw the arms of Aquitaine on the soldiers and then I saw the hawk-like features of Geoffrey of Anjou and beside him was Agnes with strands of her flaming hair escaping her headveil like fiery banners. I ran to my Lady's chambers with all haste.

'Did I hear visitors, Bernadette?'

'Yes,' I gulped some air. 'It's Lady Agnes and the Hammer,' I said. 'Pardon me, Geoffrey of Anjou.'

'Are you sure?' she asked frowning and rising from her seat.

'For certain,' I tell her.

Dia had risen too with a look of interest on her face.

'Go and find Hugh, Bernadette. He is probably on the practice field. Tell him I will conduct Agnes and Geoffrey to the hall. Be quick about it. Please come with me Dia.'

I admired her self-possession. I felt flustered and anxious. The sight of those two could never auger well. Was it war? Did they come to bring us all grief of some kind? I ran to tell Lord Hugh and then ran back fast as I could to make sure I didn't miss anything.

'Welcome Lady Agnes and Lord Geoffrey. My husband will join us shortly.' Almodis gestured to the seats on her right. I hovered with a bowl of water and an aquamanile to wash their hands. When they were seated I poured the water from the awkward brass pourer shaped like a knight on his horse, doing my best to stay out of range of the nasty red squirrel Lady Agnes had on a leash, seated on her lap. Another maid set wine and bread on the table before them. Almodis gave them time to settle and then asked, 'Have you ridden far today?'

'No,' said Agnes turning her red-brown eyes and the self-satisfied line of her smile onto my Lady. 'Only from Poitiers.'

My Lady must have been surprised and curious when she heard the word 'Poitiers' but she concealed it and waited for more information to come.

'We find you in new circumstances, Almodis,' said Geoffrey in a pleasant voice. 'Not the pretty little girl at the court now, but an *uxores* presiding over the splendid castle of Lusignan and carrying its heir.'

Lady Almodis smiled in acknowledgement but continued to wait silently. I saw her run her hand over the great round of her belly. Thank God she is so fertile and it only took those two awful nights with Hugh to get her with child. First we had tried lacing his food with the herbs my mother had told me about but that had only made him violently sick and we were afraid that we would be taken up as murderesses.

'Once children have been conceived, my Lord,' I heard her say to him, when they thought I was full out of the room, 'we might live in a state of spiritual fraternity as your priests suggest if that is what you wish.' When he did not respond she added bitterly, 'It will mean only a few brief descents into hell.'

I saw through the crack of the door that he touched her arm gently at that. 'I am sorry wife. It is not your fault.'

Dia and I had helped her to ply him with fine wine until he was near unconscious and then, she told us, she straddled him in their bed and consummated their marriage. 'It was so awful, Dia, I felt like a succubus, a prostitute,' she said and I did feel for my poor Lady. 'When it was over,' she told us, 'he spent the entire night on his knees beneath the crucifix with his rosary.' Still these horrible encounters had been enough to get her with child. I know that many nights my poor, dear Lady creeps to the *garderobe* and weeps silently there.

Audearde and Rorgon entered the hall and Almodis introduced them to Geoffrey and Agnes of Anjou. They took their seats and broke their fast but were too awe-struck by their unexpected visitors to offer much in the way of conversation. Hugh still had not come and the silence in the hall began to feel uncomfortable.

'I hear there has been some fighting around Mon Coeur,' said Almodis eventually. 'I hope you were not much engaged or injured my Lord,' she said to Geoffrey.

'Oh very engaged,' he said nonchalantly and laughing with Agnes, 'but injured? Not at all!'

Hugh entered and strode up the hall to join them. The necessary welcomes were exchanged again.

'I come to claim your fealty Lusignan,' Agnes pronounced at last. 'Eudes is dead. Slain at Mon Coeur two days ago. My son is Duke of Aquitaine and takes the name Guillaume VII. We claim your kiss of peace as Regents of Aquitaine.'

I saw my mistress bow her head briefly and a cold chill passed through me. She had played with Eudes and loved him in place of her own missing brothers. I remembered his kindness to her at her wedding. I prayed that he had died swiftly and easily. Geoffrey was regarding my Lady with intense interest. A horrible vision rose up in my mind of Geoffrey slicing Eudes' neck, hacking into his bright young face.

Hugh ordered more wine to be poured before responding to give us all time to adjust to this shocking news. I saw my Lady's gaze on Agnes' jewelled fingers curled around the fragile pink glass of one of the palm beakers that Count Ramon had sent to her.

'I will give you my kiss of fealty Lady Agnes, Lord Geoffrey,' Hugh said with careful formality. 'My brother can officiate for us.'

Agnes nodded and then she and Geoffrey turned their eyes very deliberately onto my Lady. The castle lord had capitulated easily but the lord had a Marcher wife. She is a brave lady and she did not betray her feelings to the likes of them.

'How old are Pierre and Guy now?' she asked in a neutral voice. She and I had held Agnes' baby twins and played mother to them. We had followed them anxiously around the bailey at Montreuil-Bonnin as they learnt to walk.

'Duke Guillaume VII and his brother are ten,' Agnes said, giving her plenty of time as regent. Her smile was close to a gloat. Geoffrey tapped his pink beaker for more wine.

'Give Lord Geoffrey a larger glass, Bernadette,' Almodis said. 'This pink frippery is too small for him, and Lady Agnes too.'

I guessed that she was thinking if only she could save Aquitaine, La Marche and the South so easily from them, as she saved her favourite beakers. I had heard Lady Almodis speak often about Agnes' certainty that she would rule Aquitaine despite the many heirs the old duke had left in the way of that ambition, and now they were both proved right. Eudes had been duke for barely a year before Geoffrey had slain him.

Geoffrey and Agnes stayed for two nights and my Lady arranged hunting and hawking, feasting and talk of the goings on in the Holy Roman Empire. Dia sang for them and Agnes, greatly admiring her, would have taken her off with them if Almodis had not pointed out that she was on loan from the Count of Barcelona. 'I will let him know of your admiration for his *trobairitz*,' Almodis said, effectively closing down Agnes' acquisitive attempt.

One night, going to undress Lady Almodis for bed, I came across Lord Geoffrey standing very close up against my Lady, she with her back to her chamber door, and he running his hand and his eye round the curve of her belly. My Lady had a curious look on her face, between fear and pleasure. They looked up and saw me and then Geoffrey stepped away from Almodis, as I heard Regent Agnes' steps behind me. I hoped that I had blocked her view.

12

The Season Turning, October 1038

To Audebert, by the Grace of God, Count of La Marche, your sister, Almodis, Lady of Lusignan sends greetings and the courage of Charlemagne.

The Hammer and Agnes have been here. You will have heard the news that Eudes is dead at Mon Coeur and Agnes is regent for Pierre who takes the name Guillaume VII of Aquitaine and V of Poitiers. He is ten years old so they will have a good run of it. Hugh, my lord, has given them his fealty and Geoffrey has left him a squadron of his milites *to 'assist' us. Stay in Bellac. They may not venture so far. If you can avoid fealty without battle you must. I fear that they will bring the northerners down upon us. Anjou is thick with the Capets and the Duke of Normandy. They look to the Limousin, to our rich lands and they slaver at the mouth. Wild stories of our wealth spread like wild fire in the North, of how we sow our fields with silver pennies in obscene displays of our riches. And if they do bring their war machines to you, take on your vigour! I pray the audacity of your arms will comfort your friends. Give no heed to the costs of doing this, you will recover a hundred* solidi *for every one you spend and your name will be exalted by all. I am strong who loves you. Take care of your frontier Audebert.*

The best way to create truth is to assert it, I have read, and I do believe in the power of the written word, both in war and in love. Despite my offers of a fine chamber within the castle, my love wordster, Dia, has insisted on living in a tiny house in the village. I am curious to see her home and she has invited me there for

dinner. The path up to her door switches back on itself in a steep
zig-zag. 'If I'm not there when you arrive, Lady Almodis,' she'd
said, 'just let yourself in. I won't be far behind you.' I knock and
wait, knowing though, that nobody will answer. You can always
tell, standing outside a door, whether there is anybody in the
house or not. Absence has a certain dull presence of its own that
you can always feel.

So I turn the doorknob and open the door straight onto the
back of a heavy dark curtain that I scrape away from in front
of my face. I pull the door closed behind me, an impostor, an
intruder, despite Dia's words of permission.

As I step into the room the curtain falls back, keeping out the
draughts. The room is dark and cold nevertheless. Thin sticks of
wood are piled next to the empty fire grate. Two chairs covered
in scuffed brown leather hold their arms out to the fire. It is so
dark in the room I hesitate on the threshold waiting for my eyes
to adjust to the gloom, but the gloom persists. A cheap, spherical,
glass lamp hangs low over a table between the chairs, its wick unlit.
The stark form of the lamp looks jarringly out of place amidst the
genteel shabbiness and fuzziness of the rest of the room.

I peer around curiously. If Dia were here, she herself would
be the focus of my attention but now I can look carefully at what
surrounds her in her life, in her work of composing. A faded
pink, floral shawl is thrown over an uncomfortable looking blue
day-bed. A table is covered in and surrounded by piles of parchments. Dia has to practice both her voice and her instrument for
several hours every day, and it is a great pleasure to me to have
her melodies around me so much.

Struggling to rise in the far corner and looking like upholstery
himself is Gaston, Dia's ancient dog. He is near blind and deaf
and his black coat is matted in long dreadlocks like a hermit. It
is impossible to see his eyes, and in the dark room he is merely
an indistinct darker area. Dia adopted him after the death of his
previous owner, an old, old man from the village. Eventually
Gaston makes it across the room to sniff my hand. Satisfied that
he knows me he shuffles back over to his green blanket on the
floor and more or less falls back down on to it.

I hear flies buzzing, disturbed by my entry, and look to see where they are chasing each other through dust motes floating in a strip of light from one of the windows. A few books and scrolls fail to fill the bookshelf. So few books for such a wordsmith. I have noticed an element of self-denial in Dia's character and now it gazes at me in the thinness of her belongings. I try to imagine being Dia, living her unseen life in this room.

More scrolls occupy the small low table before the fire. Dried purple flowers stand in a jar on the mantelpiece. A wooden lute-like instrument with a broken string is hanging from a nail above a very dark brown, oversized chest. Dia told me that in the past she had a lover: a musician who beat her, but she did not tell me more about this man who has left so many scars on her heart. I guess that there is perhaps some association of this broken instrument with him.

There are no mementos of family or friends anywhere in the room. Despite our many warm conversations, I know so little about her. She is estranged from her mother; her father is dead; she spent some time working in the hospital in Salerno; she has toured many places in the company of other troubadours: the Basque Country, the kingdom of Aragon, Italy, Sicily. These are sparse details for someone who has lived twenty-three years. There must be more to know. I search for clues to the mixture of profound sadness and private joy that I have observed in her. I look around the room, feeling as if I am stealing her life, rifling through her things.

I know that she keeps an eye on the old man in the village who sits by the fountain with his hose awry, drool dribbling down his chin, his mind long gone and no family to care for him. When we go to the market together I have noticed how she looks out for the grimy young man, a lunatic, who is always pacing up and down between the two queues of people and carts waiting to enter the gate. Every day, all day, he is in the same place, begging, wearing a thick hood pulled over his head even in sweltering sunshine. He too has lost his mind and has nobody. Dia always gives him something – a coin, a small flagon of wine, a bag of nuts, and a few words. He recognises her and mutters incomprehensibly in response to her queries about how he is, while she blithely holds up the people and carts behind her.

I notice a sketch on an easel standing in the meagre light by the window and move over to look at it. The pencil drawing is a detailed image of the lined and beautiful face of an old man: one of the damaged people she acquires a responsibility to nurture in small ways that probably make very big differences to their lives. It must have taken a long time to draw this. One day? One week? And all the time she sketched him, no doubt she spoke softly with him of his hard life. Perhaps he is dead now.

I hear a greeting shouted in the square below and move over to the window, careful not to step on Gaston in the gloom and see that Dia has just arrived back. She doesn't look up to see me haunting her house but is concentrating on reaching for her shopping baskets. There is a lurid brightness in the air that occurs just before rain. The ugly new fountain in the square below spurts its water with an incessant rhythm.

I move quickly through a colourful beaded curtain off the living room, wanting to cover the whole apartment before she arrives, and I emerge blinking into the tiny bright kitchen after the cave-like living room. I am looking at a spectacular view of the wide river below. The sound of water pounding over the rocks is thunderous in here and easily drowns out the pompous fountain. The water rushes in thick sheets looking like a solid surface of glass. Huge black tree trunks are snagged on jagged boulders. A man on an ass clops along the narrow road running alongside the river, waving a greeting to the fishermen. Dia's tiny balcony is crammed with brimming flower pots, bowls of crumbs for the birds, saucers of water for the lizards. I feel an envy for the freedom and independence of her life.

From up here I can look down on her wood pile neatly stacked in a small courtyard below. It reminds me of her surprising argument with Madou, the woodman. It seemed so out of character for her. I had to be a go-between, because neither of them would speak directly to the other. When he finally gave in and came to deliver some wood to her, instead of repairing the argument as I expected, Dia wound it up even further and they argued some more.

'Why are you leaving it like this all over the road? Why don't you help me stack it as you did before? What's up? I'm not paying you enough?' she yelled at him, as I watched appalled at what I hoped would be a reconciliation with someone who is, after all, the only woodman in the valley.

'You pay for the wood, not my labour or time!' he yelled back.

'It's not good enough! I'm looking for another supplier.'

I shifted from foot to foot in the cold as they shouted and gesticulated at each other, knowing that she had already tried and failed to get another supplier. Madou jumped down from the cart and came up close and whispered something in her ear. They smiled at each other and suddenly the fight was over and they were friends again. I was amazed to see her, usually so adroit, turn suddenly coy. Was I an awkward witness for some kind of fore-play? Madou rode off and *I* helped her stack the wood. She told me that an Andalucian deals with emotions and men in a different way to an Occitan woman.

'*Bonjour!*' she calls now, pushing her way through the brown curtain, knowing too the difference between the feel of presence and absence in a house. I move back through the beaded kitchen curtain to greet her. Bulging bags are hanging along her arms with warm-smelling baguettes protruding like spines.

Dia is very slender with olive skin contrasting against the enormous mass of her long, black, tumbling hair. She has a kind of fragile beauty that forces your eyes to linger there: on her face, her brown eyes, her laughing mouth. Physically she is frail but her energy and will are like sinews. I have watched how she gives precious emotion and care to the dying and the dead, to women in labour, to distraught children. Despite her surface cheerfulness, I feel that she is always trailing a grief that she deals with every day, her own secret grief.

She kisses me three times on the cheeks. '*Bonjour, bonjour*, Almodis. *Ça va? Oui, ça va bien aussi.*' There is an effortless style about her in her threadbare clothes. I have tried to give her new clothes, but she stubbornly continues to wear her own old ones. She moves into the kitchen with Gaston at her heel, rumpling his dreadlocks and vainly attempting to tuck her own hair behind an ear with one finger. She tips the contents of her bags onto the small table with relish. Garlic, onions, mushrooms, steak, potatoes, and then, an incredibly smelly cheese. We clasp our hands over our noses and mouths, and she manoeuvres the cheese quickly with her free hand onto a saucer and rushes out onto the balcony with it. '*Oui*! *This* we have to put outside!' She comes back in laughing with me. 'It will *taste* fan-*tas*-tic though, you'll see.' She wraps her Andalucian mouth awkwardly around her perfect Occitan.

'Ah you brought some wine,' says Dia, 'let's have some right away and get the fire going. It's so chilly – brrr!' She rubs her hands up and down her thin arms theatrically and the still house is suddenly, vividly, alive with her.

13

Bernadette: Confessional

I grow to love my Lady. She is a very fine chatelaine. She has the castle running smoothly and brooks no interference from her mother-in-law which is some accomplishment. That is a harridan and a half. But my heart really swelled with love for Almodis when she took care of me over Piers. She found me sobbing and insisted on knowing what was the matter. I told her how I'd seen him tupping the kitchen maid in the stable and how I'd given my virginity to him and thought he might marry me.

'Bernadette. You are well out of it,' she declared, striving to make me laugh. 'That is a man who very rarely has his hose anywhere but round his ankles.'

She made him come and kneel to her, with Dia and I as witnesses, whilst she gave him a good telling off about his behaviour. 'It has come to my attention, Piers,' she said in her best haughty manner, 'that you have been engaging in no end of illicit carnal activities with the maid servants. It is ungodly and it is disturbing the peace of the household. You will keep your cock to yourself and kept safe for your future wife from now on,' she said to him.

Well he was red in the face and so angry, I could see, but what could he say? He had to apologise to her and agree that he would mend his ways.

'There now, Bernadette,' she said when he'd gone, 'didn't it make you feel a whole lot better seeing him shame-faced?'

Now here she is birthing and so brave and I am exhausted.

We have bathed her often and kept her warm and anointed her abdomen with oil of violets. The chamber smells sweet with a fumigation of musk, amber and aloe. The Spanish woman is strumming gently on her instrument. Almodis refused to have Audearde in the bedchamber. It makes me laugh to see that old hag find much, much more than her match in my pretty young Lady. As the midwife instructed, Almodis is wearing a necklace of coral and holding a magnet in her right hand, although she scoffed at this, and said it was just superstition.

'Are you afraid, Lady?'

'No,' she huffs and puffs between the pains with sweat soaking her golden curls into draggles clinging to her pink face. 'This is just one of the things we do, Bernadette. I will do it well. I will be glad to have this burden shifted, my child in my arms and my body back again that I might return to riding and hunting.'

I'll give her that. She shows no fear. When she screamed and I asked in terror, 'Oh how is it my dear Lady?' she just said: 'It is good Bernadette. He's coming.' She was sure all along that it was a boy. Her pains began at midnight and it has been very fast. The dawn is just beginning to lighten the sky in the window and the baby slides out from her and lets out a great wail, but it isn't over. The pains are continuing and then we know that my Lady is bearing twins. Two fine boys she has birthed! We are all weeping with joy as she holds them both in her arms and looks at us exhausted and happy. Dia goes to tell Lord Hugh and bring him to see his heirs. I set about tidying the chamber and removing the evidence of her labour. The midwife has bathed the blood and stuff from the babies and wrapped them.

Lord Hugh comes in to look at his sons but recoils at the sight of the twins.

'My Lord,' Almodis says with the patience of a saint, I must say, 'I have birthed twins because I am a twin. There is no evil here. See they are both healthy and well formed. This is Hugh, your heir, and this is his brother, Jourdain.' He doesn't take them in his arms, says only, 'I am glad to see you well madame and to see my heirs.' Then he goes out again just like that.

My Lady is crying. 'It's just the exhaustion,' she says. I wipe her face for she doesn't have a free hand. We both know it's not the exhaustion and I wish I could give that lord a dressing down for her as she did for me with Piers.

Then we all hear the most ear-splitting caterwauling. 'Do you think that careless kitchen maid has caught her hand in the fire?' I say.

'It sounds like a cat in pain,' says Almodis doubtfully.

'It is Melusine,' says Dia, ashen in the face, but though she and I rush to the window we don't see anything in the moat.

'Nonsense,' says Almodis and turns back to her twin boys.

And I thought I would be bored in Lusignan! Geoffrey and Agnes are only just gone and now we have another to do. I've been watching Piers eyeing up Nadine for a few weeks. She's only fourteen and the daughter of the steward. I don't know what I was thinking but I decided to follow them when I saw them disappearing into the chapel. They couldn't be up to no good in a chapel. I could warn Nadine about him. Shout at him? Piers likes his risks. I saw that he was fondling Nadine's breast and buttocks right there, lying in the pews, in front of the statue of the Virgin. The poor girl was whimpering that it was sacrilege and they'd go to hell and then I heard the register of her whimpering shift and I knew what that meant. What should I do? Run and tell Rorgon? But then I heard the heavy door behind me and there *was* Rorgon, and Lord Hugh with him, striding up the aisle. If Piers looked this way he would see me. I ducked down behind the confessional box and heard a whisper and scurry as Piers and Nadine crawled out and made their escape. I peered round to see if I might follow but drew back quickly as I saw Lord Hugh's legs. They were going into the confessional and I was trapped. I hardly dared breathe. If they caught me I'd be whipped for sure.

'Bless me, Father, for I have sinned.'

I was appalled to find that I could hear Hugh. Rorgon's murmur was much less distinct. If I moved at all they would know I was there.

'I dreamt of her again,' he said. What could I do? I had no choice but to listen.

Rorgon must have told Hugh to tell him about his dream as he continued: 'In my dream I am lying naked in bed and a great serpent is laying next to me. Its body is thick and it has two curling tails. Above the waist it has the naked breasts and arms of a woman. I caress its horrid green scales. I place my mouth on its breast in a loathsome kiss! And it writhes and writhes, slimy, against me. I taste the tang of old, foul water on my lips. Its voice is sibilant like a snake and it slithers on the bedcovers. Ten grotesque children are standing against the wall of our bedchamber watching us on the bed. I raise my head to look in the face of the fearsome serpent and I see that it has the smiling features and the great green eyes of my wife. In her mouth are sharp and tiny pearly teeth. I feel blood in my own mouth where she has kissed me. Seaweed is tangled in her blonde hair and red leeches cling to her shoulders. Her skin is cold and wet and deathly pale. I fear that my wife is Melusine, the harbinger of my death, that she is Eve, the tempter and death of my soul. She is an identical twin, the Devil's seed. My seed mixed with hers will make children as grotesque and cursed as Melusine's!'

I could hear Hugh sobbing as well he might. I wanted to sob myself with terror at his vision. If I dreamt so I would never shut my eyes at night but keep my candles burning down to their wicks. Oh please let them finish and go away, I prayed. I can't bear anymore of this.

Rorgon must have given Hugh a fasting penance because I heard Lord Hugh said: 'But what good will that do? Fasting only seems to make my visions more lurid.'

I could just make out Rorgon's reply as he raised his voice: 'Isidore of Seville tells us that fasting is the doorway to the kingdom.' I heard them both stand and move down the aisle and out of the church. The heavy door banged shut behind them and I collapsed into a heap of stressed limbs and mind. But I pulled myself together quickly and rushed to get out of the clammy cold church as fast as I could. What should I do with this awful knowledge? I can't tell my Lady direct. Dia will know what to do.

14

Consanguinity

I sit down to write to my brother:

> *To Audebert Count of La Marche from Almodis, Lady of Lusignan.*
> *Brother, I have provided Lusignan with an heir and also with his twin brother.*

I hesitate with my stylus hovering above the parchment. I have to remind myself how hurt I am by Hugh's behaviour to me, and to think on the conversation I had last night with Dia about the possibility of repudiation and a second marriage. I continue:

> *My marriage does not please me. Men repudiate one wife after another. Might I not do the same? If you find an alliance with a lord of greater standing than Lusignan and that alliance would be of value to you, might you not broker another marriage for me? I have a fertile womb and generous lands to bring to a new husband. I can vouch that this marriage can be dissolved with honour and without bitterness from Lusignan to you. Think on it for my sake and yours.*

I sign my name, read the letter through, roll it up and seal it quickly before I can change my mind. Anything must be better than to live like this. I cannot live in the *mariage blanc* that Hugh seems to want, and Lusignan offers me little exercise for my wits.

I leave the rolled up letter sitting on my desk and turn to pull on my riding boots. Piers is marshalling the horses and hounds in the courtyard and I can hear hooves on the cobbles, the dogs' impatient yips, men shouting to each other. I stand and look down from the window. It is a beautiful May morning and today we will hunt the hart. My husband strides up to Piers, with his brother, Renaud, close behind him. They are ready to ride and waiting for me. Hugh looks up, sees me and raises his hand. I raise mine but the smile that begins to bloom in my eyes and on my mouth is halted, bereft, as he turns back to Piers, then squats to stroke his favourite hound. He flees from me who lately did me seek. Why must I keep hoping that he will return my affection? It is clear by now that he will not. I take a deep breath and smile at the decorated green hunting cap sitting on my desk, next to my letter to Audebert. Bernadette has painstakingly sewn a crown of fresh leaves all around the cap. I wind my yellow plaits round my head, pin them in place, and then pin the cap to them. I pick up my green gloves. I am wearing all green today, in honour of May. I look down at my gown: its neck, cuffs and hem are edged with gold lace and I will arrange its voluminous emerald folds grace-fully across my horse's flanks, but for who? Who will care what I look like? I was so confident in Roccamolten that Hugh wanted me but I was so wrong. I hear the one long blast on Piers' horn that means the last remnants of the hunt must assemble now or be left behind. I'm ready and the morning is waiting. I turn from the window and skip down the steps.

Renaud greets me as I emerge into the sunshine: 'Queen of the May!' he exclaims and hands me to my horse.

Piers' blue eyes rove over me with admiration too. He has been surly since I told him off for his wenching, for Bernadette's sake, but when I see how finely he has caparisoned my horse, I laugh delighted, so that he must smile with pleasure at my praise. Tram-per is a roan and my best courser. I run my hand over the rich, deep red-brown of his shoulder in greeting, and he shakes his head up and down at me. Piers has plaited and twisted the red hair of Tramper's tail and mane with green and gold ribbons. His bridle, girth and reins are made from thick bright green leather, strung with yellow tassels and tiny gold bells. I step into the stir-rup and arrange my dress around me. I disdain to ride side-saddle as many ladies do. Bernadette has tied a wine skin and a cloth with cold mutton and pigeon pie to the pommel of my saddle. I survey the mustering of the hunt. The hounds are leashed in pairs, panting and straining to be off, and each huntsmen holds four in hand. I can feel Tramper shifting beneath me, keen to be out of the courtyard, galloping and leaping in the glimpse of fields beyond the gateway. Hugh is mounted on his strong white mare, Cassie, and Renaud's mount is a black horse with a white star on her forehead. Along with Piers, we are the only riders. Lusignan is such a small household, compared to the hordes of minor nobles and followers I was used to at the hunts of the Aquitaine court and at my father's stronghold. The rest of this hunt is on foot: the dog-handlers, the huntsmen, and the beaters with their long rods. Everyone is wearing green and they all have leaves edging their caps. We look like a courtyard full of salad I think, and smile to myself.

'The white Baux hounds are best for hunting the hart,' Piers is telling Hugh, and nodding to the four he is holding in front of him.

'The white? Not the black Saint Humbert's hounds?' says Hugh, indicating his own favourites.

'No, no, my Lord. See, the black hounds have mighty bodies but their legs are short so they are not swift enough for the hart. They are good for the slower, smellier quarry such as foxes and boars. When the Trojans escaped from Troy and taught the art of hunting with dogs to the Romans, it was the white hounds they employed. The Baux are not keen on cold water, I'll give you that. That is their failing, but they make up for it with their valour. And look at them. They have all the marks of the best hounds for hunting: long-snout, big ears and nostrils, massive thighs, straight backs, dry feet and hard bellies. They are most easily trained not to chase sheep and rabbits and not to attack the other domestic animals.'

'Well, what about the dun hounds?' says Hugh.

'Yes, they are fair, not afraid of the water, but they are not so good with the noise and throng of the hunt.'

Piers' expertise on everything to do with horses, hounds and hawks is famed from here to the coast and other marshals and huntsmen come to consult with him for his knowledge. He keeps the dogs in luxury in the kennels. They have a fire to warm them in their raised hut and fresh straw every day, plenty of room to exercise, a stone water trough and a quaint arrangement of pipes and channels to bring in fresh water and take out the excrement and dirty water when the kennel lads scour their home. Those dogs live better than the lads themselves. Piers combs their coats and paws gently after each hunt, looking for thorns and blisters. He gives them a weekly herb bath to rid them of lice, fleas and other vermin so they are the most perfumed dogs you could imagine, smelling sweetly of vervain and marjoram. He gets into the river himself with the pups to teach them to swim, and he trains the young hounds with the aid of the old hounds. The cook complains to me that she is tripping over barrels in her kitchen that Piers has set near the fire, full of newborn pups, and given her orders to feed them on her best broth. 'It's not like you can even pet the pups,' she says to me, 'because their dams wander in and out of my kitchen to suckle them and they are frightening fierce and like to bite my cooking hand off if I go near their offspring.' Now Piers coats the palm of his hand with vinegar and holds it out to each of the hounds that will scent the hart. They sniff and snort. This clears their noses to help them find the trail.

An old man holds up a battered flute to show me. 'That great hart that we will find today, my Lady, he loves the music of the flute, he does, and our cries of Ware! Ware!'

I nod kindly to him. 'Let's go!' I shout to Piers and he gives two blows on his horn: the signal for us to set out for the fields. We emerge from the arched gateway into full sunshine and the dew is heavy in the grass. The sun is climbing in the sky and promising a sparkling day. We head towards the largest stretch of forest to the right of the castle, at a trot, with the dogs and those on foot running besides us. As we approach the forest's broad margin, I see row on row of pale tree trunks disappearing into darkness. Only two or three rows in, the gloom is impenetrable beneath the thick canopy of leaves.

As we pass under the roof of the forest, the sounds of our moving are suddenly hushed by the thick vegetation and debris of the forest floor and it takes a moment for our eyes to adjust from bright sunlight to the forest's permanent night. The hounds are quiet after the panting and yipping of their run here and no one speaks. Our harnesses jingle softly. Twigs crack here and there. We rein and let the men with the hounds move ahead of us to find the scent, fanning out, creeping quietly. I hear the trill of a stream to my right and Tramper steps over a fallen bough and skirts a small pond. There is no birdsong. They have heard us coming and, deep in the gloomy thicket, so has the hart. I imagine him lifting his great antlered head from the stream, sniffing the air, but we have been careful to enter where we will be downwind and no warning will be carried from our scent. The dogs are snuffling the ground, walking their handlers in circles and meanders, seeking a scent that they will surely find in a few minutes. The ground is thick with springy, green moss. The green of our clothes blends in with the leaves around us so that we appear like the carvings of green men in the church, come to life, creeping through the trees and bushes. A flash of bouncing deer passes across the path ahead of me, three or four so fast that I cannot be sure if I really saw them or if their fleeting was of my imagining.

Hugh is riding just ahead of me. In the heat of the ride he has stripped his tunic down to bunch up at his waist and is riding in a thin white undershirt, cut away close at the armpits so that the black hair under his arms can be glimpsed now and then as he moves with his horse. The skirt of his short tunic rides up high on his brown thighs. I admire the breadth of his shoulders, the muscles of his back visible under the thin shirt, the exposed muscles of his arms and legs. I watch his buttocks rise up and down in the saddle. I pull my attention away from the gorgeous form of my husband, as the dogs begin to babble and a group of young hinds and harts scatter before us, but the huntsmen hold back. These harts have their first velveteen antlers and are not what we are seeking.

'It's a pleasure to behold those harts when they go to rut and make their vault in the autumn,' the old man with the flute calls up to me. 'For when they smell the hind, they raise their noses up into the air and look aloft, at that she smell, as though they give thanks to nature which gives them such great delight.' His grin is lascivious and gap-toothed and his face is grimed with green smears and sweat. I look away, and see that Hugh is looking over his shoulder at us and has heard the old man's words. His face shows a disgust that seems to implicate me, though the words were not mine.

'Those harts will be hiding themselves in the thickets about now,' the old man continues unbidden by anybody, 'avoiding the torment of the horseflies, still growing their new antlers to their full hardness, fearing that they are without their weapons and for shame at the temporary loss of their beauty. In August, though, they'll begin to wax hot for the hinds and they'll rub the last of the velvet from their horns and fight each other and bellow. In November they crop flowers to restore and recomfort their members, overwearied with all that rutting, Lady! They don't need to drink from the stream at this time of year, for the moisture of the dew gives them sufficient for their thirst so they can stay hidden.'

I spur my horse forward to ride alongside Hugh, to get away from the old man. The lead huntsmen with the scent hounds have found hart droppings and footprints.

Piers goes forward to inspect the finds and rides back to tell us, 'It's a grand one from its hoof prints! I put my hand in the slot, its track, and it was four fingers wide.' He tips the droppings, the fewmets, from his horn, to show us. 'See, they are long and round, knotty and great. Good venison to be had there.'

'Take some wine,' I say, leaning over and handing my skin to him. We are on the track and looking now to flush our quarry from his lair.

'I've seen many a young hunter mistake the tracks of a hind with calf for those of a stag,' the persistent flutist tells me, spitting on the ground, 'for she's like to open her legs wide like a male, with the weightiness of her body, but that man of yours knows his business I see.'

'Yes,' I say shortly, trying again to escape his conversation. Usually, I would find him amusing, but I do not like this coupling of me with the lewd old man that my Lord seems to have decided upon.

Piers is following the path of the hart, visible from his tracks and droppings but also from where the branches and boughs are bowed and broken down by his passing and feeding. 'He has a long step and will stand up well before the hounds, Lady Almodis,' he tells me. Then, 'The fraying post!' he calls back and I ride up to see the tree he is indicating, where the stag has rubbed off shreds of velvet from his new antlers. 'See how high it is,' Piers says. 'This is a very good, tall, hart.' Piers has already been out the previous days, scouting, climbing trees, watching covertly for the hart's feeding and watering habits and the routes he takes in and out of the thicket.

Another cry goes up: 'Here!' I ride to the source of the call and see that Piers has found the hart's hiding place. The shape of its body is evident in the press of the leaves and soil and Piers lays the back of his hand to the indentation to feel what warmth remains. 'Five minutes, no more!' he says, knowing all the secrets and precepts of venery.

I catch a glimpse of the hart standing at gaze on a rise above us. He has a fine head of red antlers, well furnished and beamed. I hastily count fourteen tines which makes him at least six years old and perhaps one that has outrun the huntsmen before. Both antler branches end with a circle of four small croches, looking like two small crowns that he bears high above his head. He has a long brown body and looks to have very good breath for the chase. The hunted hart trusts to nothing but his heels and never stands until his wind is spent so the hounds need to be encouraged with shouts and bugles. The forest rings with the sound of our horns and hollers. 'Hi Talbot! Hi Beaumont!' the huntsmen call to the dogs. We trust to the older hounds, and not the younger. The older dogs know their work best and will not be fooled by the subtleties of the hart's stratagems, trying to throw us off by crossing its own path and doubling back on itself.

Around noon we reach the edge of this stand of forest and the hart has made a break, running into open countryside. We pursue his tracks for a while but out in the open the sun is punishing for the dogs and horses. When we reach a village, Piers tells us to rest in the shade and we will pick up the trail again mid-afternoon. The dogs pant, lapping water and feeding on gobbets of bread. I sit under a shady tree ringed with blue and pink flowers and look under my lashes at Hugh napping beside me, roaming my eyes over the thick black of his hair, the moist red of his mouth, his black eyelashes against the brown of his cheek, the eloquent curves of his ear and neck. How strange that I am not able to touch or even openly look at my own husband for fear that I would unnerve him. I am relieved when Piers assembles us again and tells us he has picked up the hart's tracks. We ride on into another forest with a broad river running through it.

Now we have been giving hard chase for two hours since our break at noon, and the hart's strength is beginning to sink. Four long blows on the horn indicates that the hart has broken cover again. 'His head's down,' calls the man who has sighted him. The huntsmen leash the young hounds again for they do not have the wisdom to know that a hart at bay is likely to turn and kill them, and there would be an end of all Piers' care of them.

'He's in the river,' Piers calls out, following the tracks on the ground. After riding for five minutes along the banks we sight the hart swimming in the deep middle of the waters. A fit hart can swim for thirty miles and they sometimes swim out to sea, but this one has been hard chased all day and has no strength left. It seems that he intends to stay and take his stand in the water so Piers begin to strip off his clothes to swim out for the kill with his dagger, but then suddenly the hart swims to the bank near to us and staggers out of the river, water pouring from its coat, its eyes roving nervously. Hugh dashes forward with his sword drawn. The hart falls to his knees at a blow from Hugh, but my husband stumbles and I see with horror that his belt is caught in the thrashing antlers as the hart tosses its head in its last agonies. I step forward, avoiding the antlers and hooves, slicing upwards with a rapid stroke through Hugh's belt and he falls back, sprawled on the ground, gasping, 'Thank you, Almodis'.

'You are welcome, my love,' I say to him smiling. 'If a hunter is injured by a boar he will be healed, but if he is hurt by a hart he will be brought to his bier, so they say.' I offer him my hand to pull him up, but he declines it and looks away from me, his face reddening as he lifts himself to his feet, dusting off his clothes.

Piers allows the dogs to close in for the kill, snarling and snapping, biting and tearing at the hart's neck and then they are hauled off again, their snouts red, and tied to trees at a distance and separately to stop them fighting each other in their blood lust. The kicking hart is finally still and the huntsmen all sound one long blow on their horns to mark his passing.

Piers steps up to flay the carcass. First he cuts off the right foot and gives it to me, his mistress, though by rights he should credit Hugh as leader of the hunt. I take it embarrassed and avoid Hugh's eyes. Piers plants a long forked branch in the ground to hang the dainties on. A bed of green leaves is made up and the hart is laid there. Piers slices off the testicles, the doulcettes, and hangs them on the forked branch. He makes a long incision down the belly, from the neck to the genitals and then he makes incisions in the skin of each leg. When the skin is removed, Piers pauses for a long draught of wine. We talk about which hound has performed the best today. After a while, Piers gets back to his business, his hands bloody past his wrists as he skilfully breaks up the venison. The hart's liquid black eyes remind me of Hugh's. Their soft beauty has congealed now to gum, their life gone out.

The old man with the flute steps forward to sing us *The Song of the Hart*. His voice is cracked and quavery, but his words are beautiful.

> Since I in deepest dread, do yield myself to Man,
> And stand full still between his legs, which erst full wildly
>   ran,
> Since I to him appeal, when hounds pursue me sore,
> Why dost thou then O hunter me pursue
> With cry of hounds, with blast of horn, with hallow and with
>   hue?
> Or why dost thou devise, such nets and instruments,
> Such toils and toys, as hunters use, to bring me to their
>   bents?
> Canst thou in death take such delight?
>
> Trapped with sundry snares and guiles,
> My swiftest starting steps in vain,
> Cruel curs with brainsick bawling,
> Hot foot follow me both over hedge and dykes.
> Horn rends the restless air

With shrillest sound of bloody blast and makes me to
    despair.
Hounds tear my life out.

Golden time does never stay but flees on restless wings.

We ride back slowly with the venison packed and slung across
the mules. Our horses and dogs are exhausted and when we enter
the courtyard I know that Piers and his assistants still have several hours work to take care of them. As I walk back into my
bedchamber, a beam of moonlight picks out the rolled letter to
Audebert on my desk. Bernadette has been slumbering in a chair
by the fire and struggles to rise to greet me, groggy. 'Send a messenger in the morning,' I say as she starts to untie the front of
my gown, 'to take that letter to Roccamolten.' I hear a sound
behind me and Bernadette's mouth drops open in a round O. I
glance to the door and see Hugh standing there, uncertain. With a
smooth movement I turn, closing up Bernadette's gaping mouth
with one finger under her chin as I go. The front of my dress
swings loose and the edges of my breasts and part of my belly are
exposed. 'Welcome, my Lord,' I say softly, extending one hand
towards him, and pushing Bernadette towards the door discreetly
with the other. He steps across the threshold and I see that his
cheeks are flushed with wine and his expression full of chagrin.
Perhaps he has been goaded here to my chamber by the sub-
tle taunts of the celebrating hunting party downstairs. He does
not disdain my out-held hand this time, taking it, and stepping
towards me.

The castle has fallen into a peaceful rhythm after the departure of
Geoffrey and Agnes and the birth of my sons. I am tired feeding
my twins (I refused Audearde's attempt to make me put them to
a wet-nurse) and now I am growing another child in my belly, but
I am contented. I begin to wish back my letter to Audebert. Relations between Hugh and myself are friendly. I could have a worse
marriage with a man who beats me or keeps concubines.
    This child I carry now was conceived with Hugh in an awkward
drunken state again, but it is done. I am resolved that after this

birth I will speak with him directly about our physical relationship to see if it might be mended. If not, then I will agree with him that now we have heirs it can be a marriage of friendship only. That would be better than this awful grappling in the dark and knowing that my husband enters my body in horror and disgust. Yet how will I bear it? I am only nineteen, condemned to live like a nun, desiring my husband and not being desired in return. I try not to think of Geoffrey's hands on me. I think instead of the consolations I have: my children will be a comfort; Dia is an excellent companion and friend; and despite her moaning, I grow fond of funny, podgy Bernadette.

I hear the clatter of horses in the courtyard: six horsemen, and eventually I make out the arms of La Marche. Audebert! I fly down the stairs to greet him and send Bernadette running for Hugh.

'Let us walk sister,' says Audebert, after dinner with the household in the hall.

I glance at him and see he has more news. Will it concern my marriage? I lead him to the fruit garden where the fountain plays and conceals the sound of conversation. 'Speak low. My mother and brother-in-law are hungry to know my business.'

'I have had an offer for you,' Audebert says coming directly to the point, 'and I am minded to accept it. It would greatly enhance your position sister and my alliances. A count offers for you.'

Ramon! It must be Ramon. 'I almost regret my letter to you now,' I say. 'As you see all goes well. Hugh and I are blessed with healthy twin sons and another child due in two months.'

'Lusignan gave his fealty easily to Agnes and Anjou and will continue to do so, even if they give their fealty in turn to the Capets and the northerners,' Audebert says.

'Yes. This is true.'

'An alliance in the South would do more good for our family, sister.'

'Perhaps.' Was 'the South' Ramon? What other count in the South would offer for me?

'Who offers for me Audebert?'

'Pons of Toulouse.'

My heart plummets to my shoes. No. No I will not accept him. No.

'His wife Majora has not borne him an heir in eighteen years of marriage. He sees that you are of fertile womb and would put her aside and marry you.'

My skin is crawling at the thought of that Count of Toulouse touching me. I must refuse but I cannot find words. What gross error has my letter to Audebert betrayed me into!

'You will be Countess of Toulouse, Almodis,' Audebert says. 'The most powerful queen in the South. Toulouse is rich with sixty castles to this one. Toulouse is the heart of the South, the centre of Occitania. Pons does not lead as he could but you would change that. I know you could. And you would be very close to Raingarde.'

'Pons is a great deal older than me.' At last I begin to muster my arguments.

'This is nothing.'

'I had thought that the Count of Barcelona might be a better match,' I venture.

'The boy Ramon? No he is just wed to Elisabet of Albi, a few months ago.'

I sit in silence with that for some time, the realisation seeping through me of how much I had been hoping that Ramon would be the one to take me out of the misery of my marriage to Hugh.

'Elisabet of Albi?'

'Yes it is an obscure marriage for a Count of Barcelona. No doubt Ermessende has engineered it to keep her control. His wife does not bring him any powerful allies to help him throw off the yoke of his grandmother. So what do you say to Pons?'

'There is no just cause for my separation from Hugh,' I begin, but Audebert interrupts, pulling a rolled parchment from his tunic.

'Look. I have had a consanguinity chart fabricated. It will convince Lusignan.'

Yes, I think, my heart sinking further, it certainly will. Hugh lives in abject fear of sin. A consanguinity claim would allow him to explain to himself his inexplicable repugnance for me. Despite its disadvantages, might marriage to Pons be an improvement on my current situation? There is Raingarde, only two days ride away.

'If I am repudiated for consanguinity, my son will be disinherited.'

'No,' Audebert tells me. 'You conceived him in innocence. We will ensure that Hugh confirms your children as his heirs. It will be a written agreement. This marriage to Toulouse will be greatly to your advantage and to mine. Pons offers you large tracts of fertile land in the Tarn Valley and all its castles as your marriage portion and I will add my own gifts to you. You could found an Occitanian dynasty, Almodis, to rival Agnes' illegitimate Aquitaine line and the Capetians in the North who are merely barons really! You could preserve Occitania. You will be a wise and effective ruler.'

I think with sadness of Ramon's words to me long ago of needing an effective woman as his countess.

'You will be sung about in the *chansons* of the troubadours, chronicled by writers like Adhémar, the episodes of your life depicted on enamelled caskets!' Audebert finishes smiling broadly.

I could oppose my brother but my misery with Hugh makes me uncertain. 'I will take my children with me? That will be part of the written agreement?' I say doubtfully.

'Of course. They are babies and must stay with you until they are seven and then you can send Hugh and Jourdain to me for training.'

Yes they would receive a better military training with my brother than with Hugh and they would learn allegiance to the southern culture. I am carrying a new child in my belly. Mine and Hugh's child and I am plotting to marry another man. Pons is not an appealing prospect. Old, ugly, but he appeared dignified at his coronation. I imagine myself as Countess of Toulouse. Yes I could revive Toulouse as the greatest power in the South, as it once was. I could visit Raingarde almost every day. I close my eyes and recall Hugh on our wedding night, naked and beautiful, the candlelight glinting on his black hair. But his beautiful hands have never touched me with love. I know that the Hugh I want is a chimera of my own mind. A few tears squeeze beneath the lashes of my tightly shut eyes. When I open my eyes Audebert is watching me, patient for my considered answer.

'Yes, then,' I tell him, 'with those two conditions regarding my children, and the surety of the return of my dower lands in Limoges and La Marche, I will consent to this.'

I look around me at the orchard, at the cherry tree and the plum tree, at the small pears turning ripe on the branch and the apples fallen to the ground, rotting brown, burrowed through by wasps and worms. I notice that the pale bark of the walnut tree is deeply etched with grooves and whorls, seeming to mimic the appearance of its own nuts. 'Yes, alright,' I say. 'I will.'

Audebert grins. 'Where there is one flesh and one blood, one feeling will follow. Shall we play chess sister?'

I smile feebly and take his hand as he leads me back into the hall to the red and white chessboard set on the table in front of the fire but I cannot enter into his good humour.

15

February 1040

Audearde had wanted this repudiation ceremony to take place in the Abbey of Saint Martial, as our marriage had, in the full glare of the public gaze, but Hugh has prevailed and the ceremony is small and private in the chapel of Lusignan Castle. I stand shivering with my thin shift tight across my enormous belly. The child is due any day. The stones of the chapel are freezing on my bare feet. Hugh is also barefoot, in his shift. We approach the bishop and swear the oath not to have relations with each other. As the ceremony dissolving our marriage comes to its close, I feel the powerful pains begin in my womb. I drop to my knees and grip the edge of the altar platform. The bishop looks appalled. 'Get her out of here quickly,' he gestures to Hugh and Audebert. 'She must not birth this child of incest here on consecrated ground.'

I feel arms around me, lifting me as the second wave of a contraction grips me. I bite my lip and taste blood, desperate not to cry out here in the church in front of everybody. Hugh has picked me up and carries me down the aisle and out into the bailey. With the child full-grown in my belly I am no light-weight and he staggers and has to put me down in the yard. I drop to all fours to manage the agony of another contraction. My brother takes one arm and Hugh takes the other and between them they support me up the stairs to my chamber. Hugh lifts me at the threshold and lays me gently on the bed. I grasp his hand and look in his face. What is he thinking as he loses his wife and I birth his child at the same moment? He turns my hand over and kisses me long there, then walks out of the room. At last, with just Dia and Bernadette as my witnesses, I can let out my suppressed screams and begin the business of birthing the child in earnest.

'The midwife is running here, Lady. She will be here very soon,' cries Bernadette.

'Nevertheless,' I say, gasping for breath between contractions, 'she will be too late'. I clench my teeth as the next pain begins to rise up and feel my throat already sore at my screaming.

The child came fast and furious and the birthing was over in a few hours. I am looking down into the face of my daughter. 'My poor, poor child, born at the hour that your father repudiates your mother.' I wipe my own tears from my baby's face.

'My Lady!' Bernadette says, turning from the window with her face aghast.

'What is it?'

'I saw the thrash of a great tail in the moat!'

Dia rushes to the window but shakes her head. 'I can't see it.'

'Oh Bernadette,' I say, my laughter drying up my tears.

'But I really saw it Lady,' Bernadette says earnestly.

I laugh and then I say, 'Well then, Melusine and I will be this child's parents. I will name her Melisende'. Bernadette crosses herself in horror.

'Your Lord will not like that,' Dia says.

'He is not my Lord any longer,' I reply, gently placing the tip of my finger into my daughter's waving fist and smiling into her dark eyes.

I hold my tiny daughter against my body, wrapped up warmly and snug inside my travelling cloak. I cannot look back for a last sight of Hugh and Lusignan. The twins are travelling in the wagon with Bernadette and will keep her well occupied. Melisende was born on the first day of February and now a mere two weeks later we are travelling to Toulouse. Hugh had shown only horror at the sight of his baby daughter, conceived as he believed in incest, although I am fairly certain that in truth we share no relatives. Yet Hugh wept when I closed the lid on my travelling casket and turned to bid him farewell. I wept too, touching his face, overwhelmed with an affectionate intimacy that had never come during our two years of marriage.

'I am so sorry for this,' he said.

'I also my husband, my love,' I said, finding the temerity now at the moment of separation to tell him what I had felt for him.

'You have been a good wife to me and I have not repaid you in kind. If you have need of my service in the future, Lady, it is yours.' He paused to show the serious intent of his words. 'I wish you well.' He kissed my forehead.

There was so much more I wanted to say but I knew that it was useless. I turned and left.

Part Two

TOULOUSE

1040–1052

16

Bernadette: Toulousienne

A great many things keep happening, some of them good, some of them bad. Lady Almodis read that out to me this morning from Saint Gregory and he's right: back here in Toulouse and who'd have thought it. A great crowd of people came out to see her when she rode into the city to become the count's new bride, strewing flowers in our path, cheering. The reputation of a good thing precedes it. I'm become maid to the most important countess in the whole of Occitania, Piers says.

I've been sent to the market for blue thread and it's crowded with the visitors for the Easter Assembly. I halt abruptly, balancing on one leg to wiggle my shoe around my foot and dislodge a small stone that is sharp under my heel. Around me are the sounds of the city: the jokes and enticements of stall-holders, gulls excited by the food on the wharf, fishermen and traders calling out, throwing their heavy ropes, bringing their ships to the pier. Toulouse is not a warrior court, like Lusignan and La Marche, and Count Pons is no warrior. His main interests are his belly, his wine, and bedding my mistress.

'Your Lusignan brats should have stayed with their father,' he told her. 'Your business here is to get an heir to Toulouse.'

'My Lusignan children are the sign of how well I will do that,' she said, mildly. 'The boys will stay with me until they are seven, as is custom, and then I have arranged for Hugh to be trained with my brother in La Marche and for Jourdain to enter the priory in Lusignan as a novice.' Her tone was bland but it brooked no argument. It was a trick I'd seen her learning in her battles with Audearde. I looked to my new master, to see if it would work so well here.

My mistress is looking very fine today: her dress is a deep dark red like the best wine with grey fur around the neck, and her pale blue underdress peeking through the slits in her sleeves. Pons looked her over and nodded his approval of her arrangements for the boys. 'The girl is keeping me from your bed.' (The Church orders that a man must keep from his wife whilst she suckles a child.) 'Send her to the nuns at Saint Gilles.'

'Yes, my Lord,' she says, all seeming innocent. 'I have arranged a wet-nurse for Melisende.'

I knew that she had done no such thing. Nor would she.

I hurry back with the thread, in case I'm missing a new event or argument, but Almodis and Dia are still sitting in the spring sunlight, sewing. I have new clothes and ribbons to match my grand status as countess' maid and, passing Almodis' mirror, I admire my dress.

'Stop your vain twirling, Bernadette, and get on with tidying this room.'

'Sorry Lady, I was relishing this dress you gave me.'

'You look very fine in it.'

I reach for a broom again. I'm sure that dust breeds. One day or another given its persistence dust will probably begin to gain the upper hand. She's been sharp with me these few days but she's paying a high price for her change in status with that old man in her bed.

She turns back to her conversation with Dia, her voice low. 'I felt like a virgin on my wedding night. I *was* near-virgin.' I sit down quietly, hoping she won't clam up because I've returned. 'I hoped, since he is an old man, that he might be as little inclined to bedding as my first husband, but I was not lucky in that. I am the blade and you are the chalice, he told me,' she says, smirking in disgust.

Listening to her putting a brave face on it, I remember her standing in the bedchamber on her wedding night here, her yellow hair loosed down her back. I remember how Pons commanded that her floor-length red cloak be removed, and he had made her stand there shivering, naked, on display to a roomful of strange men. I was glad that Dia and I had spent all that time the day before applying a depilatory of cucumber, almond milk and quicklime for she looked gorgeous.

'Courage, Lady,' I whispered in her ear, brushing her hand gently as I passed, leaving the room, with the rest of the wedding party.

'When I heard the rustle of *his* cloak falling round his ankles,' she continues with her story to Dia, 'I kept my eyes down, seeing only the dark brown fur beneath my toes, the edge of the quilt I first took to Hugh in Lusignan.'

She tells a good story, my Lady. I never get much work done, listening to it all. 'But even so,' she continues, 'I could not avoid seeing Pons' gnarled feet and the white sagging skin of his thin legs and knees.' She pauses, and I straighten out the moué of disgust on my mouth. 'At least he was done with me fast, grunting like a pig that had been stuck and then snoring. I pulled my arm out from under him where he was lying heavily on it. I thought of Hugh,' she says, looking up and glancing at us both, 'and I confess that tears trickled out of the corners of my eyes and pooled on the pillow at the sides of my head.'

I shift uncomfortably in my seat. Part of me wants to hear this and part of me doesn't.

She sighs heavily. 'I wonder how many nights I must endure before I conceive. My Lord spends one quarter of his time complaining about the toothache, one quarter so drunk his speech is slurred, another quarter pawing me, and the last quarter telling me what an illustrious lord he is and what a lucky girl I am.'

Dia grimaces. I haven't seen my Lady laugh sincerely since we set foot in Toulouse.

'I made this calculation of his time last night,' she goes on, with a horrible cool in her voice, 'while he claimed his marriage debt *again*, and I examined a brown stain on the ceiling, doing my sums.'

Dia is looking down at her hands and her embroidery lying neglected in her lap, like mine.

'I keep my face turned away to the wall or to the ceiling,'

Almodis says. 'The pale brown stained patch above the bed is shaped like two mountains, one smaller than the other.'

'Shall I get that stain sorted out?' I burst in, finding it hard to bear her litany of nuptial distress, and she looks up, startled at my interruption. She's forgotten I'm there, listening. 'Piers could whitewash it or see if there's a leak in the roof.'

'No, no, Bernadette. I like my stain. What would I look at without it? Girl, he calls me!' she says, indignant, 'when I am a twice-married woman with three babies.'

She is just a girl though, barely twenty and bright as spring to his wrinkled winter. He has a large bald patch on the top of his head, like a monk's tonsure, but it's the only monkish part of him.

She turns back to Dia. 'I've given him his bride-nights, and God knows what it has cost me, but I'll not be subject to his every desire. I couldn't bear it.'

'What will you do then?'

'I will keep him rationed with his visits to my bed. I must get him an heir as quick as can be and then I will keep him at arm's length. Well, hall's length would be better!' she laughs at that with us. 'After I have given him his heir perhaps you can find out some herbs to cool his ardour?'

'I already know them: chaste tree, coriander and lettuce seed will reduce his urges, and I can make an *aiguillette*, a spell that acts like a ligature around the genitals.'

'Excellent,' she says, smiling broadly with her broad mouth.

When we first came here I thought she would never rise above her grief over Lord Hugh. Her baby daughter took falling tears as much as milk when she fed her. She is as desperate to keep Pons from her bed, as she was to get Hugh in it.

'You will be with child, soon,' Dia soothes her, standing and combing her hair with a finely carved ivory comb that the Count of Barcelona has sent her as a new wedding gift, 'then he will have to leave you be.'

Almodis swings her head miserably from side to side, so Dia is forced to pause in her rhythmical combing. 'He was married to Majora for eighteen years without issue.'

Dia resumes, slowly pulling the white teeth of the comb through the shimmer of my Lady's hair. 'It will be different with you. You will see. You will be with child soon.'

Tonight we have stitched long into the evening by candlelight. My eyes feel like they are hanging out of their sockets. I huff and lay the dress aside to refocus. I'm pleased with this other tawny gown my Lady has given me now she has new ones. I've had to shear seven inches off the bottom of it, she being such a willowy giant compared to my more womanly height, but I can stitch that strip to my brown dress that is frayed and stained at the hem. There's enough to edge the cuffs and the neck too for my Lady wears her skirts full so that her dresses can easily accommodate her pregnancies when they come.

'So what did you find out this morning Bernadette?'

'About what my Lady?'

'About the city, its people. Out with all the gossip. You were gone three hours and I assume that you now know everything there is to know and are about to tell me!'

Well she's not wrong. 'The Prior of Saint Antoine has a mistress and two children,' I begin. Almodis and Dia laugh. 'The other ecclesiasticals hereabouts seem to be godly and they say that Durand, the Abbot at Moissac follows the Benedictine code most strictly. There's plenty of scandal though about Guifred, the Archbishop of Narbonne. Apparently he's more warrior lord than man of God. He girds his waist with iron instead of rope and keeps a company of knights and a noose of castles around Narbonne. His scribes are busy writing pious frauds in the Carolingian archives of the city.'

'Any more?'

'Well, it seems your Lord has taken many women in his time, poor women who only last the hour that is.'

'That's no surprise.'

'The people in the market say his nephew Bertrand has been expecting to inherit Toulouse and has hefty mortgages with the moneylenders against that expectation. His first wife, Majora, had a son . . .'

'What?' she explodes.

113

'But, but,' I hold out my hand to still her, 'he was badly born. Majora was only thirteen when she birthed him.'

'Badly born – how?'

'He could not talk or walk when it was long past time and he dribbled all day and when he was five and the doctors could make no sense of him they sent him away to be looked after by the monks at Saint Gilles and Lady Majora broke her heart with crying and never showed signs of any more babies.'

'Well, does he live?'

'I don't know. The woman I was talking with said that all the people assume he died as he was such a sickly thing and has never been heard of since.'

'Send Piers to Saint Gilles tomorrow,' she says. 'I want to know if this son of Pons lives still and what his condition is.'

Her plots with Dia don't seem to be doing her that much good. I could have given her better advice about managing a husband but I don't get a look in with the Spaniard around her all the time. I'm just good for fetching and carrying, for jiggling mewling babies. Do this, do that, Bernadette. I'm tired out each night in my bed. I close my eyes and like a mere blink it's morning again and I'm supposed to jump and run and carry all over again. I feel like an old lady. I'd like to say no just for once. No, I won't light that fire with my knees pricked by the rushes and my eyes streaming with the smoke; no, I won't run to the buttery and then bring that goblet of wine up the long staircase with my thighs aching and aching with each winding step; no, I won't have a baby screaming red in the face on each arm and in each ear; no, I won't stop kissing Piers in the stable and come running because you are calling out of a window crossly 'Bernadette where have you got to *now*?'; no, I won't get out of my warm bed and go running in the cold morning to the well and chip the ice into a bowl to warm next to the fire that you might dip your white fingers in it and splash a little, a very little, on your pink cheek. *No I won't.* If only!

We have a contradictory system regarding Count Pons and I'm fearful that we'll accidentally murder him. Sometimes we're controlling his ardour to give her relief and other times I'm mixing up potions to help him quicken her womb and what potions they are! This morning I reduced the liver and testicles of a small pig to powder and mixed it with wine. I had to grind it for ages with my wrist aching and the smell something awful. Then we had to find a way to conceal its stench in strong wine to get it down him. My Lady wears a pair of weasle's testicles in an amulet hanging around her neck and lodged between her bosoms that Dia says will get her with child. A lot of nonsense I'm thinking but my Lady says that Dia trained with the healers in Salerno and she knows her business.

At Lusignan my mistress commanded a small household but here she commands a royal court, bustling with all manner of people, doing all manner of work: solving legal disputes, scribing oaths, keeping archives, fleecing pilgrims and all the other commerce of the city.

Count Pons likes to exercise his right to flagellate servants and children for any violations and especially if the servant is a young woman that he can have stripped to the waist before him. I keep well out of his way. My Lady had an argument with him when he tried to punish her son Hugh. 'No,' she said, 'I won't have it.'

'It is my right to whip any servant, child or *wife*,' he shouted at her, 'who defies me.'

She didn't reply, just stared him out till he retreated. Indeed I think he is a little afraid of her. No one, and especially no woman, stood up to him before, like she does.

Piers has returned with news that Majora's son died in his eleventh year and is buried in the cemetery of Saint Gilles Abbey. My Lady and Dia both received letters this morning. Almodis' brother wrote to tell her Fulk has died and Geoffrey is Count of Anjou. 'Good,' she says wickedly. 'Fulk Nerra was an evil man and it is long since Geoffrey needed the power to himself. Agnes will be preening. I hate to think of him with her.' She has a letter from Raingarde, saying she will visit with her husband soon. Dia's letter is from Barcelona and she tells us that Count Ramon has been successful in subduing the revolt of his baron, Mir Geribert, and Ramon's Countess, Elisabet, has borne him a son named Berenger.

'He continues precocious then,' says Almodis.

17

Easter 1040

After my wedding and the main business of the Easter Assembly the visitors are all packed up and gone in a cloud of dust in the garrigue. Raingarde returned to Carcassonne and Audebert went back to La Marche, loaded with gifts from Pons and smug to have his sister queen of the South. I think of Hugh. How is he? How will it be for him now, without me, without his children? We were there so briefly perhaps we seem like a fleeting dream already. My new husband is not pleasant to look at or to be with and a lot of my energy and ingenuity are spent evading him, organising him to be out of my way.

I rule over a vast territory from Toulouse on the Garonne to Saint Gilles on the Rhone, from the Auvergne to the Pyrenees, but my kingdom is in disarray. The Viscount of Albi, the Count of Melgueil, the clergy of my region, and of course my sister's household, came to my wedding, but the Count of Rouergue and the nobility of Septimania all stayed away: the Viscount of Narbonne, the Lord of Montpellier and the Viscount of Millau.

'The lords of Septimania give their allegiance to Barcelona, not to Toulouse,' Raingarde told me when I complained of their absence. Her own husband was prevented from coming by illness and she came with her mother-in-law, the Dowager Countess Garsendis who, as a young heiress, brought Béziers and Agde to the House of Carcassonne.

'The nobility of Septimania are my neighbours and I would know them,' I told Raingarde.

'Pons rules the Toulousain region in name more than prac- tice,' she told me. She is right. He is not interested in the business of lordship, but entrusts everything to his lieutenant, Ranulf de Roiax, the vicar (or steward) of Toulouse and to the Capitouls of the city, the twelve Good Men selected from the leading families, who act as judges and counsellors.

Pons is close with his nephew, Bertrand. They are drinking companions, and Bertrand, no doubt, hopes I will be as barren as Pons' first wife.

'He has his spies on you, for sure,' says Dia.

'Well they'll find out nothing useful,' says Bernadette, banging down another dusty book on the table. 'Not unless reading books is considered infidelity!'

When Raingarde was still here after the wedding feast I asked her to tell me everything she knew about the politics of the region.

'Everything, Almodis? That is extravagant surely!' she laughed.

'Nevertheless,' I said, taking her hand. 'Tell me what you know, informant!'

'Well, let me see, Carcassonne,' (she pointed at herself), 'owes allegiance to the overlordship of Toulouse,' (pointing at me).

I waggled my head. 'And?'

'Carcassonne also has significant links to Catalonia through my husband's aunt Ermessende and his uncle Peter the Bishop of Girona.'

'All this I know. Tell me about the nobility in this region. What do you know about them?'

'It's very complicated,' Raingarde said.

'I believe I can handle it,' I told her, making her laugh.

'Well, let me see, the Count of Toulouse is the overlord of a whole host of other counts, viscounts and lords. The lands of Carcassonne, Razès, Agde, Albi, Comminges, Foix, Gévaudan, Substantion and Melgueil, all come under his suzerein.'

'Dia,' I interrupted, 'can you find me a good map.'

Dia left the room and Raingarde resumed her litany. 'Also the lands of Nîmes, Quercy, Rouergue, Rodez and Uzès. The lords of all these lands owe allegiance to your husband. All their gold and silver mines, their bridge and gate and road tolls, their vineyards and commerce and shipping . . .'

'So I command countless counts,' I said.

'Your husband does,' Raingarde said, looking at me askance.

'There are many female lords hereabouts,' I told her.

'Well yes, where their husbands are away or there is no eligible man in the household. In times gone past, the House of Toulouse held the title, Marquis of Septimania. Technically all the counts within this marquisate are vassals to your husband.'

'Technically?'

'Yes. Your husband has not claimed this title or enforced this vassalage.'

'No,' I said in a neutral voice, my mind racing.

'Berenger Viscount of Narbonne is vassal to the Count of Barcelona, not to your husband or mine. If you want me to cut to the chase, and I know that you do, your main competition in the region (apart from me of course) is Hugh Count of Rouergue and his wife Fides of Cerdanya. Their lineage is at least as old as that of the House of Toulouse and they aspire also, to lead the county.'

'Well, now there is an alliance of the twin countesses,' I said, taking her two hands again, 'we shall sweep all before us. Duchess of Septimania. That sounds well. To name is to claim, no? Dhuoda was the Duchess of Septimania, you know, who wrote the manual for her son.'

'I've not read it,' Raingarde said. 'I've heard of it.'

'It's wonderful,' I told her. 'I have a copy. Her husband over-reached himself and both he, and the son she wrote her advice for, ended up dead, executed.'

'Well, then,' Raingarde said, looking a little worried, not sure whether to take my musing seriously.

'Still, family history is important,' I said sitting up as Dia appeared at the door, laden with maps. 'Excellent! We'll have them here on the table with the good light.'

18

Bernadette: Breaking Fast

Fortune favours the innocent. My Lady is with child. I don't know whether it was Dia's herbs or her incantations, or just my Lady's own fertility. Who knows. I think there is some witch in Dia. But my Lady is keeping the news to herself at any rate.

This morning I'm serving at high table with Piers. We bring bread and wine for Lady Almodis and Count Pons to break their fast. I do my best to ignore Piers' winks and licking his lips at me behind their backs, and concentrate on the state of my mistress. Her face shows neither happy nor miserable, just blank, and she barely touches the bread, just drinking a little wine. I pour water for them to wash their hands from this fancy aquamanile in the shape of a naked man riding a lion. Everything is fancy here. I don't like the master. We've exchanged the silent, beautiful Lord Hugh for a noisy troll. Count Pons makes nasty sounds when he eats which you don't expect in a noble but that's because of his teeth. He seems to have twice the usual number in his head and every one of them rotten.

He taps his claw beaker peremptorily and I carefully fill it with more wine. The dark red liquid is visible through the pale green glass. The feet of the beaker curl irregularly so that the cup lists on the table, reminding me horribly of the Count's old white feet that my Lady told me about. Concealing my grimace, I turn to pour wine for Almodis.

'Thank you Bernadette.'

Her face isn't showing any misery but I fancy her voice is. I

119

try to catch her eye but she avoids my sympathetic glance. She is watching a swift that has flown into the hall and cannot find its way out. The small black shape darts every now and then across the ceiling to the window, but it cannot judge the aperture and thumps painfully into the brickwork, then flies back again to its perch on a beam, getting more and more exhausted by these fruitless attempts to regain the blue air. Perhaps, I think, I could assist it with a broom, but that might scare it to death.

She told Dia last night she wasn't happy with Pons' government of Toulouse so I know what's coming in this morning's conversation and that greedy drunk old count doesn't. I can hear his chewing and grunting. He's like a pig at swill and I clatter some plates to try to cover the noise of it. Pons is a Roman name, but he is not a cultured Roman, God knows.

'The Easter Assembly is near finished, my Lord,' she begins.

'Aye.'

'I know from my previous visit here how busy the assembly time is.'

He is nodding and chomping.

'How are the organisations for the assembly usually made?' she asks.

'Vicar, does it,' he says in between slugs from his beaker. She doesn't respond to that but I know that the vicar might find himself following my Lady's orders soon.

'I intend to leave for Saint Gilles at the end of the week,' Pons tells her. 'We will spend most of the year there. It is more comfortable than here at the Chateau Narbonnais. I leave Toulouse mostly to the vicar, de Roaix, and the viscounts, Armand and Ademar. They can conclude the justice sessions of this assembly.'

'Very good, my Lord,' Almodis says. 'I will join you in Saint Gilles in a week.'

His face registers his surprise at this. 'You will not travel with me?'

'No, it is the feast day of Saint Margaret next week, and I wish to pray at her shrine here in the city, for her blessing on my fertility.' She hasn't told him yet that she's already with child. 'I am saving that for when I need it,' she told me and Dia. He is clearly displeased that she will not travel with him, but he doesn't argue. Anything concerning an heir is paramount for him.

'So you and your Good Men of Toulouse manage the justice sessions?' she asks.

He nods, his mouth still full. 'And a deal of trouble it is every year, hanging thieves and women whingeing they've been raped and knights saying they haven't been given the cloaks they were promised.'

Almodis laughs and I can hear the insincerity of it. 'My poor dear Lord,' she says, turning her beautiful eyes on him and oh, God bless her, creeping her pretty long fingers over his warty old hand. 'How very tiresome for you.'

He nods and takes another swig and she gestures me to come forward for another fill up. I can see that Piers is taking it all in, knowing what she is about. Bacchus has drowned more men than Neptune.

'I handled the law cases at Lusignan,' she says, careful not to mention Hugh. Pons can sometimes fly into a rage worthy of my Lady's toddler son, at the mention of her former husband. It's why he don't like to see the children neither. 'I could lift some of this burden for you if you wish it,' she tells him.

'Hmm,' he says and we wait through yet another mastication. I learnt that word from my Lady's descriptions of him to Dia last night.

'The minor cases you can deal with,' he says, eventually, pushing himself up from the table, his many jewelled finger-rings glinting, his knee-joints cracking and creaking like a piece of wood cooling from the fire. 'Serious justice is not women's business,' he throws over his shoulder as he leaves the hall, but if I know my Lady she'll be dealing with it all in due course, minor and serious.

'Saddle my horse and fetch my falcon, Piers,' she tells him and he bows to her and leaves. Now she allows herself a glance of conspiratorial triumph with me and I am aglow at that. Where would she be without me?

19

A Tour of Toulouse

I have no intention of setting off to Saint Gilles for at least three weeks. I have many things to get done here. As soon as Pons is gone I go to the Capitouls' Court and join the Good Men of Toulouse for the last day of their justice hearings. They rise to their feet when I enter and look dumbfounded when I seat myself in the count's chair. I let them stare for a while.

'Continue,' I say eventually, and so they do although obviously discomforted at my presence. I watched Eustachie and Agnes act as regents in Aquitaine, and the women of La Marche, my mother and my grandmother, were accustomed to rule in the frequent absences of their men at war, so I am copying them. The Good Men live up to their title and are even-handed in their justice. We hear the case of a man who has broken into a house, and he is fined 100 *solidi*. Half of all these fines go into Pons' coffers. At the end of the day I seek out Bernard, the Bishop of Toulouse, who is one of these Good Men.

'Will you attend me tomorrow morning, my Lord Bishop? I should like to understand the workings of the city and the region and to know more of the concerns of my people.'

'Of course, my dear Lady,' he says in a tone that indulges me as if I am a little girl.

The bishop arrives in my chambers at mid-morning. Everybody seems most slack here in the hours they keep. He gives me a short summary of who the Good Men are: 'Aside from myself, of course,' he prepares to reel off a list, 'the council consists of Bertrand of Provence, your lord's nephew . . .'

'He was absent yesterday,' I interrupt him.

'He was. The Vicar of Toulouse, Ranulf de Roiax . . .'

'Also absent.'

He bows. 'You saw there, Armand and his brother Adémar, Viscounts of Toulouse; Gerald, Abbot of San Sernin; Hugh, Abbot of Daurade; and then the representatives of the leading families: Calvetus of Palatio; Bruno of Villanova; Bellotus of Castronovo, Remigius of Caramans and Aimeric d'Escalquencs.'

'How often does Pons meet with them?' I ask, controlling my irritation with the schoolmaster's tone he is taking with me.

'Never, Countess.'

'Never?' I echo.

'The count leaves his business and his trust in our hands.'

I allow a meaningful pause to form after this remark and then say, 'I wish to see the Cartulary of the House of Toulouse.'

'It is kept safely at the Cathedral, my Lady,' he says smugly.

'Then I will come tomorrow at first light.'

He looks astonished so I continue before he finds his voice, 'And I wish to see the inventory of the count's rights and holdings. Is that also kept at the cathedral?'

'There is no written record, my Lady,' he says, clearly glad that he can patronise me with my ignorance.

'Then how do the assessors know what is due at each feast day?'

'It is stored in their memories. They pass this knowledge onto their sons.'

I consider this and determine that I will have these living repositories disgorge their lists to me and I will draw up inventories. 'I require two scribes. Send me two of your monks, Bishop.'

'My scriptorium is extremely busy at the moment, Countess . . .'

'I can come and select them myself,' I say delivering my threat pleasantly with a smile.

'No, no,' he says, quickly. 'I will, of course, find two able brothers and send them to you.' He bows to make his exit but I have not quite finished with him.

'Where is The Custom of Toulouse kept?' The Custom is the law book of Toulouse.

He looks openly surprised now. 'It is also kept at the cathedral, where it is consulted by the count's four judges,' he says firmly.

'Good,' I say, ignoring his implication that it is none of my business. 'Send the Cartulary and the Custom with the scribes and I will consult them. I will return them to your safekeeping when I am done.'

He looks grimly at me, bows and leaves. I see on his face that he does not approve and will take his complaint to Pons.

'Is it wise to put too many noses out of joint, Almodis?' asks Dia when he is gone.

'The only nose we need worry about,' I say, 'is mine.' But she has a point. My grandfather told me that loyalty and friendship sustain our power. Who are my friends here? My brother and Hugh and Geoffrey, they are all far away. I have Raingarde and perhaps her husband when I meet him and no one else. I need allies, amongst the aristocracy, but also amongst the knights and *vavasours* and the Good Men of the city. I will make visits and issue invites to my neighbours and I will see what charm and learning might work on the Count of Rouergue and his wife. I send for Hugh, Abbot of Daurade. I liked the look and sound of him in the justice chamber yesterday and mean to make a friend of him.

The Abbot returns promptly with my messenger and I find him to be as intelligent and friendly as I guessed he might be. 'I am in need of a personal chaplain, my Lord Abbot, and wonder if you might recommend one of your ordained priests at the Abbey to come and attend me in that capacity?'

'Of course, my Lady. I will be happy to oblige you. I know just the right person. He is called Father Benedict. I will send him to you next week as he will need a little time to get used to the idea of his change in station and to say farewell to his fellows at the Abbey.'

'Thank you.' The abbot spends the afternoon conversing pleasantly with Dia and myself, playing chess, listening to Dia's songs. By the time we sit down to dinner I know that I have found my first ally. Next year, I think to myself, this Hugh will be my new bishop here.

Lady Emma, Pons' illegitimate half-sister, was cold to me at the wedding, following suit with her nephew I suppose. I noticed that she was with child and when news reaches me that she has birthed a son, I write to tell her that I mean to endow him that he might enter the Abbey of Comminges when he is old enough and, I assure her, I will see he receives preferment and rises to the rank of abbot if he shows himself able. A few weeks later she is visiting me, gushing with her gratitude, that I have given stability to her uncertain status as the bastard of a count. Another ally then or at least not an enemy.

'The younger men of the court are fawning enough for you surely,' says Dia.

'They are bored. All that Pons offers them is drinking, eating and whoring. They need action.'

'Will you start a war?'

'No I will start a weekly hunt which I will lead and you and I will teach them poetical games and singing. We will give them action and civilise them at the same time.'

'The Bishop's scribes have arrived for you from the cathedral,' Bernadette tells me this morning, kneeling to pull up my hose and attach them to the gold buckles on my garters.

'How do they look?'

'They're monks,' she says dismissively. I raise my eyebrows for more information.

'Well they are called Rostagnus and Osmundus. Rostagnus is a young man, perhaps eighteen and comely,' she says looking up at me archly, 'but Osmundus is fat and old and appears rather slow in the head.'

I smile. Bernadette has become invaluable to me and I enjoy the colourfulness of her language and her mind.

I explain their task to my scribes: that they will call in all the assessors who are holding the count's inventory of rights in their heads and they will write them down. Bernadette's assessment of Osmundus seems fair. He is anxious and clumsy. As soon as he came into my presence he swept a glass off a table with his habit and smashed it on the floor. He is non-plussed by my instructions and I see that Rostagnus will cover for Osmundus' hopelessness and that he will do all the work.

'So I see in Osmundus that the bishop has sent me one of his best men,' I say sarcastically to Rostagnus. Osmundus himself is far too simple to understand my meaning and merely simpers at this. 'But tell me Rostagnus, why has he sent you? What is wrong with you?'

He looks me in the eye. 'You are very direct, my Lady. I believe that the bishop thinks I ask too many questions.'

'Good,' I say. 'Are you from the city?'

'Yes. I am the fourth son of Aimeric d'Escalquencs.'

'Ah, yes, I met your father yesterday at the justice hearings. Welcome to my household, Rostagnus d'Escalquencs.'

'It is not simply a task of one day, then, Na?' (Na is what the people here call great ladies. It is short for domina. I am getting used to it but Bernadette refuses to use it. Sounds like a baby's name she says.)

'No, Rostagnus. It is not simply a task of one day. Before we begin work on the inventory I would like you to show me around the city.'

He looks alarmed.

'We can wear hoods and simple clothes, and Dia can come with us,' I add, in case he is afraid to be alone with me. 'I know that if I ask a member of the court, they will only tell me what they want me to know. What you tell me will be the truth.'

He blushes but smiles with his eyes downcast.

'I am curious to know about the people of the city. Will you show me around?'

'On foot, Na Almodis?'

'Yes, on foot, where I might see and talk to the citizens, and don't worry about my safety either. I can look after myself,' I say, lifting the fulsome hem of my sleeve to show him a dagger sheath strapped to my lower arm.

'The cathedral, abbeys and priory, we don't need to go there. I will visit them in my official capacity. This is a tour of what I might not otherwise see,' I tell him.

'Yes Na.'

From Chateau Narbonnais Rostagnus leads Dia and I left down towards the river and the mills near the Comminges Gate. Past Tournis Island in the middle of the river, we walk along the street of Joutx-Aigues, past the Jewish synagogue, and then up to the bridge that goes across to the area known as Saint Cyprien. 'The leper-house lies in that direction,' says Rostagnus. All along the water-front there is a mix of boatmen, stalls, fishermen and whores. A fat, naked woman darts past us, her flesh wobbling, her hands gripped to breast and private parts, her face in a shape of perfect distress, and a small crowd comes chasing after her.

'What on earth is this Rostagnus?'

'The woman is an adulterer, Na. It is the custom here, but a barbaric one I believe.'

'Yes, although I have seen worse,' I say, thinking of Geoffrey's mother.

Outside a tavern a group of Genoese sailors are gathered. Rostagnus goes inside to get a jug of beer since we are parched with our explorations and Dia and I sit on a bench with our hoods pulled up.

'And what about her former husband then? A sodomite I hear,' one of the Genoese is saying. 'Why else would any man let a woman like that countess slip through his fingers?'

I catch my breath, frowning at the lewd guffawing he has earnt himself, and feeling Dia's eyes on me.

'Her former husband could've just been paid off,' another voice suggests. 'The count needs an heir doesn't he?'

'No, no, I tell you. I've heard it from a reliable source. A friend of Ganymede's!'

Rostagnus comes out of the tavern with a jug and I stand up quickly and move away, so that they have to run to catch up with me. I don't want to hear any more of these spiteful rumours.

After the bridge, we pass the Daurade Abbey and then come to the Saracen Wall that used to enclose the city but now marks the entrance to the new expanding city area that is called the Bourg where weavers, finishers, candlemakers and wax merchants ply their trades. 'Up along the river, in that direction,' Rostagnus says, pointing, 'above the Bourg is the Chateau du Bazacle and more mills.' We pass through the Saracen Wall at the Portaria, the massive old Roman gate. We walk right, along the walls of the Abbey of Saint Sernin and down towards the Matabiau Gate, the Villeneuve Gate and then back through the Saracen Wall. Rostagnus points out the tower-houses and the fortified homes of the Toulouse nobility, including his father's house near the Montgaillard Gate, and finally he brings us back round to the Mint that stands neighbour to Chateau Narbonnais. I am pleased to find Rostagnus an intelligent and lively guide. Another ally.

20

Bernadette: Thwarted Men

I'm hurrying as best I can across the slippery cobbles of the bailey, carrying a jug of water on my shoulder from the well, trying to get out of the chill morning air. I've barely closed the door behind me and started to feel the blood surge back painfully into my ears and fingertips when my mistress comes banging through the doors letting the cold in behind her.

'There is much to do here Bernadette,' she says with satisfaction. I hold out my hands quickly to the fire, hoping it isn't me again who will have to do the much there is to do. 'It seems to me there are three types of people: those who do things, those who try to stop the first doing things, and those who accept far too easily that nothing can be done.'

'You'll have the household running well in no time, my Lady,' I begin.

'I wasn't speaking of a mere household,' she declares, raising her brows at me as if I am a nincompoop. 'I'm speaking of the county and the city. Pons is the most indolent in a long line of indolent lords.'

I gasp at her, frowning and glancing quickly around me.

'There's nobody here, Bernadette. You can stop your gasping.'

I think I see the tapestry at the far end of the hall move. It could have been a draught. I turn back to her. 'What needs doing?' I ask and instantly regret it. I'm exhausted long before she is partway through her list, counting up and down the joints of her fingers.

'Pons has allowed the churches to fall into disrepair and his relations with the clergy are not good. The county, that should all be under my command (hers I notice, not his) has been parcelled out to countless minor families who now think they can act independently and need to know otherwise. The *capitouls* of the city have no regard for him and he takes no interest in their concerns. The young men of the court are bored because he is too lazy to hunt and too stupid to debate and compose.'

I hear a creak behind me. 'My Lady,' I yell trying to cover her words, 'there is a great draught blowing at the back of the hall and I must see to it.'

'Fine. There's no need to shout.' She looks at me confused.

Hurrying towards the end of the hall I hear the distinct thud of a door closing, concealed by the tapestry. Piers, most like.

My Lady has summoned the butler, the chamberlain and the vicar to her that she might hear the details of their management and make what changes she deems necessary. The vicar, Ranulf de Roiax, sends word that he is out of Toulouse, meeting with the Count of Rouergue and that he will attend Countess Almodis the following week. She returns his messenger telling him that he will conclude his current business and attend her the following day at the latest. It seems that the count's household has had a very soft rein, or perhaps none at all, from Pons' first wife, Majora. Everyone seems surprised at any rate at my Lady's style though she is just doing what she did in Lusignan, on a bigger scale mind you. The butler, Gausbert, introduces her to all the servants, explaining their functions. We visit the kitchens where she charms the cooks and their assistants, demonstrating her knowledge of dariole and spiced wine.

We visit the women's workshop where five young girls are under the instruction of an older woman, Elois, working vertical looms and five more girls are spinning and three are preparing dyes. They make wool, linen and silk, Elois, tells us and Lady Almodis is pleased with the quality of their work.

'I will need cloaks, belts and robes to distribute at the Autumn Assembly,' she says. 'What do you have already made up?'

Elois shows her two chests with completed items neatly folded.

'Good,' says Almodis, 'but we will need twenty chests not two in six months time.'

The girls didn't stop their work when we entered although they stopped their chatter. The looms clacked and the thread twanged and the spindles jumped rhythmically. They are all listening intently to my Lady's words and one or two gasp aloud when she says 'twenty'. Elois opens her mouth. 'Of course,' Almodis preempts her, 'you cannot achieve that with so few weavers and spinners. You must have more workers and we will expand the work area threefold. I will send the chamberlain to plan this with you. The count and I are also in need of some items as quick as you can.'

Elois nods and picks up a tablet and stylus.

'You write, Elois?'

'Oh no Lady,' she chuckles, 'but I have my own way of making a tally.' I watch curious as she makes simple drawings of the items my Lady orders: two cloaks for herself, one blue silk for summer, and one scarlet wool for winter; one new dress, yellow; then a new wool cloak, green for Pons; a new tunic, red brocade; and two new hose. Elois draws the basic shape of the items on her tablet and makes a mark to indicate the number of each and an X to show it is for a woman and a + if it is for a man and then some symbols that I suppose represent the colours and the materials. She sees me looking over her shoulder and leads us to the dyeing area where the mordants and other materials are laid out in small containers with the symbols chalked on their sides.

'See I take the symbols of the colours and so on from here.'

'This is excellent, Elois. When will the workshop move out into the open?' Almodis asks.

'Well we don't usually do that, my Lady,' Elois says looking worried. 'Count Pons didn't want it.'

'Then how can you use the long light of summer? You will either do much less work than you could, or the girls will ruin their eyes working by candlelight, and candles are expensive. The girls need fresh air and they need the inspiration of the blue sky, the yellow flower and the buzzard soaring overhead, when they can get it. I will speak with the chamberlain to arrange this too. Next month will be warm and the days lengthening. He will organ-

131

ise an enclosed courtyard with a canopy for all of you and the new workers to move to when the weather is fine,' says Almodis with complete decision. Elois looks surprised but pleased and the workers are grinning too. They spend twelve hours, six days a week, labouring in here all year long, and it must feel like a dungeon in the summer months. They are cooped up with the odours and heat of the dyeing process. One of the dyers is so delighted with the prospect that she claps her hands and begins singing a cheerful working song that makes my mistress smile. I see that the dyer's fingernails are coloured a kind of motley purple-pink-blue that will never wash out.

'When do you shear the sheep and pick the flax?' Almodis asks. So she went on all day long, finding out the details of the household, and had to send word to the chamberlain that she was delayed and would see him the following day.

On the following day there is still no sign of the vicar and, with a great frown on her face, Almodis sends Piers to find out his whereabouts. She has another full day's work with the chamberlain, Arnaldus Maurandis. Arnaldus is a big muscly man, more than six foot with a bushy blond beard. He wears a sleeveless surcoat with the red and gold badge of Toulouse, the Occitan Cross, on top of his white undershirt and brown wool trousers. Lady Almodis seems happy with his arrangements, making small adjustments here and there. I can see that she likes him. He introduces us to his son, Gilbert, who is training with his father.

'Let me see the count's treasury now,' says Almodis.

I notice some unease creep into Arnaldus' expression. 'The count,' he says, hesitantly, 'is fond of his treasury room.'

'Room?' echoes Almodis. 'I was expecting a strongbox.' She turns to me raising her expressive light brown eyebrows. 'Well, take me to it.'

So we traipse off to a room with two armed guards outside who usher us in and I gasp out loud. It's like a treasure trove from a story: gold and jewels glittering in piles, on shelves, in chests set everywhere about the room. Arnaldus is looking uneasily at me.

'Don't worry, Arnaldus,' smiles Almodis. 'Bernadette is no thief. She wouldn't know what to do with such a hoard.' I giggle but actually I do have some ideas.

Almodis paces round the room, picking up a golden goblet, a silver reliquary, studying them and putting them back. 'Some excellent craftsmanship, that should see the light of day,' she says. Arnaldus bows in acquiescence. 'And so much of it.'

'The count has accumulated a goodly pile, yes, from taxes and gifts.'

'Then he must spend nothing and give nothing.'

Arnaldus remains silent with his eyes on the ground. Almodis nods to herself twice and slowly. 'Take an inventory, Arnaldus. I will spend the count's treasure but it will return four-fold and the inventory will show that. Very well,' she says eventually, 'I thank you Arnaldus,' and we leave the room, which is a relief in truth. The glare of all those riches was hurting my eyes and being in its presence made my mouth go dry. When we shut the door it was like closing up the sun in a dungeon. I thought I could see a yellow shine coming through the gaps around the door.

'I am pleased with your work, Arnaldus,' she tells him, giving him a gift of a ring from her own chest as a token of their new partnership, 'and you too, Gilbert,' she says, holding out a golden saucer brooch of Norse design to him, that is finely wrought in the sinuous shape of a dragon. Gilbert stands with his mouth open, not responding to her outstretched arm for some time, before coming to his senses and taking the brooch with both hands.

'Oh Lady, thank you,' he stutters. Gift-giving is obviously not a common occurrence in this household.

When Arnaldus and Gilbert have returned to their duties, Piers comes in to tell Almodis that the vicar has at last been heard of at the chateau of Ambialet near Albi. 'He is making his way back to attend you, I suppose,' says Piers.

'It is a day's ride from the castle of Rouergue, if he had come directly when I ordered,' she says. Piers says nothing but I have no doubt that she is right. 'As soon as he arrives, Piers, I want him sent to await me in the Great Hall. Straight from his horse, you understand?'

'Yes, Lady.'

'He is to have no fire. If the hearth is lit when he arrives, douse it.' Piers and I both look at her in surprise. 'Give him no wine and no bread. Do not invite him to sit. Draw no hot bath for him to wash away the dust of the road.'

'Yes Lady.' Piers voice and face are neutral, but I can imagine what he is thinking of her orders.

'Send word to me of his presence and keep him waiting there, in that condition, until it pleases me to give him audience.' Piers bows, glances at me and leaves. Well I hope that vicar might hurry now because he is already going to be standing, waiting for her for one whole day and the hall will get mighty chilly for all of us.

The vicar arrived this morning and Piers has carried out his instructions. The man has stood, fasting and parched, in his riding clothes, soaked with sweat for nigh on ten hours now. Almodis went out hunting for the day and dined out at a bower in the forest, so that she arrives back late and stalks into the hall with me running at her heels. She doesn't glance at the man, who mutters 'my Lady' as we pass and sinks to one knee. She climbs onto the dais and sits in the great carved chair and regards him in silence. After a while he looks up at her and shifts his weight, uncomfortably on his knee. She has given him no command to rise. Piers stands in the corner looking chilled to the bone himself.

Eventually, 'Get up', she says curtly, and the vicar rises with a look of great anxiety on his face. He is a stocky man with a big belly pushing at his leather tunic and threads of grey in his hair. 'Well?' she says.

'My Lady, I am Ranulf de Roaix, the count's vicar. Forgive my delay in arriving, Lady. I had business to conduct on the road here.' Despite the cold, he is sweating and I can smell him from here.

'I cannot forgive de Roaix,' she says, her voice loud in the frigid hall. 'You should have been here last morning. You are a day late. Whatever business you had, was it more important than the duty you owe to me?'

'No, Lady,' Ranulf stutters, surprise, anxiety and suppressed anger, all crossing his face plainly in quick waves. 'I offer my heartfelt apologies,' he says tentatively. Good, good, I think, but sound and look much more apologetic than that. Recognition is dawning on him that it might be his post, and not just his bath and wine that he will be deprived of here.

'I am sorry,' he says, sinking to his knees again. She lets him wallow there a while longer. My teeth are chattering and I hug my arms around myself. She must be cold too. She has flung off her floor length fur cloak and is sitting there in a dress of gold silk but she does not show that she is cold.

'Get off the floor, de Roaix. Bernadette, fetch wine and bread.' She looks at the hearth. 'It's too late for a fire tonight. Sit here for a moment Ranulf and tell me of the business that kept you on the road, then my maid will order a bath for you. Tomorrow you will attend me promptly in my chamber at daybreak to give me a full accounting of your work as my vicar. Bring your record books with you.'

Ranulf sits across from her and wolfs down the wine and bread I place before him. I admire her ability not to wrinkle her nose at his stink and the sound of his chewing. His mouth is occupied with that great work but his eyes are fixed wide on my Lady over the rim of his goblet. 'The Countess Majora did not . . .' he begins.

'The Countess Majora is a nun,' Almodis interrupts smoothly, 'and I am not in the least interested in what she did or did not do.'

'I usually organise any business of the domain with the count,' he begins again.

Oh dear, he is not catching on fast.

'The count is busy with other matters. You will deal with me now. Ranulf, I have noted that there are large expanses of land that have been left uncultivated and that many farms are abandoned. The river, that should be our great source of wealth, our artery, is choked with fallen trees not far outside the city. The waters run sluggish and not navigable for large boats. We need to clear the river.'

'A capital idea my Lady,' he says, his voice sweetly patronising, 'but I fear we cannot get to it. It is surrounded by impenetrable forest.' He beams at her smugly, his chin glistening with grease.

'Then we will clear the forest on our way to the river and we will create a new village in the clearing. People are crammed so tight in some quarters of the city that we need new settlements. We can sell the timber to the ship-builders.'

'Who would wish to move there?' de Roaix objects. 'Besides we can't afford it.'

He is still eating and reaching his fat hand out for more when she says, 'Tidy away the board, Bernadette.' I snatch it up fast and she stands up abruptly. 'It is time we all retired. I want you and your record books outside my chamber door at dawn.' She is already half way down the hall, and the fat vicar is struggling to rise from his seat, his mouth ajar, and the guards are opening the door for her exit.

She was still sleeping at dawn of course but I looked outside the door and there was no Ranulf or his books. Now she is up and dressed and broken her fast and still no sign of him. She sends Piers to find out what has happened. 'Your hair is sticking up, Bernadette,' she says to me. 'You look like something you could turn upside down and sweep the floor with.' Well I don't have a poor maid to brush and brush and brush it do I? Piers is back while I'm still smoothing down my hair.

'Ranulf's gone, my Lady. His horse too. Snuck away in the night.'

'Yes, I am not surprised. I will appoint a new vicar.' I see Piers shift his weight expectantly. 'Ask Arnaldus Maurandis to attend me.' I am seated behind Piers so that I can't see his face, but his stance betrays an intensity of suppressed emotion.

'Arnaldus is a reliable man and knows the city of course, but then who will take his place as chamberlain?' he says.

'Arnaldus' son, Gilbert, will take the role of chamberlain,' she says, fixing Piers with a stare. I see the back of his neck redden and he clenches his fist at his side. 'You are an excellent groom and mews-man, Piers, and I need you about me.'

'Of course, Lady Almodis,' he says, bowing his head but we all know that he is greatly displeased.

Next she turned her attention to the merchants of the city. Arnaldus told her they complain the count takes too much taxation and gives nothing back. 'The city and county of Toulouse,' she says to Arnaldus and me, 'was once the heart of the great Visigothic Empire, and of the Roman Empire in this region. Toulouse is the hub of the old Roman road system. All goods and travellers going north, south, east and west come through here and their tolls and tithes with them, but now bridges, roads, churches and walls are crumbling. When I entered the city for my marriage a man had to run ahead of my horse with a plank of wood to mend the surface of the roads and another was forced to place his shield over large holes in the bridge for my horse's hooves.' So she and Arnaldus put their heads together over a programme of works that includes clearing the waterways too.

Rostagnus' inventories have uncovered shortcomings and neglect in the garnering of income so more is coming in which will pay for her improvements. For days on end all her talk with them is of Peter the Brown who owes her provisions for ten fighting men plus two setiers of wine, his brothers who owe five quarters of barley, Roland who owes the fighting men breakfast, Richard who owes albergum of a pig, a sheep, three setiers of good wine, four setiers of bread wheat and a quantity of pinard, the abbot who owes provisions for fifty fighting men and brill on the table.

'Where is the library, Arnaldus?'

'There is no library, Lady, just a few scrolls in the chaplain's vestry.'

'Find me a good stonemason and carpenter then. We shall build a library, a small annexe to the hall here, on this side, well away from the kitchen and in the full light of the morning sun.'

In a few weeks she was installed in her library with the builders still working around her.

'Bernadette, go with Dia, and find the Toulouse family record books.'

I groan as I lift myself off the stool. I know that these books will be dusty, dirty, heavy and many! Other lady's maids don't have to be maid, nursemaid, librarian, dogs-body all in one go do they? I look with regret at the pristine white of my apron knowing that I will not see it again till next wash day.

She spent a week with her head in those dusty books that the bishop reluctantly sent her and, when she emerged, a cobweb hanging off her veil and her fingertips as grimy as the carpenter's, she says, 'There's not much of use here since the records have not been kept up to date since Count Pons took power.' She sets Rostagnus to remedying that, telling him, 'I do not hold with the notion that we master the art of writing in order to "improve" the documentary evidence, as they do, by all accounts, in the scriptoria of Saint Martial, Lagrasse and Narbonne, but we should at least attempt to keep true and full records.'

She has written to Pons, telling him that she is delayed, but will join him soon. She sends off letters to Carcassonne and La Marche and occasionally further afield enquiring after some new book or troubadour she has heard of. Audebert writes her that Agnes is sitting smug in Aquitaine, warming her son's throne, but we hear that Geoffrey is forever abandoning her for his northern military campaigns and they have no children. My Lady's growing collection of books is carefully arranged and looked after by Dia. All this 'busyness'. Is it to avoid thinking of her new husband, or to avoiding thinking of her old one?

There were no more dismissals after Ranulf but the laundry is whiter, the hall tables gleam and the wine tastes a good deal better.

'Wealth is not for hoarding and heaping, Bernadette,' she says, 'but for using. If we give, it will come back to us.'

'Yes, my Lady,' I say, 'what goes around, comes around.'

She took the two chests of clothes already woven and gave some to the workers in the workshop who needed them, and others to a crowd of beggars at the Montgaillard Gate. 'Saint Augustine wrote, that we must be mindful of the poor,' she told me, 'so that we lay up for ourselves in the heavenly treasury.' So she became popular with all the people because she was hard but fair and the fame of her generosity spread all round the city. I overheard people talking of it in the market and hoped that it would not reach Pons' avaricious ears.

My Lady goes early every morning up the staircase in the east tower to stand on the keep as the sun comes up and I must watch the children while she does. One morning she wakes me and takes me up the staircase with her. Together we watch the sun rise across the city and the surrounding land and river, and listen to the birds' frantic twittering and chatter.

'I will find a way, to survive this grievous marriage,' she says aloud, but more to herself than to me. 'I will devote myself to my children and to my land. Two husbands who have not matched up to my expectations, or indeed to what I give to them. My children will be the sons and daughters of *my* line, not theirs.

'Why do you come to these battlements every morning, Lady?'

'I like to look out across the city of Toulouse and the blue bends of the Garonne and the countryside all around. I like to look at what I own, what I rule and I like to dream of where the river might take me if I were not countess but instead a beggar boy and could step lightly onto one of those skiffs and hide amidst the cargo.'

'Would the river take you to Barcelona perhaps?' I venture.

She is silent and I fear I have offended her, but then she says, 'Only if it were flowing backwards, my silly Bernadette!'

21

Christmas 1040

I dismount to rest my horse for a while, and stand in pale green grass waving in a bitterly cold wind, looking towards the castle of Saint Gilles. We have had to make slow progress here because of my condition. It is near Christmas and the countryside is deep in snow. A dark red bush pushes up through the snow looking like a bloodstain against the pure white. I feel the chill and damp through the soles of my boots. I turn my arms and hands over and over in the fat flakes of snow, smiling. Underneath my fur-lined hood my hair hangs in a single plait down the back of my green tunic, and underneath the tunic is a canary yellow dress that shows through at the sleeves and at the slits on the sides. The sleeves of my yellow underdress are so incredibly long and flared that they will sweep the floor when I walk into the hall of Saint Gilles to tell my lord that I am carrying his heir. I tuck my cold hands into my sleeves. There are knights on horses in the distance in front of the castle. The sky is a mix of blue and dirty yellow; the sun is shining but the temperature is freezing. The snow gives a peculiar quality to sounds, making them carry long distances. We can hear the voices of the knights, the snorting and stamping of their horses and the clanging of their weapons on the target carrying across to us in the frigid air. I stamp my feet and wish that I had three pairs of hose on.

The castle of Saint Gilles stands on a huge granite rock that rises up out of the flatter land around it. It towers down over-looking the valley of the wide river that is lazily, greenly lapping its way around the rock. I look up the steep sides of the enormous valley that stretches as far as I can see. The sides of the valley are littered with puny trees and grey and black boulders. Some of the trees wear only snow and icicles and other conifer trees are a deep, dark green. At the top of the valley, so far above my head that I have to lean back to see it, is a plateau.

'When you are on that plateau up there,' Piers tells me, seeing where I am looking, 'this valley disappears. It's hidden by the thick covering of trees in the summer and invisible from above. A secret valley.'

I smile at him and turn my gaze back to the castle and town huddled around its walls. The rock is grey and the castle is grey so that it seems to grow out of the rock. A crenellated wall runs around its four sides and six towers rear up above the wall and the battlements. It is not a regular square because it has been built following the contours of its rocky foundation. Clustering at its foot and climbing up towards it are small houses with red tiled roofs and steep cobbled streets with haphazard steps cut into them.

We remount and as we get nearer I see the knights more clearly. They are wearing white padding and practising with a target and a spear, riding one at a time to try to hit it in the centre. I wave to them and they wave back. I lead my party towards an arched stone bridge. There are many fishing birds on the river: slim and elegant black cormorants, white and swooping gulls, cranes perching and occasionally taking off from rocks in the river on their slow, enormous wings. Slabs of ice float in the green water and ducks weave around them.

'Imagine how cold those ducks' feet are,' says Bernadette.

Unseen fish or frogs splash and make circles on the river surface. Our horses' shoes sound on the bridge and then we are over, in the stony town of Saint Gilles. We have to dismount again to climb up the steep streets and ice and snow underfoot are treacherous. People stop and stare at us. The colours of their clothes are drab browns, greens, whites but also very bright colours: reds, yellows and blues. I smell a whiff of the fuller's vats where sheep's wool is pummelled in urine for hours, the ammonia drawing out the grease and making the wool soft. Perhaps some of these people are those employed to stand up to their

141

knees in these vats all day, treading the wool. I swallow, nauseous, and lean more heavily on Piers' arm as he assists me up the slope. I am heavy with my child.

Women are carrying loaves of bread and pails of water, men carry bundles of firewood, children play on the steps of the houses with wooden toys, a cat shakes snow from its paw and blinks at me, smoke rises from the chimneys of the houses. We skirt around steaming piles of mule dung. Many of the doors are hung with circles of holly with bright red berries for the Christmas feast. There are deep drifts of snow on the street-corners and in patches on the roofs of the house and every now and then a chunk of snow slides from a roof onto the street below or once, unfortunately, down the back of Bernadette's neck. 'Eeeek!' she exclaims and Piers and I laugh.

The wooden arched door in the massive stone wall of the castle is studded with metal knobs and bands. Inside this door is like being in yet another village as the castle walls enclose more stone buildings: the bakehouse, dairy, pigsty, dovecote, stables, and one large building. Piers leans hard on the giant door of the Great Hall. Inside there are tapestries on the walls and the smell of rosemary rising from the rushes. Hanging everywhere is green ivy and the darker green of prickly holly and here and there the white berries of mistletoe. 'Shut the door!' someone yells and Piers turns and leans on the door behind us, closing it with a clang.

So I am come (but briefly I intend) to Saint Gilles where Pons and I will entertain his nephew for the Christmas feast. I take in the cavernous room in front of me: two extraordinarily long wooden tables with benches, a fire burning brightly, large shaggy dogs curled in front of the fire, people scattered, doing odd tasks: cleaning weapons, practicing on instruments, cradling babies, spinning and sewing. At the far end of the hall, on the raised platform stretching across its width, sits Pons with Bertrand. I register the look on their faces, as I glide up the hall towards them, my belly preceding me by quite some distance! After greetings, and Pons' joyful effusions, and the much less sincere congratulations of his nephew, Bernadette hands me a glass of warm punch flavoured with citron and sweet syrup, and then I excuse myself and my unborn child for a short rest. Pons is anxious that I should be treated with the utmost care. Bernadette takes me up to a small room above the hall, which has a window with two tall pointed arches. She throws up the lid of a wooden chest that stands at the foot of the bed, rummaging in it. Eventually her head re-emerges, her cheeks pink, and she throws more fur quilts onto the bed. 'I think these will do.'

'So I shall birth the heir of Toulouse in this bed,' I say.

'Are you sure it's a boy?' says Bernadette.

'Yes, Dia took two drops of my blood from my side and dropped them into spring water and they sunk. Also my right breast is bigger than my left which Hippocrates said is a clear sign of a boy.'

There is a sudden clangour of bells from the church to pronounce the start of the Christmas feast. 'The peasants are on holiday now for two weeks,' exclaims Bernadette, looking like an excited child. 'The best feast of the year!'

'Well perhaps we should rejoin the Christmas group then,' I say, not wanting to curtail her fun just because I would avoid my lord and, in any case, I am hungry. Back downstairs there is shouting near the door which bursts open giving entry to two men dragging what looks like a small tree towards the fireplace.

'The yule log,' Bernadette says, 'that will burn through the whole holiday.'

With a great effort, swinging it a few times between them, the men throw the log onto the fire where it sends out sparks and heat. People are clapping and laughing, sitting down at the long trestle tables, full now with the whole village crammed into the hall, and there is a buzz of chatter and laughter and a great deal of staring at me.

The servants are handing round chunks of bread to everyone. 'King of the Bean, King of the Bean,' children chant, and I think with a pang of my own Lusignan children, left behind in Toulouse, playing with their Christmas toys with Dia instead of me.

'This is a special Christmas game played here my Lady,' Bernadette tells me, standing at my shoulder, 'where the person who finds a small bean baked inside their bread will be crowned the king of the Christmas feast, so don't swallow it if it's inside yours.'

I take a bite of my bread finding nothing and look along the rows of faces to see who has the bean. Bernadette has seated herself just below the platform and I see that she is pushing her cheek out with her tongue, a comical expression on her face. She takes a small object from the tip of her tongue. 'Oh!' she says, looking at the small white bean on her fingertip.

'It's you!' Piers yells, hoiking her to her feet, shouting, 'Bernadette has the bean! Bernadette has the bean!'

Everyone stops talking to stare and one of the table servants places a silver plate crown on her head, laughing and bowing to her as he does so. We rise to our feet, lifting our tankards and glasses and yelling loudly together, 'Hail King Bernadette, King of the Bean!' Bernadette is clearly worried about keeping the wobbly crown on her head and has gone the colour of a beetroot.

We eat a thick vegetable soup, then chicken and roast boar, and finally cheese. Pons pokes and probes at his mouth with a wooden toothpick. 'There's another whole course in my teeth,' he says, roving his tongue under and over his lips.

Musicians play on recorders, horns, trumpets, whistles, bells, and drums. Everyone listens in concentrated silence and claps wildly when they finish. Then come acrobats who stand on each other's shoulders, juggling and playing flutes; and then, the professional farters.

'These are my favourites', says Pons, making me glad that Dia isn't here.

The heat of the fire is making my face red and my head thick with sleepiness. I go and stand near the door to give gifts to the servants and village people as they leave: parcels of food, clothing, ale and bundles of firewood.

Upstairs in my white nightgown, made from soft Egyptian cotton, and with a red woollen shawl draped around my shoulders, I lean out of the arched window gasping at the cold beauty of the night. Trees, hillside, everywhere is white with a dusting of snow, and the river is beginning to freeze over. Buildings shimmer with icicles. The cloud is white and so low it almost touches my nose. I shutter the window and turn to the huge bed, piled high with blankets and pillows. I expect the sheets to be freezing but find that they are snug and warm. Bernadette has put a bedpan of hot water in to warm them. I slide the covered pan out, balancing it gingerly with its long handle and set it carefully down on the floor.

In the morning I am ravenous. The Great Hall is full of snoring people and dogs. I go downstairs to the kitchen where a cook places a steaming bowl of porridge in front of me. 'To feed you and the heir, Lady,' she says cheerfully.

Back upstairs, the Great Hall is a scene of confusion with servants running about tidying up the mess from last night's feast. I sit down at the trestle near the fire to catch my breath amidst the commotion and then feel the first pain of my child coming. Bernadette walks me slowly up and down the hall to ease the pains for as long as possible before I must retire to my chamber. She bathes me in scented water and passes frankincense under my nose to provoke sneezing and help with the birth.

Bernadette and I pray to St Margaret of Antioch, who made her own safe passage through the belly of a dragon, as I labour to birth Pons' heir. I don't know what is in Bernadette's head, but I pray that the child will not look like his father. The baby comes quickly and I have a fine new son to add to my nursery, named Guillaume. Bernadette ties the umbilical cord three fingers from his belly to encourage the development of a large penis.

Pons comes to claim his marriage debt a mere three days after I have birthed his heir and takes me so by surprise with his cruelty and violence that I cannot find excuses or a way to deter him. When he leaves me Bernadette finds me weeping. 'My Lady!'

'Pons has claimed his marriage debt and I am in pain,' I wail.

'I will fetch some healing lily unguent, Lady. His marriage debt!' she says, her face showing her outrage. 'He should have waited full forty days before that!'

'Yes, I know,' I say feebly, 'but I could not . . .'

Bernadette has set up her mattress on the floor in my room and she has ranged Father Benedict and Rostagnus on palettes outside the door, to keep Pons from me. I try to find ways to accept my life as it is and hope that with each attempt I might gain one foot forward. My baby Guillaume is only a month old when I begin to suspect that I am already with child again.

The cooks cater to Pons' extravagant tastes. Today they serve us a feast of birds: partridges, storks, cranes and larks line up down the table and in the centre there is a peacock, its meat roasted and then presented in its original plumage. Another child rolls in my belly and my stomach churns.

'Dear wife,' Pons says to me, 'I hear that you have been worrying your pretty little head with men's business. There's no need of that. You are not a chatelaine in a minor castle now. Here, we have servants and officers doing all that for us.' As I expected the bishop has been complaining of me.

'And do you think that all that is rightfully yours finds its way through the filter of their fingers to your coffers?' I ask him. 'I am the daughter of a count and the granddaughter of a duke, my Lord. I know my business. If you will allow me I will increase your income.'

A grape is pinched between his fingers on its way to his maw, and is arrested at the moment when his mouth opens. 'Increase?'

'Yes,' I say, confidently. 'Do you know what your income was at this assembly?'

'Well, no. Ranulf of Roaix has the tally of course.'

'A wager my Lord that I can increase your income by 10,000 *solidi* or more by next Easter Assembly.' He likes that. 'And next year all your subject counts and viscounts will attend your assembly.'

'Now don't go upsetting anyone. I want no war or strife for that's expensive you know.'

He has never warred. His court is soft and enfeebled. If it were threatened with military invasion it would fall in no time. 'I have appointed a new Vicar of Toulouse,' I say and the table falls silent.

Pons looks bewildered. 'What? What's happened to Ranulf? Ranulf of Roaix?'

'He was dishonest and disloyal.'

Pons begins to shake his head. 'But Ranulf, he was always . . .'

'He has been defrauding you, my Lord, depleting your treasury.'

He gapes at me, very concerned at that, and the sight of his jangled brown teeth is not a pleasant one. 'Depleting?' he says aghast.

'Yes,' I say, although in my memory of that treasure room I can't see any cause for concern. 'I have appointed a new vicar, Arnaldus Maurandis, and I will oversee his work rigorously.'

'Yes, yes,' he says, stroking my cheek and hair, and then allowing the back of his hand to graze my breast. 'I am sure you are handling it all very well, my pretty little wife.'

I am four inches taller than him and certainly a good deal prettier.

'You are looking very well today, wife. Over your prayers eh? I will visit you tonight,' he whispers, smirking in my ear.

I decide that this is the moment to tell him I am carrying a second child. He forgets everything else and his face lights up. 'Do you think it another boy?' he asks.

'Yes,' I say.

'Excellent!' he says kissing me wetly on the mouth, trying to thrust his tongue between my teeth, his hand pushing high on my thigh. 'And a man may sleep with his wife to within three months when the birth is due,' he says.

'Do you want to ruin this son too, as happened with Majora's child,' I ask angrily, and the lewd expectation on his face drops instantly.

'Aye, aye,' he says. 'You must do what you think is right and best for the child.'

The next day I inform him that I have decided to return to Toulouse to wait for the birth as the air suits me better there.

He is angry and argumentative at first. 'How can the fetid air of the city be better than here, where we are near the sea?'

'Saint Gilles is full of sick people, carrying disease and malformity,' I say. I mean the pilgrims who come to the abbey here

147

with their staffs, their bandaged limbs, their weeping sores, to ask
Saint Gilles, saint of cripples, to aid them. He looks at me askance
but he gives in.

'I shall miss you, my sweet.' I suppress the urge to allow my
mouth to curl in hatred.

22

Candlemas to Lammas 1041

It is a relief to be back in Toulouse, getting on with the business of government with my vicar. 'If Pons continues as he is,' I say to Arnaldus, 'you can be sure that someone will see his weakness, will take advantage of it. Toulouse is rich, dripping with wealth.'

'Who would threaten Toulouse? This overlordship you speak of is in name only now, Lady, surely?' says Arnaldus.

'No it is not. These counts and viscounts have given their oath to Pons. Who will lead the region if it is threatened by the King of France, or the King of Aragon?'

'That is hardly likely . . .'

'Who?' I demand.

'Well not Pons, Domina.'

'No, not Pons, but we will be prepared to act in the count's name, to hold the region together if it should ever be necessary. I mean to appoint my man, Piers, to assist you in this.' He bows and I send for Piers and tell him that I am going to give him an elevated position and responsibility. He draws himself up, smiling broadly. 'I wish you to take on the role of Marshal of Toulouse and work with Arnaldus Maurandis to ensure that we are ready should the region be threatened by outside forces. You will see that the lines of communication and the promises of service from all the lords in the region who have given us their oaths are in good order. You will ensure that the network of rural lords coming to give us their four months guard duty is functioning well and that the *albergum*, the provisioning, is in place when we are on the move. You will train the boys sent here as foster children, for knightly training. There are few at present, but there will be more.'

'My Lady I will be glad to undertake such a role.'

'You will give me your oath then Piers. But let us be very clear. Your oath is to me and not to my husband. I want no deceit and no discord. I look for fealty.'

'I understand my Lady.'

'And Piers,' I say in a low voice, close to his ear, 'if you break your faith to me, if you betray me, I will not forgive you. I will hunt you down and string you up.' I am looking directly into his eyes, my face close to his.

He nods. 'I understand this my Lady.'

He pushes his floppy brown hair back from his face, then places his hands together inside mine and says:

'From this hour forward I, Piers, will be faithful to you Almodis by true faith without deceit as a man should be faithful to his lady to whom he has commended himself by his hands.' I kiss him on both cheeks, and am glad to see a smile on his face instead of a scowl.

I have invited the local nobility from Saint Jeury, Ambialet, Albi, Cordes-sur-Ciel, Trebas, to send their young sons into my foster care and train in Toulouse with Piers. They learn horsemanship, archery, swordsmanship and codes of conduct, and they learn to be loyal to me. They take care of the horses, clean the stables, polish armour and harness, maintain weapons. Father Benedict tries to teach them their letters and Latin. They are the entourage for my baby son, Guillaume. When they are not training, they wrestle; or I listen to the click of balls in their boule games; or they play hoodman's blind, staggering blindfold round the courtyard trying to catch one of the others and pass on the hood. It reminds me of my father's courtyard in Roccamolten. It is a delight to see them here and my Lusignan children: Hugh, Jourdain and Melisende, join in these games and become part of this junior court. It is good to see Piers flourishing in his new role and sporting a fetching pair of scarlet leggings.

This spring the rivers are swollen and the land is waterlogged. The Garonne shifts from green to muddy brown and brims its banks, overflowing into the water meadows where ducks gleefully swim on what once was dry land; and trees are half-drowned, rising straight out of the water; and small islands of land seem merely a precarious crust, like skin on hot milk. The flood waters encroach on many of the houses closest to the river, with water as high as their lintels. They are built for flood though, with their storage areas on the ground floor and the living quarters above. Nevertheless the townspeople are greatly occupied salvaging their wood and other goods usually stored downstairs and helping each other sweep out the thick mud when the waters begin to retreat. The farmers, however, are pleased since the flood is good for the soil. Gradually the land oozes back up from the subsiding waters.

'Amoravis, the minter, begs an audience with you, Na,' Rostagnus says.

'Show him in.' He is a tall and striking man with pale skin and black hair and beard. 'I am pleased to see you here Master Minter.'

'I am come to ask a great kindness of you, Na.'

'What is it?'

'We are approaching the Christian Holy Week and there is a tradition here of Striking the Jew in that week.'

'Yes, I have heard of it.'

'Last year many Jews were badly injured, Na. I ask you is there an alternative? A tax perhaps?'

'It will be difficult to enforce.' I am silent, thinking, and Amoravis stands silent, watching me. 'A tax of two *solidi* for each adult Jew in the city, half of which will go to the city's churches,' I say, meaning that the other half will go to Pons' coffers. I will be well on my way to winning my wager with Pons now.

He bows. 'That is a great kindness from a just Christian lady.'

Lammas is past and my child is due, and Pons has written to say he will return to Toulouse for the birth, so that I will have to deal with him again. I could run. I could go where nobody would find me, not him, not Audebert, no one. I could work as a peasant in a field and live in a small hut built into the side of the mountain. I could hunt my own food, write a book of my life, but I would never see my children or my sister again. I don't care about clothes and jewels and castles but I would miss my books. I could cope with cold and hunger and work. I am not afraid to sustain myself. My family name would suffer if I deserted Pons: my sisters, my brothers, my mother, would all be shamed. Perhaps my children would suffer more than the loss of their mother, perhaps my sons would be disinherited and no one would offer for my daughter. Yet perhaps to be unwed would be a blessing for her. I cannot seek refuge in a nunnery. It is a good life for some but it would be as a grave to me, a life that isn't living. I cannot hate the world and its pleasures. I would rather take my chances in the world, be a wandering troubadour . . .

I cannot run. For my children, I must stay and wear this. The bells call the workers to meals three times a day, striking the hours; they call the monks to prayers, measuring out the day and night in small pieces, and so I must bear one piece at a time.

Abbot Durand in Moissac has written to my husband protesting at my abolition of Striking the Jews in Holy Week, but I have successfully persuaded Pons of the economic advantage to himself.

'My Lady! Your sister has arrived!' Bernadette bursts in.

From the window I see Raingarde alighting from her horse and waving up at me. 'Let's go and get her!' I grab Bernadette's hand and drag her behind me. She is as slow as a slow worm.

'Take a care Lady. You are full pregnant. Like to drop any minute!'

'As if I don't know that, Bernadette, but with my sister here I feel as light as a dandelion head on a summer breeze.'

The sunlight is streaming through the doorway into the court-yard and I am momentarily blinded as we burst out to greet Raingarde. Her blonde head is hard to discern in the brightness, but blinking, I grasp her in an embrace, as best I am able with my cumbersome belly between us.

'Sister! Welcome!'

She is kissing my face and hands. 'Almodis! Almodis!'

'Well now,' says Bernadette, no doubt embarrassed at our effusions, 'shall we escort Lady Raingarde to the hall, Lady Almodis?'

I ignore Bernadette and stand holding Raingarde's hand, looking her up and down. Like me, she is a woman now and no longer a girl.

'Yes,' I say, at length, 'come in Raingarde and be comfortable.' I tuck her hand into my arm and lead her in, blanking out the noise of Bernadette supervising the baggage and Raingarde's entourage behind me. 'We've got your own chamber all ready for you.'

'My own chamber?' she glances around before we go in. 'Chateau Narbonnais is so huge Almodis!'

'It is!' I laugh. 'Massive!'

Raingarde has been with me three days and is settled with her maid, Carlotta. I wish she could stay here forever but she will want to go home to her husband as soon as I am recovered from the birth. I thought to have her here as protection from Pons too. Two days ride away is nothing. I will ride to see her in Carcassonne often. I smooth my dress over the great round of my stomach, hoping that my child will stay in there for a while, that I might have more of Raingarde for myself.

23

Bernadette: My Lady's Ideas

My Lady has established her household in Chateau Narbonnais here in Toulouse and keeps Count Pons in Saint Gilles as much as she can. He does not like to travel: bum-shaking he calls it, whereas my Lady looks like she was born in the saddle and would happily live there. Worst luck, he's back with us again now, but while she is carrying his child the count does everything he can to appease her.

Me and Carlotta are waiting at table and in between the courses I'm having a chat with the buttery servants. 'Old Pons is ogling Lady Raingarde good and proper at the high table!' I say.

'Likes the look of two of 'em does 'e the dirty bugger?'

'He keeps looking back and forth between them and poor Lady Raingarde is red as a poppy but too polite to pass comment. Not so, my own Lady though! Bless her.'

'What did she say then?'

I let them wait a moment to milk the drama and then I feign her voice and manner as best I might, with my little finger cocked out from the stem of a glass and my nose right in the air. '"Are you suffering from an infliction, husband!" she says, after her stares and tuts have not sufficed to stop him roving his eyeballs all over her sister. "Yes, we are identical twins! Yes, we look alike! Yes Raingarde is beautiful! Is there something you would like to say?"' I drop my act and grin at them.

I couldn't speak a word of Occitan when I first arrived here, but Almodis has taught me and I've got the hang of it so well,

I'll like as not be forgetting my own tongue. At Hugh's court there was a mix of Occitan and Langue d'Oil spoken depending on who was visiting or who you were speaking with, but here it's only the Occitan and Almodis always uses only that with her children.

'Oooh, bless me, what did his lordship say to that? She doesn't mince her words, your Lady does she?' says the buttery maid.

'He just smirked and lowered his eyes, but not for long before he was back at it. They made some small talk and he asked after Lady Raingarde's husband and mother-in-law, some such, you know how they do.'

'In you go now with the next course Bernadette,' Gilbert prods me. 'Do you want them going hungry while you gossip?'

Don't care if they do, I think to myself. Well the fat lord at any rate. His belly's bigger than my Lady's and he's only got hot air and wine in it. When he forced himself on her in Saint Gilles, after she'd just birthed baby Guillaume, I felt like sinking a dagger into that rotund belly, but then I imagined my feet jigging up and down at the end of a hangman's noose like I'd seen on the gibbet outside town and felt all cold and shivery. My Lady though, I thought, when she'd recovered from the birthing weepiness and the shock of what he did to her, *she'd* as like drive her dagger into him and *she'd* go for his privates if I know her. I'd resolved then and there to keep an eye on her. I didn't want her swinging for that dirty old lord.

Well that's another epic dinner over with and I'm putting my feet up, getting a bit of rest in my Lady's chambers where we've retired so's we can get in some good gossiping.

'Tell me of your husband, Raingarde. You spoke fondly of him in your letters to me in Lusignan.'

'Oh yes,' Raingarde responds all enthusiastic. 'You will meet Pierre soon, Almodis, and you will adore him too. He is a kind man.' She stops there and we all wait expectantly for more but in vain.

'Well,' asks Almodis, fishing for something, anything, 'umm, does he like music?'

Raingarde looks at her puzzled. 'Yes.'

'And riding?'

'Not so much,' says Raingarde, looking down at her hands, so now we are getting to the nub of it, for we are all thinking and can't say, how is it at twenty-one that Almodis, her twin, is on her second husband and fifth baby, whilst Raingarde is still the slim, childless, young girl who left La Marche. That's the obvious difference between them after all! She's been wed three years and no child.

Almodis is looking worried that she has discomfited Raingarde with her question. 'He is away from home a great deal on business, perhaps,' she says gently.

'I know what it is you mean,' says Raingarde, looking miserable and glancing around at Dia, Carlotta and me.

'Shall I dismiss them?' Almodis asks abruptly and I'm desperately thinking no, no! Raingarde doesn't answer for a while but looks at the flames dancing in the grate.

'No,' she says quietly. 'Carlotta knows all my business and I have no need to have secrets from old friends,' she glances up at me and Dia, but I see that there are tears in her eyes and I'm thinking about where is the nearest clean handkerchief. 'You mean, Almodis, that I have no child as yet.'

Almodis simply looks at her neutrally.

'I love my husband,' Raingarde goes on, looking earnestly into my Lady's face. 'He loves me also.'

'Oh I am glad of it,' Almodis bursts out and we all recall what she has had to bear in Lusignan and understand her relief that it's not her sister's lot.

'I do not despair of a child, not yet,' Raingarde tells her.

'No, no. Of course not.'

'If you are so fertile, then perhaps I will be too, eventually, if God wills it.' She clams up again and Almodis clasps her hand affectionately, not asking, just waiting. I pretend to be about my sewing and Dia rises to poke the fire and put another log in the flames.

When Dia is seated, Raingarde decides to speak again. 'Pierre has a condition,' she says hesitantly and I suppress the urge to yell: well what is it?

'A condition . . .?' asks Almodis.

'A skin condition. It flares up and becomes very painful and he can't move or do anything as usual when it is in that state. All over his body like a carapace,' she tries to explain it to Almodis, gesturing at her own arms and legs and head. 'It's like a shell. He can't ride, can't move . . .' she peters out.

'What do the doctors say?' asks my Lady.

'It is a family illness, inherited from his grandfather. There is no cure but there are respites when it's not so bad.' After a while she adds, 'So he tells me. And we are waiting for that.'

Almodis looks up at Dia and me, frowning, anxious for her sister.

'I believe I know of this condition,' says Dia. We all turn to her.

'Dia has studied medicine with the healers in Italy,' Almodis tells Raingarde. 'Do you know a cure, Dia?'

'No, there is none as Lady Raingarde says, but tell me is your husband's skin sometimes white and patchy on his elbows, knees, scalp, buttocks and sides?' Raingarde nods. 'And at its worse it becomes red, hard, tight, shell-like?' Raingarde nods again. 'Yes, I know this,' Dia says decidedly. 'It passes usually through the males of a family and skips a generation. Your own sons will be well. Exposure to sunlight is very good for this condition. You must persuade Lord Pierre to expose his skin to the sun every day for two hours at least and I can make you a sweet-smelling unguent and teach you how to apply it to give him ease.'

Raingarde is delighted. 'Truly, Dia! Oh I am so grateful. The doctors only bleed him and shake their heads and make him feel worse.'

'Excellent,' says Almodis, 'but have you consummated the marriage?' My Lady could show more tact sometimes.

'Yes, of course!' says Raingarde, 'but we cannot lie together as often as we wish.' I see grief cross my own Lady's face at that. Her problems have been of an altogether different cast here in Toulouse. 'And your husband, Almodis?'

'You have met my husband,' she retorts, 'and I think none of us wish to speak of him. We are having a nice evening together. Raingarde when my child is birthed, in a few months, Dia and I can come to visit you and Dia can speak with your husband herself. Do you have news from home, Raingarde?' asks Almodis.

'Yes, Audebert and Ponce have an heir to La Marche, named Boson,' says Raingarde. 'Mother writes to me that the baby is in excellent health and that Ponce is a fine organiser for Audebert, but she leaves little room for mother to have a useful role now. She talks of setting up her own household with our sisters, Lucia and Agnes who are seven and six, but Audebert won't hear of it. He says it is too much expense.'

'Mother has her own lands and castles. She could live independently if she wished to. She should,' Almodis says decisively.

'Well, then, perhaps it is not all Audebert's reluctance.'

'Mothers and daughters-in-law!' declares Almodis, casting up her eyes at the memory of Audearde. 'It never works. At least I have none of that here.'

'Well I do!' laughs Raingarde, 'but Lady Garsendis and I get along well enough.'

'She tells you what to do in your own household and you do it, no doubt,' replies Almodis, knowing her sister's gentle character.

'She has a lot of good advice for me,' Raingarde says dryly.

'Does she speak of her sister-in-law, Ermessende, in Barcelona?' asks Dia. Almodis develops a strong interest in the fire as Raingarde responds: 'Yes they correspond quite often.'

I notice from the corner of my eye that my Lady sits up a little straighter, shifts the weight of her belly and finds the view out of the window quite fascinating: stars and dark as far as I can see.

'What is the latest news from Barcelona?' asks Dia on her behalf.

'The young Count Ramon is married you know and already has two sons and his wife so young too,' says Raingarde, and Almodis stops pretending to be uninterested now.

'How old is she?'

'Elisabet was just thirteen when they married so she is fifteen now,' Raingarde tells her.

'Well,' Almodis laughs a false laugh, 'and we are such old women, Raingarde, at twenty-one.' Then after thinking on it a little longer. 'Of course if Ramon's wife is young, a pliable child, it means that Lady Ermessende can try to hold onto her regency for longer.'

'Countess Ermessende wrote to Lady Garsendis that the boys are named Berenger and Arnau. Ermessende is still regent since Lord Ramon is not yet of age, but he is already winning great military renown in campaigns against rebellious neighbours in Cerdanya.'

Dia strums her instrument and sings quietly, as if she is rehearsing:

> How I wish just once I could caress
> that chevalier with my bare arms,
> for he would be in ecstasy
> if I'd just let him lean his head against my breast.
>
> Handsome friend, charming and kind,
> when shall I have you in my power?
> If only I could lie beside you for an hour
> and embrace you lovingly –
> know this, that I'd give almost anything
> to have you in my husband's place,
> but only under the condition
> that you swear to do my bidding.

The nurse comes in with little Guillaume who is a fat baby, not yet a year old. Raingarde puts out her arms to hold him and jiggles him up and down on her knee, singing him a rhyme: 'Under the water, under the sea, catching tiddlers for my tea, up, down and around!' The baby giggles and I wonder if he knows that she is not his mother but I suppose he does somehow. 'How proud father would have been of you, Almodis.'

'Really,' says my Lady, 'and I wonder what he would think of my charming husband.' The bitterness in her voice and words are searing and Raingarde sits back looking scorched. Almodis paces the room in her discomfort, then sits down again next to her sister.

'Are you not happy?' whispers Raingarde.

'How could I be?' my Lady whispers back, leaning her forehead against her sister's, reaching across the obstructions of her belly and her child on Raingarde's lap. 'I can't *feel* anything, Raingarde. I miss feeling. I would rather hurt than have this blank *nothing*.'

I see differences growing now between the sisters. My Lady has an adamantine lustre mixed with the spring green of her eye, she has a polish, where before she had a bounce. I remember the hope of her just before she married Hugh.

Ten days later and there is another boy child fitted along her arm, his tiny head cupped in her hand and his toes pushing on the crook of her elbow. 'He is named Raymond,' she tells us, 'and my boys and I have a deal of work cut out for us, don't we?' She looks to Guillaume who is perched on his aunt's lap and then she stares into Raymond's questing green eyes.

'You and the baby need rest now, Almodis,' Raingarde tells her sensibly. 'You need to sleep.'

'Sleep,' snorts Almodis, 'that is a short activity carried out in hours of darkness. No, we shall start immediately, well tomorrow at least,' she laughs as Raingarde begins to protest.

'What is it you mean to do?' asks Dia, nevertheless, tucking in the bed tightly as if she fears Almodis might leap out straight away and begin strapping on her hunting clothes. I take the baby, lay him in the cradle and rock him there.

'I mean to persuade Pons to go on pilgrimage to the shrine of St James at Santiago de Compostela,' she tells us, her eyes glittering and indeed we are all impressed with that. 'He needs to atone for setting aside his poor first wife, Majora,' she tells us mischievously, 'and to give thanks that he has two fine heirs, Guillaume and Raymond.'

'And such a clever wife,' murmurs Dia.

'That's not all though,' says Almodis with triumph. 'I am going to announce a prize for the best poem in the Occitan language. I have a goldsmith in the city, Amoravis, who is fashioning a violet made all in gold as the prize, and Dia will spread the word to troubadours everywhere and they will come here to compete for my prize!'

'Wonderful!' says Raingarde, truly amazed.

Sounds like a lot of work, says I, in the privacy of my own head. Golden violets and troubadours indeed. There'll be pregnant maids and broken marriages like as not. I can't stop myself from tutting out loud but Almodis merely smiles at me, amused at my disapproval as usual.

24

Bernadette: Midsummer 1044

'If all the world were paper, and all the sea were ink . . .' Lady Almodis always begins her lessons with her children this way and they shout it with her, giving me a headache. It's a quotation from Dhuoda.

We are on an outing and the twins Hugh and Jourdain are fighting as usual. They are a deal of trouble for me to look after and keep from irritating the master. Not all twins love each other it seems. These two are not alike, as my Lady and Raingarde are. At five they are already showing a difference in size. It seems that Hugh got all the nourishment in the womb and Jourdain less. Hugh likes to bully his brother and Jourdain is of a gentle cast of mind. Of all of them, he follows his mother in her liking for dusty old books. My Lady says that he will go to the monks at Lusignan Priory when he is seven, if he wishes. She says it is clear that his brother will not share power in Lusignan when he grows up, and so that would only store up trouble for them both when they are men. She is teaching all her children to read and write. I can't see the point myself. Hugh will be Lord of Lusignan, Guillaume will be Lord of Toulouse and Raymond of Saint Gilles, so what's the reason? I told her that lords don't need to read and write where I come from. They have scribes to get their fingers inky but she told me and the children, 'An unlettered ruler is an ass. That is what Fulk Count of Anjou wrote to old King Louis of France, and it was twice a joke since the King could not even read the message'. She said I could learn with them but I haven't got time to fill my head with alphabets and numbers when I've got five little children to keep out of Pons' way and my Lady to look after.

'You are brothers knit together with my blood,' she tells Hugh, Jourdain, Guillaume and Raymond often. The sons of Hugh and the sons of Pons. 'When you are all grown up, you will swear your oaths using my name, I Hugh, son of Almodis or I, Raymond, son of Almodis and you will swear allegiance to each other, to support and help each other.' They love her stories of what will happen when they grow up.

'What about me mother?' says Melisende.

'We shall find you a beautiful and kind lord to marry,' says Almodis, 'and you will be the chatelaine of your own castle and have many sweet children.'

Today, she says is a maths lesson. 'See, here is our lesson!' Almodis declares, throwing her arm up towards a steep path that winds up a cliff face to the priory perched high above the village of Ambialet and the meandering River Tarn. The children are frothing excited around her. They spread outwards from her knees, five blond heads of varying heights, looking all the world like an extension of the gold lace train of her dress: Hugh and Jourdain, Guillaume, Raymond and Melisende with her long curls, just like her mother's. I am not looking forward to huffing and puffing up that steep path, no doubt having to carry three-year-old Raymond, some of the way, and he's already solid muscle and heavy so I will start to feel his weight walking uphill on a hot summer's day. The sun shines, dancing on the river, over to our left. How could a hot hill climb be a maths lesson, I wonder, and how can the children be so delighted at the idea of a maths lesson anyway?

'Shall I wait here for you, my Lady?' I ask hopefully, gesturing towards a wooden bench at the foot of the hill.

'No, no, Bernadette, you may learn some maths too today,' she says, making the children laugh.

'Where's the maths, Mother?' Hugh shouts and they all chime in noisily as his chorus, chanting his question, over and over. 'Where's the maths, Mother! Where's the maths, *Mother!*' they yell.

'Follow me!' she lifts the hem of her skirts in one hand, skirts

I'll be cleaning tomorrow, and sets off up the path with them running around in front, behind, skipping, shouting, and me, trying to keep up. Tiny brown lizards zigzag up the rocks away from us.

'Don't go near that one!' Almodis warns Raymond, as he makes towards a larger green lizard. 'The big ones bite and they clamp on and they don't let go of your arm or finger until you kill them or give them beer, and we haven't got any beer with us.'

'Got my knife, though,' he says, lifting the little scabbard hanging from his belt, to show her.

'Still,' she tells him, 'today is maths, lizard hunting is another day!'

'Where's the maths! Where's the maths!' they start again, and my head is aching and my face is hot and sweaty. The hill is very steep. I think if I stand still and look up towards the sky and the priory I might topple backwards, there is such a gradient. The path winds back and forth on itself. As we round a bend, a tall, silver pole rears up in front of us, set in a grassy niche. At the top is a finely wrought image of our Lord Jesus being condemned to death by the wicked Pontius Pilate.

'Number one!' yells Almodis and then starts running 'Where's number two?' and they all start running to catch up with her.

I give up, I think to myself, exhausted already. I will get to the top in my own time. Another bench is placed opposite the silver pole and I sit myself down to catch my breath. The blasphemy of it! We should be meditating on our Lord's suffering on the Via Crucis, not doing maths! I've only been sitting, puffing, for a moment when Guillaume comes scambling back down the path and starts heaving on my arm.

'Come on Bernadette. Mother says you are to keep up and you need to do maths.'

The cheek of it, but I know she'll only be embarrassing me in front of the children if I don't comply so I get to my feet and trudge up behind the boy, to join them all gathered around 'number two', the second silver pole with a rectangular silver plaque at the top embossed with an image of Our Lord being given his cross, his knees bending at the awful weight of it, and his poor head dripping with blood from his crown of thorns.

'So the Roman governor of Jerusalem, Pontius Pilate, ordered that he carry his own cross up a hill as steep as this,' Almodis finishes telling the children. 'So what do you think might happen in number three? Help Bernadette, Jourdain!' and off they all go again, with Jourdain pushing me from behind while I hold Raymond tight in both arms, alarmed now at the precipice to my left and the craggy unevenness of the path. This is no place to be carrying the baby of a count. What is she thinking? And no place to be tripping around laughing with four other children either. The sun beats hot on my shoulders and back. At number three I croak 'I need water!' and Almodis hands around the water skin that she is carrying slung over her shoulder and we all take a sip.

Number three shows the Lord Jesus falling for the first time under his terrible burden, and I feel just like him myself, no chance to catch my breath before we are off again to number four where we see Jesus' poor mother Mary, meeting him on his way to his terrible death, and weeping. I am struggling to keep up with them and can barely glance at the next stations of the cross: Simon of Cyrene carrying the cross, Veronica wiping the face of Jesus, Jesus falling the second time, Jesus meeting the daughters of Jerusalem, Jesus falling the third time, Jesus stripped of his garments and then the crucifixion: Jesus nailed to the cross. I should be doing this walk very slowly, meditating on every one. Oh I am so tired, I hardly see the last three: Jesus dying on the cross, Jesus' body removed from the cross and Jesus laid in the tomb and covered in incense.

Finally, my thighs aching terrible, the sweat trickling down my back, my arms trembling, we have passed all the silver stations of the cross and at the top there is a small cemetery and a little church where I can sit down in the cool shade. Eventually the pounding of my heart and at my temples starts to slow down. Almodis sits next to me breast-feeding Raymond (which is a scandal of course to do so in a church).

'What would you have me do, Bernadette? Boil the poor baby's head in this heat?' she responds, when I tutch at her.

You should stay at home in the cool calm of your chambers like a proper woman and mother I think instead of dragging us all up dangerous hills. Still there was no one in the church to see her, well only the statue of Madonna, with her own baby Jesus on her breast, I realise. So I relent. Perhaps she is in the right of it and Mary wouldn't mind a bit of baby-feeding in her church. Raymond climbs off her lap and rejoins his brothers and sister.

The children, having explored around the church in a small troop, are starting to get bored. 'Sit here,' for a moment,' their mother tells them and they obey. They always do obey her, and never me, when her back is turned. Five children all under six is a lot for me to handle and she should get a nursemaid for the job, but she won't. 'I want you to look out for them, Bernadette. You will be fair to all of them, including Hugh and Jourdain and Melisende, but a nursemaid here would favour my Toulouse children over my Lusignans, and I won't have that.' So here I am, lumbered with two huge jobs, looking after her (that's the biggest!) and looking after five young children.

'So how many stations of the cross did we see altogether?' she asks them. 'Fourteen!' Hugh answers quick as a snap.

'Yes,' she smiles at him. 'If there were two of every silver pole we saw instead of one, how many poles would that be?' There was a silent pause at that. Much too hard, I am beginning to think. I don't know the answer to that, how could . . .

'Twenty-eight,' says Jourdain.

'Yes! And what if there were three of every pole?' and so she goes on, with them calling out their answers. 'And what if half the poles were blown down by the wind, how many would there be?'

I cross myself at that. Surely that is blasphemy and we are sitting in the Lord's very house. Eventually they tire of their maths.

'Is this our land, Mother?" asks Guillaume, which seems to be one of his favourite questions, wherever we are.

'Yes. This is the chateau, the domain and the village of Ambialet, which belongs to me. Your father,' she says, 'gave it to me as part of his wedding gift, and I shall give it to Raymond when he is a man.' Raymond opens his eyes wide at that and points at his chest. She nods at him. 'Yes, the lands that were my wedding portion, will be yours one day and you must rule them well.'

'You could put in some more benches for tired nursemaids, for a start,' I grumble and they all laugh at me.

'Time to go home,' Almodis declares, 'but we will pass by the chateau for you to see it Raymond and we can swim in the river when we get to the bottom of the hill to cool down.' They are all jumping up and down with joy at that. Swim in the river indeed! She's taught them all how to swim, ignoring my warnings, and saying that Charlemagne and Beowulf were great swimmers. We're not fish, I say.

'Be careful, going down,' I shout at their backs disappearing around the bend. 'It's more dangerous going down . . .' but they are already long gone and she with them.

When we arrive at the riverbank there is a fête in preparation and the castellan of Ambialet invites us to stay overnight for the event. My Lady agrees and we watch entranced as young people in boats row on quiet oars up the river with lanterns and arrange themselves on the dark waters in the patterns of stars.

Later, in the castle, when the children have all gone to sleep, curled up on palettes near the fire with the castellan's own children, a troubadour comes to entertain my Lady with a story of Count Geoffrey of Anjou's recent victory over the Count of Blois at the battle of Nouy. The French King Henri had given the city of Tours to Geoffrey, the troubadour tells us, and Geoffrey had besieged the city for more than a year, trying to claim his property. The Count of Blois and his brother came with seventeen hundred armed men to aid the starving city. Geoffrey prayed to Saint Martin for his aid and a miracle occurred. The whole mass of Geoffrey's army, on horse and on foot, seemed to be clad in shining white robes and the Count of Blois' troops were unable to fight, feeling as though they were bound in chains, and the saintly Geoffrey won the battle. My Lady and I exchange glances at that. If Geoffrey was saintly he'd changed a bit for sure! More like he promised to give the saint back everything he'd stolen from him and got saintly intervention that way. I look down at my feet. It must be near bedtime and I am looking forward to taking my boots off.

She's had five babies in three years: the twins, then Melisende, then Guillaume born ten months after Melisende and Raymond born nine months after Guillaume. Some women would have had their health sapped by such childbearing, but my mistress is thriving and happy enough when Pons is not in the vicinity. When the cat's away the mice will play. 'You are my war-band, my *drut*: Dia, Bernadette and Rostagnus,' she tells us, 'my band of faithful friends,' and indeed, we are at war.

'Read this out, Dia.' She passes a long scroll that she has been working on all morning, getting her fingers inky, whilst we laboured at the proper work of ladies, stitching hems and hose.

'One: monsters, cripples and sickly children are conceived on holy nights,' reads Dia, and looks up. 'What is this, Almodis?'

'Read on.'

'Two: a husband must not seek the marriage debt the night before holy days.'

'That's Tuesdays and Thursdays,' Almodis says.

'Three: a man must abjure carnal relations with his wife forty days before Easter, before Holy Cross Day in September and during Lent,' continues Dia. 'Four: menstruating women do give men leprosy. Five: marriage is ordained by God, not for the sake of lust but rather for the sake of offspring. A man should abstain from sex with his pregnant wife.' Dia is laughing now, as she continues the list. 'He must abstain for three months before childbirth and forty days after childbirth. Six: the Church ordains that a husband must not have sex during the day.'

'Do you like them?' Almodis asks. 'They are my catechism of excuses. I am collecting them in everything I read!' Dia laughs, but it is no laughing matter. She sins if she denies her husband his marriage-debt. 'Yet,' she says, suddenly reflective, 'loathing does not hurt as bad as tenderness.'

'Have a care Almodis,' warns Dia, but I don't think it's the sin she is warning her about. Dia used to have her own small house in the city as she did in Lusignan, but after that Christmas in Saint Gilles, Lady Almodis persuaded her to move into the chateau. She has her own little room where she sleeps and composes.

When His Ugliness comes banging on my Lady's door she sends out Dia who says, 'It's her menses' or 'It is a holy day' or 'She is sick in the stomach and puking', or sometimes they let

168

him in and ply him with a drink laced with Dia's concoctions so that he falls asleep on the instant or, she tells us, 'He gropes me desperately but cannot have me. I prefer the sleep herbs Dia!'

Sometimes these excuses work and he stomps off swearing and I keep out of his way in case his lascivious eye should turn to me, but other times he'll have none of their excuses or their potions and Dia and I have to hurry out as he mounts her with no patience or gentleness, like the bull in the field, and we sit in the next room having to listen to the concussions of a man and a woman and him groaning and yelling in his horrible ardour for her.

'Perhaps all this coyness and denial makes it worse?' I suggest to her when she is sitting in her bath, but they take no notice of me. They like their system, and anyway, I suppose she must get heirs.

'There is another remedy for your problem, Almodis,' says Dia one day. We all know what problem she means. Almodis and I look up from our stitching.

'I have seen a whore on the waterfront, of good quality, who looks a little like you, named Alienor. We could employ her in the chateau and she could put herself in Pons' way, become his concubine, take his attention away from you.'

I stare at Dia with my mouth open. Her subtleties are surely sinful and no wife would do such a thing.

'Do it,' I hear my Lady say with great satisfaction.

I cross myself and look back down to my embroidery.

'Come along Bernadette,' says Dia.

'I'm not going amongst whores,' I say appalled.

'Do as you are bid,' my Lady orders me crossly.

I've a good mind to tell Piers how I've been sent down that Comminges Street, infested with prostitutes, but I know he is carrying tales to Pons so I resist the urge. I like bedding Piers but I know he would hurt her if he could and if he harms her seriously then it will harm me too, so we lie and lie with each other. I feed him stories for Pons that Almodis, Dia and I invent together. Due to practising a thing, my mother used to say, we become skilful thereof.

Pons has set up that town whore and treats her like the pampered lady she isn't. Once a month Alienor comes to see Dia and Almodis. Dia gives her silver and Alienor gives them a report on him, too fulsome sometimes for my Lady's liking. 'We don't need a blow by blow account of your bedding and the state of his prick,' she declares, impatient, although I'd been quite enjoying Alienor's story myself. 'I need to know what he has said of me, of my children, of affairs of state.' So this way we go on.

Dia has letters from Barcelona and the air always shifts when this happens with my Lady's anxiety to hear the news of Count Ramon, although she won't admit to it. Dia is frowning greatly and the news does not look good.

'Dia?' Almodis asks, unable to wait any longer. 'What is it?'

'Bad news from Barcelona, Almodis,' she looks up from the letter. 'Two of Ramon's little sons have died of a fever.'

'Oh no!' she exclaims and glances quickly to her own five children playing on the floor. 'Oh, poor, poor, Ramon. Poor boy.'

'He is a man now Almodis, not a boy,' Dia tells her.

'Yes,' she answers distracted by her own thoughts, 'but I always think of the boy I met here. It seems so long ago but it is only five years. But yes, if nothing else has done so, this grief will turn him from boy to man.'

'The boy is an astute man, Lady Almodis. My friends tell me that gold and silver are pouring into Barcelona with the new trading he has stimulated and the tribute he is exacting from the Lords of Lerida and Tortosa, the musulmen.'

Almodis nods. 'Yes I have heard that also. Does he not have a third son?'

'Yes. It is the eldest two who have died: Berenger and Arnau. His youngest child, Pere, is still a babe in arms and he has survived it.'

'That is something, but how sad for Elisabet, for Ramon. I will write to them,' she says and sets about it straight away.

'Take care of Piers, Lady. I think he is doing a job of spying on you for the count, like Alienor is doing for us.' I had seen him sneaking beneath her window again this morning and disappearing in his black leather jerkin through a hole in the hedge.

'Oh I know Bernadette,' she says. 'I know Piers well. I have given him preferment and he has given me his oath. If he seriously trespasses on that oath, I shall punish him. Don't worry.' But I do. She has me and Dia check regularly that there is nobody listening at our doors or happening to be examining his shoe buckle under our window, where I caught him another time.

'Why don't you dismiss him, Almodis?' Dia asks. 'It would be safest.'

I see her considering it but she has some soft spot for him. 'I keep him for my father's sake. He can't do us any real harm. We can use him to feed what we want to Pons.'

But Piers is smart as a snake and I do fear that he might harm her. I decide I will do a job of spying on him, like Alienor does for us, and he does for Pons. Besides he is handsome and my bed is cold and empty too often. The heart has its reasons that reason ignores. Dia can give me contraceptive herbs and I can sin along with my mistress.

25

Easter 1047

I am watching my children playing in the spring sunshine in the courtyard. Melisende is sitting on a bench next to the well twisting a spinning top and Jourdain sits next to her, drawing on a slate. Hugh, Guillaume and Raymond are noisily chasing each other. Raymond has the red cloth in his hand and is trying to catch his older brothers. Hugh is eight, Guillaume is seven and Raymond is six but there is not a great difference in their sizes. All my children have my own thick, dark blonde hair. Hugh has outstripped his twin Jourdain in growth and boisterousness. Although Raymond is younger than Guillaume he could be his twin and has begged that I let him go early to train with Hugh and Guillaume. When I said no, he and Guillaume gave me an arm wrestling display to show how strong Raymond is, with Guillaume obligingly allowing Raymond to win in order to prove the point. The bond between these three is tight. If I separate Raymond and Guillaume, Raymond may grow up to challenge his brother's authority and Raymond is not destined for the church; he is clearly going to be a warrior, not a monk. Raymond crashes into Guillaume sending him sprawling against an irritated Jourdain whose stylus flies out of his hand and the red rag passes to Guillaume.

'Come on Jourdain, join us,' shouts Hugh but Jourdain shakes his head, retrieving his stylus and settling into a different corner. Hugh deliberately crashes into an exasperated Jourdain again as Guillaume catches him.

'Jourdain,' I call, 'come and draw with me in my chamber. You will get some peace there.' I move to the stairway and, reaching the top, call down: 'Raymond I've decided that you can go to training early along with your brothers.'

He lets out a yelp of triumph and rushes into a hugging scrum with Hugh and Guillaume. Jourdain joins me at the top of the stairs and takes my hand. 'Then we will all get some peace and quiet eh?' I say to him.

'They are totally mad,' says Jourdain, watching his three brothers jumping up and down with their arms around each others' shoulders, their heads banging together.

In my chamber he gets all our spare sandals from the chest: mine, Dia's, Bernadette's and all the children's, and arranges them in a circle, with some tipped and propped up on pebbles as if they are dancing. We laugh at his arrangement together. 'Are you happy, my sweet son or do you wish that you also were going to train as a knight?'

Jourdain turns to me aghast. 'No Mother, please, I want to decorate books and manuscripts as Father Benedict has been showing me with coloured inks and gold leaf, and I want to read every book in the library of the Priory of Lusignan!'

'Alright,' I squeeze his hand, 'I just needed to be sure what you wanted.'

Accompanied by Dia and the boys, I am embarking on the journey back to Lusignan and La Marche. It is ten years since I saw Roccamolten and I am excited at the prospect. My emotions concerning Lusignan are more mixed. The time has come to lose my boys, all four of them at one stroke. I am taking Jourdain to become a novice at the Priory of Lusignan and then Hugh, Guillaume and Raymond are going to train with Geoffrey of Anjou. Pons objected to my choice of the Count of Anjou to stand as foster father to our sons at first. He wanted them to go to one of his cronies in Languedoc. Why can't they go somewhere nearby he said. I told him if they could survive in the crucible of Geoffrey's warrior court, they can survive anywhere. He will teach them *proeza*, prowess. They will return to us as formidable knights to rule Toulouse and Saint Gilles. I did not tell him that I want my sons bound to me and to each other, and not to him or one of his local lords. Of course Agnes of Mâcon will not be their foster mother. I would never subject them to what I had to tolerate in my own childhood. It was when I heard the news that Geoffrey had repudiated her last year that I determined to send them to Anjou. I thought at first of sending them to my brother Audebert in La Marche but he does not stick his nose outside his own territories. He maintains his frontiers and is content with that. My grandfather's blood, the blood of exhilaration and risk, runs in my veins and not in his.

We will travel as far as Bordeaux, by boat, on the river Garonne two or three days, and from Bordeaux we will continue to the fortress of Lusignan on horseback: another two days. After visiting Lusignan and leaving Jourdain there, the rest of us will journey on to La Marche where Geoffrey will come to collect my three trainee knights. They are all mightily pleased to be setting off on their life's journeys. Melisende, though, is standing on the pier with Bernadette looking miserable. 'Don't fret, honey. By the time I return,' I say, laying my hand on my stomach, 'there will be a new baby for you to help me with.' She nods her head and smiles feebly at that, still pouting her mouth at the boys strutting and packing. I kiss the top of her head. 'Oh Melisende, you don't know how glad I am that I will keep you with me. I will return soon and you will take care of Bernadette in the meantime.'

Servants are carrying supplies down to the boat which is large with a flat bottom as the river is shallow in parts, and it is named *Hearth Bound*. It has a big, yellow sail with the badge of Toulouse on it and at the prow of the boat is a bare-breasted woman with fish in her tangled hair, which Raymond and Hugh are giggling at together.

Eventually everything is loaded and we step onto the boat. We wave to Melisende and Bernadette until they are out of sight. As we journey up river I watch the steep sides of the valley give way to fields of crops growing close to the water and the occasional village where people stop to wave their hats as we glide past.

I wake the next morning in a nest of blankets on the deck and we are making haste towards Bordeaux. Several times along the way the sailors pull the boat into the bank and we stop to eat and talk of the boys' future. 'A squire's training concentrates on strength, fitness and skill with various weapons,' I tell the circle of their avid faces. 'Individual training is only part of it. A knight must also know how to fight as part of a team of horsemen.' I glance surreptitiously to Jourdain to see if he is showing any signs of misery at being excluded from this military coterie but he is looking happy with his nose in a book.

The river journey passes without incident and we step off the boat in Bordeaux three days after leaving Toulouse. Piers, who leads my escort, sends some of the soldiers to search for horses and provisions. We spend the night in the guest house of the abbey where Dia and I share a bed and the boys sleep on palettes on the floor.

After the first day's riding, we camp in the forest and the soldiers build a fire and teach the boys drinking songs. There are two men on watch throughout the night. I wake briefly when the soldier next to me is shaken awake to take over the guard. There is a full moon overhead so I can see the sleeping forms of my companions huddled around the fire, and the horses snorting cold breath through their nostrils at the edge of the camp. I see the two soldiers on guard exchanging words and mugs of hot ale and the two who have just finished their watch squirming and hunkering down into their cloaks to sleep as best they can on the hard ground. I hear an owl calling repeatedly and the occasional crack of twigs and branches. Little creatures scurry in the undergrowth.

Late the following afternoon we ride into the town of Saintes and find an inn. The soldiers are obliged to sleep in the stables with the horses, but they seem happy to have a night of drinking, playing dice, singing songs and no doubt kissing the serving wenches. Next morning we are up early and heading for Niort. 'After that,' we will be within spitting distance of Lusignan,' says Piers, and my heart tumbles at the name.

At Niort we are the guests of the lord and lady. They offer us food and wine in front of the fire and then warm and comfortable beds without bedbugs. Hugh is itching all over from the inn beds and has little red spots up and down his arms, round his ankles and in his hair.

'Try rubbing this liniment in,' Dia tells him, producing a small, round tin from her pocket filled with an oily, bad-smelling cream. Hugh rubs it all over his lice bites and then we all have to move some distance from him and his stench.

'If you get any more bites,' says Jourdain, 'they will join up and you will just be one gigantic smelly red lump.'

In the morning, Piers tells us to saddle up for the last leg of the journey. Three hours riding through forest and we will reach Lusignan.

The castle rears up ahead of us: that once familiar sight of pale turrets and walls surrounded by vineyards. I had thought never to see this place or its lord again. I remember that day when I was repudiated and birthed Melisende all in a moment, and that terrible parting from Hugh and going to a new husband I knew I would not like. Yet my worst imaginings did not do Pons justice. I do not want to see Hugh again. The wounds will reopen and I will find Pons all the harder to bear but I had to come for my boys' sake. We rein horse to look at the view. 'Your new home, Jourdain, the Priory, is close to the castle walls, and one day, Hugh, you will rule this land that we are riding through.' I spur my horse forward again, steeling myself for this meeting. At least Audearde is gone now, cold in her grave that she rehearsed for all her life.

The gates creak open and we ride through. There is bustle in the courtyard, maids craning their heads from windows or setting down pails to stop and stare at us. This courtyard is so familiar to me and its memories rush at me. It was here that I greeted Geoffrey and Agnes when they came to claim our fealty, here that my brother and Hugh had to carry me in labour, after my repudiation. And here he is, his hair a little streaked with grey but it suits him, still Hugh the Fair. He looks pleased to see me and overjoyed to see his sons. He greets Dia warmly and is friendly to Guillaume and Raymond too. What a good father he would have made. Why could he not have been a good husband? I had imagined, distant from him, that perhaps my earlier feelings were just the romantic moonings of an adolescent girl, but I have to take this idea back, now that I confront him as a woman, seven years on, and my eyes still hanker to linger on him. I reflect that perhaps I was lucky after all that our marriage had difficulties, for I know that Audebert would have pressured me to take Pons even if I had been happily married to Hugh. How much harder it would have been to be forced to leave him if my love had been returned and I were a happy wife.

Our son Hugh will inherit Lusignan and he needs to know the twists and turns of alliances and enmities hereabouts, to live and breathe them. The southern air of Toulouse politics would be of little use to him. Hugh is a handful. He has my temper, not his father's, my determination, my pride. He will make a fine ruler. His nickname is already Hugh the Devilish, not Hugh the Pious like his father or Hugh the Brown or even Hugh the Loving, like his ancestors! Ah well, if he is devilish it is from me and it will serve him and he will serve Lusignan with his temperament. He will do things, I think, looking admiringly at him as he struts around the new household like a king.

Times are changing with regard to the succession in families. In times gone by a division of rights and properties was made between all children, including daughters, and it was only the title that was handed down to the first-born son if there was one, and if not to the first-born daughter. Now, more and more, because of the weakening of holdings that these divisions have caused, everything is focussed on the first-born son and second sons, like Jourdain, usually go to the church or at least do not wed in order to keep all the family's rights concentrated on the one strong lord.

My former husband asks after Melisende and I describe her beauty and gentle character to him. 'We might look about us for a lord in this neighbourhood for her betrothal,' I say, and he begins to think about that. I glimpse for a moment a vision of he and I growing old together, just here in Lusignan, taking care of our children and our grandchildren.

When the children have gone to bed he pours us one more glass of wine, takes my hand and kisses it, and I feel the rapid burn of desire that I thought never to feel again. 'In time to come no one will remember my time as Lord of Lusignan,' he says, 'except in that I married you and you have given me such fine children.' I look into his black eyes. If he asked me to bed now I would go with him, but, of course, he does not.

The following morning we prepare to take Jourdain to the priory. With my four sons assembled, I give Jourdain a beautiful psalter. The room feels crowded and cosy as the boys bend their blond heads close together to look at the book with its red-leather cover and the gold on the edges of every page. The pages are thick vellum made from calf's skin and there are exquisite illustrations in gold, blue and red.

'Dia, tell us again about Melusine,' clamours young Hugh, when a book and sitting still become too boring.

'Melusine became the fairy Queen of the forest of Colombiers in the French region of Poitou.'

'Here!' says Hugh.

'That's right. She married Lord Raymond, with one condition: that he would never see her on a Saturday. She built the fortress of Lusignan in a single night. She and Lord Raymond had ten children, but each child was flawed. Urion had ears like the handles of a vase and one red eye and one blue one.' The boys giggle. 'The second child, Odon, had one ear bigger than the other. Guion had one eye higher than the other; Anthony had a lion's foot on his cheek.' We all gasp. 'Regnald,' Dia continues, 'had one eye,' and she screws one eye shut and glowers at us comically out of her other. 'Geoffrey had a tooth that protruded out more than an inch.' The boys are snickering at Raymond who is sticking one of his front teeth out at them over his lip.

'Froimond had a mole or tuft of hair on his nose.'

'Not so bad?' I shrug at them.

'But,' returns Dia slowly, to increase our suspense, 'the next child was named Horrible and he had three eyes, one on his forehead; and then there were two more sons Raymond and Theodoryk.'

'Many ugly sons!' I call out. 'In spite of the deformities,' I pick up the story, 'the children were strong, talented and loved throughout the land. One day, Lord Raymond's brother visited him and made Raymond very suspicious about the Saturday activities of his wife. So the next Saturday, Lord Raymond sought his wife, finding her in her bath where he spied on her through a crack in the door. He was horrified to see that she had the body and tail of a serpent from her waist down.'

They are gasping at that and Hugh falls to the floor flapping his legs together like a mermaid. When they have recovered themselves, I go on.

'Lord Raymond accused Melusine of contaminating his line with her serpent nature, thus revealing that he had broken his promise to her. As a result, Melusine turned into a great serpent, circled the castle three times, wailing piteously, and then flew away. She would return at night to visit her children, then vanish. Lord Raymond was never happy again. Melusine appeared at the castle, as a dragon wailing, whenever a Count of Lusignan was about to die or a new one to be born. It was said that the noble line which originated with Melusine will reign until the end of the world. Her children will include the King of Cyprus, the King of Armenia, the King of Bohemia, the Duke of Luxembourg, and the Lord of Lusignan.'

'Have you seen her,' Raymond asks his eyes looking like two round pennies.

'No, but I've heard her. When Melisende was born, I heard her in the moat, swimming around like a giant fish and wailing. She wails because she is exiled from her family forever by her husband's failure to keep his promise. She mourns that she can no longer take human form and play with her children and grandchildren.'

'Let's see!' shouts Hugh, and leads them in a rush out to the black waters of the moat where they try to imagine wailing and the sound of something big swimming in the water.

'Imagine,' says Dia, 'you would hear the wailing getting louder and louder as she rounded the walls and then there she would be, right in front of your eyes. Her head above the water is that of the most beautiful lady but behind her you can see the thrashing of two great, green scaly tails. Tears are falling in little waves down her face and her mouth is open in a wail and the moon glints on her sharp teeth.'

The children hold their breath in horror.

'One of her tails,' I say, 'flicks up in the air behind her, and her naked breast and head rear up out of the water close to Hugh's petrified face.'

'I'm not petrified a bit!' he objects.

I smile and continue, 'Her hair is long, blonde and tangled. She wears a golden crown studded with green jewels. She holds out her arm and hand to Hugh. It is a deathly pale white. It looks like the arm of a dead person.'

Raymond holds his own very pink and muddy hand and arm out for kissing to Hugh who spurns it.

'The serpent-woman smiles at Hugh,' I say, 'and the smile on her small red mouth is frightening too. Hugh takes a stumbling step backwards as Melusine slithers out of the moat and on to the bank. As she touches the land she briefly shimmers into the form of a normal and very beautiful woman, but this lasts only seconds before she returns to the fearsome serpent shape again. Hugh looks into Melusine's beautiful face and large green eyes. He feels he might drown in those eyes. He tries not to look at her monstrous tails dripping and slimy on the grass. There are worse things in the water than jelly fish, he thinks!'

'You should have written the book, Lady Almodis,' says Dia. 'It seems as if you have really met this lady.'

With my husband, my former husband that is, I take Jourdain to the Priory to be entered as an oblate. Hugh reassures me that he will visit our son often. The chamberlain removes Jourdain's child's clothes and dresses him in a linen shirt and a novice habit so that he looks like a comically tiny adult monk. He is presented to the prior and the formula of oblation is read to us and signed by us both. The wafer and chalice of the Mass are put into Jourdain's hands and then all are wrapped around with the altar cloth so that he and the offering might be received into the church together. The prior blesses his cowl and puts it on his head.

The boys in the oblate's school sing in the choir but they do not keep the fasts or the night-time services of the adult monks. When he is fifteen Jourdain will decide whether to become a monk or whether to withhold his consent and re-enter the secular world. He seems to be taking the whole thing very cheerfully. I kiss him goodbye on his forehead. How bitter are these partings but I must not let them see me weep. I may never see him again. I try not to think of that and to hope that I will. The boys will write to me often, at least I know that Jourdain will.

Outside the priory my boys are waiting for me and I wish goodbye to my former husband.

'I will take good care of Jourdain,' he tells me again. 'Good luck in Angers, boys, and write if you need anything.' He brings his horse close to me and drops his voice, taking my hand. 'I am glad to have seen you Almodis. I think of you every day and every night, you know.' There is a lump in my throat and I can't answer him for too long a time, but eventually I say, 'I think of you often with affection also my Lord'. Dia, the boys and I turn our horses towards Roccamolten and I do not look back to where my love sits his horse and my little boy wears his cowl.

In Roccamolten my brother's wife, Ponce, is to my liking. She manages my brother well since he is not as bright as he should be. The La Marche kin: how grand we all are these days: my brother, the Count of La Marche; I, the Countess of Toulouse; and my sister, the Countess of Carcassonne.

'And two more sisters to wed to Occitan counts,' says my mother, looking at my younger sisters, Lucia who is thirteen and Agnes who is twelve. Lucia has the same colouring as myself and Raingarde and some similarity of features. You can see that we are related. She is a little shorter in height, has a different mouth and her eyes are brown whilst ours are green. Lucia might make a good marriage, but Agnes is plain and very shy. She busies herself with her baby nieces and nephews and the puppies playing under the table. She seems perhaps fit for the cloister so I am surprised when my mother says, 'Agnes has taken a foolish fancy to a clod-hopper in Charroux.'

'He is not a clodhopper,' Agnes says through gritted teeth. 'He is the son of a respectable land-holder.' She looks at me with appeal but I cannot help her against all these, though I feel for her. Audebert will no doubt marry her to someone she does not like in a year or two.

Preparing for our homecoming feast, Guillaume and Raymond amuse my mother and brother, vying with each other for the hardest task. 'I will set the fire,' says Raymond.

'No I will set the fire. I am the eldest and the heir.'

'I will move the trestles then.'

Once we are all seated and eating, my mother remarks, 'So your former husband is still unmarried.' I do not answer. Since they are neighbours, it is not a question. 'Odd,' she goes on. 'He is still a young man.' Since this elicits no response from me she opens another topic: 'Agnes' daughter has wed the Emperor of Germany. Imagine how pleased she is with that! She intends to move to her daughter's imperial court you know, now that her son is of age and she must cede the Regency of Aquitaine to him.'

'Well it has taken him an extra few years to prise her fingers from the throne of Aquitaine,' I say.

'Umm,' my mother seems distracted. 'I was thinking of doing the same myself,' she says looking directly at me.

'You are thinking of moving to the Imperial German court?' I say with mock innocence and Audebert guffaws, spitting meat onto the clean white linen. When he stops choking I turn back to my mother who is looking seriously affronted.

'Well I'm so glad I amuse you both,' she says, but she is looking at me.

I cannot have my mother at my court in Toulouse. I need to be nimble in my arrangements to cope with Pons and continue my plans. I am past a mother. I had to get past a mother when I left home a five-year old hostage, but I feel I have been unnecessarily cruel. 'Have you considered visiting with Raingarde in Carcassonne?' I ask, trying to mollify her. 'You should see if the South suits you before making any decisions. Now that Raingarde is with child, she would be glad to have your help. You could bring Lucia and Agnes with you.' My mother nods but is still looking at me with hostility.

'Lucia, perhaps,' says Ponce, 'but I need Agnes here to help with my babies.' 'Yes,' mother says, recovering her poise, 'I will write to Raingarde and see if a visit from myself and Lucia would suit her.'

'What do you make of this scandal of three popes, Almodis?' asks my brother, bored now with where women will be and who will look after whose babies.

I can see that my mother is smarting at my rejection. For the next few days I am as kind as I can find the patience to be, but I see that she will not forgive me for refusing her and I do not care to explain why.

My child is due and I am waiting here to gain one child to replace the four I am losing. The baby is late and I wander around Roc-camolten, trying to hatch my egg, having flashes of early child-hood memories here, running laughing through long grass higher than my head in sunshine with bees and insects humming around me.

After the birth of my new son I am maudlin.

'Please, Almodis, speak to me!' says my mother. 'Nobody knows what to do with you.'

No, nobody knows. My own mother does not know for I am a stranger in the house of my family for a second time. They know nothing of me in truth. Only Raingarde is my real family. I have wept continuously for three days. I began when my mother placed my baby in my arms and I cannot stop. I am like a rusty spigot that has been turned on and cannot be turned off.

'Now Almodis,' says Dia, doing her best to cheer me up, 'you'll wash away that baby. He'll have to learn to swim early!'

I laugh but also continue to cry. I have named him Hugh much to their consternation.

'You know that you cannot name him Hugh, Almodis,' says my brother. 'He is your husband Pons' son and Hugh is not a name in his family.'

I don't respond and only continue to weep gently and play with my baby's fingers.

'Pons will take it as an affront, my dear sister,' Audebert goes on, exasperated. 'You know it!' When his irritation has no effect they try other means.

'You can't call him Hugh, Mother,' my eldest son tells me, touching his brother's tiny foot, measuring its smallness with his man-boy hands. 'We'll have three Hughs in the family then: me, father, and my brother, all called Hugh. We'll get confused won't we, when you yell Hugh you rascal! Out of the door.'

I am laughing with him but I also continue to cry. I ignore their admonitions and in the night I have Dia fetch Father Jerome to give my son a benediction and name him Hugh.

'Well,' says Audebert, the next morning when he hears of it. 'We will have to think of a nickname then.'

'You could call him Hugh the Bishop,' says Raymond, 'since he is the third son,' aiming to make it clear to me and his brother that he has no intention himself of going into the church.

I am losing my son, Hugh, and I lost his father, Hugh, I think in a burst of self-pity, so what does it matter if I name this baby Hugh.

'What is a wife's duty Mother?' asks Lucia some days later when we are all seated in my mother's chamber.

'A wife's duty is to run a household and get sons.' My mother continues short-tempered.

'How does a wife get sons?' persists Lucia.

'She lies on her back with her legs open,' snaps my mother.

Lucia starts to cry and I look at my mother, shocked. Did she suffer as I do? I had never thought of this before since she and my father seemed happy. I soothe Lucia. 'There now,' I say, but I can't lie to her and mitigate my mother's harsh words. Instead, I say, 'The scholar who divided humankind into three states: those who pray; those who fight; and those who work; he forgot the fourth state: those who breed.' My mother nods at my words.

I have a letter from Jourdain at Lusignan Priory already. He writes that he has a great friend in one of the other boys and the masters are kind to them. His father is visiting him every Saturday to see how he does and he writes me the story of his week. His writing is full of blotches and strange spellings yet he tells me he intends to work in the scriptorium, drawing angels, flowers, and ugly demons (he adds with relish), around the letters of the manuscripts.

At noon today Geoffrey arrives, with ten of his men and is greeted warmly by Audebert and Ponce and by all of us. He has been engaged in a constant to and fro of war between Anjou, Normandy and the Capetian king for many years. He looks me over brazenly as usual, so that I am glad that I wore the finest dress and jewels that I could find. 'Just birthed of a fifth son I hear, Lady Almodis,' are the first words from his mouth. 'You look very well Countess.' He bows low to me.

Hugh, Guillaume and Raymond troop in, wearing their best clothes, to meet their new foster father. Faced with his forbidding presence, they lose a little of their bounce and mischief, yet I am confident that he will be hard but kind to them. I remember his childhood kindnesses to me. There is some heart underneath his armour I believe, I hope. I introduce them and he asks them about themselves: what training they have already had, what weapons they know how to handle. Raymond trots out a long list that surprises even me. He is really too young yet, at six, to go to train, but he is precocious and eager and it is best to keep them, all three together, in Geoffrey's household, looking out for each other.

'Well,' says Geoffrey, when they have finished accounting for themselves, 'it seems my army is much reinforced!'

He does not plan to stay for long but to take them tomorrow morning and I will depart then too, back to Toulouse. The thought of returning to Pons makes my heart sink, but I console myself with my new baby and the thought of Melisende and Bernadette.

It is very late. Dia and the children have been abed for a long time and the castle is still and silent. I am sitting up feeding my baby and am surprised to hear the door creak and see Geoffrey enter.

'I want you to come away with me, Almodis,' he says, without prelude.

'What do you mean?'

'You know what I mean. I want you to be my wife.'

I control my shaking and carefully lay my child back in his cradle so that I might stand and face Geoffrey. I pull my thin nightshift across my breast. He is the kind of man who takes what he wants if it is not freely given and we are alone.

'I am wed. I am the faithful wife of the Count of Toulouse.'

'The miserable wife, Almodis. I've met your ancient husband and I know you.'

'You know nothing.'

'Let me try another tack. I am in need of an heir and a wife. I have long desired you. You know it. I would give you everything you could wish for and free you from that tedious excuse of a man. He does not share your literary passions. I can do that. You rule and he drinks. I will appreciate and nurture your capabilities and I flatter myself that you would find me a more welcome sight in your bed. Much more welcome,' he says, taking a step towards me.

My eyes linger on his mouth, his hand held out to me, the strength of the muscles in his neck.

'It's impossible,' I say, rather weakly.

Sensing his advantage he closes for the kill, taking my arm and pulling me to him, kissing me hard, breathing my name. I stumble back from him. 'I must think on it,' I say holding him at bay with a gesture.

'Yes do,' he says warmly, believing that he has already tamed me.

I run from the room and gain the battlements. My daughter is in Toulouse. I have worked long and hard for the city and the county. If I abandon Pons as I would dearly wish to do he may disinherit my sons and take his nephew as his heir to spite me. And Geoffrey, what an uncertain man is he to take to my bed? He is addicted to battle. Agnes could not keep him with her, and what if I should not give him the heir he needs so badly? Is he infertile? I have managed Pons but I would never manage Geoffrey. He would seek to control me. I have seen how he is with his sisters. If they comply with his wishes, as Adele does, he is all goodness, but if they do not, as Hermengarde does not, he is punitive and harsh. Last year he accused Hermengarde of defiling herself with an illicit liaison and took her youngest son away from her to raise him in his own court. Could he be as cruel as his father?

As a woman who had abandoned her husband, I would be a scandal, excommunicated. We would struggle to have a marriage between us and any offspring recognised. Would my brother war with Geoffrey? Would Pons? No, nobody but the Duke of Normandy willingly wars with Geoffrey.

Though I have only distaste and contempt for my husband, I love my city and my county. My life is of the South – in the lands bounded by the Loire, the Garonne, the Pyrenees and the Rhone.

I love the people and the poets of Occitania, the Corbières hills, the monuments and memories of Romans and Visigoths, the visiting Barcelonese and Aragonese, the sun, the Genovese captains in the harbours. I love its deep valleys, its rivers winding round granite cliffs and castles, the cormorants on the river, the rolling gait of the broad, short peasants with their dark visages and hook noses. I do not wish to go to the North with its excessive pieties, its cold, its masculine military culture.

I run down to my chamber and shake Dia awake. 'Pack up and bring the baby.'

She is sleepy and confused. 'Now?'

'Do it quietly and speak to no one but Piers.'

I write a note to Geoffrey. *I cannot do as you ask my Lord though I am greatly honoured that you ask it. My conscience and my religion forbid such an action. I will love you always as my brother. I beg that you will love my sons as your own.* My pen hovers. Would he be cruel to them in anger at me? I will tell Hugh to write to me immediately if Geoffrey is unkind and I will remove them to Audebert's care if that should happen. I continue my letter: *I beg you teach them the arts of war and of chivalry of which you are the greatest example in all Christendom.*

Mayhap you will ask me again, I write suddenly at the end. What impelled me to do that? I open my mouth and things fall out of it. I must let this sentence stand or start the letter over again. Geoffrey is not a man to toy with. I think of his mouth on mine, of his thigh against mine, and leave it be.

The boys are sleeping soundly, their three blond heads showing above the fur covers. I kiss their soft cheeks, one, two, three, and hope they will not be too bewildered to find me gone in the morning without goodbyes.

'Let's go,' I tell Dia.

Piers is waiting with the horses at the gate. Another departure with a newborn huddled in my cloak. As we clear the gate I look back to where my boys are sleeping and see that Geoffrey stands on the battlements watching me go. I throw back my hood so that the moonlight catches my hair and I raise my arm to him and he to me. I cannot see his face clearly, just the glint of his shoulder brooch and his sword.

26

Easter 1050

'It would be good for the House of Toulouse, husband, if our standing in Rome with this new pope were stronger.'

'Want to go gallivanting on a pilgrimage, eh, pretty?'

'No, my Lord. I was thinking that you would be the one to carry out such a delicate diplomatic mission, to travel to the tomb of Saint James at Santiago de Compostela, forging alliances with abbots and bishops along the route, and ensuring that the pope is a friend to Toulouse. That is not a job for a woman. I need to look after babies.'

'Hmm', Pons says, looking up at the ceiling, imagining himself, no doubt, lolling in a carriage all the way with two half-naked prostitutes, and I see that I have won my way.

Pons went by boat up the Tarn last week to the Abbey of Saint Peter at Moissac to begin his pilgrimage. He knows the abbot there, Durand de Bredon, and will begin his devotions for his journey. I expect that he will spend most of that journey on horseback, but he wants me to believe that he will go barefoot as a walking pilgrim. So I calculated how long it would take him to walk from Moissac and back: four months, I've told him. So now he will have to take that long or be shamefaced. I have sent one of my men, Gregor, along to give me news of my Lord's progress, so that I can be sure he does not return to take me unawares.

It is the first day of the Troubadour Court as I am calling this year's

Easter Assembly. Pons knew my plan but he thought that just a few bedraggled *jongleurs* would turn up 'to take advantage of your hospitality and win your little prize', but he is wrong. Here is a great throng of people in the bailey of the Chateau Narbonnais. Jongleurs, troubadours and *trobairitz* from all over Occitania, Italy, Catalonia, Andalucia and even a few from other Muslim kingdoms. Dia is making a list of all the entrants for the prize and she keeps rushing in to tell me excitedly that so and so is here from such and such and he is very famous or she is widely renowned or he is very handsome! My prize, my court, is a great success already. The nobility of Toulouse are here too, arriving in clumps with their servants and entourages, elbowing for precedence. Raingarde and her husband Pierre arrived last night, with my mother and sister Lucia who is growing fast, sixteen now. My mother is determined that Lucia will make a splendid marriage, and won't listen to reason that the third daughter of a countess is not such a catch, though Lucia is handsome and intelligent so we will see what can be done for her. Raingarde brings with her the very sad news that Countess Elisabet of Barcelona – Ramon's wife, has died in childbed in Barcelona, leaving him with just his eight-year-old son Pere.

I have invited Fides, Countess of Rouergue; Rangarda, Viscountess of Albi and Nîmes; Garsenda, Viscountess of Narbonne; and my sister to act as judges with me: a high court of women! Their husbands are all here with them and many others of the local nobility besides. I see Roger, Count of Foix and his brother Bernard, Count of Bigorre in the courtyard below and Richard, Viscount of Millau arrived last night too with the Bishop of Uzès. Almost everyone is here. Arnaud, Count of Comminges, sent me a charming letter in rhyming couplets, which he no doubt did not devise himself, sending apologies that he is laid up with gout and cannot attend. Everyone knows that he has a great distaste for poetry and music and prefers drinking songs but I have sent him an elegant reply, pretending that I know how distraught he is to miss the court.

And the town is here. I have made a great point of inviting the *capitouls* and the leading merchants, as well as Armand and Adémar, the viscounts of the city. At least they can all go home at night, because we are bursting at the seams. Gilbert, has everything running smoothly. He has proved to be an excellent and energetic young chamberlain. The servants have an air of team morale about them as if they are all rising to the challenge of this great event and wanting to show what they are capable of. In most households there would be moaning and complaining but my staff look as if they are enjoying themselves. Well, all except Bernadette, of course, who has gone into her most sincere and loudest level of whingeing.

'But how am I to do that my Lady, at the same time as looking after three children?' she keeps saying to me.

'Just get on with it, Bernadette, like everybody else,' I tell her. 'Involve the children in the tasks. Use it as an opportunity to teach them something.'

'What?' she says and I turn from her exasperated, to look over Dia's list of troubadours. I know that Bernadette will do the jobs I have given her and well, but she has to complain too. I watch with pleasure as my children troop out after her telling her which bits they can help with. Hugh the Bishop is three now. Melisende is ten, and holds hands with my new daughter, Adalmoda, who has just started to walk. Bernadette does not have the patience to go at a baby's pace, but Melisende does. She helps Adalmoda balance her slow and precarious way. Melisende is a good girl and has some features of my former husband, her black eyes contrasting with her golden hair. I am reminded with sadness of him every time I look at her. I have no doubt that Bernadette will sit in a corner complaining with Adalmoda and Hugh the Bishop on her lap and Melisende will do all her work.

I sit with the other lady judges on the high table with the golden violet laid on a purple cushion in front of us. Amoravis has done an excellent job and it is a beautiful object. Fides has added 200 *solidi* to the prize making it even more desirable. Dia introduces the 'proceedings' telling us that there are thirty competitors and there will be three days of poetry and on the fourth day we will give our decision. Rangarda, Garsenda and my sister have also contributed money prizes so that we can award second, third and fourth prizes too and I have decided to give each entrant some small gift to take away. We will have to place a limit on the number of entrants next year or we will be sitting here from

Easter to Lammas listening to poems. Gilbert told me that some of the merchants have been grumbling that if I am spending so many days with entertainers how will I do my duty in my husband's absence and ensure the 'serious' business of the assembly is conducted. I gathered the *capitouls* and merchants of the city together this morning before the poets began, and gave them a schedule of hearings for the disputes and other matters of justice that are coming before me.

At the end of the morning's recitations, the final troubadour to come before us gives his name as Rodriguez of Girona. He has a thick black beard, a hooked nose and a dirty cowl covering his head, with a pilgrim's broad-brimmed hat jammed on top of that. His belly is huge, perched above his legs, which seem to be the only shapely part of him. It is not a promising beginning and I hope that his contribution will be a couplet rather than an epic. He gives us a sonnet describing me as the Queen of Occitania. It is a short and surprisingly sweet poem for one so ugly, but not the best entry to be sure. It seems some flattery to name me but I feel a suspicion that he is laughing at me somehow.

'Next,' snaps Countess Fides, rapping her ring against her glass. She is unimpressed, or perhaps she is jealous that he has not called her Queen of Occitania.

'Thank you Don Rodriguez, how beautiful,' I say and he bows low and is replaced by the next competitor.

I weary of poetry. I did not think that I would ever say that! Yesterday's batch was indifferent. Many poems but no great ones. Imitations and conventional compositions. I watch my falcon circle high in the early morning mist. The blue of the sky is working to force its way through but has not won its battle yet. The sun is bright but has no heat so early. The trees are beginning to bud and green. I have ridden a long way out, needing to escape from so many people, so many demands. My stomach rumbles and I head towards the lodge to break my fast. I am come alone and carry some bread and ale with me. I need solitude and so am perplexed to find the fat troubadour Rodriguez of Girona standing near the door of the lodge. Drat! He bows low flourishing his ridiculous pilgrim's hat.

'I cannot give you audience now, here, Rodriguez,' I say, before he can begin with some tiresome request. 'Leave me and I will speak with you later today in the hall.'

'I would wish to comply with your every order my dear Lady,' he says, 'but I cannot.'

I stare at him. What does he mean? He must comply with my order. He does not drop his gaze. He stares back at me. Does he mean me harm? Surreptitiously I feel for the hunting knife at my waist.

'You won't need that Almodis. You need have no fear of me, though I look most fearful.' There is something about his voice. He is pulling off his hat and cowl and I step back and grip my knife now, assessing the position of my horse. What can he mean by this behaviour?

'You will address me as Countess,' I say in my coldest voice, 'and you will leave me immediately, now. I want you gone from Toulouse altogether before I get back to the castle.'

'Oh but I can't do that,' he persists. 'What if I should be the winner of the violet?'

I am frowning and begin to be afraid. His behaviour is impertinent in the extreme and he is shedding his clothes in an alarming fashion. I turn to run to the horse and he grabs me by the arm. He means rape.

'Almodis, Almodis. No, it's me. You know me.'

I turn, sick in my stomach, to see if I can find a way to be free. I don't know him. Is he mad? He holds my arm so that I cannot free my knife. How have I allowed this to happen?

'Please, don't be afraid. I'm so sorry to scare you. I could not come as myself and have any chance to speak with you.'

I turn in wonder and see that his black beard is hanging loose from one side of his face. A false beard. Stripped of his cowl, his hair is golden. His hand on my arm is young and shapely. The clothes he has shed are his . . . his belly.

'Ramon?'

'Yes. I thought you would know me yesterday!'

He is laughing and I remember his laugh and his blue eyes, the boy in the mews when I was still a girl. I am so relieved and amazed I cannot speak. He relaxes his grip but still holds my arm.

'I'm sorry. I have really frightened you. Come into the lodge and sit down. We will break fast together and I can try to explain myself to you. Countess,' he adds in mock politeness and I manage a feeble smile at that. My mind is blank. He has brought some fruit and wine but I cannot eat. A bee bumbles through the lodge, buzzing slowly. All the time I am taking quick glances at him and he is stripping himself of more and more of his ridiculous disguise. The hook nose, strips of cloth that padded his arms and stomach, the beard. At last there he is. Himself. With vestiges of glue hanging on his chin and cheek.

'I don't understand you,' I say, finally finding that I am angry with him. 'Why must you come like this? Like an idiotic pantomime. You would be an honoured guest at my court as yourself.'

'Yes, but where would be the fun in that?' I frown and he sees that he must say more. 'I am truly sorry that I scared you. I couldn't think of another way to encounter you alone.'

I shift along the bench, away from him. 'And why should you wish to do that? Why this subterfuge and deceit?'

'I wished to speak with you intimately, Almodis,' he says shifting back towards me and taking my hand.

I feel the cool warmth of his palm and admire the light golden skin of his hand on mine but then snatch my hand away. 'And why can you not speak to me in my chambers or in the hall? This is ridiculous Ramon.' His blue eyes smiling at me chime so strongly with my memories. A little mollified I add, 'I am pleased to see you of course, after all this time.'

'Eleven years,' he says. 'And four days.'

I swallow at that and look at him again. He has changed, for now he is a man but still a young and beautiful one. I reach up and pull a piece of glue hanging from his cheek.

'Ouch!'

'You deserve a great deal of pain,' I tell him, smiling reluctantly. 'And by the way you won't win the golden violet. Your poem was terrible.'

'No, don't say that! It wasn't bad. Dia wrote it for me!'

'What, Dia! She knew it was you and didn't tell me!'

'Don't be unkind to her. It's not her fault. The fault is all mine.'

'Well, you have amused yourself with this game, Count Ramon,' I say rising, 'and now I must return to my serious business of running my assembly.'

He rises with me and takes my hand again. 'Almodis, let me speak first. I did not do this merely for a jape, though I admit it has been quite amusing.' He pauses and grins lopsidedly at me, raising his eyebrows, but I do not bend.

'Hmmph!' I say.

'I am come to speak with you seriously Almodis. You know that my wife has died?'

'Yes,' I say, 'I am so sorry for it Ramon. You have suffered a great deal with your family.'

'Thank you, and yes. Fortune favours me in the field and in politics. Barcelona flourishes and you will love the city when you see her but I have not been so lucky in my family life.'

'No doubt I will admire Barcelona,' I say. 'Perhaps I will come next year to your Easter Assembly.'

'No,' he says. 'Come now. Come with me. I want you as my wife Almodis. I wanted you eleven years and four days ago, but my grandmother would hear nothing of it and took me away before I could speak with you. Elisabet was a good wife to me but I don't want just a dutiful wife, Almodis. I want you. I love you. I always have.'

I pull my hand out of his with force. 'What can you mean, Ramon? This is more nonsense.'

'No.' He sinks to his knees and crushes me and my skirts against him. 'Please, Almodis, consider me and say yes. I know that you are not happy with Pons. I know how capable you are, but above all, I love you and I will make you happy, as you deserve. I will give you everything. You are more shining than snow. You are radiant Almodis, as radiant as the girl I met so long ago in the mews in her nightclothes and her hair loosed down her back.'

'That was long ago,' I try to pull away from him, but he holds fast. 'I was a girl then and you were a boy. Now I am a woman and seven times a mother.'

'You are the same to me. You are that girl,' he says, a stubbornness creeping into his voice and the set of his mouth, a boyish stubbornness.

I pull violently away from him and stumble back against the bench behind me, sitting down hard. 'Ramon, you know that I am married and I am not free for you to speak to me in this way.' I grip my knife again. Perhaps he does mean violence still? To abduct me? To take me by force?

'Please, darling, be convinced that you do not need your knife,' he is laughing, on his knees, holding out his palms to me. He rises to his feet again, conscious that he is making a spectacle of himself, but he holds me fast by the arms. 'I am no threat to you. Forgive my passion. Forgive that I have made you afraid.' He shifts now to sit on the floor at my feet and speaks gently, coaxingly to me, as I heard him speak to his falcon in the mews so long ago.

'I have a ship at Narbonne. Come away with me now. Dia will send what you need on to Barcelona. Pons will bluster but he will do nothing. He will not take arms against me. I will make you Countess of Barcelona and you will make me the happiest man in the world.'

'And my children?' I say.

'Dia can bring them to the ship tonight if I send word to her now.'

I look to the window. The sun has broken through in full power and I blink in the light. The sky is solid blue. My falcon soars there. I feel that my heart might break in two.

'No. No. I cannot do this.'

'You do not love me? Like me, at least?'

I do not answer.

'Almodis?'

'I am Countess of Toulouse. I am wife to Pons. I have work and a life here. I have responsibilities and duties and I carry the honour of my family's name and I will not betray that. Thank you for your offer.' I stand and move swiftly to the door and he is scrambling up behind me.

'Please, Almodis. Wait then. Make no decision now. I can wait.'

'In your ridiculous beard? No you must leave.' He is moving towards me so I stop and look steadily at him and he halts. 'You must leave now,' I say, and I lift my skirts, turn and am running to my horse. I want to say more. I want to say how my heart sings at the escape he offers me, at his valuing of me, but I cannot trust my voice, my resolve, so I cannot speak all this to him. He runs out after me but I am in the saddle, my falcon flies to my arm and I spur my horse.

'Goodbye Ramon. I wish you well,' I call out but I cannot look back at him. I learnt in Lusignan that love is merely a poet's word, a flimsy story, and that a woman's life instead is breeding and managing, so I do not know why tears are streaming down my face. I see nothing, but my horse knows the way back. When I am far enough away from Ramon I sob aloud. Eventually, the gates of the city are ahead and I wipe my face dry. Inside the chateau I run to my rooms, furious with Dia for her deceit all these years and I tell her to pack her bags and depart by dawn tomorrow.

She is white-faced and desolate with her apologies. 'Almodis, he loves you so! I had to help him and I thought perhaps you . . .'

'That's enough,' I say. 'You have betrayed me and after all, you belong to him. You are his creature.' I slam the door of my chamber, bar it and run to my bed where I lie for two days speaking to no one, allowing no one to enter. In my dreams I see Ramon, beautiful, golden, laughing and I am laughing with him and kissing him. When I wake now and then I listen to the sounds of the Toulouse Court outside my door. Dia has tried calling to me. Bernadette has called through the door and then I can hear her standing there telling all comers that I am taken ill and they must judge the competition without me and the Good Men must hear the justice cases without me. They must come back tomorrow. The countess cannot see you today, she says. I lay with my face wet, my hair and bedsheets tangled, falling in and out of sleep and dreams. But the following day I must rise and repair myself, present myself, the countess, the mother. My distress over Ramon is replaced by my sadness at parting from my sister and I begin to recover myself. I try not to think of Ramon, of his face, of his grasp on my legs, of his offer.

'So Bernadette, is Dia gone?' I am not my brisk self but I feign it. I feel weak and feeble.

'No, Lady. She begs to speak with you one last time. And you must eat Lady. I insist.'

I sigh. Yes, then, I will keep Dia with me for she is all I have now of him and I would miss her very much if she left me. I tell Bernadette and Raingarde nothing of what has happened and I forbid Dia to speak of it. If I do not discuss it with anyone then it will begin to fade and soon I will think that it may not have happened at all.

Two months later and news comes that Ramon's earlier betrothal to Blanca of Castile has been renewed. That dream is over then and he was not sincere. Dia sings pointed lyrics:

> You stayed a long time, friend,
> and then you left me,
> and it's a hard, cruel thing you've done;
> for you promised and you swore
> that as long as you lived
> I'd be your only lady:
> if now another has your love
> you've slain me and betrayed me,
> for in you lay all my hopes
> of being loved without deceit.

'Enough! Desist!' I say to her in exasperation. I sometimes wonder if I had accepted either Geoffrey or Ramon's proposal, what would have happened? As Bernadette would say: 'If ifs and ands were pots and pans.'

When Pons returns from pilgrimage touting his lead sea shell from the shrine of Saint James, I have another idea to keep him from me. 'My Lord, for your birthday, I wish to make you a gift,' I tell him. 'There is a villa on my land, near Saint Gilles.' I have been planning this for months now and my heart is pounding. I need this to go well. 'I have decorated and furnished it, especially for you,' I say.

His eyes light up and he thrusts his hand up my skirts, gripping the bare flesh of my thigh. 'Then we should take a little trip there together, eh?' he says.

I disengage myself, covering my shudders with smiles. 'Oh no,'

I say, evading his hands, 'it is your villa, all for you, your own private palace.'

I succeed in persuading him to travel without me and wave him off the following morning, promising to come after him soon. I am wreathed in smiles, but saying in my head: 'Good-bye. Don't ever come back. Fall from your horse. May you be gnawed at by ringworms.' When he gets to Saint Gilles he will find Alienor waiting there for him and all manner of luxuries and wines and amusements and I hope that she can keep him there for a long, long, time or give him an apoplexy with her enthusiastic ministrations.

'Your Lord must be well pleased with his gift,' murmurs Dia, her head down sewing.

Pons has been gone now for three months. Alienor sends word that she keeps him drunk 'as a lord'. He has tried to return twice but I found excuses to deter him. Chateau Narbonnais was in disarray, being redecorated, I told him. Another time I wrote to say that there was a heavy slate of justices to hear and would be glad of his assistance, and Alienor told me he received my message on the road and turned back to Saint Gilles, sending me his heartfelt apologies that he was unable to come at present. It cannot last forever and I cannot return to the previous tolerance of him.

'When he does return,' I say to Dia, 'I mean to tell him that I have taken a vow for a *mariage blanc*.'

She looks at me long. 'That will not go well,' she says simply and bows her head again.

27

Bernadette: Breaking Oath

Alienor kept Count Pons in Saint Gilles for nearly a year but when he did return my Lady told him of her vow of a *mariage blanc*, which she has solemnly sworn in front of the new Bishop of Toulouse, Hugh (her bishop). My Lady is on a dangerous path now, denying the count her bed. He raged and kicked the furniture in her room, but she held her ground and I looked nervously at the knife at her belt. If he lays a finger on her now, I was thinking, it's murder I will be defending her for. She prays each evening to St Uncumber who helps wives get rid of bad husbands and she does not care who hears her or who tells tales on her back to the count. I have had a hit with my plan to wheedle information from Piers. He told me in drunken pillow-talk that Pons has commissioned him to find a reason for him to repudiate Almodis and I, of course, tell this to my Lady.

'Open this door! If you continue to behave like a nun I will ensure that you become one!'

'His threat is real, Almodis,' Dia tells her.

She is looking down at her hands in her lap. 'I know,' she says quietly.

I swallow fearfully at that. If she is put aside, then what will become of me? I'm not minded to become a nun neither.

'He has his three boys,' Dia says. 'He has what he needed of you.'

'Yes, I am a used and therefore useless wife, but he will find that they are my three boys and not his.'

There is a powerlessness in that while they are young. Perhaps when they are older it will mean something. I know that she carries on a constant correspondence with Hugh and Jourdain, Guillaume and Raymond, that she binds her boys to her with love, loyalty and the wisdom of her strategies.

'We must keep an eye on his correspondence, Dia. Send Bernadette to canoodle with his clerk or messenger, whatever works.' Dia nods and I bridle. Canoodle indeed! I picture the count's clerk and messenger. Well the messenger then.

'If he has correspondence with any of the prioresses hereabouts I want to know of it. If he is writing to a noble family with a marriageable daughter I want to hear of that.' Then she raises her head and looks at Dia. 'No, more. I want you to intercept any such letters and bring them to me.' Dia returns her look for a long silence. 'I know,' she says, 'that this is a dangerous game but I must play it. I might keep him a short while longer by giving him access to me, but it is only a matter of time before he turns his desire to some young girl-child. Fresh, compliant meat.' The air in the room tastes sour.

Dia does not ask me to canoodle. Perhaps she is canoodling with the clerk herself. He has a flushed look about him these days.

'Come in Bernadette and Dia,' she says to us in a solemn voice and I am appalled to see the red and purple bruising on her cheek, circling one eye, and a cut on her swollen lip.

'Oh my Lady,' I gasp reaching a hand to her face.

She swats away my hand. 'Don't touch me. You are here to bear witness.'

Bear witness? To what? I am shaking now. She is so unlike herself. At the end of a ditch a somersault, I think, but keep my thoughts to myself. I look to Dia who nods calmly to me and steps to one side of the fire. I see I should do the same and stand on the other side. My Lady is wearing only her white shift and I see that her hands are shaking but I do not know if it is with fear or with fury. She holds in her hands a straw as if it were a golden sceptre. I cannot understand the purport of this. Is it witchcraft?

'In the ritual of homage between men in the North,' she tells us slowly, 'a blow is considered the only good reason to break the oath of fealty.' She pauses and looks at us. I am bewildered. What have men's rituals to do with a man beating his wife? She takes one step towards us and the fire, holding the straw stretched out in the palm of one hand before her, and using her other hand to help shrug off the shift. It falls to her ankles and now we can see that it was not just the blow to her face that she is talking about. There are black and red marks about her back and buttocks and even across the soft mound of her stomach where she has carried so many babies. I gasp and put a hand to my mouth as she frowns silence to me. Tears trickle down my face. What monster would be so cruel to one so beautiful? Her breasts are pert like a girl's, only their enlarged brown nipples betraying the fact that she has borne seven children.

'I, Almodis of La Marche, Countess of Toulouse, daughter of Amelie, Countess, hereby break my oath to Pons, Count of Toulouse, son of Emma, Countess.' She breaks the straw in two and throws the pieces on the fire where they fizzle fast. She turns her back, her poor bruised back, on us and on the flames and stalks naked to the window.

'Leave,' she says without turning to us, and Dia takes my hand and leads me from the room.

Later, I stand quaking, hidden in the recess in the passage, listening to Pons shouting at her bedroom door. Dia has barred the door against him and he is threatening to slit Dia's tongue and 'silence her hysterical poetry' if she does not open up, but she does not.

A few days later the count and countess are breaking fast and I am serving them. Her eye is an unsightly green and yellow. The air between them is frigid.

'I've taken over one of your servants my dear. I hope you don't mind it,' Pons says casually.

'One of mine?'

'Yes, he seems a capable man. Not adequately challenged I thought and I needed a new vicar in Saint Gilles.'

'You have appointed a new vicar without consulting me?' She sets her fork down. 'Who?'

'Piers Fitzmarche.'

'Piers who?' she splutters.

'Your half-brother he tells me. I thought you would like to see him given preference.'

She is on her feet, shouting. 'My father never acknowledged him. He has absolutely no right to use that name. I forbid it.' She is red in the face.

'Calm yourself, calm yourself,' he pulls her back down to the bench. 'Alright I won't allow the use of that name. We'll find him another name, but he is Vicar of Saint Gilles.'

'He is *my* servant.'

'Not anymore,' Pons yells, thumping the table so that a bowl bounces off, smashing on the tiles. As I bend with a brush to collect up the shards, I hear Pons tell her in a low and threatening voice, 'Be silent woman. I will not be gainsayed in public.'

She is breathing through her nose, her chest heaving with the effort to control her temper. What shall I do if he threatens her with violence again? Will I have the bravery to intervene? I grip the handle of the broom ready to make a swipe.

'Of course I am delighted for him,' she says at length, 'and for you to have been so clever to appoint yourself such a talented servant. How good of you,' she says munificently but the graciousness in her voice drips with insincerity.

'It is well, Almodis,' Dia tells her later in the chamber. 'Piers will be out of your way. Unable to spy on you more.'

'At least we knew who the spy was. Did you know of this Bernadette?'

'No,' I say truthfully. 'He never said. Vicar of Saint Gilles! All puffed up he'll be. He'll be after one of the daughters of the Saint Gilles' Capitouls now, clawing his way up and he'll not be short of noblewomen who would bed him either.'

'Why is it that you object so to the preferment of Piers?' Dia asks her.

I often wondered that myself. Why does she care so much to keep him down? All over some scars on her knuckles? Her reasons sound lame: 'He laughed at me when we were children. He scoffed at my notions of a female lord. Have I not proven him wrong!'

'Yes, of course you have,' Dia tells her.

'You'll be needing a new marshal now,' I say.

'You must not make more of an enemy of him, Almodis, now that he is so placed,' says Dia firmly.

'Must! I must do what *I* deem politic,' she says crossly.

Later climbing into bed she says to me, 'When we returned from being hostages in Aquitaine, my father looked and looked on Piers and hardly looked at all on me.'

'That's not true, my Lady! Your father doted on you. Perhaps he was trying to find his likeness there.'

'And not finding it,' she says stubbornly. 'My father was just. He would have acknowledged a bastard if Piers were one of his. He did not.'

'Well he is out of your way now.'

'Perhaps, but likely not. He is out of your way now too, Bernadette?' she says stroking my hair and looking a question in my face.

'Good riddance, his promises are as much as the wind can carry,' I say, keeping my face unemotional. Perhaps I've been learning my lessons from her.

28

Midsummer 1052

Garsenda and Berenger have invited me to visit with them in Narbonne. The guestroom I have been conveyed to is bright with sunlight. From my window the glittering sea in the distance fills my eye, and just below the window, trees with purple- and lime-coloured leaves provide a brilliant contrast. Garsenda comes to accompany me to dinner. She links her arm in mine and, as we approach the hall, she says, 'We have a surprise for you'. I raise my eyebrows and guess at some troubadour I have not heard before, or an extravagant dinner dish. We are half-way up the hall before I look up to smile greeting at Berenger, sitting on the dais, and see that Ramon is sitting there, next to him. I stay as calm as I can, taking my seat, smiling.

'I believe you know Count Ramon,' says Berenger.

'I did not know you were in the county, Lord Ramon.'

'Ah well,' he says lightly, 'Narbonne is of course, part of my county, and not yours. I am on my way to Rome.'

'A pilgrimage?'

'Of sorts, yes, but more politics than penance, I fear.'

Archbishop Guifred is also here. Berenger has often complained to me of him, telling me that he has scribes forging documents day and night to gradually reduce the viscount's holdings and increase his own. The archbishop is the third son of the Count of Cerdanya, and Ramon was warring with his brother until recently. Berenger complains that he stripped the cathedral of all its valuables to buy the bishopric of Urgell for one of his brothers and that he takes tolls that rightly belong to the viscount. 'I begged the pope to take him to Rome in chains and punish him, without success,' Berenger told me. I am intrigued to meet this epitome of wickedness. The archbishop is a handsome man in his fifties, richly dressed and bejewelled. His hair is a thick mixture of grey and brown. He has a haughty military bearing that reminds me of Geoffrey. His powerful kin are counts and bishops in four or five counties and his father brought the archbishopric for him when he was ten years old for the fabled sum of 100,000 *solidi*. He carries a crozier of the utmost ostentation: the head is mounted on a polished wooden rod and is lavishly embellished with gold, silver, enamels and rock crystals, fashioned in the shapes of vine leaves and lizards. 'Mosan metalwork from the Meuse Valley,' he tells me, when he sees me looking at it. Between us all then, I prepare myself for an evening of hypocrisy.

The dinner passes off with small talk and music. I resist the urge to drink copiously. Inevitably there comes a moment when Berenger says, 'And so, Blanca of Castile, Ramon? Will you take your new countess with you on your return?'

I feel the bench shudder as Ramon's shifts uneasily at that and he tries, unsuccessfully, to catch my eye. 'I do not believe so,' he says eventually.

'No?' says Garsenda in mild surprise.

'The . . . the wedding,' he fumbles, and is usually so smooth, 'will not take place this year.'

'But Ramon,' Garsenda is in full surprise now, 'you have been a widower for two years. You must be in urgent need of a wife,' she pauses archly, 'to take care of your son, to manage the affairs of your court. You could send her here to us, and then meet her on your way back from Rome.'

'No,' he says forcefully. 'I have other arrangements in hand. But thank you,' he adds, realising he has offended Garsenda.

I decide, at length, to rescue him from his discomfort. 'Is your grandmother well, my Lord?' I say and he turns to me. I hold his gaze steadily.

'Unfortunately, she is,' he says, smiling wryly.

'Ramon!' exclaims Garsenda, but we are all laughing.

'Barcelona not big enough for the both of you, eh?' says Berenger. 'An excess of rule, between you?'

'Hmm,' says Ramon, good-humoured, but glancing occasionally at me, not forgetting the conversation about Blanca, that I have just diverted. 'Countess Ermessende has Girona and Vic and I hope that will be enough for her powers, now she is nearing seventy-five. She is rebuilding the cathedral in Girona.'

'Oh,' groans Berenger, 'let us not speak of cathedral building. It seems that ours will never be finished and we must live with stone dust until we die of it. My food tastes of it and my wine.'

'Lady Almodis,' says the archbishop, licking his fingers, 'Now that we have finished supping on the delights of Lady Garsenda's table, the dew of heaven and the fat of the earth, won't you allow me to give you a tour of this dusty cathedral that is so interfering with the viscount's digestion?'

It would be difficult to refuse such an invitation so I rise and go with Guifred into the half-built edifice. The workmen are packing up their tools and leaving as we go in. A man goes past us with a squeaking wheelbarrow and touches his cap to the archbishop. The central nave is completed and magnificent. I stand in front of the altar admiring it.

'Do you need to give confession?' asks Guifred, taking my hand and stroking it in a decidedly unclerical manner.

'No . . .' I begin, surprised.

He raises my hand to his lips, saying, 'No, a lady such as yourself, so very beautiful, must not describe her sins in too much detail for fear of tempting a priest, even an archbishop.'

I pull my hand from his grasp, look at him, at the crucifix above the altar, and back to him in contempt. What is written of how high clerics throw what is holy to the dogs; fatten on the sweat of others; devour the fruits of the earth without charge; is true then. I turn away.

'One moment, Lady Almodis,' he says, 'before you leave me standing at the altar, I have some information that you need to know. Let's sit,' he says, leading me to a pew. 'It concerns your husband, Count Pons.'

'What of him?'

'He is planning to repudiate you, my dear.' When I do not

respond, he goes on, 'Ah, and you already thought so, eh? Such an act would have to have religious sanction of course. Sanction from the highest cleric in the domain.' He nods, raising his eyebrows at me. 'I don't ask for much, Almodis. In return for my refusal to your husband, won't *you* give me your consent, for one night only?'

I rise in disgust. I cannot even voice an answer to such sacrilege and blackmail. I stride down the aisle and hear him laughing softly behind me.

Archbishop Guifred does not return to the viscount's palace and the next day's hunting and dining passes pleasantly enough. At dinner I am wearing my new blue gown and the earrings and necklace that Hugh gave me for my dowry, so long ago.

'Oh, beautiful!' exclaims Garsenda. 'Where did you get them?'

'From an admirer!' I say laughing, but this is the first time I have worn them since I left Lusignan, the first time I could bear to raise the lid on them. After dinner, I excuse myself and make my way up the staircase to my chamber. I cannot blame Berenger and Garsenda for this encounter with Ramon. They were not to know how it would embarrass us both. I suppose that Ramon only found out that I was here or coming when he could do nothing about it. It is the obvious place for him to stop on the way to Rome. I pass into a narrow passageway leading to my room. There is only a stub of a candle on the wall and it falters and goes out with the breeze of my passing. I should have carried a light with me. I put my hand to the cold stone to steady myself in the darkness and continue forward.

'Almodis!' Ramon comes up behind me so fast, taking my arm, that I am just turning with surprise at the sound of his running footsteps when he is already arrived. I open my mouth to speak but he crushes me to him and his mouth is on mine, my back against the wall. I am so surprised that it takes me too long to react. I am already losing myself in this kiss. The sweet scent of him. His hands are in my hair, pulling at the shoulder of my gown, on my breast. I place my palms flat against the wall at my sides, allowing his body to push against mine, feeling the jutting stones of the wall against my shoulders.

207

I raise my hands to push at his shoulders and twist my mouth away from him. 'Stop!' He steps away from me and I feel the loss of his heat. I can just see his eyes, his breath in the cold air.

'My love!' he says.

I am shaking my head, smoothing my dress, calculating the distance to the end of the passage. He steps towards me cupping his hands to my breast and hip again. 'No,' I say and turn away swiftly, moving forwards. He holds me back by the arm. 'Let go of me!'

'I must speak with you, Almodis. Explain myself.'

I shake him off and keep going. 'There is nothing to explain.' He runs around in front of me so that I must halt again. We are at the end of the passage and over his shoulder I can see Bernadette peeking from the door of my chamber.

'Yes, there is much to explain. Please I must speak with you.'

I place my hand flat on his chest, on the brown brocade of his tunic, and push him hard, out of my way.

'I will wait for you, in the passage later,' he says, low, under his breath, gesturing back to where we stood panting against the wall. 'My room is off that passage.'

I glower at him and pass by, slamming my door behind me so that Bernadette looks up startled. Who does he think I am? A chambermaid that he can tryst with in the dark? Why should I speak with him? I don't want his explanations and excuses. Why should I grace him with my forgiveness? Anyway, I suddenly remember, what is it to me, the wife of Pons of Toulouse, who Ramon is betrothed to?

'Oh Bernadette!' I say flinging myself down in the chair and staring at the flames flicking the back of the chimney, the new logs cracking and hissing like snakes.

'What is it, my Lady?' She's unlacing my boots and unfastening my garters. I suddenly feel shy to have my body stripped of its concealments, my treacherous body with its groanings and its openings that should be closed tight shut. I close my mouth inadvertently and grip the arms of the chair. Am I like Bernadette to be taken up against a wall by Piers? I try to shake the images and sensations from me.

'It's nothing,' I tell her, as she stands looking at me wide-eyed, a comb in her hand.

'Has something upset you, Lady? Lord Ramon?'

'No, no. Nothing.' I am glad Dia is not here for she would worm it out of me, questioning me until I yielded it all up.

Bernadette slips the nightshift over my head, combs out my hair, places a glass of wine beside me on a stool. 'Do you need aught else, mistress?'

'No. Thank you.'

'They've given me a pallet in the servants' dormitory, but I can stay here with you, if you'd like it,' she says, looking with desire at the feather bed, loaded with quilts and furs. 'You seem upset and in need of company tonight?' she says eagerly.

'No, I'm fine,' I say firmly. 'Go to your bed, Bernadette. You need your rest now.'

Her face falls but she curtseys and turns to the door but then stops again.

'What is it?'

'I . . . you are looking a little flushed, Lady Almodis.'

'There's nothing wrong with me.'

'No, I don't suppose there is. I just wanted to tell you that you are looking so very lovely tonight, my Lady. Oh my!' she claps her hand to her mouth. 'And I've forgotten to take off your jewels.' She starts back towards me.

I place one hand on the necklace at my throat and hold the other out stopping her approach. 'It's alright, Bernadette. Leave me. I want to keep them on for a moment and I will take them off myself, before I get into bed.'

She laughs. 'Aye, I'd sleep in them if it was me,' she says, and I stand and kiss her which surprises her so much that she goes out without saying another word to me.

I walk over to the mirror that hangs above the fire. It is not as good a mirror as some of the ones I have at home. My face is blurry in places and the light from the fire dances in the room, reflecting back, quivering my image. The pink and blue gems of the earrings and necklace shimmer gloriously and my loose hair looks aflame in this light, almost red. I remember when Hugh gave me these jewels. I remember my hope and pride at that moment before we were led to the bedchamber, before I stopped being a girl and became a woman, but not in the way that everybody thought. How proud I was to think that I would be wife to that beautiful man holding out his marriage gifts to me. I see tears pooling in my eyes in the mirror, competing with the gleam of the jewels. How I had thought that Hugh would love me, in my girlish ideas; how he would kiss my neck where his necklace nestled against my bare collarbone, enslaved by my beauty, my charm, my wit. 'Oh what a fool,' I say aloud to my image in the mirror. 'You poor fool.'

Lurking in the back of my mind now is Pons and I do not want to let *him* into my thoughts. Even though my memories of Hugh, my disappointment then was so bitter, I would rather stay there with him, thinking of that past, than let myself remember my present. I close my eyes on the unwelcome memory of my wedding night with Pons. No. I pick up the wineglass and gulp down its contents.

I am walking out the door, wiping my eyes. I want no wet tears spilling down my face. I take the trailing sleeve of my nightshift and blow my nose on it, laughing at myself, remembering Agnes chiding me as a child for this nasty habit. I smile, cherishing my seven-year-old self. I walk back into the darkness of the passage. No one has replaced the candle. The castle is silent. The dark grows darker. I walk swiftly, feeling with pleasure the swish of my silk shift against my thighs, round my ankles, seeing its vague whiteness in the gloom, hearing the tiny chinkings of my jewels. A door cracks and then Ramon opens it wide for me to enter his room which is dimly lit by two candles.

'Almodis,' he says softly, his arm about my waist.

'You look surprised,' I say. 'Were you expecting someone else? Did you mean only to flirt and not to act?'

He is shaking his head, smiling at my questions. 'No. No.' And then after staring at me for some time: 'We might lay with *épreuve*,' he says meaning that we could lay chastely with a sword between us, its cold metal touching our hot flesh.

'We might,' I say, unlacing the ties of his shirt.

I wake before him at first light and look at the tufts of his blond hair and his brown eyelashes against the brown and pink blush of his face on the pillow beside me. I sit on the edge of the bed and put my shift on quickly, scooping up my jewels with one hand, wanting to get back to my room before anyone else in the household awakens.

'Almodis?'

'I must go quickly.'

He raises himself on one elbow, 'Sweet Almodis. You are like your birthland in the Limousin: strong as granite, secret as the bosky woods, modest as the mountains.' I smile politely to him and start to stand but he holds me back. 'Tell me, if I had asked you to marry me all those years ago in Toulouse, would you have said yes?'

'No,' I say, watching the smile extinguished in his eyes. 'I was betrothed on my father's oath. Our lives are not for our desiring.' I neglect to mention how I had desired Hugh of Lusignan at that time, my chimera.

'And now?'

I do not reply.

'We can find a way, Almodis, if you wish it.'

'I don't have time for conversation, Ramon, I must go.'

I move swiftly to the door and hear him jump out of bed behind me. He comes around me, holding his shirt comically to his groin, and opens the door gallantly for me.

'Another time, then?' he says.

Later that morning I go down to the dock with Berenger to see Ramon off on his journey to Rome. He leans close to kiss me goodbye on both cheeks. 'My love,' he says in my ear. He has given me a thick gold ring that I am wearing on my little finger, but only for today. Inside it is engraved with the words: 'I am wholly yours'. When I turn back for a last sight of him I see that his hand is still cupped, in the same position, as when I left his embrace, cupped to the shape of my hip, to the shape of my absence. I smile at that and turn away. A boy. He is a sweet boy still, and I am glad that I have stolen one beautiful night for myself.

I pace my room, horrified. There is no doubt. I am with child.

Pons has not lain with me for over two years. I could birth the child in secret and send it away. Or I must expose it in the forest as poor mothers do, so that it dies of cold or is eaten by animals. I pull my lips in tightly and begin to weep silently to myself. If I send word to Ramon what good would that do? He is betrothed and he will wed Blanca. He must now. He told me in Narbonne that he had betrothed himself to Blanca in despair at my rejection at the Troubadour Court but then found that he could not forget me, could not marry her. He has found excuses each year to put the marriage off: a military expedition last year, a pilgrimage to Rome this year. 'I will keep finding excuses, Almodis,' he said, 'until you marry me.' What nonsense he speaks. What did he expect? That I would leave my husband and marry him? We would be disowned by everyone, our people, our families, everyone. My sons would be shamed. My sister, my poor sister: she would not be able to show her face anywhere. People would spit on her, mistaking her for me, the Count of Barcelona's whore, a woman of unbridled lust. No one would recognise a marriage between us. He would lose all the respect he has earned so hard over the last years. He is ridiculous. He still thinks like a boy! Because he wants something he thinks he can have it, he can have me with none of this weight of the world mattering. Now if I tell Ramon of this child what would he do? He will not own a bastard got on the wife of another lord. I am undone. Ramon could not risk war between Barcelona and Toulouse for my sake.

I sit hugging myself and weeping for a long time. In my head I chant Dia's litany of contraceptive herbs: birthwort, Queen Anne's lace, lupine, pepper, myrrh, licorice, pennyroyal, rue, parsley, cypress. Unfortunately I used none of them. Dia is outside the door calling to me. 'Leave me be now,' I call back and her footsteps retreat down the passage. Perhaps I will miscarry in my misery. Perhaps Dia can help me miscarry. Must I pay so hard for one small pleasure?

I stamp my foot. I have only to look at a man and I am pregnant! I am so tired of carrying children: the pains in my ankles and back, the swellings and unswellings, the difficulty of sleeping in the late stages, and now I must sleep with Pons to conceal my infidelity and stop him from making me a nun. I dash my pink glass to the ground at that horrible thought and cry some more, realising that it is the glass Ramon gave me for my wedding to Hugh. How I have loved the way it fitted into my hand. I cry for it as if it were a dear friend, ruined and shattered on the cold ground.

'My Lady?' Bernadette comes in looking anxiously from me to the pink shards.

'It's nothing. An accident. Clear it up.' I wipe my face and shake my head. 'It's nothing.'

I try to write a letter to Ramon to tell him of my predicament and ask him for his help. I begin with a quotation from Dhuoda: *If sky and meadows were unfurled through the air like a scroll of parchment and if all the gulfs of the sea were transformed, tinged like inks of many colours I could walk across this floating parchment like a bridge, crossing the inky sea to you* . . . Ridiculous. Love is ridiculous and not real. I scrunch up the blotched sheet of paper and throw it in the fire.

29

Moissac 1052

Pons and I have travelled by boat up the Tarn to the abbey at Moissac where we will sign a charter to join the abbey to Cluny. It was my idea and greatly welcomed in letters to me by Abbot Durand. We are shown into the abbot's office. Durand de Bredon is very tall, taller even than me and thin, so that he gives an over-all impression of longness. His face is long, his nose is long, his fingers, held out to us in blessing, are very long. He is a fanatic, talking to us of a return to the rigours of the early church, of the need for self-deprivation.

'You will be interested to know that we are preparing for the beatification of a saint here, my Lady,' he says, 'a sister of great faith.'

'Oh?'

'Sister Dolores. She lived in utter solitude for nigh on twenty years, not touching a living soul, not speaking except to whisper her visions to us, wonderful visions of the angels and seraphims.'

I try to look impressed but recoil at his description. I do not believe that God wishes such self-deprivations. God made us and the world that we live in. It and we, I think, cannot be all as bad as some preach.

'Come and see her cell,' he says. 'It is quite extraordinary.'

I am not at all interested to see a nun's cell but politely I must feign my fascination. Pons, on the other hand, is intrigued. 'Imagine that,' he says to me pointedly, 'not touching a living soul for years.'

When I step over the threshold into the church time seems to slow and stop, partly because of the weight of history here, but also because of the sheer volume of still air. The columns, buttresses and vaults rise up around me like a great stone forest. Demons cavort in its stained glass windows, an orchestra of angels play their instruments in the ceiling above the choir. Inside the church are forty carvings of green men and outside, hideous gargoyles funnel rainwater away from the walls.

The abbot leads us on to the cloisters where birds are singing in the green square. Monks pace the quadrangle underneath the intricate stone latticework of the fan-vaulted ceilings, or are seated at the stone carols contemplating the enclosed garden through a colonnade of arched windows. The order is mostly silent so the church is the sounding space where voices can burst out. The abbot brings us to a place mid-way down one side of the quad and turning his back on the grass and sunshine, faces the wall, declaring with relish, 'Here it is!'

I am confused. There is no nun's cell here. I see two rectangular openings in the wall, one above the other.

'This one here,' he says, 'placing his hand at the top opening, 'was at eye-level, so that she could see out, and then this one,' he gestures at the larger opening below, 'was for her prayer books and letters.' It takes me a moment to understand him.

'She was walled up here?' I say slowly. 'Inside this wall.'

'Yes. Astonishing isn't it? She was a true saint.'

I feel sick and turn away from the wall. Unspeakable.

'Would you like to try it my Lady? The access is from the side here . . .'

'No. I would not.'

'Yes, yes,' Pons says. 'She would love to try it.' He takes my arm tightly, bruising it. 'Try it,' he hisses at me.

'No need to be afraid.' The abbot is humorous. 'We won't leave you in there, will we count?'

'Oh certainly not. How would I cope without my wife?' There is an opening and Pons thrusts me into it so that I am tightly encased front and back by stone.

'You have to sidle sideways, countess, to get to it. Yes that's right, down that way, until you reach the stone that she perched on. That's it.'

The narrow stone passage opens out into a room that is only slightly wider. In the middle is a stone bench long enough to stretch out on and suspended on the far wall, a large, dark crucifix. A chamber pot and a water jug are the only objects in this sliver of a room. If I sit on the bench with my back to Pons and Durand, facing towards the church, I can see through a squint hole where I have a view of the altar. She would have been able to hear mass and the music of the choir. If I swing my legs over and face out to the cloisters I have a narrow framed rectangular view. The lintel I had stepped over would have been bricked up when Sister Dolores occupied this living grave, mortifying her flesh, in hope of paradise. A small hatch beneath the crucifix would have allowed her servant to take her pot and pass through her water and food. Sister Dolores would have stayed here with not even room to pace on either side of the bench for twenty years. I am doing my best not to imagine it.

My hands are at the opening now and my eyes at the eyehole. I try to slow my breathing. I am overwhelmingly hot. 'Of course Sister Dolores was smaller than you,' the abbot rattles on.

I imagine the long, long years. I imagine spiders weaving strands of my hair into their webs.

Pons is standing in the line of my vision, enjoying himself hugely. 'Suits you,' he says nastily. He thrusts his hand into the lower hole poking about my lap. 'Is this how she was fed?'

I bat his hand away. There is barely room to bend my arm and raise it to my mouth. Her muscles must have wasted, her bones must have ached. She would see the monks coming and going on their way to mass. She would see a butterfly or dragonfly skid across the green quad. She would see snow fall and leaves fall, year in, year out. The horror of it. Only a loss of her mind could have sustained her, only a feverish dwelling in visions. I scuttle sideways back out.

'Mind your dress, my dear.'

I lean my back against the wall, outside, taking deep breaths.

I ignore Pons' grins and stare at the abbot. He stares back at me, stony, long. I say, 'And does God wish this, Father?'

'Sister Dolores will be beatified in a matter of weeks,' he says in a tone that disapproves of my challenge. 'Female flesh, in particular, requires mortification, driven as it is by godless female itches,' he says, his eyes on my heaving breasts which are already starting to fill out with milk for Ramon's child in my womb.

'You are quite pale, dear,' says Pons, clearly pleased.

I walk quickly down the cloister needing to escape the sight and thought of the anchorite cell. I am disgusted. In the guest chamber Bernadette rushes to find a bowl for me but she's too late and I have to vomit into one of Abbot Durand's ornate vases decorating the room. I order Bernadette not to clean it.

30

Lammas 1052

I have returned to Toulouse, and Pons to Saint Gilles. My sister, Lucia, has come to stay with me. The muggy, hot weather has broken and I lie in bed listening to the sound of summer rain beating down hard on the cobbles and roofs. It is not light yet. The sound must have woken me. I relish the warmth of my bed, of my body, and the fact that I need not get up just yet.

'My Lady!' Bernadette is through the door with her words. Something is wrong. I sit up, pulling my shift up my shoulders, blinking against the candlelight that she has brought in with her.

'What is it? Is it Raingarde? One of the children?' But not Raingarde. I would have felt her long before anyone came to give me news of her. Is it my mother?

'It's Alienor, Lady!'

I struggle for a moment trying to place Alienor in my household. I am still half asleep. 'Alienor?' I repeat.

'She's outside and begs urgent audience with you.'

'In the middle of the night?' Is Pons dead? Hope rises in me. 'Quickly, show her in and bring us some water.'

'Big with child she is,' Bernadette, says her eyes round. 'And wet through with the rain. Shall I light the fire? She's in an awful state.'

'Yes, light the fire.'

The commotion has woken Dia and she comes in just behind Alienor and helps her take off her wet cloak and hood, but the clothes underneath are soaking wet too.

'Get Alienor some clothes from my chest, Dia. You mustn't stay in those,' I tell her.

Bernadette helps her to strip. As the mound of her belly is exposed she is looking at me mutely, her eyes wide and afraid and I begin to fear too. When she is clothed in my gown and has stopped shaking with cold I say, 'Sit here on the bed, Alienor and put this blanket around you too. What has possessed you to ride here in the middle of the night in this terrible storm?' I settle the blanket around her.

'He's thrown me out,' she says, 'and you can see why. He said he would run me through the town naked if I didn't do what I was told. Said he didn't want to know nothing of my bastard. *My* bastard,' she says indignant. 'Well it's his, isn't it my Lady?'

'Yes,' I soothe her, drying her hair. 'Never mind him, Alienor. You are safe now. You have served me well and I will take good care of you and your child.'

'That's just it,' she says. 'You won't. Not if his plans and plots all go to schedule. I thought me and the babe would be done for if I didn't get word to you in time.'

'What plans do you mean?'

'I heard him talking with Piers.' I glance up at Bernadette at that and she looks anxious.

'He's meaning to put you away, Lady. Lock you up. You wouldn't be able to help any of us then.'

I sit back against my pillows. 'Tell me what you heard.'

'I thought he loved me just a little,' Alienor sniffs. 'I thought he might like a babe of mine to dandle on his knees and give him a job as a cook when he's old enough.'

I wait as patiently as I can for her to tell her story.

'He was going to ship me off to the nuns in the morning. "I've got you a good place as convent servant at Saint Gilles," he says to me. Me! With nuns! I don't think so. Had to leave in the middle of the night, didn't I?' She looks around the room at Dia and Bernadette, gesturing dramatically.

'Half those nuns are former prostitutes, anyway,' mutters Bernadette.

Warming to her story, Alienor continues, 'I picked up these letters that were waiting for Piers in case they help.' She reaches for her saddlebag and gives me two letters with Pons' seal. 'I don't know what they say. They might not be the right ones. He says to Piers, the bit I heard, my Lady, the sleeping draught will make it easy till you can get the countess to the boat.'

I swallow hard at that and look at Dia and Bernadette huddled close together in the dark room lit only with one candle and the young fire. This is very bad. The fire is still struggling with the frigid night air and our breath comes white before our faces.

'Then he says,' continues Alienor, '"keep her bound and gagged on the boat, Piers. It will be the only way."'

Dia and Bernadette exclaim at this and I feel cold to my bones.

'"Durand will meet you at . . ." But I couldn't hear that part clearly. Maybe it says something in the letters. It was something beginning with M. Piers was shuffling papers and I couldn't hear it.'

'Did you hear anything else?'

'No, that's it. But he's said to me many times in the last months, "I'm going to put her in a nunnery. That's where she belongs with her books. Time for a new wife."'

'You have done well,' I tell her quietly, calmly. 'Bring me the letter knife, Bernadette.' I slice open one of the letters.

'From the Count of Toulouse to Eli, Captain of *The Tarn Trader*,' I read out.

'I've seen that boat at the pier,' says Dia. 'It plies salt and the like up and down the Tarn.'

'My servant, Piers, delivers to you the cargo I spoke about with you. I charge you, as we discussed, to ship it to Moissac, with all haste and deliver it to Durand de Bredon.'

I pause and Bernadette is exclaiming, 'Moissac! He means to incarcerate you with those stone demons!'; and Dia is saying at the same time, 'Durand de Bredon, Almodis! They mean to do worse than make you a nun'; and I am thinking, 'Ship the cargo'. I take a deep breath.

'What time is it, Bernadette?'

'The sun's not showing yet,' she says, peering out of the window. 'Must be an hour yet or more before sunrise.'

'Wake the groom and saddle our horses. We will ride to my

sister in Carcassonne. Alienor, you will come with us. You will be safe there and Raingarde will give you a position in her household. Wake the girls, Bernadette: Lucia, Melisende, Adalmoda, and also Hughie. We must all go and before first light when Piers will discover his letters missing and Alienor fled, and he will be hard on her heels then.' Bernadette stumbles out into the dark of the corridor. 'You have done so well, Alienor.' I press her hands warmly and she is smiling brightly at me, with tears on her cheeks. I wipe her face with a corner of my bedsheet.

'The second letter, Almodis?' asks Dia.

I slice it open. 'From Pons, Count of Toulouse to Durand de Bredon, Abbot at Moissac. My dear friend, I am in your debt for this service you do me. My wife is greatly in need of God's enlightenment. She has grown unwomanly and unchristian in her overweening pride.'

I stop at that, wanting to rip the letter in two, to have Pons' ugly head between my hands that I might bounce it against the stones of the wall.

'Dia will you take Alienor to get a bite to eat before we ride out. She looks in need of it.'

Alienor starts to shake her head, but Dia coaxes her out. I swing my feet to the cold floor, the letter gripped in my hands and Bernadette is back now.

'They're all up and getting dressed in haste. I'll get your clothes. What's it say?'

I don't reply but read the rest of the letter to myself. Bernadette fusses around me pulling on my hose and boots, laying out gowns and my riding cloak. *Some time with you*, Pons continues to his dear friend, *in the anchorite's cell* . . . I feel nauseous at that but read on . . . *will be the salvation of the Countess' soul.*

'They mean to wall me up in a living grave!'

Bernadette clamps her hand to her mouth. 'Oh Lord, oh Lord!' she says, wringing her hands. 'We've got to get out of here.'

'Be calm. Alienor has given us two or three hours. I am forewarned now, but we will need protection. I'll finish dressing. Dress yourself and find the Sergeant at Arms. Send him to me.'

'What should we take with us? Your jewels? Your clothes?

'We'll worry about that later. For now we need to think of our hides.'

She dashes off and I finish the letter. Pons writes to the abbot that he should keep me in the cell with whatever spiritual instruction he deems necessary for as long as it seems needy. I remember Durand's long, stern face and my hands are shaking. *If she should show true repentance*, writes my dear husband, *perhaps one day you might release her to a suitable closed community of nuns, but have a care and full judgement for she may never show true humility and she will attempt to trick and manipulate you.* I fold the letter up, and then again, and again; I fold it until it is a tiny square, and I secure it in the purse at my girdle. I have to make an effort to calm my fury and finish dressing. I smooth the folds of my skirt over my growing belly. Oh and what would happen to you little Ramon in such a scenario? I could not hide you for long from my monk inquisitors. They would see my swelling and my sin would be confirmed in their eyes. They would rip you from me as soon as you were born and expose you or discard you, and I would suffer the fate of a wife proven to be faithless in every sense. I shudder, feeling Geoffrey's hand crushing mine, smelling the stench of his mother's burning flesh. I swallow hard and stride to the door.

In the courtyard my household is assembling. Despite the summer season, the weather is still wet and gloomy with low cloud grazing the rooftops. Splendid cream and brown snails have come out to slip across the rain-slicked pavement and long pale bloated worms have been washed into cracks between the cobbles and appear like the marks of an unknown language.

Raingarde is running out, frightened to see me here in Carcassonne, unannounced, with all my household, and I am in her embrace.

'I knew there was something wrong,' she says looking enquiringly into my face. 'What has happened?'

'Let's go in.'

This is just a temporary respite. I can't stay here. He means to repudiate me, to incarcerate me and if he cannot do it in the night by subterfuge and violence, then he will seek to do it with the law and with bribes, and all the while, my belly will begin to betray me.

There is a pheasant in the orchard this morning, strutting inquisitively amidst Raingarde's herbs and fruit trees. Yesterday an eagle soared and circled above me as I stood looking out across the valley from the castle parapet. These birds are some portents but I don't know what they mean. I don't know what anything means anymore. There is nothing and no one on the road to the north, where Pons is, and nothing and no one on the road to the south, to Ramon. I picture Ramon hand in hand with his new wife, Blanca. Garsenda came last night to stay for a few days and Berenger with her, though he did not stay. He escorted her here and is gone now.

'A word with you in private, Countess,' he murmured in my ear, as my sister and Garsenda were greeting each other loudly by the hearth.

I rose quietly and took him to my chamber, gesturing to a stool. 'Please.' Yes Ramon would send word to me through him. He knows he can trust him. But his information was not from Barcelona.

'I am perplexed by some news I have heard, Countess, and I know not whether this will be of value to you, in which case I would wish to impart it, for I am your servant, Almodis,' he says with great sincerity (and I believe him), 'or perhaps this news is idle gossip and will only irritate you and have no grounds.'

My thoughts tumble through the possibilities.

'It is a sound source,' says Berenger, watching the expressions on my face, so I struggle to control them, to present a bland mask.

'Please tell me your news, Count. I will not hang the messenger,' I smile and he laughs lightly.

'My correspondent is in the Court of Aragon,' he says, 'in attendance on King Ramiro.'

Now I am bewildered and shake my head, raising my eyebrows, asking him to continue.

'Your lord, Count Pons, is in a delicate negotiation with Ramiro it seems.' Berenger stops.

'I know nothing of this,' I say. 'Pray continue. What is the nature of this negotiation?'

'It is concerning Ramiro's youngest daughter, Dona Infanta Sancha, concerning a marriage.' Berenger halts again, looking to me with anxiety on his face. 'A negotiation of marriage,' he repeats, to ensure that I have understood him. 'Perhaps it is on behalf of your son, Guillaume?' he ventures. 'Sancha is young. Thirteen or so.'

I clear my throat, trying to gain control of my voice before I speak. 'Yes, perhaps,' I say. 'Thank you, Viscount. This news is of value to me.' We look at each other. We both know that Pons is not negotiating marriage with the thirteen-year-old princess of Aragon on behalf of my son. Even if Pons does put me aside and get more heirs on this child, he will not disinherit my sons. They are near men now and he will not be able to displace them or wish to expose his house to the vulnerability of a child heir; and Audebert and Geoffrey would give Guillaume and Raymond their military support to enforce their rights if it were necessary. I rise and convey Lord Berenger back to the company where he takes his leave. I know Pons' plan in full now but what is mine? For once, I am a blank, an empty vessel. I must resolve on some course of action. I cannot remain in this state of limbo. My head aches and is full of fug. My side aches. I have not slept for three nights.

Three days comforted with Raingarde, safe for now. I have told no one, not even my sister, of my condition. She knows I am holding something back.

'Can I help you Almodis? Please tell me what you are not telling me.'

But I cannot. It will not help to let go of my secret. It will just make me mope and feel sorry for myself and I can't afford that.

'A messenger is here,' Dia comes in quickly, 'from Lord Ramon.'

'Show him in,' I say feigning calm. The man she brings in has the look of a sailor and is a musulman, his skin dark brown like stained wood. He introduces himself as a captain in the service of the Emir of Tortosa.

'Please sit,' I say. 'Bring us sweetmeats and wine, Bernadette.'

She circles him at a distance as if he is a wild cat that will pounce on her suddenly if she comes within his reach. She places his wineglass so far from him that even stretching he could not reach it. I know, in her xenophobic little mind, she is thinking 'long ways, long lies'. I frown at her and move the glass to his hand.

'You are very welcome, Captain Alfaric.'

'Thank you gracious Queen,' he says. 'My master is an ally of Ramon of Barcelona. They are also great friends.' He sips his wine. 'It is not often that one comes across a man so open, so intelligent, full of such a grip on life, as the Count of Barcelona.'

I nod and keep my face neutral.

'I have a ship at Narbonne, Lady, a fine ship named *Wave Walker*, and it is my wish, my very great wish, to place this ship, at your command.'

I cannot believe what he is saying for a moment. Escape? Ramon is offering me escape? But to what? I wait but he says no more. 'Do you have orders for the destination of this ship,' I ask eventually.

'I have only your orders, Queen Almodis,' he bows. 'I and the ship know the way well to Barcelona of course. The tide is good to sail at daybreak but we near the edge of the sailing season and soon it will be dangerous to put to sea. I will wait for you for three days, three daybreaks starting tomorrow,' he says.

I need to be alone, to think. What does Ramon mean by this? He does not come himself. 'Thank you, Captain,' I say, rising. 'You may leave now and I will consider your kind offer. If I should decide on a voyage I will be with you in Narbonne before daybreak, before the tide, on one of the next three days.'

He rises with me, bows low, kisses my hand, and is gone.

What would Ramon do with me if I reached Barcelona? Perhaps he means to 'retire' me too. I would be an inconvenience. He would offer me a kinder retirement than Pons' anchorite cell to be sure: abbess of a luxurious convent near Barcelona or offered as wife to one of his allies. My stomach churns at the thought of yet another man, not of my choosing, with rights over my body.

Or, I will not be Ramon's unwed paramour bearing him bastard children, hidden away, whilst Blanca is his countess. If he thinks that he is mistaken.

My children need me to be out in the world, negotiating their marriages and legal matters, giving them advice, standing as regent for them if – and here I indulge myself in a prolonged fantasy: if Pons should die in agony from a disease that attacks first his genitals and then his bowels – then Guillaume who is yet twelve would need me to stand regent for him. I would have to act as Regent of Toulouse.

I return to my own situation. If Ramon's intentions are not to my liking then what options do I have? None of my children are old enough to offer me a home. Would Hugh take me back? Again I linger in a fantasy of that, but no, he could not. He could not shelter scandal, raise the enmity of Pons and the Court of Aquitaine against himself. I could write to Audebert and he would have to take me but what then? I would be a shamed and repudiated wife in his household, a single woman with no role, no point, with less status even than my youngest sister. Audebert, would I fear, be inclined to send me to a nunnery himself, to avoid embarrassment. Perhaps my mother and I could set up house together in one of my properties, but whilst I was in Occitania, with no military, no male, protection, I would be vulnerable to any violence Pons cared to make against me. So I am facing Ramon's offer, whatever that is, or a nunnery. I could buy the post of abbess somewhere agreeable I suppose, but again I would have to leave my children to fend for themselves in worldly matters if I did so and I have no inclination to it.

At dawn, two days after Alfaric's visit I know I must go to the ship at Narbonne. I have no choices. I must leave behind everything I have built here in my county of Toulouse over the last twelve years. I rouse my household and Dominic, my Sergeant at Arms, with his cohort of five soldiers, and I tell them to prepare to ride with me. I creep to Raingarde's door and rest my head against the wood. I cannot go in. Her husband would wake and then the whole house. I have left her a farewell note telling her not to worry.

226

We have left the city far behind. The road is still dark and not far ahead I can just see that it enters thick woods. We have been riding for an hour. We all have our hoods raised against the heavy rain but even so I feel like I have been dunked in a puddle. Everything is dripping: the trees we are riding through, the edge of my hood, my nose. My hands are cold and underneath my cloak, my thighs are wet. We bedraggled women and children ride in the centre of the group on five horses, with the soldiers around the edges, protecting us. Bernadette has four-year-old Adalmoda clutched in front of her. Five-year-old Hugh is perched in front of his aunt Lucia. Dia is riding her beautiful Spanish horse and Melisende, who is twelve now, manages her own horse well. As the trees around us become thicker and thicker the soldiers crowd closer to us and I sense they are on the watch for trouble.

'Are you watching out for bandits?' I ask Sir Dominic.

'Them and the pixies, trolls and hobgoblins also,' Dominic responds with a completely serious look on his face.'

'Th-th-uu-tt!'

An arrow wings past my ear and strikes deep into a tree behind him.

'Defense position!' shouts Sir Dominic.

'Th-th-uu-tt! Th-th-uu-tt!'

There are more arrows in the air twisting at high speed and clanging against armour. One of the men falls from his horse, an arrow protruding from his neck. My soldiers raise their shields over the heads of their charges and maneuvre the whinnying horses towards the cover of the trees. They draw their swords, so I follow suit, dragging my knife out of its scabbard. Reaching the edge of the trees, I see that one of my soldiers has Dia on the ground, sheltered under his shield. Bernadette, Lucia and Melisende have dismounted and run a little way into the trees with my two young children. I glimpse Hugh's wide eyes and Adalmoda with her face buried in Bernadette's skirts. I stay on my horse and wonder if flight is an option.

A large group of well-armed men ride out of the trees on the other side of the path and they far out-number us. 'Stay back, Lady,' Dominic shouts to me and he and the five soldiers advance to engage in combat. Swords ring loudly in the cold air, spears are flung and thrust, maces and axes whirl and slice horribly above men's soft heads. Soldiers fall from horses, squelching in mud, gasping in pain, rolling to try to avoid the bucking hooves of bloodied horses. Shouting and the clashing of arms echo loud in the quiet wood but it is all over quickly. The ground is strewn with my dead men and their horses are running aimlessly. Sir Dominic lies with his eyes open to the sky, a lance sticking from his ribs. The attackers circle behind us and herd us close together. They hold us at swordpoint, catching their breath. The leader rides up to me and wrenches the knife from my hand, lifts his visor, and I see that it is Piers.

'Vicar Piers, what is the meaning of this? Is this *paratge*?' I say, meaning what is right and honourable.

'Off the horse,' he says brusquely, as if he has never met me before. Afraid for my children, looking at the terror in Melisende's face, I comply. 'Tie their hands. Put the hoods and gags on them,' he says, emphasizing the word 'gags' as he looks at me.

The men have placed brown wool hoods over Dia and Lucia's heads and I can see Lucia desperately sucking her breath in and out through the fabric. Forcing a confidence into my face and my voice that I do not truly have, I call out to my children before they lose sight of me. 'Do not fear little ones. You are the royal children of the House of Toulouse.' I turn to hiss quietly to Piers, 'And only a craven fool would touch you.'

'They'll not be harmed,' he says to me, avoiding my eyes.

Piers pauses with a hood in his hands in front of Bernadette who is shaking and weeping. 'Piers!' she implores piteously. He gently caresses her hair out of her eyes, tucks a few strands behind one of her ears and then places the hood over her face and her muffled cries. His expression shows that he finds he does not have as good a stomach for terrorising women and children as his master, Pons.

I step towards Piers, and the soldiers bruise my arms in their struggle to restrain me and keep me from him. I spit my words at him: 'You swore an oath of fealty to me, Piers, you proven traitor, you low-born bastard! You will not see February. I will cut off your arms and legs . . .'

I lay jolted in a carriage with the itchy hood over my head and face. My hands are tied tightly in front of me, a gag is forcing wide my lips and tastes foul. There are other bodies and muffled noises around me in the carriage. I long to reassure my children. I breathe hemp and will myself to stay calm. I want to vomit but then I would die.

31

Flight from a Window

The cart stops. We have arrived somewhere. Hands pull me roughly from the cart and drag me on unsteady legs across wet grass. The hood is pulled off and the gag removed. I can't see for minutes and double over coughing, heaving. My hands are still tied in front of me. Eventually my eyes adjust and I see a grass square surrounded on all sides by red and cream brick cloisters. Piers, looking ashamed of himself, and a stern-featured nun, are standing before me. I cannot be in Moissac. It is much further than we have travelled.

'Where am I?' I demand.

'You are a guest of the Abbess of Lagrasse, Countess,' the nun says, 'on the orders of the Count of Toulouse. Please come with me.'

'It is impossible for me to walk like this,' I say. 'Untie my hands.'

Piers looks at the nun hesitant, but she nods and he cuts the rope around my wrists. The pain in my wrists becomes worse now that my arms are freed. Piers no doubt has not fared well for his failure to take me straight from Toulouse to Moissac last week and looks determined to brook no dereliction of his orders now. I go meekly enough with the nun but I determine that no sleeping draught will pass my lips and I will be making no onward leg of this journey to Moissac. I size up the nun.

We arrive in the guest dormitory on the first floor where I am relieved to find my household is unharmed, although they are shocked and afraid. The dormitory is flooded with morning sunlight and there are two neat rows of beds. It seems almost normal. Bernadette is holding Adalmoda on her lap. Dia is holding Melisende's hand and Lucia and Hughie sit close to Bernadette. I see on the other side of the room that there are two other maids who I do not know. Other more willing visitors I suppose. Perhaps they could take a message of our plight to Carcassonne or Narbonne.

'You will be served food in here and you should rest, Countess,' the nun says. 'You have a long journey ahead of you.'

'What of my family and women? Will they travel with me?'

'Back to Toulouse, I think,' she blurts out and bites her lip, no doubt under instruction to tell me nothing. She hands me a goblet of wine.

'Thank you,' I say. 'Leave us now.'

She looks at me in surprise, unaccustomed to being commanded perhaps, and she glances at the goblet which I have set down on the trestle.

'Go,' I say menacingly, taking a step towards her.

When she is gone, I empty the contents of the goblet into the unlit hearth and turn back to the dishevelled huddle of my women and children. 'There was a sleeping draught in it,' I say. 'They mean to ship me to Moissac.'

'So I will go in your stead and you will make your escape on this ship that is waiting for you in Narbonne.' I am amazed to hear Raingarde's voice and to see her throwing back her hood. She is one of the unknown 'maids' on the other side of the room. 'Why didn't you tell me,' she demands, and there is real anger in her voice.

For a moment I am speechless. I see that the other woman is Carlotta. 'How did you get here?' Then, only just realising what I have heard her say, 'And no, you will go nowhere in my stead.'

'I knew there was something wrong. I had Carlotta watch you and when you all slunk off at dawn, we came with you. Two more maids. It made no difference to the men at arms at the back of the company.' She is looking very pleased with herself. 'You see,' she says, 'you are not the only clever one.'

'Oh, Raingarde, I do not wish you here! Embroiled in my troubles.'

'Dia has explained everything to me: that Pons plans to incarcerate you and to take the Aragon princess to wife,' she finishes, looking unreasonably cheerful. 'We change clothes,' she says. 'You go now. I will feign sleep and let them take me to the boat. I have left word with my husband that bad business is afoot and he will need to rescue me. You must send him word when you reach Narbonne to wait for me at the dock in Moissac.' With Carlotta's help she has already taken off half her clothes and is handing them to Bernadette, who puts down Adalmoda and approaches me with them. 'Come on, quick. We don't know how long we have and the boat will only wait for you until sunrise tomorrow.'

I protest and refuse but they all assist her in disrobing me and swapping our clothes. I am desperate at the thought of Raingarde walled up in that cloister.

'My husband will find me,' she says, certain.

'They will mistreat you. You have no idea what could happen to you.'

'And you should suffer it but I cannot?'

'I will go with her,' says Carlotta, surprising us all for she is usually so silent, and she draws a vicious hunting knife from her boot and then sheathes it again.

'They will notice one maid is missing.'

'If they do, we shall say that she climbed out the window but the rest of us were too afraid to follow.'

I look dubiously at the window. An old oak stands close by and it is just conceivable I suppose to leap across and climb down through its branches. If you were an acrobat.

'Go on,' says Raingarde, pushing me to the window.

I resist her, but she does not give up shoving me. 'I can't do that!'

'For large evils, great remedies, mistress,' Bernadette cries out.

'I will ensure that the children and your women are sent on to you. They will not suffer. Do it, Almodis, now!'

All this time I thought she was my shadow, a pale reflection, my gentle sister in contrast to my hard grip on life and power but

I see her standing there in my clothes and I see that I have been wrong. She is my brave sister. I look round quickly at each of their faces, I take a deep breath, I wriggle my feet in my boots for good purchase, I grip the window frame and haul myself up onto the sill. Unfortunately I look down and am immediately dizzy and irresolute. I should tell them I am with child and just can't . . . but then without thinking about it, without deciding, I am flying, really flying. I collide with a branch and the wind is punched out of me. I slither ungainly down the tree, coming to the ground with a thud that winds me again. I look up at their faces crammed into the stone frame of the window, signal that I am fine and set off running to the trees.

In the forest I find an ass tethered outside a hut. I dare not wake the people sleeping inside and ask for help in case they betray me back to the abbey. I silently slip the animal's rope, coax him into cover and make my way, travelling close to the river, looking for a boat that might carry me to Narbonne, thinking all the while that I should surely miss Tortosa's captain, that he will sail without me. I think of the story my father told me of how on campaign once he tricked his pursuers by putting cloven cow-shoes onto his horses' feet. I pass a small cave with a shrine to the Virgin strung with flowers and small offerings: a baby's shoe, a rotting veil. 'Protect me mother Mary,' I whisper to her. 'I wish to be a mother to this child.'

At last I see a small, shallow-bottomed boat bobbing near the bank. It has a long pole and a paddle. I loose the ass to find his way home; I thank him and regret the loss of his living company as I face the river to continue my journey alone. I step into the rocking boat and pole myself away from the bank and into the centre of the river where the current takes me forward swiftly. It is nearing twilight and clouds of mosquitos and midges hover above the surface of the water. Green trees and rushes rise up on both sides all around me, green reflected in the water, even the sky is tinged with green as the light fades. I feel a sense of unreality moving through this shrouded world. I fear at any moment that armed men will burst through the green curtain to the water's edge and haul me by my hair from the river to a stone prison.

This is the river Orbieu which eventually will join with the Aude and take me all the way to the port of Narbonne. I am hungry, thirsty, weary, chilled to the bone and my ankle throbs where I landed badly on it. I need only fend off the bank or fallen trees on occasion or pole myself through choked and shallow parts of the river. Cicadas begin their frictions. At dusk the Devil is abroad is one of Bernadette's sayings. I wish I hadn't remembered it. I must go on through the darkness in order to get past the towns of Fabrezan and Ferrals unseen. At Ferrals a watchman calls out, 'Who's there?', but I pole myself into the centre of the river where the current is strong and pass by silently in the gloom.

Before the Orbieu joins the Aude, I haul my boat onto the bank, meaning to rest a moment before I attempt to pass Narbonne and anyone watching for me. I am bone tired. 'Lady!' A hiss in the trees terrifies me but I see that it is Captain Alfaric.

'How did you know I was here?' I say amazed.

'A letter from your sister, told me you were in trouble and to look out for you,' he says, giving me more cause for surprise at Raingarde's effectiveness. She must have sent this letter as we were leaving Carcassonne. He helps me haul my boat further into the trees where it will not be seen and then tells me to follow him a little upriver where his own boat is waiting. As we walk I explain what has happened: how my sister Raingarde has taken my place with my kidnappers and how I must get word to her husband. Alfaric frowns and grimaces all the way through my story. 'Such deceit and betrayal. Such violence to a beautiful lady,' he says tasting the words as if they are curdled milk in his mouth.

'You cannot go to Berenger,' Alfaric says. 'Pons is in Narbonne and the city is swarming with Toulousain men-at-arms. They must be watching to make sure you do not break from your captors and attempt a sea escape. We must carry on along the river straight to the port and my ship, and elude them.' He points out another small boat, waiting for us, but this one has four oarsmen for speed. Alfaric hands me to a cushioned seat in the boat and takes his own seat behind me at the helm. The four oarsmen smile at me. At Alfaric's soft commands they quickly pick up a pace, moonlight glinting on the sweat of their faces, biceps and thighs as they move back and forwards together, and the boat thrusts and jerks ahead. Now that I am become a passenger, I begin to shake with cold and stress. My teeth chatter and my stomach is churning on its own hunger. Alfaric drapes a thick blanket around my shoulders and hands a wine skin to me. I take a long draught of the strong wine and feel warmed.

As night falls we draw near the walls of Narbonne. On one bank is the city and on the other its new town, the Bourg. We travel under the seven-arched Roman bridge that carries the old Roman Road, the Via Domita, that splits in four directions, to Spain, Toulouse, Aquitaine and the Atlantic. In the gloom I can just make out the butchers, at the end of their day's work, discharging blood and offal into the river.

Alfaric changes the sail on the mast to a plain red one and the soldiers cover the coat of arms of Barcelona on their surcoats with their large woollen cloaks. I cover my head and part of my face with a hood. The soldiers look uneasy. If we are caught now we will be in a world of trouble. Everyone keeps as silent as possible and the lamps are doused. I listen to the lap of the water against the boat and against the walls.

I recognize the shape and position of the guest chamber where I stayed the night that Ramon was there. 'That's likely Pons' chamber, up there,' I whisper. This is the most dangerous part, if someone should happen to look out at the river and see me. I try to keep my eyes on the deck and hold my breath, catching a glimpse of that window slowly opening. A woman's head appears and then a bucket and a stream of urine is thrown into the river, close to where our boat is hugging the wall.

'If it comes to a fight there's nothing to worry about,' one of the soldiers whispers. 'We've got Morning Star and Good-day and Holy Water Sprinkler here to safeguard you.'

'What's that?' I ask puzzled. 'Is it magic?'

'No Lady, this here is Morning Star,' says one soldier holding up his huge mace, a club with blades sticking out of the top.

'And this is Good-day,' says another in a low voice, holding up an equally evil looking weapon, 'and Captain Alfaric's,' he says pointing at another mace leaning against the boat's side, 'is the one called Holy Water Sprinkler. Do you get it?'

'Quiet,' hisses Alfaric. 'We don't want to be using our

weapons on the townsmen if we can help it, whatever their damned names are.'

They fall silent. When the boat has passed the city we heave a collective sigh of relief.

At its mouth the Aude opens up into the great bay of Narbonne where ships lay at anchor protected by the hills from winds from the north, and by islands and a line of sand bars from the Mediterranean sea storms. I hear the sound of a treacly, lazy sea washing back and forth across rolling pebbles.

The rowers pull us into a dark pier and one man takes a note that I have written to Raingarde's husband and a purse from Alfaric and disappears towards the harbour front in search of a safe messenger. We wait in silence. Two of the rowers grip the edge of the pier, holding the boat in place; the third is crouched on the pier with the rope in his hands ready to cast us off in seconds if we are threatened with discovery. I can hear drunken singing from a nearby tavern, a wild shriek of a woman's laughter, the boat bumping gently against the pier. Thick clouds have covered the moon and it is pitch-dark. I begin to wonder if the man with my note has been taken. Then he jumps softly into his place, nods briefly to me and Alfaric, and we are moving again, making for the black expanse of the harbour.

We are running dark, relying on the sweep of the lamp from the lighthouse to help us navigate our way between the other boats. Alfaric must remember the position of anchored ships and our route through them, with each brief flash of illumination. We pass through narrow gaps between vast warships that could crush us to kindling in seconds, their curved wooden sides disappearing far above our heads like mountain slopes, the eagle's nest lookouts at the top of their high masts dipping and swaying. Occasionally we bump and scrape against another boat. I keep my hands clenched in my lap, away from the edge of the boat.

The rowers bring us alongside a cog: a round, tub-like merchant's ship with a single bank of thirty-two oars and a square sail. 'Attracts less attention than a warship,' Alfaric grins at me, handing me carefully to the knotted rope ladder that dangles against the side of the swaying ship. I swallow, feeling gray with exhaustion, desperately trying to muster the mental energy for the climb.

My arms and legs feel powerless as I climb but I hang on. I feel stabbing pains in my womb and fear that I will miscarry my child. Nearing the top, grinning faces crowd the edge of the ship, and strong arms and hands reach down to haul me up. I lean, gasping on the ship's rail, nodding at the sailors, unable to speak.

Alfaric comes up beside me. 'We are only days, perhaps hours, ahead of the bad weather when all ships take to the harbours for the winter, but never fear, Lady, we shall get you to your destination.' The sailors are swarming around us, tying ropes, unfurling sails, setting the oars. There is barely any wind and they row us towards the narrow mouth of the harbour. It seems to take forever as the ship creaks and lumbers but steadily picks up speed. I look back towards the harbour front and the towers of the city, straining to see any signs of pursuit.

'Lay down, Lady, quickly,' Alfaric says urgently. I do so and a blanket falls over me. The ponderous rhythm of the boat slows and stalls again. I hear voices: Alfaric calling out his business to an interrogator, giving plausible replies to someone on a boat guarding the harbour mouth. I lie still and silent, breathing damp wool and wood and the faintly acrid scent of a man who has lain recently in this blanket. I think we are moving again but I am disorientated and uncertain. We may be going backwards or forwards or it may only be the rock of the sea that I detect.

Alfaric lifts the blanket from my head and I blink like a woodlouse found under a log. 'We're safe,' he says, pointing to the harbour mouth, dimly discernible and now behind us. He takes my hands and lifts me to my feet, conveys me to a narrow cabin with a bed piled high with blankets and pillows, a flagon of wine and a basket of bread and meat on the table.

'This looks like heaven,' I say. 'I am greatly in your debt Captain Alfaric.'

'No, Lady. I am honoured to serve you. You look very tired and I will leave you to rest.'

He's right. I fall back on the soft pillows, too exhausted to reach out my hand and eat, too exhausted to close my eyes and sleep.

I wake, my back aching, to a dull, overcast morning and an expanse of open sea all around us. This grey sky, this grey sea, look beautiful to me; they look like freedom. I taste the salt in the air and it is freedom. I watch curious as the sailors try to use a board with the shadow of the sun to find the way. They navigate without sight of land. 'And in fog and heavy cloud?' I ask Alfaric, when he approaches me.

'We have a sun-stone,' he says, mysteriously. 'It shows us north. Or failing that, we have these ravens,' he says pointing to three birds staring at me fiercely from a cage. I shake my head, not comprehending. 'We release them and follow them till they find land. That works,' he says cheerfully. He hands me a packet. 'For you, Lady, from the Count of Barcelona.' He bows and leaves me.

Inside there is a short letter: *Dearest Almodis, I trust you are safe with the sea-captain of my ally Tortosa. He will bring you to me.* I am a cargo again, I think. Me and my unborn child. *Know Almodis that I would give every river in Catalonia and risk all if you will have me.* I sit up straight. Not a paramour then? *I ask you for your hand in marriage. I do not sue for you to your brother or your mother, for you are your own captain and will answer for yourself.* I am smiling now. Ramon! He knows me. *If you will have me, radiant Almodis,* (again I smile, he was ever full of flattery and hyperbole) *I will endeavour to make each of your days, henceforth, happy ones. I await you and your reply. Ramon Berenger, Conde de Barcelona.* Almodis, Condessa de Barcelona, I think, rolling it aloud on my tongue. It sounds good.

There is more: a scroll on fine vellum with the seal of Barcelona depicting a walled city by the sea. I break the seal and begin to unroll it. It is a contract of betrothal. A memory of my marriage contract with Hugh flashes in my mind: me, a girl laughing in the kitchen, reading it to the cooks, scolded by my mother. This contract begins with the arms of La Marche and Barcelona entwined. Ramon has signed it at the bottom and there is a place for me to sign.

Not yet. I will savour a few more days when I belong to no man. I watch the sailors swinging the sail to find the wind. I roll the contract up carefully and stow it back in its packing. I, and the child in my belly, are lulled by the rhythm and roll of the sea.

Yet still I doubt him. Is he not also betrothed to Blanca and does he not treat that betrothal lightly?

Part Three

BARCELONA

1052–1071

32

Michaelmas 1052

I sit on the pink marble window-seat in my new chambers in the Comital Palace, bathing in the early morning sun that streams into the room. 'Good morning world,' I say aloud. I close my eyes, breathe in the citrus smells of Barcelona, knowing that to the north, in Toulouse, winter is closing in. The caws of seagulls mingle with the bells of the city's towers, the honking of geese, and the hammers and shouts of workmen at the cathedral building site next door. I open my eyes again and look about me. Ramon has prepared these rooms for me with great care. Cheerful ceramic tiles cover the floor, decorated with pictures of salamanders. Twenty or more pitchers stand about the room filled with white and red roses. 'The flower of submission,' he said. A large platter on the seat beside me is heaped with green apples, purple plums and oranges. I pick up an apple, savour its scent and bite into it. The view from the window is glorious: immediately below is a walled garden lined with lemon and fig trees with paths made from tiny shells, and then I can look out across the maze of city streets to the blue of the sea beyond and the shimmer of heat rising.

When I arrived last night, the wooden wharf was lit by a hundred torches and lamps, revealing the pale stone of the high city walls in the near-distance, and close by, the massive shipyards where the war fleet was being variously built, repaired, docked, for the winter. Myriad merchant ships were rocking at anchor in the harbour, their riggings clanging and whizzing in the high night wind. Ramon stood on the wharf and handed me off the ship. He took me in a long embrace and then straightened out his arms to hold me back and look at me.

'Thank God and his saints. Are you alright?'

'It is your child, my Lord,' I said, seeing him eyeing my stomach, and not bothering to give the evident answer to his question.

'My child?' he said, looking at me with wonder in his face, 'and you did not write to tell me so?'

I made no reply. I was tired and inexplicably cross with him.

'Well,' he said eventually, necessitated by the awkward silence, 'I am doubly delighted and amazed. Welcome to your new home, my Lady, my Countess?' he said.

Is he laughing at me, I thought. I am bedraggled, filthy and fat. Stubbornly, I kept my silence. I am alone in a strange land, stripped of my household, made vulnerable by my pregnancy and my flight from convention. I hate the notion that I am dependent on him.

He handed me to a carriage that took us to the palace. We passed through the gate of the new walls and then, soon after, another gateway in the old Roman wall that rings the centre of the city. On the journey I had to break my silence: 'Raingarde? Have you news?'

'She is safe in Carcassonne. Her husband was at Moissac, waiting to rescue her from that stone cell. I understand that she gave the abbot a red-hot telling-off.'

I smiled at the thought of Raingarde, indignant with that long hound-faced Abbot.

'Your children and women are safe too in Narbonne. They will come on to Barcelona as soon as the sailing season begins again.'

Inside the entrance to the palace, there was a small, brown-eyed girl curtseying to me. 'This is your maid, Marta,' he said. 'She will take care of you until Bernadette arrives. It is late and perhaps you would wish to retire now, or,' he hesitated, 'would you grace me with a short visit later?' he said hopefully.

'I am very tired my Lord and need to bathe after my journey.' I indicated my clothes which were the same maid's clothes I had been wearing since I left Lagrasse. I had done what I could to keep them fresh but they were tattered and grimy nevertheless. Looking down at them, I felt humiliated. 'I beg you, that we might speak tomorrow.'

'Of course,' he said, 'you will find everything you need in your chambers. I cannot tell you how glad I am that you are here and safe, Almodis.'

In my sunny window-seat I am lost in reverie, wondering at my cold behaviour to him last night, when he was so courteous to me, so that Marta's appearance in the doorway makes me jump. 'Count Ramon asks to visit you this morning my Lady, if he may?'

'Please show him in.' I feel more myself now and sit up straight in anticipation. He takes me by surprise, dispensing with small talk: 'May I ask Lady Almodis why you didn't write and tell me of the child? What would you have done? Passed the child off as Pons'?'

'Perhaps,' I say with irritation. 'In truth, I hadn't yet decided what I would do.'

He looks flabbergasted. 'I don't understand why you didn't write and tell me!'

'I assumed that you could not, would not, act. That you would have to marry Blanca.'

He looks distressed. 'You assume too much.' He rearranges his face into an expression of tenderness. 'It is possible to be *too* independent you know, Almodis.' He reaches out a hand to stroke my cheek with the back of one finger, and I feel a little softened at his touch.

'Nobody looked after me from when I was five,' I say. 'I felt the loss of Raingarde like a wound when I was a child. I grew used to surviving without help, to nursing my own troubles.'

'Well now you will have to grow used to a smothering love instead,' he jokes.

I smile wanly. For some reason I cannot explain to myself I am holding out against him. We don't really know each other. I have thrown myself into a strange place. I am a scandal and a repudiated wife. I am stripped of my possessions, my rights, my children. Ramon reassures me that he intends to negotiate all for me and everything will be well, but I cannot stop myself from thinking that perhaps he weds me only because he must, a shamed fugitive from my life because of one moment of weakness with him.

'Will you meet my son?' he asks.

I smile at that. 'Yes of course, I would be delighted to meet him.'

He gestures to Marta who returns five minutes later with Pere, a tall, gangly, ten year old. He has black hair and brown eyes, perhaps like his mother. He looks around the room as if he is searching for something. He is quiet and when he does speak he is a little surly. 'This is my mother's room,' he says to me, a hint of challenge in his voice. It will take time for him to get used to me, and he clearly resents that I am encroaching on his father's attention. 'Will you show me your horse and falcon?' I ask him trying to win him around.

'Tomorrow, perhaps,' he says.

Ramon shrugs cheerfully. 'He misses his mother.'

I would like to hold Pere, kiss his soft cheek, inhale his child-scent to remind me of my own absent children, but it is clear that he would not welcome any such attention from me.

'I have arranged for us to wed at the monastery of Sant Cugat in two days time,' Ramon says, 'if it pleases you.' He looks uncomfortable, uncertain.

'Two days,' I say, surprised.

'Does it not please you?' There is irritation in his voice now.

'Such haste,' I say after a moment's hesitation. 'Should we not rather delay it until next week so that we might invite your allies to attend?'

He looks at me with admiration. 'You're right,' he says. 'We shall do just that.'

I ask Marta to bring us two goblets of Vin d'Orange and we toast our betrothal.

Pere sits silently in the window-seat that I have vacated, swinging his legs, staring at me.

I arrived with nothing and Ramon has given me a queen's trousseau and along with it, a new horse, falcon, and groomsman, which makes me think bitterly of Piers' betrayal. When Ramon and Pere have left me, Marta shows me a yellow wedding dress with very fine Spanish lace, and this reminds me of my lost husband, Hugh. Perhaps it is the pregnancy that is making me so emotional and yet so cold and lacklustre to Ramon. I am clearly puzzling him, and myself too. He has given me betrothal gifts that took my breath away with their beauty: a shoulder brooch made from gold, tiny pearls and emeralds; a gold and black enamel cross pendant; a ring set with a turquoise which Marta tells me protects against riding accidents, poison and drowning; a minature padlock of gold and white enamel engraved with the words: 'of all my heart'.

In the days before my marriage I talk to Marta and sometimes to Ramon to find out as much as I can about my new home. I savour the distinctive smell of almonds as I enter the kitchen, on a tour of inspection of the palace. Everything is in good order and this is quite unlike my arrival in Toulouse. Barcelona has four gates, two of which belong to Ramon and two to the bishop. The market takes place next to one of Ramon's gates and brings in a great deal of income. I put on plain clothes and a maid's apron and accompany Marta there that I might see the place and listen to the Catalan, subtly different to my Occitan. I go arm in arm with her down narrow winding streets with houses rising up high on either side, colourful laundry strung above our heads, birds swaying in cages, children and grandmothers dressed in black, sitting on doorsteps. The market is bustling and we stroll past stalls with sacks of buckwheat and peas, jars of olive oil, baskets of garlic and cabbages, bags of prunes. One stall is hung with rabbit and squirrel furs and the pelts of cats, wolves and ermine. Everything is here, from small to large, from scissors and needles to masts, oars and anchors.

Barcelona was a Muslim city before it was conquered by the Frankish king Charlemagne and there are signs of its mixed heritage everywhere around me. The city is surrounded by vineyards, and farmland where the harvest is just beginning. A water channel flows along the route of the old Roman aqueduct from the Besòs River. Commerce flourishes alongside the walls of the city and also in the new part known as the Born. Merchants, moneylenders, craftsmen, shopkeepers cram into these spaces selling and buying hides, iron, food, cloth, spices, silver, skins. Ramon tells me that there are near 4,000 people living here. Ramon's vicar, who is called a *vaguer* here, collects his taxes and tributes for him, managing his mint, market, mills, ovens and water mills.

'Our domain extends along the Llobrigat and Cardener Rivers, as far as the Montsec Mountains,' Ramon tells me. 'The main trade routes are the spice route and the route of the islands, from the Balearics, Sicily and Sardinia. Barcelonese merchants compete along these routes with the Genoese, Pisans and Toulousains. We hold an annual trade fair in July and have to build a special compound for all the visiting merchants,' he says. 'The city exports fustian and linen cloth, cereals, olive oil, wine, figs, leather, woollen cloth from Languedoc, naval supplies and weapons from Southern Spain and Italy. And,' he says, 'we import cumin, goat hides, fruit from Maghrib in North Africa and ginger, cinnamon, pepper, dyes and alum from the East. Our shipyards are famous, our wood apparently impervious to rot and insects.'

I laugh at his humorous, hyperbolic descriptions, amazing myself with the sound of my own laughter that it seems I have not heard in ages.

He explains that his military campaigns to the south have resulted in annual tribute being paid in gold by the Taifa lords from Lleida, Tortosa and Saragossa in exchange for peace and protection. The city's advocates and judges use a book of Visigothic legislation handed down from the sixth century, the *Liber Iudiciorum*. The people take an afternoon siesta and live life at a slower pace caused by the heat of the sun and the brighter bluer light. One afternoon, Ramon came into my rooms at siesta time and Marta scuttled out. 'Might I stay with you?' he asked and, at my nod, climbed onto the bed, behind me. He put his arms around me and his body against mine and kissed the back of my neck lightly. I felt a shiver of pleasure but stubbornly did not turn to him.

'Well, Marta, if I am to be a bride we must make some preparations.'

246

She bites her lip cheerfully, all smiles and anticipation. The night before my wedding I have her mix up the ingredients of Dia's recipe for golden hair: boxwood, broom, crocus and egg yolk cooked in water. Marta anoints my hair with the froth that collects on the top of this concoction. She lays out the yellow wedding dress with silver lace around the edges and a silver ribbon tying it up at the front. It flares out under the breasts in full folds so that my pregnancy is concealed. Ramon has given me a pair of gold filigree basket earrings that I put on and Marta admires. My slippers are gold and silver, but I put them in my saddlebag for the ride to the monastery and pull on the old riding boots that I arrived in. Ramon is looking splendid in a dark red velvet tunic with a jewelled sword at his waist. His buttons are fine enamels and his cap is adorned with a peacock feather. People line our route to the monastery cheering and waving flowers and hats. We are a romantic couple: the dashing count and his stolen bride.

'The counts of Barcelona are always married at Sant Cugat,' he tells me.

I try to respond to his conversation but find myself struck mute. He must think that he is marrying the most miserable woman in the world. We are wed with a blessing from Abbot Guitard. Now I have given my assent and am no longer Countess of Toulouse, but Countess of Barcelona.

We return to the city for the wedding feast in the Great Hall of the palace attended by his allies, including William, Lord of Montpellier, who I made an ally when I was in Toulouse. He gives me a tactful version of how my departure from Occitania and Toulouse has been received by my old neighbours there. The halls at Chateau Narbonnais and at Saint Gilles were enormous spaces full of people and bustle, but this Barcelonese court is even bigger, perhaps three times bigger and jammed full with visitors. Everywhere I look I see gold and silver thread, glinting in bright candlelight, faces that I do not know looking at me with curiosity. This court is dripping with prosperity. Unlike Toulouse and Lusignan, there is no obvious task of reorganisation necessary for me here. The people's warmth of feeling for their count is genuine. The great fire is tended by red-faced boys. Occasionally the log burns a brighter red and lets out a sudden bang and spark and the boys rush to ensure that the embers do not catch alight as they hit the sweet-smelling rushes.

I sit on the high table next to Ramon, wearing a gold crown on top of a thin green silk veil over my hair. My hands are covered with rings with green and red jewels. Ramon, too, wears a crown. He is clean-shaven and has a gold ring in one of his ears. I smile a very little because he is in fact a very handsome man.

Musicians play in the minstrel's gallery, accompanying the singers, the *jongleurs*; and *ioculators* or jesters, cavort between the tables. The giant door of the hall groans again on its hinges and a single man, with an instrument, strides up the aisle. 'Ah, the troubadour!' says Ramon, taking my hand. 'Music is essential to aid the digestion of food.' I laugh at that and he laughs with me, looking relieved. The troubadour sings about Ramon and myself. 'This is the lovers' music,' Ramon whispers to me. 'The music of *fin d'amour*, fine love.'

'I thought the convention was that the lover should love someone *other* than their marriage partner,' I say.

'We are the exception.'

'Such a great love had the lord for his lady,' sings the troubadour, 'that nothing could stand in its way. The mountains, the rivers, the snow and the ice must part for the love of the lady.'

The stories and singing come to an end and everyone is yawning and stretching. People start to lay out their cloaks to sleep on the floor.

'Shall we retire, my Countess,' he asks me with great courtesy. I rise and keep the wobble from my smile, remembering two other nightmarish wedding nights, but why should I worry with this husband? In the bed-chamber he sends the wedding party away as soon as the priest has blessed us and the bed, and he locks the door. He holds me gently. 'Perhaps you would wish to be left alone, since you are with child, darling?' he says, clearly not wishing it himself.

'No,' I say, forcing myself to unbend. 'I would not wish that.'

The light in his eyes at my response, is like a boy presented with his first puppy. Why is my mind so old and his so young? I run my hands over his blond head, tracing its beauty. Our loving in Narbonne had been done in the dark, in secret, but now we are man and wife and the candles are blazing, the room warm and scented with the perfume of so many roses. I place his fingers on the bow of silver thread at the top of my bodice.

33

Correspondence

Despite the kind companionship of my husband, I feel alone and exposed without my household – my women and my family who have always been around me. This is the first time I have been separated from Bernadette since I was ten years old. I remember when she arrived sullen and miserable from Paris. 'Don't you want to be here with me?' I asked her, but she would not answer me, just hung her head with tears trickling down her cheeks. 'Are you missing your mother and home,' I tried in Langue d'Oil.

She nodded her head at that, looking at me in surprise that I could speak her tongue. I took her hand. 'We shall be friends,' I told her and she looked abashed and curtseyed. In truth, it was hard for me to like her in the beginning with her complaining and her ridiculous sayings. If she hadn't done her work so well, I would have sent her back to her mother. She grew on me little by little and now I am bereft without her.

The ladies of the court keep me company but I miss the easy and intelligent company of Dia. Yet to be rid of Pons, I thank Saint Uncumber. Not to be walled up in the anchorite cell in Moissac, I thank the Virgin. To have Ramon to husband . . . yes, I warm to him. I look to where he is standing in the passage talking to a huntsman. Ramon is flamboyant in a tunic of orange trimmed with black. I like him. It would be impossible not to like him.

Pere lingers close to his father's elbow. He is always with him, like a faithful hound. He refuses all my invitations to come and speak with me, to play at tables or chess, to ride together. 'Not now,' he says, or just shakes his head. 'Sorry,' he says, but there is no remorse in his voice or his gaze.

'Tell me something of the history of Barcelona my Lord, and of the Taifa lords,' I say to Ramon.

'My father sought peace with the Taifa lords but my grandmother wished to drive them from their lands in the name of God.'

'And you?'

'I must strengthen my comital control first, stabilise my relationships with my neighbours across Catalonia before I can consider the border with the south. The frontier lords, my neighbours, castellans, even some factions within the city have taken advantage of the years of minority rule, first by my father and then by me. Ermessende's base is in Girona and she has been intent on holding her own rights and not especially on holding mine for me, and what she has held she will not give up. Tribute from the Taifa lords is greatly enriching my counting house. I see no need to war in the south at present. I am on very good terms with Tortosa and the ruler of Dénia. My grandfather gave too much to Ermessende. His testament left her lands and powers well beyond her dower, lands that in custom would have gone to my father. The little that was left over when he died was divided between me and my two brothers. My brother, Sancho, decided to enter the church a few years ago and gave over his rights in the Penedès to me.'

'Your grandmother acts against you, against family.'

'Yes, it's true she does. She incites the rebel lords, Mir Geribert and Besalú, against me.'

'Why? What will she gain in the end by this?'

'She wishes to hold onto her own power. She thinks I innovate too much and should continue to defer to her advice. I have not thought so since I was fifteen. Since I saw you in Toulouse in fact and she disagreed so violently with me then, taking me away against my will. Now, of course, I have offended again and proven her view that I am not fit to rule by kidnapping you, causing a great scandal.'

251

'Perhaps she has a point,' I say.

'Am I not fit to rule with you my glorious queen?'

'Now you flatter me!'

'No, I don't think so. All Occitania sings praise of your government of Toulouse.'

'All Occitania! Berenger of Narbonne perhaps!'

'All.'

He is thoughtful for a moment. 'My grandmother is looking for ways to avoid relinquishing her power. She does not wish to be a dowager countess.'

'I can sympathise with that.'

'My father tried, unsuccessfully, to limit her to Girona.'

'She is a remarkable woman.'

'Oh certainly. My father died when I was eleven and she took control as my regent, even though my father had wanted the Count of Urgell to act for me. When I came of age I initially allied myself with the rebel lords in an attempt to challenge her. Then those same lords, led by Mir Geribert, rebelled against me; and factions in the city, led by Bishop Guislabert and the Viscount of Barcelona, who is married to my father's widow, his second wife, also rebelled against me. People went so far as to lob missiles from the clock tower of the cathedral at the comital palace!'

After a pause, I say, 'The system of the Council of Good Men works well in Toulouse. You could introduce that here. It is a way of acknowledging the leading men of the city rather than allowing them to grumble against you.'

'Will you organise it?'

'But you know the leading families, the personalities of people,' I say in surprise.

'And you will find it out,' he replies with certainty.

In every way he has involved me fully in government since I stepped off the ship. All orders and documents are issued in both our names, Conde Ramon and Condessa Almodis de la Marca, as it is in Catalan. I am getting used to this sound and the change in my fortunes.

It will be six months before my household can risk themselves to the sea voyage and they cannot come overland over the mountains in the winter or the spring mire and floods. Father Benedict has asked if he might return to the abbey and I have given him leave. I am very pleased that Rostagnus has asked to come to me. The bishop has given him permission and he will travel with Dia, Lucia, Bernadette, Melisende, Hughie and Adalmoda. Dia writes to me that they are the guests of Berenger and Garsenda in Narbonne who are lavishing affection on my children. Hughie and Adalmoda must be bewildered at my sudden disappearance. My poor babies, they will hardly remember me and will think that Bernadette is their mother. By the time they get here I will have another baby in my arms, Ramon's child, that will come in March. He asks me about my children.

'Adalmoda is four and Hughie is five. I have negotiated for him to go to Cluny. We have nicknamed him Hugh the Bishop. Melisende is the child of my first marriage and she is twelve now and betrothed to the son of the Lord of Parthenay.'

'You can be sure that Garsenda is taking good care of them.'

I am jealous at the loss of six months of Hughie's time with me. I have so little time with my sons. Ramon suggests that I keep him with me here in Barcelona until he is twelve or thirteen and then send him to Cluny.

'Dia was my principal *trobairitz* here,' he says, 'before I sent her to you as the gift of my love,' he kisses my hand. He besieges me with his love and kindness at every opportunity. 'It will be good to have her back here again.'

I must acquaint myself with Ramon's court and the political situation. Whilst I ruled in Toulouse, covertly and behind Pons' back, and in Lusignan because my lord could not, here it is clear that Ramon regards me as his co-lord and that my counsel is of the utmost importance to him. 'What,' he jests, 'did you think I married you for love! Did I risk all the opprobrium that is being heaped on our heads because of your beauty. No, no, it was merely your ability to write, count and organise that appealed you see.'

Despite his jokes, his every word and action breathes his love and yet I cannot allow myself to trust to it.

Ramon has received a letter from Countess Ermessende and passes it to me:

253

As you well know a marriage of inclination is strongly condemned in Catalonia and it is a miserable situation that you, the Count, should so fail in your duty. This marriage that you have engaged in is no marriage. Your true wife, Lady Blanca, waits for you to return to your senses and turn away from this lunacy. Children born of this outrage will be bastards.

I place my hand on my stomach. Ah good, I think, now I have something to do, something to contest.

The second letter he opens seems to cause him much more concern. 'It's from Rome,' he says, his face serious for once as he looks up and hands it to me. 'We are excommunicated and our marriage ruled illicit.'

I scan the document. This will undermine his authority.

'The church should stay out of the business of lords,' he says angrily.

'It is not entirely unexpected,' I say to him.

'It is my grandmother's doing.'

'With or without her intercession, it was inevitable.'

'My grandmother took Lady Blanca with her to Rome to complain of me to the pope.'

'It will not last,' I say. 'We will weather it and next year we will sue for it to be lifted. We will send emissaries to the pope. And gifts.'

He nods.

'We will hurry on the building of the new cathedral. Its dedication will win us favour.'

'Yes,' he says, squeezing my hand, 'you're right.'

He shows me around the new, half-built cathedral. 'If we die before its completion,' I say, 'since we are excommunicated, we would go to hell. What if I die in childbirth?'

'You won't die,' he says, blasé, 'and neither shall I. We have too much living to do together now.'

We knew that our marriage would carry a heavy price. The bad news continues to roll in over the next weeks.

'Besalú has broken fealty with me again.'

'Still, the majority of your neighbours have reconfirmed their allegiance.'

He nods. 'Thanks to your efforts.' Shortly after my arrival I began working on this, inviting and corresponding with the Counts of Urgell, Empurias, Pallars Sobirà and Pallars Jussà and all the neighbouring lords.

'Any good news?' he asks, gesturing at my correspondence.

'Yes. Dia has made the arrangements for my household's journey here in the spring, and my sister, Lucia, is coming with them.'

'Good!' he says, his expression brightening.

'My mother writes to offer us her allegiance.'

'Excellent!' he says and I smile wryly at him. It is hardly recompense for being excommunicated.

My brother has remained silent, neither condoning nor condemning my marriage. He sent me no wedding gift. I do not suppose that the scandal has been especially helpful or pleasant for him. However, my sons have all written to me. They seem so far away now.

'My son Jourdain writes from the Priory of Lusignan to tell me that he is working on a history of his grandfather, Hugh IV, and my sons who are training with Count Geoffrey in Angers, that is Hugh of Lusignan, Guillaume and Raymond of Toulouse, they have written together.'

Ramon raises his eyebrows, surprised I suppose that Pons' sons should write kindly to me.

'They are all *my* sons,' I say to him, jutting out my chin.

'So I shall be of little consequence, then,' he laughs, 'with our children?'

I shake my head, smiling. 'Shall I read you their letter,' I say.

'Please.'

'Chère maman, La Condessa de Barcelona, we greet you and kiss you and send you our happy wishes that you are safe and well. We decided to write to you together and tell you how dearly we love you and cherish you and will cut off the heads of anyone disparaging your name.' I look up laughing to Ramon. 'It is a boys' letter: Hugh is fifteen, Guillaume fourteen and Raymond thirteen. They tell me about their dogs and hunting and their bruises and scrapes from training and who is good at this and that.' I hand it to him to look at, to cheer him up. 'I suspect that the letter itself is the work of Raymond but they have all three signed it. And then there are five postscripts.'

'Five!'

'See: Raymond first writes in a postscript that his cousin, Audebert's daughter Almodis, is named for me and is very beautiful and Guillaume is mooning over her. Guillaume has written under that: Raymond is an ass. Then Raymond writes that Hugh has been chastised by Count Geoffrey for kissing the cook's daughter and seems to have gained some training from my old groom, Piers, who was well known for his womanising. So Hugh writes: Raymond is an ass. Finally Raymond adds that Hugh is rightly named 'The Devil'.'

News of my children lightens the bad news. Last week I received a formal letter from Pons repudiating me, signed by the Bishops of Toulouse and Albi. We hear that Sancha of Aragon will take ship in the spring to wed him, poor child. Pons' letter demanded the return of all his children, but in the case of Hugh the Bishop and Adalmoda I have refused on account of their age and in the case of Guillaume and Raymond they have written themselves from Geoffrey's camp at Domfront where he is now resisting the siege of Duke William of Normandy, to say that they cannot leave. Raymond wrote to me, 'I told father we will of course attend him when our training is completed and Count Geoffrey can spare us. I expect that to be quite a few years yet, Mother.'

Of course none of my family know the full circumstances of my flight, of Pons' threats to me, my adultery and pregnancy. Though they may all start calculating when my baby is born in March, none of them can prove it or be sure now that I am safe here with Ramon.

'Since a marriage of inclination is very much condemned here in Catalonia,' I say, 'why did you send Alfaric for me, especially since you didn't know that I was carrying your child.'

'I thought you might be convinced by the romance of me sending a musulman to whisk you away,' he says with characteristic levity.

I am surrounded by strangers again, including my husband and must get to know him. He is beautiful to look at. He is fair where Hugh was dark haired. His skin is olive brown and slides like silk under my hands. He is gentle, humorous, open-minded, quick-witted. I keep waiting for him to show some bad trait but, so far, none is evident.

34

Christmas 1052

'I have a surprise for you.'

'A surprise?'

Ramon takes my hand and I follow him out of the hall and into the wing of the palace where I knew he had some building work in hand. We reach a door, a high arched double door made from shining wood, faced with intricate silver metalwork in the shape of flowers with a gem at the heart of each.

'Oh, this is beautiful, Ramon,' I say, running my fingers along the maze of metal and jewelled blooms.

He laughs. 'That's just the door!' He hands me a large key, kissing me on the lips. 'This is my morning gift to you Almodis.'

'You already gave me a morning gift,' I say, bemused. 'And this one is rather late!' I fit the key to the lock which turns smoothly, push open the heavy door and step in with Ramon behind me.

'A library!' I look around me dazed, delighted. Winter sunlight floods the centre of the room from arched windows opposite, that reach from ceiling to floor. A long table of fine wood stretches the length of the room. Ten men could lie end to end on it I guess, marvelling. Exquisite lamps of green glass are placed at regular intervals in the centre of the table. Around the walls, the shelves are set back, protected from the sun, but I see glinting there their promises of worlds I can enter, ideas I can argue with. On the table is a complex golden contraption, driven by water wheels, a clock of some kind with the metal figure of a small man in Arab dress holding a pointer to show the time.

'It's a water clock,' Ramon tells me. 'In Greece they call it a water thief. It is a wedding gift to you from the ruler of Dénia. He writes that it has been designed by the engineer Ibn Khalaf al-Muradi. In the ancient world they were used to time the pleadings of lawyers in the courts, a sick patient's pulse, or a client's allotted time in a brothel!'

I look at Ramon, shaking my head. I am speechless.

'There's a ladder,' Ramon says, pointing it out, 'to reach the highest shelves.' Some of the shelves hold books and scrolls and others are empty. Four caskets stand alongside the empty shelves. I pick up one of the books nearest to me and look at its gorgeous cover, its title page. There are books here I have longed for, heard about.

'This is William's copy of Dhuoda's Manual,' Ramon says, handing a small book to me.

'Her son's?' I say astonished.

'Yes, he died here in Barcelona.'

I open it and wonder at what I am holding. 'This is perhaps her handwriting,' I say.

'Very likely.'

I replace it carefully. 'Oh Ramon, I am overwhelmed. Thank you.'

'This is your library,' he says. 'All yours,' and he is beaming at me. 'No one else will set foot here without your invitation. Not even me.'

I step close to him and hold him by his upper arms, looking into his eyes. 'Thank you.' I kiss his mouth for a long time, but when he begins to respond, I pull away playfully, biting my lip.

'Look in the caskets,' he says. He is like a boy on his birthday, gleeful at my pleasure.

I open the lid of one casket and see familiar books there. 'My collection from Toulouse! How?'

'I sent Berenger to negotiate it with Pons,' he says. 'Of course he was reluctant. He told him at first that he had burnt them.'

I heave a groan.

'But Berenger had a letter that my lawyers drafted asserting your rights to your property and threatening legal suit. Berenger persuaded him it was for the best. The couriers brought them over the mountains through the winter weather. I couldn't be sure if they would arrive in time for Christmas, but they have.'

I wander away from him picking up old friends, exclaiming at new ones.

'I will leave you to your unpacking and send Marta to help you.'

35

Bernadette: Reunion

It's late March 1053 when we reach Barcelona. The ground is tipping up and down, up and down, as I try to regain my land legs. Through waves of nausea, I realise it is my dear Lady that I see coming to me, her arms wide to greet me. I thrust the baby at Melisende and run helter-skelter to her, bending this way and that, sure I shall fall at any moment, for I've been on the rolling ship so long I don't know what is earth or sky anymore. 'Oh, after the rain, nice weather,' I cry out, reaching to hug her but then noticing how vast is her belly. 'Already?' I say muffled against her shoulder, puzzled.

The rest of the party arrives and she is exclaiming over them all with more hugs and kisses: 'Lucia! Melisende! Hughie! Dear Dia! Hello Rostagnus, I am so glad you are here!' And then in a quieter voice, 'Hello my little Adalmoda, and, oh, who is this?' she is saying, gesturing at the baby in Melisende's arms.

Oh Lord, I've forgotten all about that. My face is red and hot and I can't seem to speak. I stare at my boots all white-spattered with salty sea spray. There is a moment of silence.

'The baby is Bernadette's,' Dia says quietly. 'He is named Charles.'

'Bernadette's?'

I glance up at her and straight back down at my boots, seeing her perplexity. 'Happened last summer,' I mumble, but I can't go on.

'The father is . . .' Dia begins in a quiet, measured voice again.

'Piers,' pipes up Hughie.

Another silence. Eventually I look up fearfully, for I must to make sure she isn't dashing my boy's brains against a rock or aught else, but I'm surprised to see instead that she has taken hold of Charles and is staring into his eyes, all smiles.

'Hello Charles, hello Charles,' she coos to him. 'I am your Lady Almodis. Oh Bernadette, you fool,' she turns to me, 'why didn't you tell me?'

'Why didn't you?' I respond, as the penny finally drops that she must have been pregnant before she left Toulouse and Pons wasn't the father. She smiles briefly at that too.

'I'm so glad to see you all.' She hands Charles back to me.

Count Ramon has been standing back, waiting for her to finish her exclamations and steps forward now with a tall boy, older than Hughie. What a handsome man the count is. 'With a change in age, comes a change in fortune, my Lady,' I say to her with relish.

Count Ramon and Dia are greeting each other warmly and Almodis introduces him to her sister and her children, and then to Rostagnus and me. 'And this is Bernadette's son, Charles,' she says, as if she's known about it all along.

'You are come in the nick of time, Bernadette,' the count says to me.

'A stitch in time saves nine,' I respond, 'and I can see that.' I am eyeing her great stomach. 'You should be in bed right now,' I tell her.

She laughs. 'The same Bernadette.'

The same lady more like, I think, ignoring good advice. The count looks a little concerned at this exchange.

'You think she should be abed, Bernadette?' he asks me, but then quickly drops the subject when she gives him her basilisk stare that says don't anyone even think of telling me what to do.

He introduces his son, Pere, to us. Melisende and Lucia are at once fussing over him but he draws back, staying close to his father and saying as little as possible. He does not smile. I'll have my work cut out with him sure enough. Another household swarming with children to wear me out then. I tot it up on my finger joints. Six when the new baby comes, but at least Melisende is of an age to help me and I've got an assistant named Marta.

Three days later and my mistress is brought to bed and I have to increase my additions to seven. She is delivered of twin sons who have been named Ramon Berenger and Berenger Ramon. Too many same names I say, and tell her I will call them Towhead and Beren to make my life easier. She laughs at me. They look just like their father and she would have had a very hard time passing them off as Pons' children. They are not identical, as she and Raingarde are, but similar instead, like Hugh and Jourdain. Ramon Towhead has her green eyes and Beren has his father's blue ones.

The count is beside himself with joy at the birth of two sons and with relief too that my Lady is well, though she is tired for longer than usual after this birth. It gets harder the older you get, I told her, which she wasn't best pleased about. For the first time she asks me to find two wet-nurses for the twins, rather than nurse them herself. My heart swells with love for the count seeing how he dotes on her. It's high time she had some good loving. Oh Lord when I think of her flying out of that window, carrying these two babies in her womb, when I think of that knave Piers putting the hoods over our faces and intending to send her into that stone cell. 'I haven't slept properly at night the whole time we've been apart,' I tell her, 'worrying about you.'

We relive together the drama of her escape and Raingarde's bravery. I tell her how Raingarde feigned sleep at Lagrasse and they came and trussed her up and carried her out to the boat and didn't let Carlotta and her big knife go with her after all, but that soon the Count of Carcassonne's soldiers came to release us and gave that nun and the prioress a clear idea of what the count thought of this treachery, and he took away loads of rights he'd given them. 'Oh but we were so afraid for Raingarde and what was happening to her on the ship with Piers and if he would notice it weren't you,' I say.

'Did he notice?'

'Yes. He saw her hand had no scars as they were nearing the pier where the Count of Carcassonne was waiting to rescue her and he realised in a trice that he'd been outwitted and he jumped overboard and swam for it rather than be taken.'

'Did he drown?'

'No. She saw him stagger out on the bank and we heard since that he's back with Pons but stripped of his honours as vicar.'

My Lady is sitting in her white nightgown with a pale green silk dressing gown on top of that, so I think she's warm enough and doesn't need my scolding for a change. She is talking and laughing with Dia, and they look up to greet the count and Pere who have come to visit the new babies. Ramon lifts them from their cradle one at a time, talking softly to them, kissing their sweet-smelling heads. 'Would you like to hold your new brother, Ramon?' he asks Pere, and I notice my Lady swivel in her seat with a look of concern on her face.

'No,' says Pere, shortly, 'I wouldn't.' He sits down heavily on the stool beside the cradle. 'Why's he called Ramon?' he demands. 'He shouldn't be called that.'

A still silence descends on the room that had been so cheerful before. 'That's his name,' says the count. 'They are all names in the family of Barcelona: Pere, Ramon, Berenger.'

'He's not first,' says Pere.

'No,' Ramon glances uneasily at Almodis. 'No, of course not. You are first.'

'No, I'm not the first either,' the boy says angrily, rising to his feet. 'I already had two brothers that died.' He walks quickly from the room, shaking off the hand that his father reaches out towards him.

We exchange worried looks.

'What shall I do with him?' Ramon says to Almodis. 'I don't understand why he feels so threatened.'

'He's had you all to himself for eight years,' she says, 'and now suddenly he must share you with a new wife and five other children. And he sees that he was the sole heir and now he has two brothers. He will adjust in time,' she reassures Ramon.

This Barcelona city is foreign but I suppose I will get used to it eventually. Other times, other customs. Another foreign tongue but not too different from Occitan that took me so long to learn. At least they can understand me in the market, though they laugh at me or ask me curiously where I am from. Dia is glad to be back in Barcelona and has gone to remake her old acquaintances and find herself lodgings.

The palace and my Lady's chambers are wondrous excellent but I've got the rough end of the deal as usual. Lucia and Melisende are sharing a room, whilst I sleep in the nursery with Adalmoda, Charles and the new twins. I don't get a wink of sleep of course between all them. Hugh the Bishop has been sent to share Pere's room but complains of it often. 'Can't I sleep with you, Bernadette?' he says plaintively. 'Pere pinches me and tells me ghost stories to frighten me.' Sometimes I let the poor boy climb in with his cold toes and his wet nose from crying. Sometimes he climbs in with his mother and Count Ramon and they don't seem to mind it.

Already Toulouse seems like a distant memory. We are all so immersed in our business here. News comes from Raingarde that their mother Amelie has died and I comfort Lucia. My mistress does not shed any tears over it. I think of my own mother far away in Paris. How she'd laugh to know all the adventures I've been through and where I am now.

36

Martinmas 1054

At the eleventh minute of the eleventh hour on the eleventh day of the eleventh month, the feast of Saint Martin begins, with bonfires and children carrying lanterns in the streets. We celebrate the new wine and the bounty of the earth. Bernadette swears by the old belief that if you stand at the back of the church and look at the congregation you will see an aura of light around the heads of those who will not be among the living next Martinmas. 'That's good,' she pronounces, after her pagan survey, 'none of you are for the chop.'

Our third son, Arnau, was born two months ago. My eighth son and my tenth child. Eight pregnancies are enough now I hope. Pere has gone from being sole male heir to a potential division between four male heirs and he makes it quite plain what he thinks about all these alien children in his palace.

'Why is your son still here, Ramon?' I ask, 'He should have gone to another household for training long ago.'

'I would not send him to my grandmother,' he says, 'to have her use him against me and I could not bear to part with him before when he was seven. I had lost two sons and a wife. He lost his mother and I could not let him go.'

'Perhaps he should go now? Perhaps to Berenger in Narbonne?'

'No he would take it too hard now. He would see it as a punishment and he is being well trained here after all.'

'He is unkind to Adalmoda and Hughie.'

'I will speak to him,' Ramon promises, but I doubt this will make any difference. The boy is becoming a problem that I must find a solution to but for now I am distracted by the arrival at court of Guillem, Count of Besalú, who comes to give homage to Ramon and to me. Now that Ramon has forced his surrender, the insurrection that Ermessende has incited against us is quelled. Other lords are here to witness the new accord between Ramon and Besalú, including Berenger and Garsenda's son, Raymond of Narbonne, who has recently been betrothed to Raingarde's eldest daughter. Besalú approaches us: he is dark haired and short but his main feature, of course, is his nose. Or lack of it. Where his nose should be he wears a silver replacement, with curving nostrils etched into the sides, held in place with a thin black strip of leather that is tied at the back of his head. It is very hard not to stare but I do my best to hold his gaze and not to gawk at the nose. I imagine the exposed bone and gristle underneath.

'I am your solid man, Count Ramon,' he says, giving my husband his hands in oath. 'I seal this agreement with my *foi*, my faith.'

Ramon tells me that Besalú is a violent and volatile man and has killed his brother and two of his counsellors in violent rages, but today he is all smiles and graciousness. He was stunned by your beauty, Ramon tells me later. 'Your Radiance' he calls me.

'How did he come to lose his nose?' I ask. 'Disease?'

'No. In battle.'

'I was well used to battle scars with my own father. Have you seen him without his fake nose?'

'Urrgh!' says Ramon. 'You are too curious by far, darling.' And then, 'It won't last.'

I raise my eyebrows. 'He seems sincere in his homage and the county likes me now.'

'Oh yes, they do like you indeed but this is the third time that Besalú has given me homage and it didn't stick for long the other times. He's left us two hostages as pledge of his allegiance: Adémar the castellan of Finestres and Bernat the castellan of La Guardia. Ademar has had a document drawn up saying that if Besalú violates his oath, then Finestres will not be forfeit. What does that tell you? Even his hostages expect him to be treacherous.

If there is peace, then he feels compelled to pick an argument and when he rises then other lords do the same and the whole tedious round begins again.'

'Then you must bind him to you closer,' I say. Lucia walks into the room with Melisende who is carefully carrying a jug of wine for us.

'Oh no,' says Ramon, following the direction of my gaze. 'Don't think it.'

'I am thinking of Lucia.'

She hears her name and looks up smiling at us. How could I even think it? To wed my gentle little sister to such a horror.

'No, no,' Ramon is frowning at me. 'You would inflict on Lucia what you have suffered yourself?'

Besalú stays with us a week and we see no sign of his temper. The idea of betrothing Lucia to Besalú grows in my head and will not go away. I want to solve this problem for Ramon. 'A peaceweaver, like me,' I tell Ramon. 'How can we go forward if we must deal with the same problems over and over again?'

'It won't be enough for his pride. The third daughter of the Count of La Marche.'

'You think he is inundated with marriage offers? She is pretty and young.'

'Your sister deserves better,' says Ramon, looking at me askance. 'You know that.' I know what he means and turn away angry that he should mention my marriage to Pons to me.

'My gracious Countess Almodis,' Besalú says this morning, bending over my hand awkwardly to avoid dislodging his nose.

'I heard that was not your description of me last month, sir.' I heard that he had called me 'an unbridled whore'.

He looks up and drops my hand, taken aback at my directness, but then he recovers and smiles unctuously. 'I did not know you then, my dear lady. Forgive my gross errors of the past. I am prostrate before you.'

'You are not wed my Lord?'

'Alas, no. Who would have me?' he throws his arms out comically.

'My sister Lucia, perhaps,' I say without thinking. Ramon has

not sanctioned this. He will be furious with me. And Lucia . . .
Besalú is studying me.

'A beautiful young lady,' he says.

I keep my lips firmly clamped together, trying not to worsen
my actions any further. Bernadette would have said: You should
turn your tongue seven times in your mouth before you speak.
Perhaps it will all blow over. Perhaps he will not take me seriously.

'Almodis!' Ramon comes in abruptly and I drop my book in my
lap, seeing his face and knowing what it is. 'Besalú has asked me
for Lucia in marriage.' He is very angry. 'You planted this idea
with him. He suggests it as part of our peace settlement! I seriously doubt the wisdom of it for your sister and have no confidence that it will seal peace between us, but now I must agree. If
I refuse it is another cause for him to break with me.'

I know that I am in the wrong but there is no way back and I
cannot bring myself to admit that I am wrong.

'You will have to tell her,' Ramon says, when I say nothing, and
strides out again, as abruptly as he came.

Not surprisingly Lucia is appalled when I tell her and cries and
screams at me.

'Lucia,' I soothe her. 'You will be a peaceweaver like me. This
marriage will be the glue to bring peace to the whole region. It is
a grand marriage since he is with vast lands and you will be
Countess of Besalú. I will teach you how to manage him.' I ache
at that idea. I know that I should retract her from this.

'I want none of your teachings,' Lucia shouts at me. 'I have
seen where that has got you. Trussed up in a cart with a hood over
your face! Excommunicated!'

However, in November the Synod of Barcelona, attended by
all the bishops, meets to ratify the Peace and Truce of God. Their
presence here at our court is a tacit acknowledgement of the legit-
imacy of my marriage to Ramon.

Arrangements for Besalú and Lucia's betrothal roll inexorably
on. Rostagnus helps me to draw up charters detailing the dowry.
I watch him as he carefully adds my seal to the documents. My
bronze seal is double-sided, finely engraved on one side with an

image of me on my horse carrying a lily in one hand and a falcon in the other, and on the other side it has an image of Barcelona, the city and the sea. Rostagnus softens the red wax, sandwiches it between the two parts of the seal die, which are slotted together with pegs, and squeezes the wax into the engraved surfaces with a seal-roller. He attaches this wax seal to red silk laces that are threaded through slits at the end of the document. The betrothal feast is held and the wedding date is set for 18 November but has to be delayed to December because of the time it takes to draw the documents up correctly. I write to Audebert and to Raingarde to tell them of the marriage and later I show Lucia their letters of delight that she will marry such a great lord, but she turns her face from me and has not spoken willingly to me since I first broached it with her. The palace seems a chilly place. Ramon is not pleased with me. Yet Besalú's allegiance and his marrying into our family stills the last of the rebellion against Ramon, and Ermessende is left without allies so that surely she must come now to give her fealty. But she does not.

'Lady!' Bernadette bursts in screeching.
    'What is . . .'
    'Fire. Fire in the library!'
    I run as fast as I can, my head empty, pursued by Dia and Bernadette, shouting for help as I go. As I approach the door, maids are screaming in the passageway. The fire is small and the male servants are beating at it with tapestries that they have ripped from the wall. Ramon is in the thick of it, passing buckets of slopping water, and soon the flames are damped down. The servants troop out looking dejected, some muttering to me, 'So sorry my Lady'. They know how much time I spend in here, how treasured are my books.
    'Not too bad,' says Ramon trying to cheer me up.
    I am looking in horror at the damage.
    'Bernadette, Rostagnus, help your Lady sort what is damaged and what can be saved, please,' he says. 'Not so much is gone, Almodis. We can replace some things.'
    'Not everything.' I feel cold with grief as I see the burnt remains of some of my grandmother Adalmode's books, some of the

270

treasures Ramon has brought for me reduced to ash and sodden illegible pages. I pick up Dhuoda's Manual, the actual one she wrote in her own hand for her son William. It has been doused with water and as I pick it up the ink swims and the words fall from the page. 'Oh, no, no,' I am sobbing now.

Ramon hugs me and tries to cheer me. 'It could have been so much worse.'

I pull myself together and step out of his embrace. 'Ramon, there is malice here and we cannot ignore it. I fear,' I say hesitantly, 'it may have been Pere's doing.'

'That's ridiculous, Almodis!' he says angrily. 'I know you are upset but how can you make such a wild accusation? Pere would not do such a thing and you offend me greatly to suggest it.' He looks at me with disgust, looks around at the devastation, throws his arms up and walks out. I exchange looks with Bernadette and Dia. Silently they agree with me.

Later Ramon summons me to the hall and I think that our argument concerning Pere will continue but instead he is sitting there with a letter in his hand and Lucia is standing before him. 'I have received a letter from Count Besalú,' Ramon tells us. 'He writes to break his betrothal to Lady Lucia.'

'Oh thank you Jesu!' Lucia says.

I reach for her hand but she pulls it away from me.

'Well, good,' says Ramon and stares at me.

'It is not good, to be thus jilted,' I say.

Later we talk together without her present. 'Lucia's position is very awkward now. Who would have her, in these circumstances?'

Ramon says nothing.

'Alright!' I say, cracking under the unremitting pressure of his disapproval. 'I was wrong and it is all my fault!'

'And?' he says.

'And I shall write to the pope and ask for an annulment for her, and I shall find her a better marriage.'

'You write to the pope, yes, but I will find her a better marriage.'

I am chagrined. 'That is my job.'

'Well then I have a suggestion for you to consider, Your Radiance,' he says, taking my hand, so that I must smile at last with him. 'The Count of Pallars Sobirà.'

'Artaldo? He is already wed and is aged!'

'He is a mere fifty and a pleasant man. His wife has borne him no heirs and is past raising his desire. He will put her aside for Lucia. It would cement my alliance with him. How are things looking in your poor library, my love?'

Our daughter Inés has been born and Ramon has lavished me with gifts including Girona, a share in the annual Taifa tribute, and many of his castellans have sworn fealty to me.

'Isn't Girona part of Ermessende's domain?' I ask him.

'I've sent her charters withdrawing her rights in the city. She shows us no favour and so she shall have none of ours. She still has Vic and can retreat there and continue her plots against me, her own flesh and blood.' He is angry because the Council of Bishops in Toulouse has reconfirmed our excommunication. It is time that I did something about Ermessende.

To the most excellent Ermessende, Dowager Countess of Barcelona, by the grace of God the most revered female lord in all of Occitania and Catalonia, may you be saved by Him who gives salvation to lords, from Almodis, Countess of Barcelona,

I begin by laying claim to kinship with you through my sister's marriage to your nephew, Pierre of Carcassonne and through my marriage to your grandson, Count Ramon. I trustingly write to you about the things that concern me. Forgive that I must be plain. When we are assaulted by necessity we should seek the most certain help. If you do not make peace with my lord, you leave opening for rebellion, and the diminution and dishonour of our rights. Is that what you want for your house? If you come to us in peace and we agree an accord then everything you have achieved can be joined to everything we have achieved, and are. I long to meet and converse with you and learn much from your judicious wealding of power as a woman. I earnestly entreat you, won't you come to us and meet also your great grandchildren? Farewell Countess.

We hear that Count Guillem of Besalú has married Etiennette of Provence. I try not to think of how it would have been for Lucia if the marriage had gone forward and how it must be for Etiennette. It seems that God has been kind to me in my errors.

37

All Hallows 1057

The harvest moon this year was spectacular: a huge orange disk so low in the sky that it seemed to touch the ground. Bernadette almost fell from her horse as we rounded a bend and saw it hanging there, come down to take a look at us.

Ramon and I have another daughter, named Sancha, after his mother. Jourdain has written to tell me that Geoffrey has knighted his brothers, Hugh of Lusignan, and Guillaume and Raymond of Toulouse, so that they are all men now. I imagine Geoffrey dubbing each of them, striking a hard blow on their cheeks, and giving them their armour and their spurs. Hugh has gone to live in Lusignan and Guillaume and Raymond have gone to Pons in Toulouse, and I wonder how they will find their father, now that they are men.

'We must send them gifts,' says Ramon. 'Horses?'

Raymond writes to me from Toulouse to tell me about his last campaign with Geoffrey:

> It was not a great success. We made foray into Normandy with the Capetian King Henri, and part of the army forded the River Dives near the tidal estuary, but then the tide came in and divided our forces on either side of the river, so that William of Normandy was able to decimate and defeat us. The King and Count Geoffrey were forced to withdraw empty-handed.

Raymond writes that I am sorely missed in Toulouse by many people, including himself.

It is the feast of All Hallows and people spend the day 'visiting' with their dead relatives in the cemeteries, laying mounds of bright flowers for them that will then rot for weeks afterwards.

We received news last week that Ermessende has interceded on our behalf in Rome and our excommunication has at last been lifted. We have brokered a deal with Ermessende and she has sold her rights in Barcelona, Girona, Ausona and many castles to us. She is at the city gate and, in moments, I will meet her for the first time since I saw her in Toulouse when I was seventeen.

She is carried into the hall on a litter and her servants help her to rise from it. She is greatly bent with her age, her back rounded over her stick. I see that Ramon is shocked at her looks. Her eyes are sunk in their sockets. I make her comfortable on a soft seat beside me.

After the greetings she says to me: 'You seem to be doing a good job, Lady Almodis. I am old now and tired.' It is a grudging concession but it is one nevertheless.

'I have greatly admired your rule, Countess,' I say. 'You have been a model for myself and my sister, Countess Raingarde.'

She nods, acknowledging my reference to our kinship and my sister's rule of her homeland. 'Let us be at peace, grandson,' she says. She reaches out a gnarled hand to me. I take it carefully, fearful that I might hurt her for she looks so frail but her grip is hard like a soldier's. She holds my hand for some time looking into my face. 'Well,' she says eventually, 'perhaps I made a mistake all that time ago in Toulouse. Three sons and two daughters in a mere four years of marriage is a goodly brood, and a third marriage at that. Too bad about your sister Lucia and Besalú but he will always be trouble that man until somebody kills him.'

She is a grim old lady. The skin of her hands and face are blotched with brown patches. She is held together by sheer will. She has ruled for sixty-four years and much has changed in the world around her since the early years of her life.

'Do you have marriage negotiations in hand for the children?' she asks me.

'Yes. Pere will marry Mathilde of Urgell next year.'

She nods her approbation of that in Pere's direction, where he is sitting with us on the raised dais, next to Melisende and Hugh.

Melisende is seventeen now; Pere, fifteen; and Hugh the Bishop, at ten, has recently been promoted to the high table from the ranks of the nursery. He looks pleased with himself and swings his legs under the trestle, since they do not quite reach the floor.

'My daughter Melisende, here, is betrothed to Simon of Parthenay and they will marry next year. My son, Hugh of Toulouse, will enter Cluny soon. The other children are yet too young for betrothal.'

'I was betrothed at seven.'

'And I at five,' I respond. 'I will look to their marriages in good time.' I will not be forced to gibber by her. I am a match for her toughness.

'Well, you have plenty on your hands.'

'Yes. Of my other children in France, I have already betrothed my son Hugh of Lusignan to Hildegarde of Thouars, a neighbouring lord. My son, Guillaume of Toulouse is betrothed to Mathilde of Auvergne.' I beckon Marta over with the younger children. 'This is my daughter Adalmoda of Toulouse and these are your great-grandchildren: Ramon Berenger, Berenger Ramon, Arnau, Inés and Sancha of Barcelona.' I say each of their names with great pride, smiling at them. They all stand in a line, in order of their ages from Adalmoda who is nine, to Inés who is nearly two, looking wide-eyed at the old lady. Marta holds my new-born, Sancha, in her arms.

'Extraordinary,' she says in a tone that is not all approbation, and shows them no affection. 'An army of children,' she says, addressing Ramon over their blond heads.

They are getting bored by their neglect so I signal to Marta and they troop out throwing longing glances at me and Ramon. 'Playtime later,' he calls and they brighten at that.

'Will you give us your oath, Countess?' I say, deciding that the niceties are over.

'That's what I'm here for,' she says, as little inclined to niceties as me.

'I cannot kneel,' she says to me, and I see in her face a bitter pride disgusted with her own feebleness.

'There is no need, Grandmother,' I say kindly, offering my hands that she might place hers between mine.

'I, Ermessende, daughter of Countess Adelais, swear to you Countess Almodis, daughter of Countess Amelie, that henceforth I will not disappoint either you or your life, nor the limbs of your body nor your descendents.'

Ramon smiles but doubtless he is thinking, as am I, that she only concedes now because she will die soon.

In October we receive another letter from the pope, this time annulling Lucia's betrothal to the Count of Besalú. I decide that time is passing on and I must broach the topic of another marriage with her. 'Lucia you are twenty-three and must be wed soon or you will have to take the veil.'

'I don't want that,' she says quickly. 'I want children and I suppose I must have a husband to get them. Can't you send me home to Raingarde or Audebert to find me a husband?'

'They would struggle because of Besalú,' I say and she looks at me coldly.

'Yes, now I am a scandal, near as much as you are.'

I do not respond to her hard words. After all, I deserve them. 'Ramon and I will take no action unless you wish it, but we suggest to you Artaldo, Count of Pallars Sobirà. You would have your own household, your own family.'

'He is an old man, but if I am to be your glue, well at least he is a kindly old man and he has a nose.' She goes out, banging the door behind her.

'Is there someone younger?' I ask Ramon. 'Someone she would like?' but he shakes his head.

When I raise the subject of Pallars Sobirà with her again a few days later, she says, 'Alright then, marry me to the old codger!' and breaks into a smile. The first I have seen on her face for months.

'That's the last time you say that!' I say laughing.

'I can say what I like in my head,' she says, 'and perhaps I will take a young lover!'

'Have a care!' I say surprised. Is she jesting?

I gather my children about me for my meeting with Artaldo, Count of Pallars Sobirà. The children are evidence of my fertility and suggestive of Lucia's. Pere's dark head stands out amongst my blond children, the cuckoo in my nest. I begin by speaking to Artaldo of my absent sons. 'I have five other sons,' I say proudly. I tell him of my Lusignan twins: Hugh who is a knight now and Jourdain, who is the most skilled in his scriptorium. I tell him of my three Toulouse sons: Guillaume and Raymond who also trained with Count Geoffrey of Anjou, 'and Hughie here who is going to the Abbey of Cluny and is destined for high office in the church,' I say.

After more small talk and refreshments, I nod to Bernadette and she turns and leads in my sister who is wearing a short veil over her face and a dress of fine scarlet cloth with black embroidery at the neck and waist. After curtseying to the count she slowly lifts up and puts back her veil. Not surprisingly Artaldo is delighted at the prospect of bedding my young sister and getting himself an heir. Because of Lucia's broken betrothal he haggles down the dowry outrageously but Ramon more than compensates for that with his promise of a marriage gift to her.

I have been engaged in a delightful correspondence with Ali ben Mochehid, the ruler of Dénia, ever since I thanked him for the gift of the water clock for my marriage. We have never met but I feel as if I know him. My letters bear fruit this year as he agrees to allow the Christian churches in his domains to be subject to our bishop here in Barcelona.

The winter is passed when we were all trapped for long periods of time indoors by the shorter days and bad weather and with the roads and sea routes impassable. Just before the Easter Assembly we receive news that Ermessende has died at her castle of Besora on the first day of March. She has sent her testament to us: *I beg the master Ramon, Count, my grandson, together with the mistress Almodis, Countess, your wife, for God and Saint Maria, his mother, to take care with my soul for God knows that I have loved you more than anybody of your people, and you may know this through what I have done for you.*

I resist the obvious response to this that she must have been deluded in her last days, and instead I simply exchange looks with my husband.

The Easter Assembly this year is a splendid one. We are out from the shadow of Ermessende, our excommunication lifted and Ramon making a new alliance with Ermengoll, Count of Urgell. Count Artaldo has repudiated his wife, Constanca, and attends court to finalise the betrothal contract with my sister. Rostagnus ensures that the documents insist he cannot abandon Lucia for any reason. Lucia herself does not seem adverse to him and I am glad of that. We have more betrothals to celebrate: Pere is betrothed to Mathilde and I hope that it will be the making of him to wed; Simon of Parthenay has come to Barcelona to claim my Melisende as his bride. He is the heir to Parthenay since his oldest brother died two years ago and the second son of the family, Joscelin, has become Archbishop of Bordeaux. Simon is a young and pleasant man, not much older than Melisende, and I am glad to see that she likes him, but it is a terrible wrench for all of us – for her to leave; for me and for Dia, Bernadette and Adalmoda to lose her. 'Every cloud has a silver lining,' sobs Bernadette, unconvinced by her own wisdom as we wave goodbye at the port.

Raymond writes me that Agnes' son Pierre (Guillaume VII of Aquitaine) has died from dysentery whilst besieging Count Geoffrey at his mother's urging, so now his twin Guy has become Guillaume, the eighth Duke of Aquitaine and is determined not to suffer the interference of his mother. He has repudiated my cousin, Aina of Périgord, and sent her to a nunnery. Perhaps he will do the same with his mother. My son, Guillaume, has wed Mathilde of Auvergne and Raymond, never to be outdone by his older brother, has wed his cousin, Bertranda, Pons' niece. There will be trouble from the church over this marriage to a first cousin I am sure, but Raymond will do what he wishes, not what anyone tells him to do.

38

Thaw 1060

It has been a hard winter and the Court has been quiet with few visitors and little news. When the snow begins to clear from the mountain roads the news flows down through the Pyrenees with the thaw.

From Raingarde Countess of Carcassonne to Almodis Countess of Barcelona

   Alas my dear sister, my beloved husband Pierre has died and left me and his children bereft. He should have lived many more years. I wish that I could retreat and weep for him but instead I must rule as regent for my son, Roger, who is not yet of age. I have arranged the marriages of my two older daughters. Garsendis will wed Raymond, the son of your good friend Berenger of Narbonne, and Ermengard will wed Raymond-Bernard Trencavel, Viscount of Albi and Nîmes. The Count of Cerdanya has offered for my youngest daughter, Adelais, which will be a fine marriage for her but I have said that at thirteen she is yet too young and he must wait a while. You will be interested to hear that Archbishop Guifred of Narbonne has been excommunicated . . .

From Raymond of Toulouse to Almodis Countess of Barcelona:

   I am sorry to say that I have two deaths to tell you of Mother, one that will mean much more to you than the other. The northern king, Henri, has died and been succeeded by his little son Philippe, so that Bishop Gervais of Le Mans and Baldwin Count of Flanders act as his regents. And I am grieved to tell you that Count Geoffrey of Anjou has died.

*He took ill and knew his time had come and asked me to go to him.
I took him to the monastery of Saint Nicholas d'Angers where he was
shriven and received into the brotherhood. In his testament he left you the
vineyard of Najac saying that you were the woman he had loved most in
his life and you were the wife that he let slip away and never be one.*

I am grieved to think of Geoffrey, the Hammer, dying a monk
and with no heirs, despite taking three more wives after Agnes.
I imagine how furious she will be when she hears of his legacy
and statement concerning me. Ramon is not too pleased with it
either. 'What were your relations?' he demands.

I answer angrily: 'At the court of Aquitaine, he was a foster
child, like me. He was like my older brother. When I took my
sons to train with him he asked me to leave Pons and marry him
but I refused. Those were our relations.'

'Forgive me. I am jealous.' He turns to leave, but then turns
back. 'Indeed Almodis I am jealous of your heart that you do not
give to me. It makes me think that you have given it to someone
else.' He looks at me with challenge and I stare back. 'Did you
love him?'

'As a brother,' I say truthfully, 'no more.'

'The truth is Almodis your heart belongs to you and you do
not give it to me.'

I lower my eyes at that. He's right. He waits for me to respond.
I look up. 'I have given you five children and good counsel.'

'Yes.' The word is bitter in his mouth. He wants more. He
relents and takes my hand. 'I don't want to argue, Almodis. You
are the most wonderful woman and partner on God's earth. I
adore the ground you walk on, the cup that touches your lip, the
bedsheets that caress your limbs and belly. You know that.'

I smile gently at him but do not speak.

'You don't let me in Almodis. You keep me at arm's length.
Outside. I risked all for you. Will you ever give me your heart,
wife?' he asks in quiet despair.

'My heart has been injured,' I say eventually to break the
silence, 'through my two previous marriages. And it was already
well guarded after growing up in Agnes' hostile household. You
must give me time.'

He looks me in the eye, kisses my hand: 'All the time we have is yours, my love.'

We have been wed eight years now and I can see the disappointment plain and painful in his face.

'Can you make me love my husband?' I ask Dia, later that day.

Bernadette looks up from her sewing with her mouth open and her eyes wide. 'Never look a gift horse in the mouth,' she says earnestly.

'Don't you love him already?' asks Dia.

'Yes, a little perhaps, but he wants more. I would like to give him what he wants but I don't know how.'

'He is a fine and loving husband,' says Bernadette in a tone of great disapproval.

'There are spells and potions,' says Dia, 'that can cause a temporary madness of love but that is not what your lord wants. He does not want the empty, evaporating passion of a drug.'

'What then?'

'You must want to love him. You must let go of your defences. If you wish it, it will be so. Bernadette is right. He is a good man, a great man, and he does sorely love you.'

'Well,' I say, doubtfully, 'I'll try.'

Pere's marriage to Mathilda has taken place today. I have given him a very fine black stallion and one of my castles and its vineyards near Girona as a wedding gift. 'Thank you, Mother,' he says as if I have handed him a slug. He has taken lately to calling me Mother – the word thick with irony in his mouth. I have tried to like him but I do not, and his dislike of me is not at all concealed. He has his own gaggle of followers now in the court, young, ambitious men, fawning on him, sniggering at his jokes, bolstering his pride. When Ramon is present, he conceals his venom towards me, but if his father is not there, he is brazen in his enmity. He raises his goblet to me now at the table, his young wife swathed in veils beside him, and I smile back, as insincere as he.

'Perhaps you would like to establish your own court now,' I said to him yesterday, 'in one of your own holdings.'

'Oh no, Mother. I think I will stay here and keep an eye on my inheritance,' he responded, smirking at me.

'Your inheritance is a matter for your father to decide,' I said, goaded by his attitude. 'He will decide what division to make in his testament, amongst his four sons.' I wished the words back as soon as I had said them.

Pere scowled darkly at me and leant close to hiss at me, '*I* am his heir,' he said.

He is a tall, broad man of eighteen now, well-practised in the tournaments, skilful with his weapons, praised by his father. My boys are still children: the twins are seven and Arnau is six. I stood back from him, trying not to show that I felt threatened. 'Of course,' I said.

From Guillaume Count of Toulouse to Almodis Countess of Barcelona I write to tell you Mother that my father, Count Pons II of Toulouse, has died after a short illness. He has been buried at Saint Sernin and I have been invested as Count by the Good Men of Toulouse and crowned by Archbishop Guifred. My father's widow, Sancha of Aragon, has departed Toulouse and taken the veil at the Monastery of Santa Cruz. Guillaume of Aquitaine has had the temerity to demand my oath of fealty as if I am his vassal and not a prince in my own right. I have refused and am preparing to march on Poitiers now. My brother, Hugh of Lusignan, and his father, your former husband, have given me their allegiance and will stand against Aquitaine with me. I have hopes that my uncle Audebert will also join me. Raymond will hold Toulouse whilst I am in the field.

I dump the letter into my lap. 'Ramon!'

'What is it?'

'Read, this!' I am shaking and my mind whirls. Dia and Bernadette have come running to see what the commotion is. Dia takes my hand, and I am surprised to find that my response to Pons' death is to sob and sob.

'Gone, Almodis,' she says raising my helpless hands up and down. 'Absolutely gone.'

'Yes. Then my sons, all my fine sons,' I say in terror, 'preparing to go to war, and Hugh with them!'

Ramon has finished reading the letter and looks at me with concern.

'Will you give them your support, Ramon?'

He looks down at his boots and I see that he will not. 'It is a rash move on Guillaume's part. He would do better to treat with Aquitaine than risk everything so early in his reign.'

'He cannot give fealty to Aquitaine. A fealty that is not owed.'

'Nevertheless, he should seek arbitration, not offer battle rashly like this.'

'Yes, you are right, and I must go to advise them so. He has no sound advice now.'

'He is a man, Almodis. He will not want a mother's advice. He has made his choice and we will see how it falls out.'

'See how it falls out!' I am furious. 'Three of my sons at risk, my Lord!' *And* my former husband, Hugh, I think to myself.

'Let me think on it,' he says. 'Perhaps we can send envoys to treat, to assist . . .'

I cannot sit and wait while he thinks and they are all in such danger. I turn from him and stride up the hall.

'Almodis, I require you to take no ill-conceived and hurried action in this matter!' he calls after me. *He* requires *me*!

39

New Lords

I have intended to send my twins, Ramon Towhead and Beren, to Toulouse to train with Guillaume and Raymond, and it is long since time that Hughie made his way to his calling in Cluny. I see that everything might be achieved at once. I tell Dia my plans and she remonstrates with me but will do as I ask. She finds us plain clothing that we may travel incognito. Rostagnus will accompany us. Dia and I stitch money into strips of cloth that we can wear around our waists: silver *solidi* and a few gold *mancusos*, only for emergencies. If we bandy about gold we will be conspicuous. I write a note for Bernadette telling her to take care of Adalmoda, Arnau, Inés and Sancha while I am gone. I leave Ramon a note telling him that I am taking Towhead and Beren to Toulouse and Hughie to Cluny and then I will return, although in truth I have not decided on that last point as yet. I wait until Ramon is sleeping and I slip out of bed and join my party at the northern gate. *He* requires *me*!

In darkness we take the road towards the mountain monastery of Montserrat with its miraculous Black Virgin and then, skirting the mountain, we head on to Berga and the foothills of the Pyrenees. We ride past trills of water in peat. At dawn I pause at a stream to refill my water skin and the bouncy moss is moist under my fingers. On horseback we eat bread and cheese in the wind. Clouds love the mountains and flow into their gullies. We stay in monastery guest-houses and the boys think it is a great adventure. Ramon will have expected me to take ship at Barcelona harbour and go to Toulouse via Narbonne. If he has realised that I would come this way then the realisation has come too late and there is no sign of pursuit.

We ride on and on, up and up into the mountains, getting colder and colder. I hear the distant sounds of dogs barking and donkeys braying in the clear air. Weather moves fast across the face of the mountain and then clouds swirl grey, shrouding us all before rain begins to lash us. The damp creeps into me. The rain eases and the mountain looks different after its washing: the brown is more prominent, the green refreshed, the white rock more vivid, and then there is a rainbow arching above it all. When night falls moonlight bathes the landscape, going in and out of cloud so that alternately there is inky blackness and then sparkling illuminated hills without any colour. We sleep in a farmhouse with pilgrims making their way towards Santiago de Compostela.

Next morning a herd of deer are silhouetted black on the horizon in the first light. Water runs down the mountain looking like white veins. Towards the end of this day's riding we rein our horses to look at the view and the sunset with its pink-tipped clouds, and Dia exclaims, 'It is too beautiful. I couldn't write a poem here.' The sky is variegated red and palest blue with black silhouettes of trees, and the reedbed reflects that vivid sky. At nightfall we approach Puigcerdà, a jewel of a town in the darkening valley.

We are up in the dark, breakfasting on burnt porridge, and I employ a boatman to take us in a small boat along the Ariège River into Occitania. The sun rises behind us. In the early stretches of the river we pass swiftly through the gorge with high granite and straggling trees and vegetation rising up on both sides and then the river banks begin to lower until we can see far across the countryside. We travel through Foix and Severdun, until the Ariège joins with the Garonne and flows into Toulouse. The river is in spring spate and we have made fast time.

There is a brooding, threatening sunrise when we arrive in Toulouse, and I find Raymond in charge. He has grown into a fine young man with a strong build and blond hair that he wears long to his collar, under a coronet. 'Guillaume's taken Bordeaux and declared himself Duke of Aquitaine,' he tells me with relish.

'Oh God and his saints, we must get him back here. Men cannot be regrown or reborn. This is folly.'

'Don't be ridiculous Mother. What do you know about it?'

'Why has he done such a rash thing?'

'He has taken the title Duke of Aquitaine and obviously Poitiers is not happy about that.'

'Obviously,' I say agog.

Raymond says, 'I can hold Toulouse.' He is seventeen years old and so absolutely certain. 'Do not forget that the Poitiers family murdered your grandfather, and the northern king gave away our honours to them. You know that we are by right the ruling family of Occitania and Aquitaine.'

I am nodding at him dumbfounded. These are my words, told in childhood stories to them over and over again. Oh what have I done with my pride, with my stories of our greatness? I have put my boys, my young warriors, in jeopardy. They are so young and they underestimate their enemy.

'They are a bastard race from generations back,' he says.

'Who told you that?'

'Audebert.'

'And is Audebert in the field with your brother?' I demand, sceptical.

'No, but Lord Hugh of Lusignan is. The first thing Guillaume of Aquitaine did was force Hugh to declare for him or for us, and he sided with us.'

Gentle, peace-loving Hugh was caught in a web of kin. He had no option. Our son, Hugh the Devil, trained by Geoffrey, growing up with Guillaume and Raymond, yes he would have urged this.

'The Count of Poitiers is marching on Toulouse now,' Raymond says eagerly, confident that he can repel an army.

'We will lose all,' I say.

'No Mother, we will gain all.'

I must go on to Lusignan, try to persuade Hugh and my son, Guillaume, to seek a truce with Aquitaine. 'This is madness. Toulouse is not prepared for real warfare. Look at the walls. It has not suffered siege for 150 years.'

'I'm fixing the walls,' he says irritated. 'The city withstood siege from Abd al-Rahman, the emir of Córdoba, and from the Magyars in the past. We are not fools or children. What do you think we were doing all this time with Count Geoffrey? Hugh, Guillaume and I are seasoned at warfare. Guillaume just killed 100 knights at Bordeaux.'

I nod at him and try to recalibrate, to acknowledge this transformation from a six year old to a ruling warrior, but what did I expect sending them to Geoffrey? I am drawn to look at Raymond over and over again, with a mixture of admiration, disbelief and loss of the small boy he was. I look at my Barcelona twins and see that the same transformation will take place with them, out of these pretty child chrysalises will come toughened men.

'My father left a wonderful bequest to the Abbey of Moissac,' Raymond says, trying to change the subject. 'He left them his big toe nail.'

Now I am laughing and scrunching up my nose. 'Eew, how lovely.'

At dinner Dia makes a song for Raymond's pleasure:

> It pleases me to see the lordship change
> And the old relinquishing their mansions to the young.
> It is this, and not some flower or twittering of birds
> Makes me feel the earth is new again.

Before I leave Toulouse, Raymond and I make a grant to Cluny as a gift for Hughie's entry there as a monk. I leave the twins in Raymond's care and travel on with Dia, Rostagnus and Hughie. Dia and I wear monk's habits over our gowns. Raymond wanted to send a company of soldiers with me, but I told him we would be safer, travelling as an inconspicuous small group of clerics.

We continue on the Garonne all the way to Bordeaux and then up the great estuary and take ship north along the coast, past the enemy territory of Aquitaine and Poitou. Rostagnus treats with the sailors and the inn-keepers, to maintain our disguise. When we land again we are two days ride to Lusignan. 'The problem will be how to get in, past the besieging army,' I say.

I decide it would be best for us to head to the Monastery of Notre Dame and speak with Jourdain. Rostagnus is flummoxed by my suggestion.

'But my Lady, we cannot practice deception on the monks. I mean, deceive them that two women are two monks – men!' he stutters.

'Don't worry Rostagnus, I don't mean for us to pass ourselves as brothers, but we need to speak with Jourdain.'

'We could go into the church and then I could go in search of Jourdain,' says Hugh the Bishop, 'and bring him to speak with you there.'

Hugh's idea is sound and so now Dia, Rostagnus and I wait in the church in our monks' habits, trying to keep a low profile, whilst Hugh searches for his half-brother. He is soon back, bringing Jourdain with him, and I am overjoyed to see my dear son, my second-oldest son (by minutes).

'He was in the scriptorium, as you said,' Hugh tells me, grinning, pleased to acquire yet another big brother that he has never met before and one of his own calling.

Discreetly, in the shadow of a column, I embrace Jourdain and am glad to see that he looks well. I am growing accustomed to seeing my little boys transformed into men now. He has ink stains on the second figure of his right hand and a smudge on his left cheek-bone.

'What are you doing here, Mother? No, I know *why* you are here, but what can you *do*?'

'Tell me everything you know about the situation.'

'Well, better than that, I will show you,' he says and we follow him to the staircase that leads to the bell tower. At the top we have a clear view of the castle and the army gathered before it. From here the ground slopes up towards the promontory where Lusignan Castle stands in the great loop that the River Vonne throws around it. Hugh's blue and silver crest flies on myriad flags set on the towers and along the allure, the walkway topping the pale stone of the walls. Steep valleys fall away on either side of the castle. The river protects the castle from assault on three sides so that it can only be approached from this side, across a very narrow neck of land formed by the meandering river. The army that has marched the short distances from Poitiers and Montreuil-Bonnin is massed here, near the narrow neck of land, where the land broadens out, and where my former husband's father built the Monastery of Notre Dame de Lusignan.

'See,' Jourdain points out to me, 'the river is blockaded on either side of the castle, so that no supplies can get through. Obviously nothing can get through from here on the north side of the castle with the main Aquitaine encampment down there.'

I look to where he is gesturing, where the vast army is gathered: pennants and banners flying, spears bristling; their tents and pavilions planted on the meadows, trampling the fields of crops and the vineyards that I knew so well. 'Their shining arms like glancing ice,' I say, quoting a poet. From up here the thousands of soldiers moving around the camp swarm like ants. Two tall siege engines sporadically fire boulders at the great curtain wall of the castle and the relentless thud and thrum bounces in my head painfully. The wall is showing some damage, but there are two more layers of wall yet beyond the outer skin.

'And then,' Jourdain goes on, 'behind the castle, on the other side of the river, there's a big garrison of Aquitainian troops in Lusignan village. The castle walls will withstand the stone-guns for a long time yet, and their wells draw straight from the river so they won't die of thirst, but their supplies of food must be getting very low now after two months of siege. They aim to defeat them by attrition.'

'Have you heard anything from your father or brother?' I ask.

'No, nothing is getting in or out. Melisende was here to look, as you are, a few days ago but we could think of nothing except to hope that Father will treat for peace and Agnes will accept.'

'Agnes!' I say astonished.

'Yes, she commands those troops down there, on behalf of her son, who is chasing your other son and my other brother, Guillaume, back to Toulouse.'

'I need a closer look.' They all look at me aghast. 'Don't worry,' I say, 'I will just look like a monk, passing through the soldiers.'

'We,' says Dia firmly. 'You're not going alone.' In the event Rostagnus and Hugh the Bishop accompany me too. As we approach the back end of the Aquitainian host, we can see small groups of other monks walking amongst them. We should be unremarkable, as long as Dia and I do not speak, keep our cowls covering our faces and hair, and our hands concealed in our sleeves. The back of the army consists of the baggage carts, women washing clothes, cooking; grubby children playing in puddles. There don't appear to be any sentries posted and we pass through without any problem. Peasants are here with carts, trading food and other goods. We move inconspicuously forward, passing soldiers who are resting, playing cards, gossiping.

'Got his young son in there,' I hear one of them say. 'Fine boy, trained by Geoffrey of Anjou. Be a shame if he up and dies 'cos there'd be no heir then. His brother's a monk up behind us.' He gestures with his thumb to his companion in the direction of the monastery. 'Got a sister somewhere, nearby, but that's not much use.'

'I suppose Lady Agnes wants that beauty of a castle for herself,' the other soldier says.

I nudge Rostagnus.

'Um, has the Duke and the Dowager Duchess of Aquitaine, offered Lord Hugh any terms of surrender, do you know?' he asks, nervously.

'Nope,' says the soldier, nonchalantly. 'Don't intend to I reckon. She wants that castle and she'll just string up the Sire of Lusignan and his boy when they surrender, I'd say.'

We pass on.

'What about your brother, Audebert?' Rostagnus whispers to me.

I snort humourlessly and keep my eyes on the ground. Rostagnus and Hughie give the odd soldier a brotherly greeting as we pass by. Soldiers are fitting feathers to arrows, greasing shield straps and helmets, loading boulders onto carts to move up to the siege engines. Nobody gives us a second look. A large red tent is pitched ahead of us. As I come around the corner of it I almost collide with Agnes of Mâcon.

'Forgive me brother,' she says, side-stepping around me and striding on.

I mutter a blessing low and quiet, my heart thumping and then turn to look after her.

She is wearing a solid silver armoured vest that must have been made especially for her slender frame and to accommodate her breasts. Her hair is almost white with faded vestiges of its fabulous red clinging in places like old rust. It flies loose about her head and face, held in place only with a gold circlet. The chain mail of her hauberk comes down to her knees, skirting the tops of solid riding boots which sport wickedly spiked silver spurs. From the quick glimpse I saw of her face before averting my own, I saw that it was lined and deeply grooved at the corners of her sour mouth. We continue forwards, getting well out of the line of her vision. Where the rows of Aquitainian soldiers end, just out of the range of the bowmen lining the castle walls, there is a narrow strip of scrubby ground between the army and the outer wall of the castle. Over to the left is the barbican gate. There is a sudden flurry amongst the idling soldiers around us and sergeants start to bark orders.

'What's happening?' says Hugh the Bishop.

I look to the barbican and see that the portcullis is rising and a group of horsemen are clustering to pass under it. A convoy of wheat carts is heading across the open ground, aiming to make a delivery to the Aquitaine encampment and the party of Lusignan riders are trying to make a daring sortie to intercept them.

'Is it Hugh?' Dia asks the question that is uppermost in my own mind. A detail of soldiers from Agnes' army are ready and setting off to confront the raiders. The portcullis has clanged back down behind the Lusignan soldiers.

'They will be slaughtered,' I whisper into my cowl, shivering as a chill passes through me.

'I don't see a white flag,' says Rostagnus in a worried voice.

The Lusignan horsemen are still on the path near the gate and look as if they have decided to go back in. They are looking at the portcullis but it is still firmly in place. Perhaps the mechanism has jammed. I can hear frantic shouts from inside the gatehouse. The Aquitainian troop is nearly upon them and the Lusignan soldiers turn their horses to face them, one man coming forward on a white horse. The blue and silver crest of Lusignan is blazoned on his armour.

'Oh God, no,' I say. It could be my oldest son, Hugh, or . . . I start running across the open ground.

'Almodis, no!' I hear Dia cry behind me. Swords and shields are clashing, a mace whizzes through the air, the horses are snorting in the narrow space near the gate. The fighting men are an indistinguishable melée. The portcullis is slowing rising again behind them and I can see that inside, the bailey is crowded with soldiers and my son, Hugh the Devil, is at the head of them, shouting with impatience to the men working the chains of the gate. The Aquitaine troop see that they are about to be swamped by the men inside and a horn sounds a retreat. The group of twenty or so Aquitainian horsemen are disentangling themselves and coming back fast towards me, so that I must swing myself around a post close to the gateway to avoid being crushed. I cower on the ground as they thunder dustily past me. I look round wildly for Hughie, Dia and Rostagnus and see that they are similarly crouched, taking refuge beside the post on the other side of the path. When the troop have passed I clamber back onto the path and move towards my eldest son who is kneeling in the dust next to a fallen man. Blood seeps into the ground around him and trickles in long lines down the incline towards me. As I get closer I see the fallen man's visor is up and I see his face.

'No!' I'm running, pushing startled men out of my path to reach them. My cowl has slipped back and my hair is flying behind me. 'No!' I scream and throw myself down beside my beloved first husband, catching a glimpse of my son's bewildered expression.

'Mother?'

'No,' I whisper and touch my fingers to Hugh's face. His eyes are open and afraid and he looks at me.

'Mother?'

Dia, Rostagnus and Hughie come up behind me.

'You probably don't remember me,' Hugh the Bishop says to Hugh the Devil, gasping for breath, 'but I'm your half-brother, Hugh of Toulouse.' They clasp hands above my head.

'Dia, Dia, for God's sake, help me get him inside so that you can staunch his wounds!'

Soldiers lift him up and he groans terribly. The pool of his blood left soaking into the ground is very large. I lift the skirts of my habit and run in beside him.

'Mother, what are you doing here?' asks Hugh the Devil, but

I ignore him. As he predicted, I am bewildered by all my Hughs suddenly together, and yet I am focussed on just one of them.

Hugh's men carry him up the stairs and lay him on the bed, the same bed where I lost my maidenhead by slitting the stomach of a rat. His breathing is shallow and his skin a deathly pale. The doctor shakes his head to us. I send a messenger bearing a white flag and the news that the Sire of Lusignan is sorely wounded, to first send Jourdain from the monastery with a priest, and then go on to Parthenay and fetch Melisende. When Jourdain arrives, he looks at his father, kisses my forehead and eyelids, and orders that candles are lit at the foot and head of the bed. The priest gives Hugh the last sacraments but he remains unconscious, and perhaps hears nothing although I keep telling him, 'I am here Hugh, I came back, I am here Hugh.' The priest traces the cross in holy oil on my beloved's eyes, ears, lips, nose, hands, feet and chest. Suddenly he opens his eyes and looks at me and I look into their gentle blackness once again. His hair is threaded with grey but he is not much changed. He is still beautiful. 'I am here,' I whisper and then he closes his eyes again and breathes no more. I fall wailing on his body. 'No, no, no, oh no.' If only I could have spoken with him one more time. I feel the grief drawing tight around my throat. I weep and wail over him for a long time.

My son Hugh begs me to desist. 'You are making the men uneasy Mother. They think you are mad. You're not even his wife,' he says crossly when I continue wailing and ignore him.

Dia takes me gently by the shoulders, pulls me up and half carries me from the room. She gives me a potion in wine and I sleep. When I wake I go back into Hugh's chamber. They have carried his body in his shroud to the priory. I climb into his bed and will not rise from it, staring blankly at the wall, knowing I am indulging my grief, but it seems that I have never given enough room to my emotions. The pain of my brief marriage to Hugh wells up inside me like a river compelled to travel underground and then finding itself burst free into the open air again.

In a desperate effort to shut up my continuous keening, my son Hugh marches in his wife, Hildegarde, with three little children. 'Your grandchildren, Mother,' he says brusquely, knowing that I will dry my eyes for them. They look at me, bewildered, a mad, wailing woman in their grandfather's bed. I swallow back tears, sniff and blow my nose on my sleeve. 'Won't you comb my ugly hair for me, little one,' I say to the girl, the youngest.

'She's Yolande,' Hugh says, putting an ivory comb in her hand. 'Go on,' he says, prodding her forwards, 'Grandmother won't bite. She just *looks* like a shaggy old dog.'

Yolande laughs and climbs up on the bed next to me, saying in her little voice, 'Pretty hair, Grandmother, golden.' The boys come forward to be introduced. Hugh (of course, again!) the eldest, is four, Rorgon is three and Yolande is two. They all have their grandfather's dark hair and eyes. I am grateful to my son for forcing me to close up my misery and distracting me with my grand-kin.

40

Under the Ground

My son is Lord of Lusignan now and he means to offer fealty to Aquitaine, which he must. Guillaume's army have headed back to Toulouse to assist Raymond, so he has no allies here now. Audebert is clammed up tightly inside Roccamolten and will not venture out. The Duke of Aquitaine has returned to rejoin his army and his mother, camped all around Lusignan. From the battlements, I watch Agnes riding in her armour and wonder if she will give my son his life and his castle. Dia and I disguise ourselves as men. The chain mail I wear weighs heavy on my shoulders and breasts, but not as heavy as the weight of Hugh's death. Black pennants fly from the castle towers to mark our mourning.

Agnes is with her son when he rides into Lusignan to take my son's surrender and his homage. 'I heard that your mother was here, Lord Hugh?' she says.

'No,' he replies, lying smoothly. 'I believe she is in Toulouse.'

'I heard that she had left Toulouse and was coming here.'

'Well she is quite conspicuous,' says Hugh, enjoying himself. He throws his arms open. 'Do you see her here?'

'Oh yes, she would be noticeable,' says Agnes. 'Such a renowned lady.' There is sarcastic venom in her 'renowned'. I see that Hugh is rising to this bait and caution him to silence with my eyes. Agnes turns her head quickly seeing that he is glancing at someone behind her. I lower my eyes, but do not move. She would recognise my eyes. She walks over towards me. 'Not here, my Lord Hugh?' she says, standing right next to me.

'No. In Toulouse,' he says firmly.

Agnes casts another dissatisfied glance around the hall and will no doubt have her servants searching every room in the castle before nightfall.

'We have to leave, immediately,' I tell Hugh and Dia, when we are back in the safety of the solar. 'She doesn't believe you.'

'She would not dare to harm you,' Hugh says.

'Yes,' I say, 'she would. She incarcerated my uncle for five years in a dungeon. He was Duke of Aquitaine at the time.'

'Is there any way out of the castle?' asks Dia.

We stand in silence thinking of the routes we know but they are all closely guarded.

'There's the well,' says Hugh finally, 'but you can't go that way. I did it when I was fourteen but I'd baulk at it now.' He is looking doubtfully at me, but I gesture for him to tell me about it.

'It's a tunnel, hidden at the bottom of the well. It goes out under the wall, to the river. You'd never make it.'

'It seems I must.'

'Spiders, rats, dirty water, tight squeezes,' he says looking anxious.

'Psshh,' I say. 'Let's go.'

After dark, seven of us walk towards the stone dome arching above the well: myself, Dia, Rostagnus and four of my children: Hugh of Lusignan, Hughie of Toulouse, Jourdain and Melisende. We are leaving behind a clear night with a near-full moon haloed in rings of brown and yellow and the smaller bright white circle of Venus. A night-lit roiling blanket of earth and bumpy moss covers the warren-like tunnels beneath us. Preparing to go underground I gulp in the view of the sky.

Hugh and Jourdain lift off the heavy cover and hold up their lights so that we can look into the well, descending far down into the earth. The moonlight and the candlelight pick out the glint of metal rungs descending down one side. I select a stone and toss it in and the wait is very long, the splash almost indistinguishable.

'Is the ladder safe?' asks Dia.

'No one has been down it to my knowledge since I did it four years ago,' Hugh says. 'It was alright then.'

The mouth of the well is protected with a heavy metal grate

that swings in the middle, so Hugh and Jourdain must hold it open while we each crouch under and in. I go first, then Hughie, then Dia, then Rostagnus. We estimate two hours of walking, wading, crouching, crawling in and out of the tunnel to get to the river and safety.

'So,' I say and prepare to start moving down the ladder.

'A torch?' whispers Hugh.

'No, we need both hands. Dia has a flint for when we need a light later.'

'Just before you reach the water,' Hugh reminds me, 'there is a wooden hatch to the left of the ladder'. He has given me the key. 'The tunnel is very narrow in places. You will have to slide through parts on your belly. At the end of the tunnel you will have to swim the river and then get to cover without the garrison in the village seeing you.'

'Is Melusine in the river?' asks Hughie, half-joking, half-afraid.

'No, or if she is she will give us a ride,' says Dia.

I begin to move down the ladder, followed by the others. 'Farewell, my Lusignan children. Rule well, Hugh, for your father's sake.'

'I will.'

The glint of Hugh and Melisende and Jourdain's eyes and torches, and their soft calls, are soon gone. Everything is gone in dense blackness. There is only the rungs beneath my hands and feet. 'Go slowly,' I say quietly to Hughie above me. 'Steady and careful.' If the rungs can take my weight they can take his. At last I feel cold water around my ankles and call out, 'Stop!' and hear it passed up the line to Rostagnus. I grope to my left for the hatch and its lock. The key is in my pocket tied to my girdle. Carefully I balance myself with one hand gripping the ladder and grope over one-handed to fit the key into the latch. If I drop the key now in the water then all is lost. I feel the contours of the lock with my fingers and fit the key. The door creaks open.

'What's that?' squeaks Hughie above me.

'It's the door to the tunnel,' I whisper. 'It's alright. It right here as your brother said.' I pass the key carefully to Hughie who passes it to Dia and she to Rostagnus who locks the door behind us, when we are all safely transferred from the ladder to the tunnel. Dia strikes her flint and hands us each a small light.

I am wading knee-deep in water through the dramatic subterranean architecture. Our boots splash in concert. Behind me, Hughie has a deliberate and considered energy and a way of moving and being that is very comforting. Warnings are called down the line, our only verbal communication (apart from some swearing and anxious mutterings to ourselves): 'deep hole to the left!', 'boulder under water!', 'rock protruding from the ceiling!', 'don't touch the walls here!'.

The tighter parts of the tunnel where we have to crawl become harder and harder. I marvel at the astonishing geology around me, our lamps lighting up streaks and nubs of Galena and Quartz glittering in the dark rock. Every now and then we encounter a spectacular mineral-encrusted rockface: Ankerite, Calcite, Cerussite, Chalcanthite, Malachite, Namuwite, Sulphur. Jewels in dirt. We pass the calcifying remains of the tunnellers' tools: wooden buckets and shutes. These old human objects are slowly being absorbed, becoming one with their wet, rocky surroundings, part of the slow flow of rocks. I try to imagine being a thing that always lives in the dark like the plants and insects down here. The adamantine hardness of the rock rubs against the soft fragility of our bodies. Footing and balance is difficult with the uneven ground. When we stop in a relatively open space to pass around water, we examine each others' faces in silent communication.

It gets very hot as we squeeze through tunnels where we cannot stand. In places, loose stones litter the floor from previous cave-ins. At some junctions with two tunnels the wrong tunnel has been marked off with loose pieces of wood. Eventually we reach the hardest part: ten minutes of very low tunnel where we must crawl and slide on our stomachs, where the air thins with the four of us grunting, kneeling on razor sharp stones. Then we emerge into a wet tunnel where we can stand again.

I try to imagine the many *lieues* of rock above the ceiling over my head. Down here it is necessary to be totally in the present, to focus on what is happening right now. We have journeyed into the tunnel, but also into our own interiors. Our bodies come into sharp focus as we are intensely confronted with our dependency on them. They are our only reference point and our vulnerability. I find it difficult to still my senses, to coalesce them to a point where I have enough control to use them. I am overwhelmed, disoriented.

The air is totally still and silent. Every tiny noise that we make reverberates in the clear acoustics: a sniff, a cough, a fart, a nervous hum, a throat clearing, a tapping of rocks together. Some of these noises are involuntary and some of them are nervous attempts to reassure ourselves that we are still alive. Down here, entombed in rock, thoughts of death and burial are inevitable but I feel surprisingly comfortable, whilst Dia's anxiety is palpable. One by one our candles are exhausted and we go forward in complete darkness. Opening and closing my eyes makes no difference at all. Am I even awake? I can see images generated by my own eyes: wheels of light, tiny revolving suns, bright lines that cross and interlace, that roll up and make circles. The air smells and tastes like cold metal. Saltiness on my lips. Coldness on my face. I can hear the gentle shuffling of the others. Wafts of cold air grip me and I shiver uncontrollably for minutes but there are no draughts and no movements in the air.

'I've found two more candles,' Dia calls, and we pause while she strikes her flint again. Hughie points out a fabulous rockface of white and red crystals, a deep red sediment in the wall that we dip our fingertips into, a brilliant cold, tiny waterfall that he drinks from and I follow suit. He picks up a piece of wood, turns it over and finds a finely etched arrow there – a long-gone tunneller's mark. He shows me all his finds. It is his way of reassuring me and I enjoy these moments of combined experience. I can look about me more now I know we are nearing the end. What goes in must come out, Bernadette would say.

When we begin to wade through knee-deep water again I know that we are in the last stretch of tunnel before the exit. Hughie indicates that I should blow out my candle and we are plunged into darkness again. I touch the wet wall to help me keep my balance, my sense of moving in the right direction. We progress up the tunnel, splashing rhythmically and the white light of the exit grows. The anticipation of emergence and the sun is enormous. There is another metal swing gate here. I hold it open for my son, then Dia, then Rostagnus. Hughie takes the weight from me so that I can crouch under and out.

We are all outside, up, in the light. The light is extraordinary. We scrabble to rapidly undo and throw off our cumbersome, sweat-drenched cloaks. We are standing in early morning sunshine diffused through white mist. The low clouds hug the green, so green, land that waves and rises and dips like the sea. We gaze in amazement at each other, at the newly vivid world around us. The sound of the river is loud. Birds. It has been a frosty night. I touch the ice on the surface of a puddle and the frost on a lichened stone. I bury my face in frosted moss and smell it. Slowly we are grinning and clasping hands, hugging. Our faces are smeared with mud and sweat. Our fingers are grimed with the many materials of the tunnel. Our clothes are covered in gray, green, black, red streaks and smears. My eyes feel stripped, clarified, pinned open. The air smells terrific.

Quietly we wade into the cold water of the river suppressing our gasps and start to swim. I think of Dhuoda's description of a herd of deer swimming across a river with turbulent currents: how one stag after another lays its head and horns on the back of the one in front and when the leading stag tires, he is replaced by the rearmost. The river however is placid enough. Hughie, Rostagnus and I are strong swimmers. Dia is less confident and we shepherd her across between us. Quickly we are out of the water and into the cover of the trees and make our escape from Lusignan. We are tottery with fatigue and adrenalin. Our wet, muddy clothes are beyond rescue, streaked with grey and green slime, red sediment and sweat, and we abandon them for new clothes we buy with the gold sewn into our belts. Gold will survive anything: tunnels, river-water, war, death and grief.

The journey from Lusignan to Cluny takes several days on horseback and this is a parting that is hurting me in prospect, for I may not see Hughie again.

'Yes, you will, Mother,' he insists, 'because I intend to become the abbot of a great abbey within riding distance of Barcelona.'

'Oh you do?' I laugh, but am very pleased with him nevertheless. I had no qualms giving Jourdain to the church. I knew it was what he wanted and that his twin would never share Lusignan with him, but with Hughie, perhaps because I have kept him with me about the court for longer, I worry.

'Don't Mother,' he tells me. 'I mean to be an abbot, if not a bishop, and I would not have anything like that much range if I were the secular third son, would I? Do you think that Guillaume and Raymond would share with me? I don't.'

I know that he is right. Saint Gregory of Tours describes the bloody history of the royal Merovingians with brother killing brother. I don't want that for my boys.

At the great monastery of Cluny, set in its lusciously green valley, I am received with great courtesy by Abbot Hugh (another Hugh!) and I see immediately that he and my son will get along. Rostagnus, Dia and I spend a night in the guest-house and in the morning I say farewell to my dear son. The abbot has arranged a boat to take us down the Rhone to Saint Gilles and then we travel by road to Toulouse where I find Guillaume and Raymond shouting at each other.

'I *had* to promise to betroth my first-born daughter to his son,' Guillaume is shouting, and talking of the Duke of Aquitaine.

'Well, why didn't you refuse?' Raymond shouts back.

'How could I? Those were the terms of the treaty. I had to agree.'

'Ye gods!' shouts Raymond and Guillaume crosses himself at this pagan outburst. 'Are you a complete fool?'

'What does it matter? When I have a son he will inherit Toulouse.'

'And if you don't have a son, but have a daughter, the blasted Aquitainians will inherit Toulouse you idiot!'

'Enough.' I say. 'Guillaume, you will make Raymond your heir until you have a son.' I am as determined as Raymond that no grandchild of Agnes of Mâcon is going to lay claim to my family's patrimony through this ruse. I counsel Guillaume to give Raymond power for his capabilities, for if he does not, I see that his brother will take it forcibly. They agree that Raymond will be invested Count of Saint Gilles. It is a good plan if they can stay allies rather than enemies.

My twins, Ramon Towhead and Beren, are already at home

here and enjoying their new duties as pages. They are impressed with Guillaume and Raymond and ape their every move, attempting to be precocious warrior men.

I ask Rostagnus if he wishes to return to his abbey in Toulouse but he answers, 'I beg that you will allow me to stay with you, Na. I would not leave you for any reason, after everything we have been through together!' He, Dia and I spend one night with Raingarde in Carcassonne, regaling her with our stories; and another night with Berenger and Garsenda in Narbonne, before we take ship to Barcelona. I had sent a letter to Ramon from Cluny with news of events and now I begin to feel anxious at how he will receive me.

41

Bernadette: The Great Round of Life

We've heard that they've disembarked and are on their way here. Count Ramon is pacing up and down at the far end of the hall with a furious energy. When my Lady, Rostagnus and Dia enter the hall, I see at once that she is exhausted and dusty from the journey. At sight of her the count's face shows a rapid procession of pleasure, relief, anger. The anger wins out. 'You have endangered yourself and my name, Almodis!'

She meets his anger with her own. 'I had to do it. For my sons.'

'You lied to me!' he says incredulous, for she did do so in her letters, concealing the fact that her lengthy absence was occasioned by her decision to join the battle at Lusignan. I realise that this is the first time in eight years that he has shouted at her.

'Whatever led you to believe, Count Ramon,' she says injecting as much sarcasm as she can muster into her tone, 'that *I* would obey *you*.' She turns her back on him preparing to leave. He grasps her arm and turns her around forcibly, places his two hands on her buttocks and pulls that part of her body to that part of his, so that I have to drop my eyes to the polished floor.

'Yes,' I can hear the smile in his voice now, 'whatever could have led me to have such a ridiculous notion. Don't I know you well enough? Don't I know that you are an unstoppable force of nature? And after all, the journey cannot be untravelled. I've been so afraid for you,' he whispers into her dirty hair, 'but here you are. Thank God, here you are.'

I look up to see that she is leaning away from him, as far as his arms will let her, but then she smiles slowly and moves back into his embrace, kissing him, so I have to lower my eyes again. The hall, it seems, has been transformed into a bedchamber.

'Are your sons safe?'

'Yes. Guillaume rules Toulouse and Raymond most of the rest of the county. They are very capable, although the assault on Aquitaine was foolish and has come to nothing.'

'So all is well,' he says.

'And Hugh rules Lusignan.'

He looks puzzled.

'My son, Hugh. My . . . Hugh, his father, was killed in the siege.' She extracts herself from his embrace, but he pulls her back in and kisses the top of her head, holding her against his chest.

'I'm sorry, Almodis. I know that you cared deeply for him.' He looks at her. 'I am sorry.'

'I must change now, and at dinner I shall regale you with such tales of escapes in wells and the like.'

'I will look forward to that. I am beyond pleased to have you home, darling.'

She nods mutely, holding onto her emotions, and beckons for me to follow her.

I take the children to church with Rostagnus, and it's like herding geese, with this gaggle of small children before me: Charles, Arnau, Inés and Sancha: our second young family now that our first are all grown up and new lords and ladies over the Pyrenees in Occitania. We hear often from them all. My Lady reads out their letters.

> *To Almodis, Countess of Barcelona from Hugh of Toulouse, monk at Cluny:*
>
> *Chère Maman, never fear, I am happy here in Cluny. I found all manner of novices hoping to be worthy of entry as monks: boys who have been here as oblates since they were six, and others just arrived like me, but also men who weary of secular life. Last year Guy Count of Mâcon entered Cluny as a novice with thirty of his knights and their wives all took the veil at Marcigny. We have been given instruction and no*

euphemisms about how hard is the life and how strict the rule. We were taught when to allow our hands out of the sleeves of our habit and when they must be covered, how to dress and undress, the sign language that is used to maintain silence, and that we will likely only ever leave the cloister to go in processions on feast days. After my silks and soft marten furs the woollen robes I wear now chafed at first, but I'm growing used to them. I study grammar, music and dialectics. You would love to roam in the library, although the monks of course would not be best pleased to see you there. On the second day that I was here, after Mass, I gave my consent to becoming a monk and my tonsure was cut. I wrote my act of profession, my Benedictine vows of poverty, chastity, obedience, and the virtues of simplicity and cheerfulness. I processed to the altar and prostrated myself three times and Abbot Hugh blessed my cowl and put it on me. The abbot is a great man, a great statesman, and gentle and patient with us all. When we cross paths with him we must bow down low and kiss his hands.

I had to maintain three days of dead silence and then I entered the daily life of the community. At first I was followed around by another monk, a custos, *who checked that my conduct was everything it should be. I had some trouble with being silent and was chastised more than once by the provost for muttering to myself or trying to talk to one of my fellows, but I am becoming proficient with the signs now and I sign even to myself. We are allowed half an hour of speech each day after Chapter. Some of the signs would amuse you – ruffling your hair means pancakes, pressing your hands together means cheese! We eat no meat, as you know, but there is plenty of fish.*

On Saturdays we are shaved and have our linen washed. Our names are marked in our clothes with thread by the tailor. I have been tasked to work on a grange for the summer so I am out in the open and enjoying the physical labour. It is my job to take care of the fishpond too. When winter comes, Abbot Hugh says that he will make me assistant to the cellarer. I will get a new habit and cowl each Christmas. They tell me that on Maundy Thursday new shoes are set on four long poles in the chapter house and we have to rifle through them looking for ones that will fit us. I enjoy the daily round: nine services when the bells ring us to the church: Matins at dawn, Prime one hour later, Tierce two hours after that, Sext three hours after that, Nones another three hours after, Vespers at sunset, Compline at nightfall, Nocturnus and Vigils in the night. It took me a while to adjust and I had to be woken up often by the circatores. *Do write mother and tell me if yours, Rostagnus' and Dia's journey home was as eventful as the rest of our trip! And how are Bernadette, Adalmoda, Arnau, Inés and Sancha? Your son, with great affection, Hugh of Toulouse.*

We hear news from Lusignan, too, from Jourdain and Melisende who make us laugh with tales of the exploits of their brother, Lord Hugh. Jourdain writes to tell his mother that he places fresh flowers on his father's grave every week on her behalf: snowdrops, forget-me-nots, May blossom, roses, he tells her, as the seasons come and go.

From Raingarde, Countess of Carcassonne to Almodis Countess of Barcelona:

The painful news from here, sister, is that my daughter Garsendis has sickened and died. She would have been wed this Easter to Raymond of Narbonne. It happened so quickly, without warning, that I wake and think for a moment, that she is still here.

My daughter Ermengard is wed to the Viscount of Albi and Nîmes and this seems a happy match. There is news that Agnes of Mâcon's daughter, the Empress of Germany, who has usurped her own son's power (just like her mother) has been deposed by her bishops. You will no doubt hear this news soon enough from your sons, but the heiress, Bertha of Rouergue, Hugh and Fides' daughter, has died and your sons are claiming all her lands and rights in Narbonne, Agde, Béziers, Uzès and Rouergue. This is a great expansion for them. Bertha's husband, Robert of Auvergne contests their claim but he is no match for such fierce men trained in the anvil of Anjou.

Your two Barcelona boys come on apace and I am especially fond of Ramon Towhead who comes visiting often with Count Guillaume. They are great friends with my daughter, Adelais, and I am glad to see them all laughing and conversing. It lightens my heart after the loss of my eldest daughter.

'My poor sister,' exclaims my Lady, over this letter. 'So hard: to lose a child. I have been lucky. I know that Ramon is scarred by the early loss of his two infant sons, but how much worse to see a child grow to womanhood, to be close to marriage and then to lose her.'

There's been a to-do in the mews this morning when my Lady discovered her falcon dead, lying on its back at the foot of its perch. The mews man was bewildered. 'Were fine yesterday,' he says.

'Please bury her. Perhaps she was older than we thought,' Lady Almodis says frowning. 'Although she wasn't long trained, a young bird when Ramon gave her to me.'

Perhaps my Lady, very, very slowly is falling in love. 'We can't push her to it, Dia, she'd only resist,' I say, when she's gone out riding. 'You can lead a horse to water but you can't make it drink. We must let her fall with her own gravity and grace, in her own time.'

'I'm sure you're right, Bernadette,' says Dia.

'Will you not marry, yourself?' I ask her.

'No, marriage is not the life for me.'

I sometimes wonder if Count Ramon himself is the man she sings of so often in her *planhs* of unrequited love, but if he is she keeps it deep.

The seasons come and go in the great round of life, blown round and round by the fat cheeks of the four winds riding on their windbags. All the men and women and children of the earth, all the birds in the sky, the fish in the sea and rivers, the creatures roaming the forests and grasslands, see the days go round from light to dark and angels watch over us. Every year in January we are feasting and giving gifts, chopping wood and collecting faggots for the fires. After Epiphany, there's Plow Monday with a race at sunrise, oxen pulling the plows and making the land fertile for seed. We trim the vines, and the rains and the sun make the wheat grow, and the lambs run in the fields with their mothers: white lambs and black lambs. At the Easter Assemblies come betrothals, the start of journeys and pilgrimages, and the fruit trees blossom. In May, flowers everywhere fill the eye with colour, and the villagers beat the bounds. We wear gay green dresses and garlands of leaves for

May Day and then come weddings. Fishermen line the riverbanks with their rods and baskets and the sun in his chariot reaches his longest day. We cut and gather the hay and time slows down for the long, long, golden days of summer when red poppies wave in the wheat. We shear the sheep and reap the crops and cool down in the stream. Falcons fly and lords and ladies ride to hunt. We harvest the year's goods and store up our surpluses for the icy times ahead. The purple grapes are gathered in the vineyards. The sun hides more and more before his shortest day and All Hallows Eve when we remember the dead lest they rise up and walk the earth and scare us out of our wits. We harrow and sow for the early spring crops and chase away the birds. The trees and earth turn every shade of red and orange and the leaves fall and the hogs gorge themselves on acorns. Then comes the blood month when we slaughter the animals that we cannot feed through the winter, and salt the meat and taste the new wines. When the north winds of winter blow, Saint Martin comes riding on his white horse and with him comes snow. We put on all our clothes and stop up the draughts with tapestries and warm our toes at the fire. Then we make ready for the great feast of Christmas and the birth of Our Lord and then we're ready to start all over again at Plow Monday. My son Charles grows apace with the round of each year, as do my Lady's children, and she and I grow older.

My Lady is good friends with Lady Mathilde, Pere's wife, but relations are still icy with him. Pere and Mathilde have been married for five years and no sign of children. She is in my Lady's chamber today, talking in a low voice with Dia, seeking advice to help her conceive. She is a pretty, slender woman with fine brown hair and great brown eyes like a doe. Pere strides into the room without announcement or invitation, shouting, 'Is my wife here?' We all look up at him. He is wearing hunting clothes. 'I thought you were hunting with me today?' he says to Mathilde. 'We're all waiting for you.'

'Oh, forgive me, my Lord,' she says, 'I forgot my engagement and I have a headache and am not minded to hunt today.'

'Hmmph,' he says, looking around the chamber and at us women with an expression of dissatisfaction on his face.

Almodis rises. 'I could ride with you, Lord Pere,' she says. 'I could be ready in five minutes and help officiate at your luncheon in the bower.'

'No thank you,' he says rudely.

Lady Almodis sits back down again and turns her face away, struggling to control her expression. I look crossly at him and would like to box his ears.

'Well,' he says to Mathilde, 'I'll leave you to your women's lore then.'

When he has left, Almodis rises abruptly and strides about the room but has to contain her anger in front of his wife.

'I'm sorry, Countess,' Mathilde offers her timidly.

'Oh never mind it, Mathilde,' she says, but the atmosphere in the room is awkward and Mathilde makes her exit soon afterwards.

'It's fixed now, Almodis,' Dia says. 'It won't mend or get any better now that he is a man.'

'Well,' Almodis says, contemplating the toe of her boot and then looking up, 'I think it would mend a little if Ramon would agree to give Pere certain reassurances of his inheritance, but he is reluctant to do so. He says he's barely grown up himself yet!' Her expression suggests that she is both exasperated and charmed with her husband's position.

At Easter this year, we hear from Hughie, who in just a few years, has risen all the way to be the abbot's deputy:

To Almodis Countess of Barcelona from Hugh of Toulouse, Grand Prior of Cluny:

On Good Friday we went to Prime all with bare feet and, believe me Mother, some of those monks have very, very dirty feet. We bathe only twice a year, before the feasts of Easter and Christmas. Yes I can imagine you pinching your nose at that. Still we can wash plenty and in truth I get in the river fairly often if no one is looking.

Last week I was sent to the nunnery of Marcigny to hear confessions. There are ninety-nine nuns there so it was a long visit. In their dining hall they keep a seat and set a place at dinner for the Virgin. The abbot has decided to send me to the Abbey of Saint Gilles. He tells me they are in need of new leadership and I should go and make myself useful. I thought I would be anxious and sad to leave Cluny that I have grown so used to, but in truth I am excited at a new prospect and to be in my own lands, close to Guillaume, Raymond and Adalmoda, now that she will be coming here to wed. Your loving son, Hugh.

42

Pentecost 1066

Ramon and I are onboard ship heading to Narbonne, taking Adalmoda to Toulouse for her marriage to Pierre, the son of the Count of Mergueil, and also to attend the investiture of Hughie as Abbot of Saint Gilles. We have, with some concern, left Pere in command of Barcelona in our absence. I recall that it is thirteen years since I made my escape from Toulouse and Pons. Thinking on it I slip my hand into my husband's and he smiles at my touch. Before we left we received news that Guillem of Besalú had been assassinated by his own servants. I shudder to remember that I would have wed Lucia to such a monster. How cold and callous my own problems had made me, but then, I think, perhaps my comfort now with Ramon makes me soft and complacent. I take my hand out of his and grip the edge of the ship, breathing in the rush of cold, salty air, the breeze whipping strands of my hair into my mouth.

Adalmoda's wedding is a joyful day, as is Hugh's investiture as abbot the following week. Raingarde is at both events and I am so happy to spend time with her and to introduce her properly to my husband. She tells me about her daughter, Adelais' betrothal to the Count of Cerdanya which she has just contracted in the village of Davejean in the Pyrenees. 'Your old friend, Berenger of Narbonne, came with us as one of the witnesses. I've left her there,' she says, 'and her husband will conduct her to her new home. All my children gone now.'

'I still have two more daughters to go,' I say, telling her about Inés, who is ten, and Sancha, who is eight.

'Well, I suppose children will keep coming if you have yourself three husbands and not one, Almodis,' she teases me. I tell her something too, of my concerns regarding Pere.

Ramon and I travel on to spend some time with Raymond in Saint Gilles where I sign a grant to Moissac with Guillaume, and another to Cluny with Raymond. Raymond's wife has recently presented him with a son, Bertrand, so I have four grandchildren now. News comes that William of Normandy has invaded England and become its new king.

'I am thinking to set aside Mathilde,' Guillaume tells me. 'She gives me no children. I have opened negotiations for Emma of Mortain, William the Conqueror's niece.'

I nod with approbation at this move. Yes, he must get heirs. 'Be kind to Mathilde,' I say to him. 'Offer her the choice of a nunnery, another marriage, or going home to her family. Let her choose.'

'Very well, Mother,' he says, 'for your sake, I will do as you ask.'

Raymond snorts at him and at me. He is happy in his marriage with his cousin Bertranda despite the pope's opprobrium.

'My Lady,' Bernadette begins hesitantly, interrupting my reading.

'Yes, what is it?'

'I've found something out.'

'Well, what is it Bernadette?' I am growing impatient with all this delay.

'I think it's Piers,' she blurts out, and starts crying.

'Piers? What do you mean?'

'I think he's here in the dungeons. Been there a long time. He's my boy's father after all.'

I open my mouth and close it several times. 'Well, let's go and see.'

She looks at me in horror. 'I can't go down in no dungeons, Lady. I just thought I should tell you. Mayhap you would see your way to forgive him.'

'Well I must see first if what you say is true. If you will not come with me then I will go and look alone.' I walk swiftly through the castle to the dungeons. Bernadette tags along reluctantly behind me. There is a guard on the gate. 'Open the gate.'

'Begging your pardon, my Lady. I must obey the commands of Count Raymond only regarding this gate,' says the guard, who is a youth, and looks very alarmed to see his usually boring guard duty disturbed in this way.

'As you well know, boy, I am the mother of Count Raymond, I am the dowager Countess of Toulouse and Saint Gilles and the Countess of Barcelona. You will open the gate now or I will ensure that you are thrust behind it yourself.'

His eyes goggle at that and he swallows, looks at Bernadette, fiddles with an enormous bunch of keys at his waist and opens the gate for me with great difficulty. 'There's nobody in there, Lady, but one man,' he says. 'I give him his supper and water . . .'

I push him out of my way, take a lit torch that is set in the wall and move down into the darkness, hearing the scattering of small creatures in the dark as I move forward. I turn to look back and see that the guard and Bernadette are still huddled at the gateway watching me. At the end of the narrow passage is an arched entry to a dank stone chamber and here are the remains of the trencher and water jug. Rats run off the crumbs at my approach and black beetles scuttle back into the damp walls. I step over the jug and into the space beyond. There is a grate high above my head, letting in a little light and against the far wall I can just see a wooden palette and the huddled shape of a man. 'Hello,' I say tentatively. There is no response. Perhaps he is dead. I move a little closer and hold the torch to try to see the prisoner. I see that he is filthy and in rags, manacles around his ankles attach him by a long, heavy chain to the wall. It would give him scope to reach the jug at the archway and to drag himself around this space, but no more. His arm is flung over his face and I cannot see it. I am loathe to go any closer but I must know if it is indeed Piers. 'Piers?' I say. The shape shifts at that. He moves his arm away and reveals a grime-covered, aged face. Not Piers then. He sits up slowly and with obvious pain and shrinks further against the wall. Poor man but perhaps he has deserved such punishment. 'What is your name?' I ask gently. 'Don't be afraid,' although in truth I am afraid myself. If he is a murderer or a madman the chain would not stop him from suddenly throttling me. I move back a few paces, anxiously. 'What is your name?' I insist.

'Water,' he croaks out at last.

I reach back for the jug which still has some liquid in it and pass it to him, trying not to think of the rats and the bugs that have supped on it before him. His hands are black with grime and there is a stench coming from him that makes me gasp when he moves.

'You don't know me?'

'No, I . . .' I stop. A cloud has cleared the sun and a ray of light hits the massive stone blocks above his head, where he is leaning. His eyes. His eyes are pale blue and I do know them. I am filled with a great grief and cannot speak for a long time, just looking on him. 'Oh Piers,' I say eventually. Images of us as children fighting in the stable in Aquitaine, his silky brown hair, his wenching, his skill with horses, hounds and falcons, rush through my head. 'Piers.'

'Lady Almodis.' I take the jug from him and his voice has gained some strength, so that I recognise his voice now too, but this is a wreck of a man I am looking at, not the handsome knave who accompanied me into Toulouse for the Easter Assembly so long ago, before I ever married, before Hugh and Pons and Ramon. 'Piers.' I don't know what to say except keep repeating his name. An image of my father, flashes before me and in the shape of his head, his eyes, even in this wretched condition, I see my father's echo. I always knew it was there. 'Oh, Piers, I am so sorry to find you so wretched. I will take care of you now. It was Bernadette who found out that you were here and sent me to you,' I say. 'How long?' I am afraid to hear his answer. 'How long have you been here?'

'I hardly know that,' he says. 'I kept some tally sticks in the beginning,' he gestures to a pile of whittled sticks by the bed, 'but couldn't go on eventually. I hardly know mistress.'

'When did you enter in here?'

'When your old husband died, Lady, and your son became the lord here.'

Six years I think but do not say it aloud. 'It has been hard for you,' I say inadequately. What words can comprehend it?

'The cold sucked me into sleep night after night,' he says, 'but I wanted to stay awake to see how dark dark is.'

'Bernadette,' I yell, 'get down here now!'

Piers looks afraid.

'It's alright,' I soothe him. 'I am going to find the key for these manacles and to bring you out of here, but I don't want you left alone whilst I do that.'

His eyes are huge in his wasted face. 'Out?' he says and my heart knots in my chest.

'Bernadette!'

She is coming through the arch with the boy-guard holding her hand and a torch above his head, and she is staring open-mouthed at Piers.

'Do you have the key to these manacles?' I demand of the boy.

'No Lady. That's the Lord Raymond that has them.'

'Very well. I will go and fetch them. Bernadette, you will stay here and talk with Piers for a while. Tell him of your son.' She is shaking her head and weeping and wailing but I grip her by the shoulders and sit her down on the bug-infested bed beside him, this poor skeleton. 'Bernadette!' I slap her lightly round the face and she looks at me shocked. 'Take care of him!' I tell her firmly. 'Boy, go and fetch a jug of clean water for him, bring another man and a stretcher.'

'Yes, Lady.'

'Leave the torch here for them and the door open. Bernadette, if you desert him, I will dismiss you,' I say firmly and then in a gentler voice: 'I will be back, Piers.'

In the hall, I pause to send Dia to fetch a doctor to my chambers and to send a messenger to my son, Abbot Hugh, to please come to me quickly and then pass swiftly up the hall to Raymond.

'Mother?'

'I need the key to Piers' manacles.'

'What?' he says, rising to his feet.

'Now, Raymond, I appreciate that you did it for me and that Piers should have been punished for his treachery but six years

316

is enough. He is dying and I intend for him to die in peace and comfort, with my forgiveness.'

'He is my prisoner and I will see fit . . .' he begins, but then thinks better of it, looking at my face. 'He does not deserve your forgiveness,' he says, handing the key to me.

I do not reply but turn on my heel and go back to the dungeon where Bernadette, bless her, has forgotten her fears of the dark and the spiders and is wiping Piers' face with her best white apron and holding the water jug for him.

'Oh Lady, he's very ill,' she says, looking up at my entrance.

'Yes.' I unlock the manacles and remove them as gently as I can, trying not to retch at the stench of the wounds underneath. The young guard is back with the stretcher and Rostagnus, and they lift Piers up and carry him to my chamber. There Bernadette and Dia prepare a bath tub, padded with soft clothes, set before the fire. Rostagnus lifts him from the bed and into the tub as if he were a feather, and holds his head above the water, for he has no strength at all. He lets out a groan as the warm water stings his wounds, but after a while he looks up at me and attempts a grin, that old, blue-eyed grin. Oh the change, the ruin of his beauty is so great I can hardly bear to see it, but I grin back and hold onto my tears. 'Welcome back to the world, Piers, you knave,' I say.

His face is serious now. 'Forgive me Almodis? I have regretted it and not only because your son threw me in that hole.'

'I do forgive you,' I say, and then in a low voice I ask him, 'and will you forgive me?'

He looks at me uncomprehending.

'I should have acknowledged that you are my half-brother, Piers. My father should have acknowledged it, but when he did not, I should have done so.'

I look at his decimated mouth, so beautiful once, that had kissed so many foolish maids. 'Oh Piers, I am so sorry. What have we done to each other, brother?' Tears trickle over the bones of his cheeks when I call him that name.

My son, Abbot Hugh arrives. So strange to see my boy with his tonsure and his habit, but also with a great authority and cheerfulness about him. 'My Lady Mother,' he says, kissing me on the forehead, 'what trouble are you in now? Last time you had me crawling through tunnels and swimming a river. Some more of the same?' He glances with concern at Piers who is being lifted back onto the bed, where Dia begins to lay salve on his wounds.

I take Piers' hand. 'You will be well again,' I tell him, though I know I lie.

And so does he. 'What traces am I leaving in the world, Almodis? A few strands of hair, drops of my sweat, ongoing resonances and vibrations of sounds I made in that dungeon, my thoughts of another chance at life still there, absorbed and stored by the rocks like a stony library. My absence is waiting there for me, mistress, like the negative space left by lead in a mine, like my open grave.'

'No,' I say to him firmly. 'No.'

Hugh has taken Piers back to the abbey now where he will care for him. Bernadette told Piers that he has a son, a lovely strong son, Charles, and he smiled at that and called her 'little Bernadette, little Parisienne'.

Raymond thinks I am too soft. 'I would have strung him up if I'd known you'd come along and let him out,' he says.

'He will not live,' I say, 'and he is my kin, your kin.'

'Would he have come and let you out of that anchorite cell my father intended to put you in?'

43

The Crisis of Carcassonne 1067

We have been back in Barcelona barely a week, when a letter follows us from Raingarde, sent by fast messengers:

From Raingarde Countess of Carcassonne to Almodis Countess of Barcelona

Sister, I helped you once when you were in dire need. I ask you now, can you help me? So many things have happened so quickly and brought such change, I hardly know where to begin. Except in that I must begin in telling you that my son, Roger, is dead. He was ill for two weeks and took to his bed a few days ago and now, Almodis, he is lying cold in his shroud in the cathedral and I must bury him, alongside my husband and my eldest daughter. I did not think that I had lived such a blameful life that I should be so punished by God.

Roger's wife, Sybile, has borne him no child, so I am ruling Carcassonne for the time being. Ermengard is the rightful heiress and I have urged her with her husband to come to me soon to consider what we should do.

Soon after Roger passed, another calamity has befallen me: the Count of Cerdanya took my daughter, Adelais, and wed her but when he undressed her on their wedding night he found her with child and has repudiated her. She is waiting in great distress in his palace and writes to me to help her. She tells me that the child is your son's, Guillaume of Toulouse.

Now I fear that many of my neighbours will covet Carcassonne if it is held only by a dowager countess and a female heiress. I have not kept the army here I should have. I did not foresee this. My nephews, and Peter of Foix, Guifred of Narbonne, the Viscount of Narbonne, the Count of Cerdanya, and perhaps, even your own sons, could challenge me and Ermengard for control of the city. I ask your advice in great distress, Almodis.

Most likely my own sons, I think, especially Raymond. Carcassonne is the lynchpin of all the trade routes. It will be a rich prize and yes, she is right, they will all seek to take it from her. Things are changing. Men challenge the right of women to rule now and the church argues against it. There is likely to be war and instability.

I read all this and I think, oh yes, sister, I must help you and your daughters, I owe you that and much more besides. I put aside my anger with Guillaume: to seduce his cousin and then abandon her to her fate because he has a rich wedding on the horizon with the niece of William, King of England, Duke of Normandy! What is to be done to undo all this? I have ideas and stand to begin to implement them, but then I still myself. This time, I will speak with Ramon, act with him, ask his counsel and try to follow it if it should differ from mine. Do my best at least. Well I will listen to it at any rate.

When I returned from my escapades in Lusignan he could have greatly resented my lies and defiance of him, but he did not. Another husband would have taken a rod to a wife who acted as I did. He would have been within his rights. Of course our marriage would have been over for me if he had, but he did not. Instead he forgave me, laughed and marvelled at my adventures, commiserated me on my losses, was impressed by my resourcefulness. 'Don't do it again, though,' he'd said to me. 'I did not know what to do with myself each day you were away. I was in such terrible anxiety for you.'

I go to seek out my husband and discuss my sister's dilemma with him.

'I don't want Cerdanya laying claim to Carcassonne, building up a new power-base for himself,' he says. 'Clearly your sister is right, Ermengard and Raymond Bernard Trencavel, should take the city, but they will be beset with counter-claims that will be supported in arms.'

'You, yourself, are one of the potential heirs, through Ermessende.'

'I don't intend to lay claim to it, against your sister.'

'I have a plan,' I tell him, and he raises his eyebrows. 'See what you think of it.'

Happily Ramon has concurred with my plan, for if he had not I suspect my new-found wifely obedience would have dissipated fast. Ramon sent an emissary with a heavy guard to Cerdanya carrying bags of gold, 4,000 *mancusos*, and the emissary has returned with my niece, Adelais, who is big with child, and with a quit-claim on Carcassonne signed by the count.

'Well, that was quite easy,' says Ramon, congratulating me on my strategem.

Adelais begins greatly ashamed when she first arrives but I tell her that to love a man and to bear a child is no shame, it is the way of the body of a woman. I am not so kind in a letter to my son, who claims that he has no way to know that the child is actually his and is proceeding with his marriage plans to Emma of Mortain. When Adelais' child is born, I will send them back to Raingarde and she must make shift to live with her abandonment. 'Your mother and I will take care of you,' I soothe her, 'I will have five grandchildren now.' But she knows that her reputation is irretrievably damaged and her child will be an unacknowledged bastard.

Bernadette tells me that Pere's court contingency are whispering in corners that my niece is a whore, like her aunt. I do my best to shield Adelais from these calumnies, although it is clear from the cold way that some courtiers look at her, what they are thinking. I resist the temptation to retaliate by pointing out to Pere that his own wife's belly remains flat and girlish.

Raingarde has drawn up formal charters acknowledging Ramon and myself as the overlords of Carcassonne. Guillaume and Raymond have objected of course, since Carcassonne was at least nominally in their suzerein. Guillaume, I have silenced with the pressure of his guilt over Adelais and the promise of some gold. I have written to Raymond to tell him that Ramon and I intend to take possession of the city and install our son Ramon Towhead as count. He has not replied. He knows that a Barcelonese garrison in the city would not be so easy a target as my sister presented alone. Raymond has allied himself with Archbishop Guifred and together they are eeking out their domains little by little.

The other contenders to Carcassonne will have heard of the changed situation and will, I hope, draw back and decide that though rich, Carcassonne, is not worth a confrontation with us. I have sent another letter to Guillaume and Raymond making them a very generous offer of a share each in the trade routes and rights through the city. I hope this will work. The thought of warring with my own sons is not a pleasant one and I sense that once in the battlefield, Raymond might show the resilience of his mentor, Geoffrey. Everything depends on our acting quickly, with decision and on a show of force. Our garrison troops are already assembled in the city and Ramon and I will travel there next year to take the oaths of allegiance from all the main castellans on the routes between here and Carcassonne.

On the first day of March 1068 Ramon and I invested Ermengard and Raymond Bernard Trencavel as viscounts of Carcassonne, with the condition that the *usufruct* of the city's rights remain with my sister. We have had to pay off her Carcassonne nephews but they came a great deal cheaper than the Count of Cerdanya.

Ramon is pleased to advance the Barcelonese frontier in Languedoc beyond Narbonne and to have his trade routes thus assisted. I think there will be some benefit too in demonstrating to Pere that he will indeed inherit Barcelona if my sons are suitably invested with rights elsewhere. Raingarde has grown very fond of Towhead during his time of training in the region and is not displeased to see her nephew take up her husband's and her son's title.

'Though I have doubts about Pere, Almodis,' Ramon says to me.

'Doubts?' I have plenty of doubts too, but it is not for me to criticise his son.

'I do not know that he will rule Barcelona well.'

I stay silent for a while. 'It is his right; he is the heir. We must help him to learn to rule well.'

We are due to begin our journey to Carcassonne when a great tragedy befalls us and delays our departure. Our son, Arnau, has died. Ramon and I are inconsolable together. Now I am like Raingarde again: we have both lost our sons this year, and I long to be with her. Ramon understands my longing and resumes the plans for our journey. The doctors can give us no explanation. Arnau was well and then suddenly he complained of pains in his stomach and was dead so quickly.

'It could be poison,' Dia tells me when we are alone and I am done crying, cried dry.

'Poison? No. Why would anyone poison Arnau, a little boy?'

'For practice,' says Dia.

44

Autumn

In the early autumn of 1069 Ramon and I cross the Pyrenees with more Barcelonese reinforcements for Carcassonne and the landscape is transforming dramatically all around us. The flaming colours of trees in the valleys shift to muted fustian browns and dark greens. The trees along the river are nearly all bare so that it becomes possible to see more of the surrounding landscape. Many little birds congregate in the branches preparing to fly further south. Instead of the route I took into my homeland a few years ago, we follow the coast for some way and then crossing the mountains we head for the tower of Dourne, high above the gorges of the upper Aude. After that we wend our way through Razès along the river, taking oaths from the castellans at Niort, Auriac and Rennes. Heading towards Conffoulens, we ride through the thick trees and the forest floor is littered with mushrooms of all kinds: red and white, brilliant white like angel's wings, shiny brown caps, and mushrooms decaying so that they look like the faeces of an unknown animal.

In Carcassonne I reunite Adelais and her new son, William-Jourdain, with her mother. She will live with Raingarde, and Ermengard has also promised her a home. Raingarde is well, despite the terrible losses she has sustained over the last few years. She is confident in our new strategem to protect her and her family's rights.

Ramon and I continue our journey of oath-taking to the castle of Ornaisons near Narbonne. 'I keep expecting to see your son's army camped on the road before us,' Ramon tells me, meaning Raymond, but there is no sign of him. When we visit Garsenda in Narbonne I am sad to see her alone, now that my dear friend Berenger has died. After Narbonne we strike back towards Toulouse, taking oaths from the castellans at Caberet and Saissac on the southern slopes of the Montagne Noire and at the fortress of Cintegabelle on the road from Foix.

In Toulouse my Barcelonese twins, Ramon Towhead and Beren, are knighted by Guillaume and will travel back to Barcelona with us. Towhead is excited to find that he will be Count of Carcassonne when he comes of age. Guillaume tells me he will not meet Adelais or look at his son. 'I can't do that, Mother,' he says gruffly and my heart aches to think of him as a boy and now this unkind man, dishonouring his cousin.

'You will regret it,' I tell him and he is angry with me.

Adalmoda arrives to see me with her husband Pierre and two baby boys named Raymond and Pons. I try not to show her how I dislike the last name. She looks well and happy and is very proud of her sons.

Guillaume gives me news that Agnes of Mâcon became a nun at her Abbey of Notre Dame de Saintes near Poitou and that she has recently died there. Though I had good cause to loathe her all my life, I go to the cathedral and say a pray for her soul for she, like Ermessende, was a very great lady.

On our return to Barcelona the city is in uproar with the news that Seljuk forces have taken control of Jerusalum from the Fatimid caliph of Egypt. The Seljuk will be even more intolerant of Christian pilgrimages. 'The pope must act,' are the words in the mouths of many people.

Shortly after our return my daughter Inés was married to Guigues Count of Albon and has left me. 'She is too young,' I had protested to Ramon since she is only fifteen.

'I was that age when I first married,' he told me. 'I've talked it over with her and she is more than happy about it. You know I would not let her go otherwise.'

I hug fourteen-year-old Sancha to me, my only child left of twelve! 'Sancha will not wed early,' I tell him and he bows to us both. 'You know that your word is law in this household,' he says. Pere stands scowling against the wall.

The atmosphere of the court has shifted substantially since our return with Towhead and Beren, and not for the better. Now there are the *conroi*, the followers, of three young princes jostling and vying with each other daily. My Barcelonese twins have returned moulded to the military bearing of my Toulouse sons, who in their turn were moulded by Geoffrey the Hammer. They wear their hauberks and gambesons most days, despite the heat, as part of their toughening regime, and the young men of the court and the city who Pere has not favoured, flock to them instead.

Bernadette tells me she has overheard an argument between Pere and Beren. 'Pere taunted Beren that his brother is Count of Carcassonne and he will have nothing.'

'Tsch! He is wicked.'

'Beren more than stood up to him though,' she tells me proudly. 'Clouted him round the head he did, and told him he'd have Barcelona and his mother would see to it.'

'In the spring,' I say to Ramon, 'we will send Pere on a mission to Rome on our behalf. He needs responsibilities and to see the world.'

Ramon and I ride out alone from the city for a rare day off from our own responsibilities. We ride past olive groves where children are knocking the ripe olives down with sticks, until we reach a secluded place on the river with willows dipping their leaves in the water. I take off most of my clothes and lie on my back by the riverbank, watching a procession of wispy clouds across the blue sky, while he tethers the horses and unpacks a picnic. My chemise barely comes down far enough to cover my privates. I have a pair of Ramon's short breeches on to do that and I stretch out my bare legs feeling the sun hot on my skin, although these will be the last days of this summer and the air has a hint of the coming chill.

'Come on then,' I say, 'are you coming in?'

He is divesting himself of his clothes. His legs, and his bare chest when he pulls his shirt up over his head, ripple with muscle.

'We are in good shape for two middle-aged people,' I say smiling at him. 'We are a happy middle-aged couple.'

'Really? Feels to me somedays as if I am in a marriage with a hedgehog.'

He throws himself down beside me laughing, wearing only his breeches, luxuriating with his eyes shut in the sun. He opens one blue eye and squints at me. 'It'll be cold.'

'Nonsense,' I say, standing up and pulling him up with me and down to the river's edge. The sun sparkles on the surface. Frogs are mating noisily. Blue dragonflies skid along the water. Fish jump and splash back down. Large black and white butterflies flap along the bank like handkerchiefs. I stand hand in hand with him like the earth's first man and woman.

'Here,' he says, pointing to a place where a flat rock juts out from the bank into the water. 'It'll be easiest here.'

I go first, slipping into the water, gasping at the initial full immersion. 'It's lovely!'

He looks doubtfully at me, dipping a toe in, but then somersaults spectacularly into the water, so that I am drenched. He swims up beside me. 'Whur-huh-huh! It's lovely and cold!'

Ducks look at us with amusement, that we have assumed duckness for the day. 'Or fishness of frogness,' says Ramon, demonstrating fishy and froggy swimming moves. I laugh and the sounds echo up from the water, bouncing off trees and light.

45

17 November 1071

A plate of pink and green and vermilion marzipans fashioned in the shapes of flowers. The sweetmeat is sweet on my tongue but now I feel a burning sensation in my throat, coughing, choking.

Poison.

I turn my head to where I know Pere stands, holding the plate, but my vision blurs and I cannot see him. I fall and lie on my back, looking at the intense blue of the sky. Shouts and running feet come to me muffled, and then silent, but still vibrating through the ground. Something obscures my vision, gossamer cobwebs I would like to wipe away from my face, but I cannot move my hand. A small oval of blue, contracting.

'Almodis!' A quiet shout. I know he is kneeling at my side, but it seems that he is standing on a distant mountain, calling to me. The blue oval of the sky, has become the blue circle of Ramon's eye, washed and swimming in tears, his tears, my tears.

I try to move my hands to leave some trace of my fingers in the dust.

I think: but I haven't finished yet.

Epilogue

The Castle of Parthenay
31 December 1099

I, Dia, *trobairitz* of Barcelona, am dying with the old century. It was all so long ago and I forget so much, but I remember everything about Almodis. Every word. I remember her, my dear friend. I remember Ramon's grief, as deep as a gaping well sunk far into the ground, as black as a moonless night.

'*L'heureuse Almodis, resplendissante sur terre, est passée, par sa mort, a la demeure de la vie,*' he wrote on her epitaph in Girona Cathedral: Happy Almodis, radiant on earth, is passed by her death, to the residence of the life.

'Though one may seem to live long in the world,' wrote her favourite author, Dhuoda, 'one's life is short, like that woven cloth that is measured and snipped off in the market place.'

We all knew that Pere had murdered her and Ramon's grief at that was terrible too: that the warnings had been there, but he hadn't been able to believe them. Pere was banished and forbidden to bear arms for twenty-five years. He lost the kingdom that he had lusted after and hoped to gain by his wickedness. He died young, just thirty-five, and alone, in Muslim Spain. When he was on his death-bed Pope Gregory gave him a pardon for Almodis' murder. But God will not pardon him. I do not pardon him.

Ramon outlived her only five more years, years of unremitting grief and loss. The people called him Count Ramon the Old, but he was not old. When she died his hair turned white and the youth dropped from him like a silk shift. I stayed with him for those years and when he too died and went to join her, I travelled with Rostagnus to Parthenay to make our home under the patronage of her daughter, Lady Melisende.

At the moment of Almodis' death, Raingarde let out a great cry in Carcassonne and never spoke again and died herself a week later.

Some say Almodis was a serpent, a scandal, a whore. They say wrong. She was a sweet lady and worked her whole life for the good of her subjects, her friends and her children. Before she died, I think she learnt to love her husband. She left a great legacy behind her: her sons, daughters and kin are rulers in Occitania, Catalonia and the Holy Lands. She never liked women's work and was happier with a pen in her hand rather than a needle and thread, but she wove together an empire and a society. Those who come after her now do not have her skill to hold it together.

Bernadette laid out her beautiful lady in her shroud and sat with her in the Cathedral of Barcelona for ten days, rocking herself backwards and forwards, and then she blew her nose, took her son, and set up a hostel on the Santiago de Compostela route. Her business flourished and Bernadette's sayings were famous amongst pilgrims across Christendom. She died peacefully in her sleep a few years back and Charles continues in the hostel still with his large family. He looks very like Piers.

In Catalonia, after Ramon's death, the twins became joint rulers of Barcelona and all its domains and they left Carcassonne to Raingarde's daughter, Ermengard and the Trencavels. Ramon Towhead married Lady Mahalta of Apulia, the daughter of the Norman, Robert Guiscard, who ruled Sicily. Through these contacts Barcelona's commerce grew more and more and the city's population with it. Ramon Towhead, Cap d'Estop, was loved for his boldness, kindness, joyfulness and his attractive appearance. He was much like her.

After six years of joint rule, the twins quarrelled and Beren demanded a division that Ramon Towhead would not agree to. After the birth of his son, Towhead was murdered while hunting in the forest on the feast day of Saint Nicholas. Many believed that his brother Beren was the murderer. Beren ruled as regent for his nephew and never married, but he was not all bad. He formed a tight-knit *drut*, a war-band with his half-brothers, Hugh the Devil of Lusignan, Guillaume and Raymond of Toulouse. They fought together in Spain and Beren was with Guillaume six years ago when he died on pilgrimage. A trial by combat found Beren guilty of his brother's murder and he died seeking penance in Jerusalem two years ago.

All the children of Almodis and Ramon are gone now: little Inés, she died in childbirth a few years after her marriage to the Count of Albon; Sancha was married off by her brothers to the Count of Cerdanya who had repudiated Raingarde's daughter Adelais all those years before. Sancha had two sons and one of them is Count of Cerdanya now, but Sancha is gone in childbed too. The only survivor of their dynasty is Almodis' grandson, Ramon Berenger III, a great king, Count of Barcelona and Duke of Provence. Lucia was regent in Pallars Sobirà and ruled well, and the Count of Urgell made her guardian to his children, such was her prestige. Her son, Artaldo, is the count now.

In Toulouse, Guillaume tried to atone for his sins with his cousin Adelais by building a great cathedral but his first wife was barren and his second wife, Emma of Mortain, gave him a daughter, Philippa, and no living sons. So, according to the treaty contracted after the siege of Lusignan in 1060, Philippa has been wed to Agnes' grandson, Guillaume IX Duke of Aquitaine, who is called the troubadour prince for his poetry.

Guillaume of Toulouse named his brother, Raymond, as his heir some time back and now that Guillaume is gone, Raymond is Count of Toulouse and Saint Gilles and much more besides, and names himself the Duke of Septimania, Provence and Narbonne. Of all her children, Raymond reminds me most of her: a fearless autocrat. When the pope excommunicated him for his consanguinous marriage to his cousin Bertranda, Raymond ignored the ruling saying, 'The church has no right to pontificate on my marriage.' He has become a great warrior in the mould of Geoffrey the Hammer of Anjou. Raymond lost an eye in one of his battles. He was the very first lord to take up the pope's call for a holy crusade and he left Toulouse four years ago with his third wife, Elvira and their baby son, leading the forces of all Occitania. He discovered the Holy Lance and this summer he was triumphant, taking Jerusalem from the heathens. He turned down the offer of the title King of Jerusalem, saying it made him shudder for that name belonged to Christ. He hasn't come back from the Holy Land. He is still out there fighting for other kingdoms with a name he'd like. He left his son Bertrand ruling Toulouse, and sure enough Bertrand's cousin Philippa and her husband, the Duke of Aquitaine are fighting him for it. So Almodis' children and grandchildren fight on between themselves when she would have woven peace.

Hugh the Bishop, well he is at least an abbot and a most kindly and revered one, and still in Saint Gilles. Adalmoda was Regent of Melgueil for her son Raymond, after her husband died. She had two more daughters after Almodis was gone and named them Ermessende and Adela. Her second son, Pons, entered Cluny and is rising steadily through the ranks, aiming for abbot.

In La Marche, Audebert lived a long life. His son Boson became count but he died in battle a few years later and then Audebert's daughter, named Almodis, and married to the Welsh Norman lord, Roger of Montgommery, became Countess of La Marche in her own right. My Lady's youngest sister, Agnes, finally married her heart's desire, Ramnulfe of Montmorillon, when they were both in their sixties, and her brother and nephew were gone and could not gainsay her.

I live now in Aquitaine with Lady Melisende who is chatelaine of the Castle of Parthenay and has her own lively family. Brother Jourdain comes often to visit us from the Priory of Lusignan. His twin, Lord Hugh the Devil of Lusignan, continues a steady policy of aggression against his neighbours. Jourdain says he is more like his grandfather, than his father. He holds his own against the Duchy of Aquitaine and even annexed a small part of La Marche a few years back.

'Now he is away with Raymond of Toulouse in the Holy Land, the neighbourhood can relax for a while,' says Melisende laughing at her rumbustious brother.

'All her children,' I say. 'I remember your births and your childish pranks. And I remember the men who loved her, the men who she would not love, and the one who she could not have.'

ALMODIS DE LA MARCHE GENEALOGY*

Adalmode of Limoges 971–1005
Countess of La Marche, Duchess of Aquitaine

m 1. Audebert I 971–997
Count of La Marche

m 2. Guillaume V 'The Great' 969–1030
Duke of Aquitaine & Count of Poitiers

Bernard I 991–1038
Count of La Marche

m

Amelie of Montignac 996–1053
Countess of La Marche

Guillaume VI 'The Fat' 1004–1038
Duke of Aquitaine (see Aquitaine Genealogy)

Audebert II 1017–1088
Count of La Marche

Almodis of La Marche 1020–1071
Lady of Lusignan
Countess of Toulouse
Countess of Barcelona

Raingarde 1020–1071
Countess of Carcassonne
(see Carcassonne/Barcelona Genealogy)

Lucia 1034–1091
Countess of Pallars Sobirà

m 1. Hugh V 'The Fair'/'The Pious' 1010–1060
Lord of Lusignan
repudiated 1040

m 2. Pons II 995–1060
Count of Toulouse
repudiated 1053

m 3. Ramon Berenger I 'The Old' 1024–1076
Count of Barcelona
(see Carcassonne/Barcelona Genealogy)

Hugh VI 'The Devil' Lord of Lusignan
1039–1106
Jourdain monk
1039–1119
Melisende Lady of Parthenay 1040–1108

Guillaume IV Count of Toulouse
1040–1094
Raymond IV Count of Saint Gilles,
Count of Toulouse 1041–1105
Hugh Abbot of Saint Gilles 1047–1119
Adalmoda Countess of Melgueil 1048–1132

Ramon Berenger II Count of Barcelona
'Cap d'Estop' (Towhead) 1053–1082
Berenger Ramon II Count of Barcelona
1053–1097
Arnau 1054–1068
Inés Countess of Albon 1056–1076
Sancha Countess of Cerdanya 1057–1087

* Dates, especially birth dates, are often undocumented, and there are also variant dates in original documents and historians' accounts. The dates shown in these genealogies are my best guesses based on these variations. For clarity, these are selected genealogies.

AQUITAINE GENEALOGY

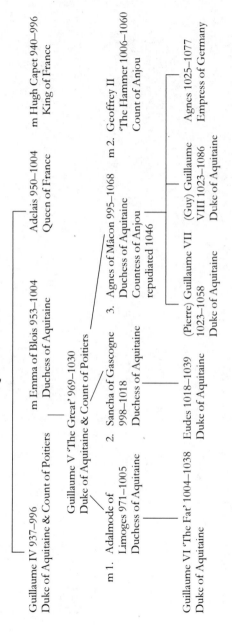

Guillaume IV 937–996
Duke of Aquitaine & Count of Poitiers

m Emma of Blois 953–1004
Duchess of Aquitaine

Adelais 950–1004
Queen of France

m Hugh Capet 940–996
King of France

Guillaume V 'The Great' 969–1030
Duke of Aquitaine & Count of Poitiers

m 1. Adalmode of Limoges 971–1005
Duchess of Aquitaine

2. Sancha of Gascogne 998–1018
Duchess of Aquitaine

3. Agnes of Mâcon 995–1068
Duchess of Aquitaine
Countess of Anjou
repudiated 1046

m 2. Geoffrey II 'The Hammer' 1006–1060
Count of Anjou

Guillaume VI 'The Fat' 1004–1038
Duke of Aquitaine

Eudes 1018–1039
Duke of Aquitaine

(Pierre) Guillaume VII 1023–1058
Duke of Aquitaine

(Guy) Guillaume VIII 1023–1086
Duke of Aquitaine

Agnes 1025–1077
Empress of Germany

m Eustachie 1002–1062
Duchess of Aquitaine

m Heinrich III 1017–1056
Emperor of Germany

CARCASSONNE/BARCELONA GENEALOGY

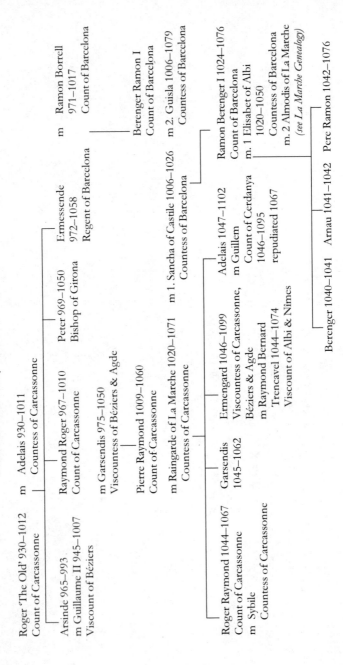

Roger 'The Old' 930–1012
Count of Carcassonne

m Adelais 930–1011
Countess of Carcassonne

Arsinde 965–993
m Guillaume II 945–1007
Viscount of Béziers

Raymond Roger 967–1010
Count of Carcassonne

Peter 969–1050
Bishop of Girona

Ermessende
972–1058
Regent of Barcelona

m Ramon Borrell
971–1017
Count of Barcelona

Berenger Ramon I
Count of Barcelona

m 2. Guisla 1006–1079
Countess of Barcelona

m Garsendis 975–1050
Viscountess of Béziers & Agde

Pierre Raymond 1009–1060
Count of Carcassonne

m 1. Sancha of Castile 1006–1026
Countess of Barcelona

Raingarde of La Marche 1020–1071
Countess of Carcassonne

Ramon Berenger I 1024–1076
Count of Barcelona
m. 1 Elisabet of Albi
1020–1050
Countess of Barcelona
m. 2 Almodis of La Marche
(see La Marche Genealogy)

Ermengard 1046–1099
Viscountess of Carcassonne,
Béziers & Agde
m Raymond Bernard
Trencavel 1044–1074
Viscount of Albi & Nîmes

Adelais 1047–1102
m Guillem
Count of Cerdanya
1046–1095
repudiated 1067

Garsendis
1045–1062

Roger Raymond 1044–1067
Count of Carcassonne
m Sybile
Countess of Carcassonne

Berenger 1040–1041   Arnau 1041–1042   Pere Ramon 1042–1076

Historical Note

Almodis de La Marche was a real historical person. That she was repudiated, kidnapped and murdered, that she was three times married, had twelve children, played an active role in the government of Toulouse and Barcelona, and was literate, are all documented facts. It was a story that needed writing! Everything in between these basic facts I have imagined and am responsible for any historical inaccuracies. I am not a medievalist and have drawn only on sources in modern English and French, and whilst based in research, this is a work of fiction rather than history.

Almodis was the ancestor of Eleanor of Aquitaine, and Geoffrey of Anjou was the ancestor of Henry II King of England, who married Eleanor. There is no historical evidence that Almodis was herself a twin, but it is likely that she gave birth to at least two sets of twin sons, and it is possible that her sister Raingarde was her twin. For nineteen years Almodis and Ramon ruled Barcelona, consolidating its power base. Their tombs are in Barcelona Cathedral. The eleven children who survived her went on to rule large parts of northern Spain and southern France, and played significant roles in the Crusades. Her sons by her three husbands were strong allies. Her descendents through the Lusignan family ruled Jerusalem and Cyprus in the thirteenth century and eventually gained control of the county of La Marche.

The lords and ladies in this story are based on historical people, whereas the characters who are not nobility: Dia,

Bernadette, Piers, Alienor, Carlotta, Rostagnus and others, are my inventions, although Dia has been inspired by the female troubadours of the twelfth century. The events and personalities described in this book are a mixture of fact and fiction. There is one piece of conscious poetic license: Elisabeth of Vendôme *was* burnt at the stake in her wedding dress by Fulk of Anjou for infidelity with a goatherd, however Geoffrey's mother was Fulk's second wife, Hildegarde.

Diverse spellings of names are used by historians and in original documents ranging through Catalan, Occitan, French and Anglicised. The use of surnames had not yet developed in the eleventh century and first names were passed down in families resulting in a profusion of Hughs, Ramons, Berengers and Garsendas for instance. In order to avoid confusion I have slightly altered some names or used their real nicknames, except in the case of Hugh The Bishop, which is my own invention.

Places and geography are a mixture of fact and fiction. Whilst descriptions of Toulouse are based on eleventh-century maps of the city, for instance, my description of Saint Gilles in Chapter 21 is fictional and based on the village of Brousse Le Château in the Tarn Valley.

I have aimed to create a portrait of the time and culture that Almodis lived in, which were very different from stereotypical ideas about 'the Middle Ages'. Southern France was a separate country from the territory north of the River Loire. South of the Loire a different language was spoken, there were different laws and a different culture. The counties of southern France had far greater ties with their neighbours across the Pyrenees in northern Spain than with northern France.

In the ninth century Charlemagne's empire had extended through the modern-day territories of Germany, France, Italy and northern Spain, but the cohesion achieved by Charlemagne had fallen apart and noble families were fighting for control of small regions. Kingship was beginning to re-emerge with the Capetians in the North of France, but in the South there was no king, and counts such as La Marche were independent rulers, and lords such as the Lords of Lusignan gave only a fragile homage to their overlords, the Dukes of Aquitaine. The battles for control were based as much on establishing lineage and allegiance through marriage and heirs, as they were on war.

One of the most distinctive features of this southern country was the prevalence of female lords, inheriting and ruling in their own right and as regents for their sons, or as co-lords with their husbands. It is clear from surviving documentation that Occitanian and Catalonian women were actively involved in political and economic life. Oaths were sworn on the matrilinear line; wives, sisters and mothers all had to give their consent to legal and fiscal acts undertaken by their men, as well as often acting themselves in these matters.

Eleventh-century southern French (Occitan) and northern Spanish (Catalan) society was sophisticated and intellectual, as well as a military and hierarchical mileau. The courts of Aquitaine and Anjou in particular were literate, where noble women learnt to read and write and were patrons of writers and book-makers.

Occitan was the language of the troubadours. Troubadours are usually associated with the twelfth century since this is when the first named poets such as Guillaume IX of Aquitaine (who married Almodis' granddaughter), Bertran de Born, Bernart de Ventadorn and the Comtesse de Dia lived, however Peter Dronke has argued that, by 1000, all the basic types of medieval and Renaissance lyric had evolved and we can 'reject any suggestion that the birth of secular vernacular lyric in western Europe was a sudden event that took place (as many people believe) at the end of the eleventh century' (1996: 30). Both Martin Aurell (1995) and Jacques Le Goff (1980) have suggested that Almodis was the canvas for the *Roman of Melusine,* which was associated with the castle of Lusignan. The Jeux Floraux competition was founded around 1323 in Toulouse by seven troubadours and awarded a golden flower as its prize. The Occitan language is still spoken today in southern France and other areas. In the nineteenth century it was systematically suppressed in the *vergonha,* the shaming. It is still not recognised as an official language by the contemporary French government, although it is recognised by Spain.

The eleventh century was a time of relative peace in the region after the invasions by Muslims, Vikings and Magyars in the previous centuries. It was a time of transitions: transition from the warrior caste of Almodis' father's generation to the more ordered and peace-seeking society of her own generation with the spread of the Peace and Truce of God which sought to reduce constant warring; transition in the traditions of inheritance from cognate division, in which all children, including daughters, inherited part of their parents' rights, to agnate primogeniture which focussed inheritance on the eldest son; the beginning of shifts in the church from a priesthood with wives, to a celibate priesthood; from a church manipulated by the secular aristocracy, to a church that sought to control that aristocracy, and the gradual move towards the totalitarian church of the thirteenth century with the concomitant erosion of women's rights and status.

The country of Occitania was wiped out 170 years after Almodis lived, in the Albigensian Crusade, when northern France, acting at the behest of the pope, repeatedly invaded and brutally subdued the South. Although presented as a religious crusade against the Cathars this was in effect a territorial invasion, a cultural subjugation of the South and of Almodis' and Raingarde's descendents who were the rulers of Toulouse and Carcassonne.

Selected Bibliography

The work of historians and medieval writers were influential on my attempt to create a picture of this lost culture and I have put some of their choicest phrases into the mouths of my characters, especially Aurell, Bachrach, Bloch, Bogin, Bonnassie, Cheyette, Duby, Kosto, Painter, Adhémar of Chabannes, Dhuoda of Uzès, Gregory of Tours, Raldophus Glaber, Trota of Salerno, George Turbevile and William of Malmesbury. These and other key sources are listed below. Bernadette's description of the great round of life was inspired by *The Creation Tapestry* in Girona Cathedral and the Duc de Berry's *Very Rich Hours*. A full bibliography is on my website http://traceywarr.wordpress.com

Aurell, Martin, *Les Noces du Comte: Mariage et Pouvoir en Catalogne (785–1213)* (Paris: Sorbonne, 1995).

Bachrach, Bernard S., *State-Building in Medieval France: Studies in Early Angevin History* (Aldershot: Variorum, 1995).

Bloch, Marc, *Feudal Society*, 2 vols. (Chicago: Chicago University Press, 1961).

Bogin, Meg, *The Women Troubadours* (New York: W.W. Norton, 1980).

Bonnassie, Pierre, *La Catalogne du milieu du Xe a la fin du XIe siècle*, 2 vols. (Toulouse: University of Toulouse, 1975–76).

Cawley, Charles, *Medieval Lands Project* online at: http://fmg.ac/Projects/MedLands/index.htm

Chabannes, Adhémar de, *Chronique*, 3 vols., transl. Yves Chauvin et Georges Pon (Turnhout: Brepols, 2003). Written in the eleventh century.

Cheyette, Frederic L., 'The "Sale" of Carcassonne to the Counts of

Barcelona and the Rise of the Trencavels', *Speculum*, vol. 63 no. 4, 1988, pp. 826–64.

—— *Ermengard of Narbonne and the World of the Troubadours* (Ithaca and London: Cornell University Press, 2001).

D'Arras, Jean, *Mélusine*, compiled 1382–94, English translation c.1500, ed. A.K. Donald (London: Kegan Paul, Trench, Trubner, 1895).

Dronke, Peter, *Women Writers of the Middle Ages: A Critical Study of Texts from Perpetua (d. 203) to Marguerite Porete (d. 1310)* (Cambridge: Cambridge University Press, 1984).

—— *The Medieval Lyric* (Cambridge: D. S. Brewer, 1996).

Duby, Georges, *The Knight, the Lady, and the Priest: The Making of Modern Marriage in Medieval France* (London: Pantheon, 1983).

Duoda Women's Research Centre, University of Barcelona http://www.ub.edu/duoda/

Evans, Joan, *Monastic Life at Cluny 910–1157* (Oxford: Oxford University Press, 1968).

France, John, ed., *Rodolfus Glaber: The Five Books of the Histories* (Oxford: Clarendon Press, 1989).

Gies, Joseph & Gies, Frances, *Life in a Medieval Castle* (New York: Crowell, 1974).

Goldin, Frederick, *Lyrics of the Troubadours and Trouvères* (New York: Doubleday Anchor Books, 1973).

Green, Monica H. ed., *The Tortula: A Medieval Compendium of Women's Medicines* (Philadelphia: University of Pennsylvania Press, 2001).

Gregory of Tours, *The History of the Franks*, tr. Lewis Thorpe (London: Penguin, 1974). Written in the sixth century.

Herlihy, David, *Opera Muliebra: Women and Work in Medieval Europe* (New York: McGraw-Hill, 1990).

Karras, Ruth Mazo, *Sexuality in Medieval Europe: Doing Unto Others* (London: Routledge, 2005).

Kosto, Adam J., *Making Agreements in Medieval Catalonia: Power, Order, and the Written Word, 1000–1200* (Cambridge: Cambridge University Press, 2001).

Le Goff, Jacques, *Time, Work and Culture in the Middle Ages* (Chicago: Chicago University Press, 1980).

Leighton, Albert C., *Transport and Communication in Early Medieval Europe AD500–1100* (Newton Abbot: David & Charles, 1972).

Lewis, Archibald R., *The Development of Southern French and Catalan Society, 718–1050* (Austin: University of Texas Press, 1965). Published online at Library of Iberian Resources Online http://libro.uca.edu

Martindale, Jane, *Status, Authority and Regional Power: Aquitaine and France, Ninth to Twelfth Centuries* (New York: Variorum, 1997).

Moline de Saint-Yon, Alexander Pierre, *Histoire de Comtes de Toulouse*, 4 vols. (Paris: A. Bertrand, 1859).

Morichon, René, ed., *Histoire du Limousin et de La Marche*, Volume 1: De la Préhistoire à la Fin de l'Ancien Régime (Paris: René Dessagne, 1972–76).

Mundy, John Hine, *Liberty and Political Power in Toulouse 1050–1230* (New York: Columbia University Press, 1954).

Oldenbourg, Zoe, *Massacre at Mongségur: A History of the Albigensian Crusade* (London: Phoenix, 2000).

Painter, Sidney, 'The Lords of Lusignan in the Eleventh and Twelfth Centuries', *Speculum*, 32: 1, Jan. 1957, pp. 27–47.

Redon, Odile, Françoise Sabban, and Silvano Serventi, *The Medieval Kitchen: Recipes from France and Italy* (Chicago: University of Chicago Press, 1999).

Reynolds, Susan et al., 'Translation of "Agreement between William V of Aquitaine and Hugh IV of Lusignan"'. *Medieval Sourcebook* online at http://www.fordham.edu/halsall/sbook.html

Robinson, James, *Masterpieces of Medieval Art* (London: British Museum, 2008).

Thiebaux, Marcelle, ed., *Dhuoda, Handbook for her Warrior Son: Liber Manualis* (Cambridge: Cambridge University Press, 1998).

Thompson, James Westfall, *The Literacy of the Laity in the Middle Ages*, University of California Publications In Education, vol. 9 (Berkeley: University of California Press, 1939).

Turbevile, George, *Noble Arte of Venerie or Hunting (1576)* (Oxford: Clarendon Press, 1908).

William of Malmesbury, *De Gestis Regum Anglorum* (London: Bell, 1847).

Acknowledgements

The Song of the Hart on p. 97 is an adaptation of a verse from George Turbevile's 1576 *Noble Art of Venerie or Hunting*. Dia's song on p. 288 is an extract from a poem by Bertran de Born, translated in Goldin (1973, p. 241). All other poems quoted in the text are by the female troubadours translated by Meg Bogin in Bogin, Meg, *The Female Troubadours* (New York/London: W.W. Norton and Co., 1980) reproduced by kind permission of Meg Bogin as follows:

p. ix: 'Now we are come to the cold time . . .' by Azalais de Porcairages (Bogin, p. 95)
p. 37: 'It greatly pleases me . . . ' by Castelloza (Bogin, pp. 119–123)
p. 73: 'Of things I'd rather keep in silence I must sing . . .' by Countess de Dia (Bogin pp. 85–87)
p. 159: 'How I wish just once I could caress . . .' by Countess de Dia (Bogin p. 89)
p. 197: 'You stayed a long time friend . . .' by Castelloza (Bogin, p. 127).

I am grateful to my self-styled muse, Bob Smillie, and to my daughter Lola, my dad, my mum, my writing and reading nephew Jack, the rest of my lovely family, my other fabulous friends and my cat for their various invaluable support. Thank you to Rob La Frenais and Zoe Benbow for loaning me their house near

Ambialet, to Hester Schofield for driving me there and being a writing inspiration, to Andrew and Bodil Humphries for their 'writing shack' in Pembrokeshire, to Alan Smith and Helen Ratcliffe for getting me down a deep mine. In Ambialet and La Condomine I am grateful to Bernadette Goy, Jacques and Keltoum Fabas, Nadine Lefloch, and Régis and Françoise Mas for their warmth that sustained me through a frigid winter in the Tarn Valley and inspired me to try to write about those lovely valleys, mountains and people.

I am grateful to the staff on the MA in Creative Writing at University of Wales Trinity Saint David in Carmarthen who set me off on this endeavour and especially Menna Elfyn, Helen Carey, Paul Wright and Robert Nesbit. All my fellow Creative Writing students and especially Amanda Miles, Anthony Jones, Karen Carmichael-Timson, Caroline James, and Helene Ifanca James, were important inspirations and critics.

I am grateful to the Musée des Augustins in Toulouse for supplying me with an eleventh-century map of the city. I would like to thank Abbey Santander for a Scholarship to pursue my research in Spain and Maria-Josep Balsach at University of Girona and Imma Prieto and Denys Blacker in Girona for their support. I am grateful to Esther Ferrar for an illuminating conversation in Girona about being an identical twin. I would also like to thank Oxford Brookes University.

Finally, I am immensely grateful to all the staff and sales representatives at Impress Books for their enthusiasm about the book and for their careful editorial, design and marketing work.